The Beggar's Opera
and other
Eighteenth-Century Plays

SELECTED BY
JOHN HAMPDEN

INTRODUCTION BY
DAVID W. LINDSAY
Lecturer in English, University College of North Wales, Bangor

DENT: LONDON
EVERYMAN'S LIBRARY
DUTTON: NEW YORK

© Introduction, J. M. Dent & Sons Ltd, 1974
All rights reserved
Made in Great Britain
at the
Aldine Press · Letchworth · Herts
for
J. M. DENT & SONS LTD
Aldine House · Albemarle Street · London
This edition was first published in
Everyman's Library in 1928
Reprinted 1975

Published in the U.S.A. by arrangement
with J. M. Dent & Sons Ltd

No. 818   Hardback ISBN 0 460 00818 8
No. 1818   Paperback ISBN 0 460 01818 3

INTRODUCTION

The seven plays collected in this volume were all produced for the first time in London between 1708 and 1779. Taken in conjunction with the comedies of Goldsmith and Sheridan (which have also been published in Everyman's Library) they give a representative picture of English drama between the Restoration and Romantic periods. As a whole this was an age of relative stability in English society and the English theatre. The major dramatic achievements of 1664–1682 had reflected the values of a courtly and sceptical intelligentsia; and in the dramatic revival of 1693–1707 those values had been re-asserted and re-defined within the new moral and political context produced by the Williamite revolution. From 1780 onwards, the theatrical atmosphere was to be rapidly transformed by the expansion of London, the proliferation of minor theatres, the rebuilding of the patent theatres, the histrionic techniques of the Kembles, the spread of democratic sentiment, and the growing appetite for Gothic sensation. For most of the intervening time, however, the English theatre was dominated, like English life as a whole, by the spirit of cultural and social compromise whose greatest literary spokesman was Joseph Addison. That spirit is manifest in Augustan tragedies which dramatize the political theories of Locke, and in sentimentalized comedies of manners which celebrate marital reconciliation. It is manifest, too, in the civilized and unaggressive tone of most eighteenth-century drama, and in the continuing predominance of established dramatic forms. Even in this age of compromise and stability, however, individual writers made their distinctive contributions, and the drama as a whole continued to evolve. Moreover, there were two short periods (1728–37 and 1768–79) during which innovation and controversy became rather the rule than the exception in the London theatre; and it is therefore necessary, in considering the works collected in this volume, to distinguish the principal phases of eighteenth-century dramatic history.

From the death of George Farquhar in 1707 to the death
of King George I in 1727, the English drama remained in a
state of suspended animation. The more conspicuous new
plays of these twenty years are for the most part either
deliberately unambitious like the intrigue-comedies of
Susanna Centlivre or heavily untheatrical like the neo-
classic tragedies of Ambrose Philips. Unimpressive as the
period was in dramatic achievement, however, it was a
period in which the theatre flourished and the drama held a
central place in English cultural life. Since 1690, the English
theatre had been increasingly dominated by Whig influence;
and Whig sympathies were certainly prevalent among the
leading dramatists and actors of the years 1708–27. The
alternation of Whig and Tory governments was thus
reflected in the theatre not by an alternation of Whig and
Tory propaganda but by an alternation of Whig propaganda and discreet impartiality. The three main phases of
political influence can be defined by reference to the theatrical
career of an archetypal Whig play, Rowe's *Tamerlane*: having been performed intermittently until 1710, this work was
excluded from the repertoire during the last four years of
Queen Anne's reign, but performed several times each season
from 1715 onwards.

During the first of these three phases, dramatists were still
allowed to praise Marlborough and propagate Whig political
theory. After the 1710 election, however, Bolingbroke himself undertook to 'survey all the Plays before they were
acted'; and during the next four years the Whig dramatists
had to respect his views. The most remarkable exercise in
reconciling Whig principle with Tory supremacy was
Addison's *Cato*; but comparable negotiations with the new
régime appear to have been conducted by Cibber, Rowe and
Steele. The tendency towards domestic themes was accen-
tuated, since dramatists like Rowe and Philips were
unwilling to present a Tory view of political history and
unable to present any other. After the death of Queen Anne,
Whig propaganda was again admitted to the theatre: the
Drury Lane plays of the next few years included Rowe's
tragedy *Lady Jane Grey*, which celebrates a Protestant
martyr, and Cibber's comedy *The Non-Juror*, which
exposes a Catholic villain. A further stimulus to propa-
gandist drama was provided by the Jacobite rebellion of

1715: several neo-Shakespearean works of the years 1720–1723 exploit episodes of Roman and English history as vehicles for anti-Jacobite argument. In the theatrical journalism of the time, Tory attitudes are plentifully evident; but in the theatre itself such attitudes were rarely expressed. The Drury Lane group tried around 1716 to associate the new Lincoln's Inn Fields theatre with the political opposition; but an epilogue spoken there rejected the charge. The situation began to change, however, after the 1720 crisis and the emergence of Walpole as First Lord of the Treasury. The new opposition included not only Tories but also dissident Whigs; and it attacked not the Hanoverian dynasty but the Walpole government. In the journalistic propaganda of this movement, the attack on Walpole was often associated with an attack on Button's Coffee-House; and it was also associated with an attack on the Cibber-Wilks-Booth management at Drury Lane, whose commercialism was considered symbolic of the Prime Minister's.

During the years 1693–1707 the social context of English comedy had been transformed by the influence of the various Societies for the Reformation of Manners. In the last years of Queen Anne's reign the work of these societies was continued, in a more civilized fashion, by the periodical essayists; and it is noteworthy that moral protests were now directed not against new plays but against such established favourites as Ravenscroft's *The London Cuckolds*. By the beginning of George I's reign, the new morality was being supported or reluctantly accepted by all practising dramatists: we can see its consequences thereafter in Steele's propaganda against duelling, Rowe's celebration of marriage, and Susanna Centlivre's superficially respectable form of intrigue-comedy. Williamite attacks on the contemporary stage, however, had mentioned not only Restoration comedy's immorality but also its persistent contempt for the merchant or citizen class; and the re-fashioning of comic tradition in favour of that class proved more difficult than the devaluing of promiscuity. The old image of the citizen was still dominant in such plays as Vanbrugh's *The Confederacy*; and it was only when the *Spectator* essays had popularized the new attitude that Whig dramatists began, in the years following the Treaty of Utrecht, to present

London merchants as intelligent and honourable men. An early example of the new approach can be found in Act II of Rowe's *Jane Shore*, where Hastings's assault on the heroine is interrupted by Dumont: the licentious nobleman is here opposed and disarmed by an honest citizen. Similar tributes to the merchant class are to be found in many plays of George I's reign, including Steele's *The Conscious Lovers*; but the anti-acquisitive attitude emerges again in some 'patriotic' plays of the 1720s. Thomas Southerne, who had begun his career in the age of Titus Oates with a tragedy celebrating the Duke of York, concluded it in the age of Walpole with a comedy denouncing avarice.

The development of journalism has a place not only in political and social history but also in the history of dramatic criticism. Defoe's *Weekly Review*, which continued until 1713, confined itself to attacks on theatrical immorality and extravagance; but the various periodicals associated with Addison and Steele made a more positive contribution. In *The Tatler*, which ran from 1709 to 1711, we find Steele dissociating himself from the extreme-reformist position: 'I cannot be of the same opinion with my friends and fellow-labourers, the Reformers of Manners, in their severity towards plays.' While maintaining a reformist attitude towards immoral comedies and improper audience behaviour, *The Tatler* assisted the Drury Lane company by advertising new productions and special performances; and we know from Cibber that the 'force and influence' of these advertisements did the stage 'very considerable service'. In *The Spectator*, which ran from 1711 to 1712, theatrical subjects are even more prominent. Addison ridicules the conventional costumes of theatrical kings and queens, and the excessive use of 'drums, trumpets and huzzas' in battle-scenes. Steele attacks Etherege's *The Man of Mode* as 'a perfect Contradiction to good Manners, good Sense, and common Honesty', stressing in particular Dorimant's discourtesy to the orange-woman. John Hughes, who was later to achieve some fame as a tragic dramatist, condemns Shadwell's *The Lancashire Witches* because it invites audience approval for young women who marry 'without consent of parents'. Whenever *The Spectator* turned its attention to theatrical matters, in fact, the main emphasis fell on the theatre as a social institution; and because *The*

Spectator was so influential, this emphasis helped to confirm the tendency which it reflected. In *The Guardian*, which ran for some months in 1713, theatrical issues are dealt with in similar terms: two numbers are devoted, for example, to the current enthusiasm for ADDISON's *Cato*.

Cato was performed at Drury Lane in 1713, in somewhat unusual circumstances. Writing a political play at a time of intense political conflict, Addison had taken a lot of trouble to ensure that it would not be interpreted as partisan. His own sympathies lay, of course, with the Whigs; but he had consulted Bolingbroke to ensure that his text was acceptable to the ministry. The prologue was supplied by a Tory poet, Alexander Pope, and the epilogue by a Whig poet, Samuel Garth. At the first performance, Whigs and Tories in the audience competed in applauding Addison's praise of liberty and virtue. There was a storm of Whig applause for the lines:

> Where vice prevails, and impious men bear sway,
> The post of honour is a private station.

But Bolingbroke, to show that he too endorsed Addison's principles, presented Booth, who acted Cato, with a purse containing fifty guineas. John Dennis attacked the play for its neglect of poetic justice; but the general attitude to it was admiring. Throughout the eighteenth century it was taken for granted that Addison's *Cato* was at the very least a great dramatic poem. Since modern taste tends to underestimate the play, it may be worth stressing that this verdict was not wholly absurd. *Cato* has many of the ingredients of a serious political drama; and it is written with an authority, a mastery of phrase, not to be found in any other eighteenth-century tragedy. In the formal debate which opens Act II, for example, Addison establishes the different modes of rhetoric characteristic of Cato, Sempronius and Lucius; and we can sense the falsity of Sempronius' enthusiasm in the extravagance of his language. In the dialogue between Juba and Syphax in Act I Scene IV there is not only a clash between honourable virtue and conspiratorial self-interest but also a conflict between Numidia's chivalric ideals and the civilizing virtues of Rome. The conflict between Cato and Caesar, between republican freedom and lawless imperialism, encompasses the whole play and is often defined with an epigrammatic vigour reminiscent of Lucan.

If *Cato* is an easy play to denounce, this is in part because it insists on being judged by high standards; but with all its virtues it does have obvious faults. The crudity of the love-scenes is comparatively unimportant, because amorous themes are not central to the play; but there is also something subtly unsatisfactory about the play's treatment of its political theme. It is as a political play, clearly, that *Cato* must stand or fall; and there can be no doubt that it is the work of a man with some political insight. But for all that one cannot feel that Addison is trying to communicate any real political understanding to his audience. He is rather inviting them to admire his hero, and persuading them that they can all admire him, whatever their political principles. His attitude, in fact, is at once too deferential and too complacent; and one cannot feel, as one often does in reading *The Spectator*, that the tone of address is a legitimate and clearly conceived strategy for the reconciliation of opposite opinions on the author's terms. As the occasional lapses in *The Spectator* reflect Addison's uncertain relationship with his public, so the vices of *Cato* result from the uneasiness Addison felt about putting his most serious beliefs into a form suitable for Drury Lane. The play is a conspicuous example, with few English precedents but many successors, of the literary mind failing to come to terms with the theatre. The trouble with Addison's political thought is that, although it has its roots in a desire for reconciliation, it turns outwards all the time to a vague use of abstract nouns like 'liberty' and 'virtue'; and the trouble with his central character in this play is that he seems not to manifest virtue but rather to lay claim to it. As one reads the play, therefore, Pope's devastating couplet rings in one's ears:

> Like Cato, give his little senate laws,
> And sit attentive to his own applause.

The play is one of Addison's most ambitious works; but it is also, I think, the work in which the limitations of his character are most clearly evident. Its triumphant first run came to an end, according to Berkeley, because Mrs Oldfield was unable to continue, having for several nights had a midwife behind the scenes. One feels that this event has a symbolic value, as re-assertion of human reality, which it would not have in relation to a wiser play.

The Tragedy of Jane Shore, with which NICHOLAS ROWE returned to the theatre in 1714 after completing his edition of Shakespeare, records the sufferings of Edward IV's mistress at the hands of his successor Richard III. The subject had been handled by Thomas Churchyard in the most popular tragedy of *The Mirror for Magistrates*; and it has its place in Shakespeare's *Richard III*, though it is there only slightly touched on. Rowe's *Jane Shore* is typical of that phase in English tragedy which began with *All for Love*, in that it takes its inspiration and its style from a single work of Shakespeare's, but develops its theme in terms rather of pathos and domestic drama than of tragedy and national destinies. The villainous schemes of the Duke of Gloucester provide the political framework for Rowe's plot; and the fears of civil war caused by uncertainty about the succession are as relevant in Anne's reign as they were in Elizabeth's. But the focus of interest is a domestic drama like that of Southerne's *The Fatal Marriage*: the injured husband, returning in disguise, proves his courage against an overbearing nobleman and is reconciled to his adulterous wife. *Jane Shore* is a celebration of domestic virtue, set in a context of ruthless tyranny. It aims, like Rowe's earlier play *The Fair Penitent*, at moving the audience to tears; and like *The Fair Penitent* it operates both dramatically and poetically.

The reign of King George I was a time of stability and prosperity in the English theatre, and of uniformity and stagnation in the English drama; but it was followed, in the years 1728–37, by a period of insecurity, disorder and astonishingly various experiment. The first and most successful dramatic experiment of this time was JOHN GAY's *The Beggar's Opera*, which was produced at Lincoln's Inn Fields in 1728. *The Beggar's Opera*, like *Gulliver's Travels* and *The Dunciad*, is a characteristic product of the Scriblerus Club; and one sees its mode of operation most clearly if one takes it in this context, being prepared for the same complex structure of implied comparisons as one finds in Swift and Pope. It was Swift who suggested that Gay write a 'Newgate pastoral', thus combining the town pastoral and burlesque pastoral which were among the new literary forms of the day. *The Beggar's Opera*, though far removed from eclogue, uses the pastoral method of oblique reference from one social world to another; and the incongruity of subject and form suggested by Swift's phrase is made even more acute by the linking of opera, which at this date meant legendary characters and a consistently elevated tone, with the world of London's prisons and taverns. The preliminary conversation between the beggar and one of the actors serves chiefly to point this incongruity: like all good burlesques, *The Beggar's Opera* begins and ends with a strong emphasis on the absurd.

Through the greater part of the first act, Gay's attention is focused on a satirical presentation of the Peachum household. This household is seen, in the first instance, as a place of business. Peachum in his first song tells us he has a job like other men, and ends with Scriblerian impertiuence:

> And the Statesman, because he's so great,
> Thinks his trade as honest as mine.

Peachum's actual business is to buy goods from thieves and then sell the thieves to the law when they don't bring him enough. He discusses all its details in a thoroughly practical way, however, making it clear that he is legitimately on both sides like a lawyer, and that he is essentially without malice, being governed simply by sensible calculations about profit and loss. This is a portrait of the criminal as businessman; and it implies a portrait of the businessman as criminal. It suggests, too, that the statesman who operates on merely commercial principles is the greatest criminal of all; and no one, in the age of Walpole, could fail to see where Gay was pointing. The song of Peachum's servant,

> 'Tis woman that seduces all mankind,

subordinates love as well as law to monetary criteria; and when Peachum's wife has been brought in by her husband's condemnation of 'Robin of Bagshot, alias Bob Booty', this theme of love and money is developed further. Mrs Peachum does not venture to appeal for her favourite. 'Women', she says, 'are bad judges in these cases, for they are so partial to the brave that they think every man handsome who is going to the camp or the gallows.' That phrase establishes the connection between hero and highwayman which is to be exploited later, and the notion is developed in her song:

> The youth in his cart hath the air of a lord,
> And we cry, There dies an Adonis!

But any hint of idealism here is quickly suppressed by Peachum's mercenary morality—'If business cannot be carried on without murder, what would you have a gentleman do?'—and Mrs Peachum is soon apologizing for her 'over-scrupulous conscience'. The highwayman-image leads into Mrs Peachum's concern about her daughter's fondness for Macheath, which is expressed in a more or less orthodox way:

> If soon she be not made a wife,
> Her honour's sing'd.

Peachum's reaction, however, is far from orthodox: the practical morality which in respectable society makes marriage financially expedient works the other way in the underground. And when Mrs Peachum presents her arguments against this position, it becomes obvious that she too is concerned with 'honour' only where it is synonymous with 'profit'. When Polly's marriage is revealed, her parents unite against her in furious indignation, using arguments which at once parallel and invert those of respectable parents condemning a daughter for taking the opposite course. Because of the burlesque framework, it is possible for Polly to express her romantic idealism in the simplest and most improbable terms; and though we see the force of Mrs Peachum's comment, 'Those cursed play-books she reads have been her ruin', we are able, because the scene is avowedly absurd, to sympathize completely with the heroine. Our sympathy with her is confirmed when her parents proceed through their usual practical arguments to the conclusion that she can redeem her failure only by turning it to good account and selling her husband to the gallows. Mrs Peachum drives her daughter off with the angry command, 'Hang your husband, and be dutiful'; and we are left with a sense of the destructive force of those

purely commercial values which Peachum shares with Sir
Robert Walpole and the South Sea directors.

In the rest of Act I, Gay draws out of this sordid criminal-
commercial world an image (made acceptable by the burlesque scheme) of the romantic and heroic values which the
new age is destroying. When Polly soliloquises about her
parents' cruelty, for example, the incongruous references to
'Jack Ketch' and 'the cart' permit an extravagant expression of that conflict of motives which is a constant theme of
heroic tragedy. Similarly, in the first songs and speeches of
Macheath, the childish diction and the references to pistols
and horses provide a context for the assertion of heroic
idealism and eternal devotion. The lovers' duet, too, is
prepared for by a discussion on transportation, and contains
allusions to it; but its argument is one which descends from
Horace and appears in poems by Petrarch and the Earl of
Surrey. And as the burlesque technique enables Gay to re-
vivify the Renaissance lyric and draw from his Newgate
world a heroic and romantic idealism which it is impracticable at this date to present directly, so it frees him from
Augustan constraints so that he can draw his audience into
the simple emotion of sadness at a lovers' parting. The first
act concludes, however, not with the melancholy notes of
'O what a pain it is to part' but with a more obviously
parodic lyric beginning 'The miser thus a shilling sees'.

In the second act the scene changes to 'a tavern near
Newgate', and the burlesque-heroic note is sounded more
decisively. Macheath is surrounded first by highwaymen and
then by prostitutes; and these groups offer their own versions of military rhetoric and fashionable repartee. On the
one hand, there is the philosophic radicalism propounded by
Mat of the Mint: 'We retrench the superfluities of mankind.
The world is avaricious, and I hate avarice.' On the other
hand, there is the elegant modesty with which Mrs Vixen
accepts a tribute to her skill as shop-lifter: 'Lace, madam,
lies in a small compass, and is of easy conveyance. But you
are apt, madam, to think too well of your friends.' Such
double-edged ironies are immediately comprehensible to
anyone familiar with Scriblerian techniques; but there are
other effects in Act II which twentieth-century readers can
easily miss. In particular, we cannot experience the shock of
recognition that the first audience must have felt on realizing

that the highwaymen were setting off for the heath to the tune of the march in Handel's *Rinaldo*, that Macheath's delicate sentiments about woman were being sung to the tune of a well-known bawdy song, and that the prostitutes were not only singing an elegant lyric on the 'carpe diem' theme but also dancing a very fashionable dance recently imported from the Continent, Gay's allusions are simple beside those of his friend Pope; but some of them are worth noticing.

The opera's central event is the arrest of Macheath; and here we find Gay's burlesque-allusive method at its richest. Coming after the satirical treatment of Peachum in the first act and the celebration of Macheath in the second, this arrest is clearly an emblematic presentation of heroic-romantic civilization's defeat by the power of commercial legality. It is a tragic event, but it is seen in burlesque terms; and Macheath's response to it is both absurd and noble: 'Was this well done, Jenny?—Women are decoy Ducks; who can trust them! Beasts, Jades, Jilts, Harpies, Furies, Whores!' Cleopatra is there, of course; and so is the ranting warrior of heroic tragedy. The sequence of abusive terms, in fact, is very much that of a Restoration hero—except that the last term becomes comic and negates the whole statement because in this context it is literally appropriate. The absurdity is emphasized by Peachum's comparison of Macheath to the 'greatest heroes'; but this is still a martyr- dom, and the kiss of betrayal and the phrase about suffering on the tree associate it (tactfully) with the archetypal martyrdom. In addition, of course, it is a historical event; and if we want a gloss on this aspect of it we can find one in Macheath's final speech in Brecht's adaptation *Die Drei- groschenoper*: 'Was ist ein Dietrich gegen eine Aktie? (What are the tools of a criminal compared with the shares of a joint-stock company?).' Peachum's parting words, which appear unaltered in the Brechtian version, make the values of the new order clear: 'Ladies, I'll take care the reckoning shall be discharged.' And the tavern scene ends, in Gay's text, with a sordid yet pretentious quarrel among the prostitutes over the thief-taker's reward.

The second half of the opera, which is set principally in Newgate, employs the same burlesque-allusive technique but communicates a rather harsher atmosphere. The New- gate world is a world dominated by money, a world where the weight of fetters is inversely proportionate to the prisoner's funds. Gay maintains dramatic and topical interest through the story of Macheath's escape and recapture, through the quarrel between Peachum and Lockit, and through the quarrel between Polly and Lucy. These quarrels were recognized by the early audiences as referring to a notorious one between Walpole and Townshend, and to one between two opera-singers who had forced Handel to write exactly balanced parts to keep them both happy. The climax of the opera's second half is the scene in the condemned cell, where Macheath sings to a medley of familiar tunes, swinging absurdly between courage and despair as he drinks and then remembers his situation. The medley culminates in a new song to the tune of 'Greensleeves'. Despite the common belief that Gay's satire is merely topical, this song was effectively used by Dickens in *Little Dorrit* as a comment on his financial swindler, Mr Merdle. There was a rumour in the eighteenth century that it had been written by Swift or Pope; but there is no evidence for this at all. Being a burlesque, of course, *The Beggar's Opera* cannot end on a decisive note of this kind. Like *A Tale of a Tub*, *Tristram Shandy* and *A Vision of Judgment*, it has to be resolved in absurdity; and Gay achieves this by bringing the player and the beggar on stage again, and arranging an operatically improbable reprieve. Before the performance concludes, the beggar-librettist is allowed a meditative speech on the implications of his work; but the opera ends not in didactic speech but in exuberance and a burlesque expression of hope.

Many dramatists wrote ballad-operas in imitation of Gay; and one of them was a London goldsmith and jeweller named GEORGE LILLO. Lillo's ballad-opera, *Silvia or The Country Burial*, was not a success; but he followed it in 1731 with a prose tragedy entitled *The London Merchant or The History of George Barnwell*. *The London Merchant* was produced at Drury Lane, with Theophilus Cibber in the central role; and because the play was based on a popular ballad, the first-night audience came to the theatre prepared to laugh. 'Many gaily-disposed spirits', we are told, 'brought the ballad with them . . . intending to make . . . ludicrous comparisons between the ancient ditty and the modern play . . . But the play spoke so much to the heart, that . . . they were

drawn in to drop their ballads, and pull out their handkerchiefs.' The historical importance of that first night can
scarcely be exaggerated. Lillo's play, although conceived as
a tragedy, was cast entirely in prose; and its central character, George Barnwell, was a London apprentice. It thus
departed from the orthodox procedures of neo-classic
tragedy in more radical terms than such works as *Jane
Shore*. To appreciate the distinctive qualities of *The London
Merchant*, one has to compare it with some of the more
characteristic tragedies of its age—works like Addison's
Cato and Home's *Douglas*. At the same time, the play is not
to be regarded as a merely eccentric work; for it has important links both with the sixteenth century and with the
nineteenth. Lillo's knowledge of Elizabethan literature was
extensive; and in this play and others he manifests that
knowledge both through his choice of subjects and through
his dramatic techniques. In particular, he was profoundly
influenced by such domestic dramas as *Arden of Feversham*,
The Yorkshire Tragedy and *A Woman Killed with Kindness*.
By temperament and by social background, he was well
qualified to respond to these works. His desire to emulate
them made him reject the currently accepted principles of
dramatic art; but it also led him towards a new conception of
tragedy. That conception was very different from Addison's;
and at a deeper level than that of articulated theory, it was
more consonant with the spirit of the age. *The London
Merchant* deals in sober and sententious terms with the
career of an Elizabethan apprentice who is tempted first to
fraud and then to murder by his association with a harlot.
It is marred by frequent *longueurs*, and by a tendency to
moralistic rant; but it differs from most eighteenth-century
tragedies in being genuinely tragic, and not merely pathetic
or heroic or sensational. It remained popular in the London
theatres for many years; and by its impact on Diderot and
Lessing it affected the subsequent development of European
drama.

Lillo's other domestic tragedy, *Fatal Curiosity*, exercised
no comparable influence; but it contains fewer irrelevancies,
and might well be more acceptable today. It had its first
performance in 1736 at the Little Theatre in the Haymarket;
and the prologue spoken on that occasion shows how such
works were viewed by management and audience:

No fustian hero rages here to-night;
No armies fall, to fix a tyrant's right:
From lower life we draw our scene's distress—
Let not your equals move your pity less!

The author of this prologue, HENRY FIELDING, was in
1736 at the height of his brief but sensational career as a
dramatist and theatrical manager. Before 1730 he had produced only a bad neo-Congrevian comedy; and after the
1737 Licensing Act he was to write nothing of real importance for the theatre. Between 1730 and 1737, however, he
wrote some twenty-six works in dramatic form. These included ballad-operas, comedies of manners, and adaptations
of Molière; but the best of them were the Haymarket burlesques in which Fielding satirized first the contemporary
theatre and then the Walpole government. The liveliness of
his theatrical satire can be seen in two works produced at
the Haymarket in 1730, *The Author's Farce* and *The Tragedy
of Tragedies*. The first part of *The Author's Farce* deals with
the attempts of a penniless dramatist to have his play
produced; and the second part shows that play being re-
hearsed as a 'puppet-show'. Fielding thus combines a
personal attack on the Drury Lane management with a
satirical review of contemporary entertainments. *The
Tragedy of Tragedies*, which is a burlesque drama in the
tradition of Buckingham's *The Rehearsal*, is less informative
but much easier to read. When Fielding published the text,
he added elaborate prefaces and notes in the manner of
Pope's *The Dunciad Variorum*; and his book was thus an
attack both on contemporary tragedy and on contemporary
dramatic criticism. By comparison with the great Scriblerian works which it imitates, this is a trivial and superficial publication; but both the text and the secondary
material are highly entertaining. Similar qualities can be
found in the two political satires, *Pasquin* and *The Historical
Register*, which Fielding produced at the Haymarket in
1736–7. The attacks on Walpole in these plays, however,
helped to provoke the 1737 Licensing Act, which brought
Fielding's theatrical career to a premature end.

The Licensing Act established the patent theatres of
Drury Lane and Covent Garden as the only centres of
dramatic production in London; and it thus inaugurated a
new age of theatrical prosperity and dramatic mediocrity

which was to last for some thirty years. The presiding genius of the mid-century theatre was David Garrick, who arrived in London in 1737 and achieved his first great triumph in 1741. The art of acting developed much more interestingly at this time than the art of dramatic composition; and contemporary work occupied a relatively small place in the theatrical repertoire. The big theatrical events of the age were not new plays but new performances of *The Merchant of Venice*, *Richard III*, *Hamlet* and *Lear*: it was with reference to these works that the leading actors were judged. The new drama of the period is for the most part professionally conservative, showing nothing of the inventiveness which marked the last years before Licensing. The regular forms are the blank-verse tragedy, the sentimentalized comedy of manners, the comic opera and the farce. Successful excursions outside these forms are infrequent; and within each of them the established themes and techniques are generally adhered to.

The most original work of these years is Edward Moore's prose tragedy *The Gamester* (1753), a bourgeois drama about the disastrous consequences of gambling. *The Gamester* never attained the popularity of *The London Merchant*; but it is in many ways a better play, more accomplished in its dramatic technique and less extravagant in its moralistic speeches. Nothing so individual is to be found among the new comedies produced in London between the Licensing Act and 1768; but the best of these are nonetheless civilized and actable. Benjamin Hoadly, son of the Bishop of Winchester, achieved in *The Suspicious Husband* (1747) a blend of libertinism and moral sentiment which exactly fitted popular taste; and in the part of Ranger Garrick gave one of his most famous performances. Arthur Murphy, treating the marital-reconciliation theme in *The Way to Keep Him* (1760), showed the skill of a practised craftsman in adjusting theatrical convention so as to advocate orthodox morality and practical common sense through comic techniques. GEORGE COLMAN the elder, combining in *The Jealous Wife* (1761) a marital-reconciliation plot and a number of borrowings from *Tom Jones*, produced an efficient and lively piece of stage craftsmanship with just enough human reality to hold an audience's attention. Colman again, assisted by GARRICK, composed in *The Clandestine*

Marriage (1766) a comedy which is at once sentimentally moral and genuinely entertaining; and in the part of Lord Ogleby he provided a new vehicle for Garrick, now approaching his fiftieth birthday.

While plays of this kind were maintaining a balance between comedy and sentiment, however, the cult of sensibility was developing both in the French drama and in the English novel; and at the same time the Johnsonian circle was mustering its conservative arguments against that development. In January 1768, with the production of Hugh Kelly's *False Delicacy* at Drury Lane and Oliver Goldsmith's *The Good-Natured Man* at Covent Garden, there began a ten-year contest between sentimentalists and anti-sentimentalists for the approval of the theatrical audience. The major plays of the years 1768–79 were the comedies of Goldsmith and Sheridan, which in their various ways reasserted the ideals of humour and wit which had prevailed in the age of Congreve and Farquhar. The most talented representative of the opposite party was RICHARD CUMBERLAND, who in 1769 began a long and productive career as a dramatist. Cumberland's *The West Indian*, which was produced in 1771, is a much livelier and more theatrical work than *False Delicacy*: it has more characters, more plot, more action, more dramatic surprises, more social reality and more linguistic vigour. Belcour, the central figure, is a young man of vast fortune and unknown parentage, newly arrived in London from the West Indies. The confusions of the plot arise from his impetuous generosity, his inability to see through metropolitan deceptions, and his readiness to woo the first attractive woman he meets without sufficiently ascertaining who she is. He is a sentimental hero, in fact, of the same kind as Ranger in *The Suspicious Husband*; and Cumberland's treatment of this good-natured but imprudent youth owes something to *Tom Jones*. To compare him with the hero of Goldsmith's first play is to realize how intimately the sentimental and anti-sentimental traditions are related. The trait of character which distinguishes Cumberland's hero is his libertinism, which makes him eager to enlist the heroine as his kept mistress; and this motif—the impetuous man who makes advances to a respectable woman hypocrites have told him is for sale—comes straight from Farquhar's *The Constant Couple*. The sentimentalism of

Cumberland's treatment is in his attribution to this impetuous libertine of 'a heart heaving with benevolence': the claim is made too insistently, and one is forced to reject such a contradictory character as incredible. Cumberland's sentimentalism is not confined, however, to this use of the dual-character technique of the reformed-rake tradition; he is equally concerned to refute popular and theatrical assumptions about 'national character'. One of the play's main arguments in defence of its hero is that he must not be condemned for those traits which result from his West Indian background. In the same way, Cumberland grants the privilege of exposing the plot's villains to a man named O'Flaherty, a stage Irishman with a heart of gold; and in the prologue he tells us how to react to this figure. Cumberland's self-conscious anti-racialism, which continues to make certain racialist assumptions, involves a self-deception by dramatist and audience very like that which is demanded by the sentimentalist's brand of sexual morality; but it is clearly the result of a confused attempt to find a more humane system of values. That attempt was to be continued, during the Romantic period, by such dramatists as Thomas Holcroft and Elizabeth Inchbald.

DAVID W. LINDSAY

FURTHER READING

BIBLIOGRAPHY

A detailed bibliography of English drama from 1660 to 1800 will be found in *The New Cambridge Bibliography of English Literature*, where it occupies columns 701–864 of the second volume. Additional information may be gleaned from the relevant sections of *The Annual Bibliography of English Language and Literature*.

TEXTS

The more important plays of the years 1708–79 include the following: Susanna Centlivre, *The Busy Body*, 1709; Charles Shadwell, *The Fair Quaker of Deal*, 1710; Ambrose Philips, *The Distressed Mother*, 1712; Joseph Addison, *Cato*, 1713; Susanna Centlivre,

The Wonder, 1714; Nicholas Rowe, *Jane Shore*, 1714; Joseph Addison, *The Drummer*, 1716; John Gay and others, *Three Hours after Marriage*, 1717; Susanna Centlivre, *A Bold Stroke for a Wife*, 1718; Richard Steele, *The Conscious Lovers*, 1722; Allan Ramsay, *The Gentle Shepherd*, 1725; John Gay, *The Beggar's Opera*, 1728; Colley Cibber, *The Provoked Husband*, 1728; Henry Fielding, *The Author's Farce*, 1730; Henry Fielding, *The Tragedy of Tragedies*, 1730; George Lillo, *The London Merchant*, 1731; Henry Fielding, *Pasquin*, 1736; George Lillo, *Fatal Curiosity*, 1736; Henry Fielding, *The Historical Register*, 1737; Benjamin Hoadly, *The Suspicious Husband*, 1747; Edward Moore, *The Gamester*, 1753; John Home, *Douglas*, 1756; Arthur Murphy, *The Way to Keep Him*, 1760; George Colman, *The Jealous Wife*, 1761; George Colman and David Garrick, *The Clandestine Marriage*, 1766; Hugh Kelly, *False Delicacy*, 1768; Oliver Goldsmith, *The Good-Natured Man*, 1768; Richard Cumberland, *The West Indian*, 1771; Oliver Goldsmith, *She Stoops to Conquer*, 1773; R. B. Sheridan, *The Rivals*, 1775; R. B. Sheridan, *The Duenna*, 1775; R. B. Sheridan, *The School for Scandal*, 1777; R. B. Sheridan, *The Critic*, 1779. Many of these are available in modern editions, such as the Regent's Restoration Drama series.

HISTORY AND CRITICISM

A classic account of the English theatre from 1690 to 1740 is Colley Cibber's *An Apology for the Life of Colley Cibber*, which was edited by B. R. S. Fone in 1968; and a lively critique of the English theatre in the 1760s can be found in Charles Churchill's poem *The Rosciad*. Allardyce Nicoll's *A History of English Drama 1660–1900*, 1952–9, is the standard modern work in this field; the second and third volumes deal with the eighteenth century. The most comprehensive and reliable work of reference, however, is the Southern Illinois University Press compilation entitled *The London Stage 1660–1800*. The five parts of this work, which were published between 1960 and 1968, cover the periods 1660–1700, 1700–29, 1729–47, 1747–76 and 1776–1800. Valuable books of a less expansive kind include: F. W. Bateson, *English Comic Drama 1700–1750*, 1929; F. S. Boas, *An Introduction to Eighteenth-Century Drama*, 1953; John Loftis, *Comedy and Society from Congreve to Fielding*, 1960; and John Loftis, *The Politics of Drama in Augustan England*, 1963. There is an essay on *The Beggar's Opera* in William Empson's *Some Versions of Pastoral*, 1936; and a full account of Fielding's dramatic career can be found in the first volume of F. Homes Dudden's *Henry Fielding: His Life, Works and Times*, 1952.

CONTENTS

The plays here printed are modernized in spelling, punctuation and the use of capitals and italics. Apart from this they follow the first editions, except in the case of *The Tragedy of Tragedies* (see p. 164). A number of insignificant corrections have been made without notice, but editorial additions of importance are enclosed in square brackets.

CATO

Joseph Addison, the great essayist, was born on 1 May, 1672, at Milston, Wiltshire, and was educated at Lichfield Grammar School, Charterhouse, and Queen's College, Oxford. As a demy and Fellow of Magdalen he made various essays in literature, and attracted the notice of the Whig leaders. After four years spent on the grand tour of Europe he returned to win sudden fame and an excise commissionership by his poem on Blenheim, *The Campaign*, which was written in 1704. Thereafter he held various political offices, including that of Secretary of State to the Lord Lieutenant of Ireland, which led to his making the acquaintance and earning the friendship of Swift, and in April 1717 he was appointed Secretary of State.

But his political activities are now of little interest compared with his literary work and its humanising influence upon the life and letters of his time. He wrote a good deal for *The Tatler*, which his old friend and schoolfellow, Richard Steele, started in 1709, and when this was succeeded by *The Spectator* (1711–12, 1714), Addison became the leading contributor, writing De Coverley papers and the other essays whose grace and charm and gently ironic humour give him his high place in English literature: for it is as essayist, and not as dramatist and poet, that Addison is rightly remembered.

In 1716 he married Charlotte, Countess of Warwick. This marriage was probably not as unhappy as it was reported to be, but Addison's last years were darkened by failing health and a quarrel with Steele.

He died at the age of forty-seven, on 17 June, 1719, and was buried in Westminster Abbey.

CATO.

A
TRAGEDY.

As it is Acted at the

THEATRE ROYAL in *Drury-Lane*

BY

Her Majesty's Servants

By Mr. ADDISON

Ecce Spectaculum dignum, ad quod respiciat, intentus operi suo,
Deus! Ecce par Deo dignum, vir fortis cum malâ fortunâ
compositus! Non video, inquam, quid habeat in terris Jupi-
ter pulchrius, si convertere animum velit, quàm ut spectet
Catonem, jam partibus non semel fractis, nihilominùs inter ru-
inas publicas erectum.

Sen. de Divin. Prov.

LONDON:

Printed for J. Tonson, at *Shakespear's Head* over against
Catherine-Street in the *Strand*. MDCCXIII.

CATO

A

TRAGEDY

As it is Acted at the

THEATRE-ROYAL in Drury-Lane

by

Her Majesty's Servants

By Mr. ADDISON

LONDON

Printed for J. Tonson, at Shakespear's Head over-against
Catherine-street in the Strand. MDCCXIII.

PROLOGUE

BY MR. POPE

To wake the soul by tender strokes of art,
To raise the genius, and to mend the heart,
To make mankind in conscious virtue bold,
Live o'er each scene, and be what they behold:
For this the Tragic-Muse first trod the stage,
Commanding tears to stream thro' every age;
Tyrants no more their savage nature kept,
And foes to virtue wondered how they wept.
Our author shuns by vulgar springs to move
The hero's glory, or the virgin's love;
In pitying love we but our weakness show,
And wild ambition well deserves its woe.
Here tears shall flow from a more gen'rous cause,
Such tears as patriots shed for dying laws:
He bids your breasts with ancient ardour rise,
And calls forth Roman drops from British eyes.
Virtue confessed in human shape he draws,
What Plato thought, and God-like Cato was:
No common object to your sight displays,
But what with pleasure Heav'n itself surveys;
A brave man struggling in the storms of fate
And greatly falling with a falling state!
While Cato gives his little Senate laws,
What bosom beats not in his country's cause?
Who sees him act, but envies ev'ry deed?
Who hears him groan, and does not wish to bleed?
Ev'n when proud Cæsar 'midst triumphal cars,
The spoils of nations, and the pomp of wars,
Ignobly vain, and impotently great,
Showed Rome her Cato's figure drawn in state;
As her dead father's rev'rend image passed
The pomp was darkened and the day o'ercast,
The triumph ceased—tears gushed from ev'ry eye;
The world's great victor passed unheeded by;
Her last good man dejected Rome adored,
And honoured Cæsar's less than Cato's sword.
Britons, attend; be worth like this approved,
And show you have the virtue to be moved.
With honest scorn the first famed Cato viewed
Rome learning arts from Greece, whom she subdued;
Our scene precariously subsists too long
On French translation, and Italian song.
Dare to have sense yourselves; assert the stage,
Be justly warmed with your own native rage.
Such plays alone should please a British ear,
As Cato's self had not disdained to hear.

DRAMATIS PERSONÆ

MEN

Cato	Mr. Booth
Lucius, *a senator*	Mr. Keen
Sempronius, *a senator*	Mr. Mills
Juba, *Prince of Numidia*	Mr. Wilks
Syphax, *General of the Numidians*	Mr. Cibber
Portius } *Sons of Cato* {	Mr. Powell
Marcus	Mr. Ryan
Decius, *Ambassador from Cæsar*	Mr. Bowman

Mutineers, Guards, etc.

WOMEN

Marcia, *daughter to Cato*	Mrs. Oldfield
Lucia, *daughter to Lucius*	Mrs. Porter

SCENE—A large hall in the Governor's
Palace of Utica

It will be noted that the first edition, which is followed here, abandons the French method of scene-division after Act I.

CATO

ACT I

SCENE I

PORTIUS, MARCUS

Por. The dawn is overcast, the morning lowers,
And heavily in clouds brings on the day,
The great, the important day, big with the fate
Of Cato and of Rome. Our father's death
Would fill up all the guilt of civil war,
And close the scene of blood. Already Cæsar
Has ravaged more than half the globe, and sees
Mankind grown thin by his destructive sword:
Should he go further, numbers would be wanting
To form new battles, and support his crimes.
Ye gods, what havoc does ambition make
Among your works!
 Marc.   Thy steady temper, Portius,
Can look on guilt, rebellion, fraud, and Cæsar,
In the calm lights of mild philosophy;
I'm tortured, even to madness, when I think
On the proud victor—ev'ry time he's named
Pharsalia rises to my view!—I see
The insulting tyrant, prancing o'er the field,
Strewed with Rome's citizens, and drenched in slaughter;
His horse's hoofs wet with patrician blood!
Oh, Portius! is there not some chosen curse,
Some hidden thunder in the stores of Heaven,
Red with uncommon wrath, to blast the man,
Who owes his greatness to his country's ruin?
 Por. Believe me, Marcus, 'tis an impious greatness,
And mixed with too much horror to be envied:
How does the lustre of our father's actions,
Through the dark cloud of ills that cover him,
Break out, and burn with more triumphant brightness!
His sufferings shine, and spread a glory round him;
Greatly unfortunate, he fights the cause
Of honour, virtue, liberty, and Rome.
His sword ne'er fell, but on the guilty head;
Oppression, tyranny, and power usurped,
Draw all the vengeance of his arm upon 'em.

Marc. Who knows not this? But what can Cato do
Against a world, a base, degenerate world,
That courts the yoke, and bows the neck to Cæsar?
Pent up in Utica, he vainly forms
A poor epitome of Roman greatness,
And, covered with Numidian guards, directs
A feeble army, and an empty senate,
Remnants of mighty battles fought in vain.
By Heaven, such virtue, joined with such success,
Distract my very soul! our father's fortune
Would almost tempt us to renounce his precepts.

Por. Remember what our father oft has told us:
The ways of Heaven are dark and intricate,
Puzzled in mazes, and perplexed with errors,
Our understanding traces them in vain,
Lost and bewildered in the fruitless search;
Nor sees with how much art the windings run,
Nor where the regular confusion ends.

Marc. These are suggestions of a mind at ease:—
Oh, Portius, didst thou taste but half the griefs
That wring my soul, thou couldst not talk thus coldly.
Passion unpitied, and successless love,
Plant daggers in my heart, and aggravate
My other griefs.—Were but my Lucia kind——

Por. Thou seest not that thy brother is thy rival;
But I must hide it, for I know thy temper.   (*Aside.*
Now, Marcus, now, thy virtue's on the proof;
Put forth thy utmost strength, work every nerve
And call up all thy father in thy soul:
To quell the tyrant Love, and guard thy heart
On this weak side, where most our nature fails,
Would be a conquest worthy Cato's son.

Marc. Portius, the counsel which I cannot take,
Instead of healing, but upbraids my weakness.
Bid me for honour plunge into a war
Of thickest foes, and rush on certain death,
Then shalt thou see that Marcus is not slow
To follow glory, and confess his father.
Love is not to be reasoned down, or lost
In high ambition, in a thirst for greatness;
'Tis second life, it grows into the soul,
Warms every vein and beats in every pulse;
I feel it here, my resolution melts——

Por. Behold young Juba, the Numidian prince,
With how much care he forms himself to glory,
And breaks the fierceness of his native temper,
To copy out our father's bright example.
He loves our sister Marcia, greatly loves her;
His eyes, his looks, his actions, all betray it;

But still the smothered fondness burns within him;
When most it swells, and labours for a vent,
The sense of honour, and desire of fame,
Drive the big passion back into his heart.
What! shall an African, shall Juba's heir
Reproach great Cato's son, and show the world
A virtue wanting in a Roman soul?

   Marc. Portius, no more! your words leave stings behind them
Whene'er did Juba, or did Portius, show
A virtue that has cast me at a distance,
And thrown me out in the pursuits of honour?

   Por. Marcus, I know thy gen'rous temper well;
Fling but the appearance of dishonour on it,
It straight takes fire, and mounts into a blaze.

   Marc. A brother's sufferings claim a brother's pity.

   Por. Heaven knows, I pity thee. Behold my eyes,
Ev'n whilst I speak—do they not swim in tears?
Were but my heart as naked to thy view,
Marcus would see it bleed in his behalf.

   Marc. Why then dost treat me with rebukes, instead
Of kind condoling cares, and friendly sorrow?

   Por. Oh, Marcus! did I know the way to ease
Thy troubled heart, and mitigate thy pains,
Marcus, believe me, I could die to do it.

   Marc. Thou best of brothers, and thou best of friends!
Pardon a weak, distempered soul, that swells
With sudden gusts, and sinks as soon in calms,
The sport of passions. But Sempronius comes:
He must not find this softness hanging on me.   (*Exit.*

SCENE II

SEMPRONIUS SOLUS

   Sem. Conspiracies no sooner should be formed
Than executed. What means Portius here?
I like not that cold youth. I must dissemble,
And speak a language foreign to my heart.

SEMPRONIUS, PORTIUS

Good morrow, Portius; let us once embrace,
Once more embrace, while yet we both are free.
To-morrow, should we thus express our friendship,
Each might receive a slave into his arms.
This sun, perhaps, this morning sun's the last
That e'er shall rise on Roman liberty.

   Por. My father has this morning call'd together
To this poor hall, his little Roman senate,

(The leavings of Pharsalia) to consult
If yet he can oppose the mighty torrent
That bears down Rome, and all her gods before it,
Or must at length give up the world to Cæsar.
 Sem. Not all the pomp and majesty of Rome
Can raise her senate more than Cato's presence.
His virtues render our assembly awful,
They strike with something like religious fear,
And make even Cæsar tremble at the head
Of armies flushed with conquest. Oh, my Portius!
Could I but call that wondrous man my father,
Would but thy sister Marcia be propitious
To thy friend's vows, I might be blest indeed!
 Por. Alas, Sempronius! wouldst thou talk of love
To Marcia, whilst her father's life's in danger;
Thou mightst as well court the pale, trembling vestal,
When she beholds the holy flame expiring.
 Sem. The more I see the wonders of thy race,
The more I'm charmed. Thou must take heed, my Portius;
The world has all its eyes on Cato's son;
Thy father's merit sets thee up to view,
And shows thee in the fairest point of light,
To make thy virtues or thy faults conspicuous.
 Por. Well dost thou seem to check my lingering here
On this important hour—I'll straight away,
And while the fathers of the senate meet
In close debate, to weigh the events of war,
I'll animate the soldiers' drooping courage
With love of freedom, and contempt of life;
I'll thunder in their ears their country's cause,
And try to rouse up all that's Roman in them.
'Tis not in mortals to command success,
But we'll do more, Sempronius, we'll deserve it.   (*Exit.*
 Sem. (*solus*). Curse on the stripling! how he apes his sire!
Ambitiously sententious——But I wonder
Old Syphax comes not; his Numidian genius
Is well disposed to mischief, were he prompt
And eager on it; but he must be spurred,
And every moment quickened to the course.
Cato has used me ill; he has refused
His daughter Marcia to my ardent vows.
Besides, his baffled arms, and ruined cause,
Are bars to my ambition. Cæsar's favour,
That showers down greatness on his friends, will raise me
To Rome's first honours. If I give up Cato,
I claim, in my reward, his captive daughter.
But Syphax comes——

SCENE III

SYPHAX, SEMPRONIUS

Syph. Sempronius, all is ready;
I've sounded my Numidians, man by man,
And find them ripe for a revolt: they all
Complain aloud of Cato's discipline,
And wait but the command to change their master.

Sem. Believe me, Syphax, there's no time to waste;
Ev'n whilst we speak, our conqueror comes on,
And gathers ground upon us every moment.
Alas! thou know'st not Cæsar's active soul,
With what a dreadful course he rushes on
From war to war. In vain has nature formed
Mountains and oceans to oppose his passage;
He bounds o'er all, victorious in his march,
The Alps and Pyreneans sink before him;
Through winds and waves and storms he works his way
Impatient for the battle: one day more
Will set the victor thundering at our gates.
But tell me, hast thou yet drawn o'er young Juba?
That still would recommend thee more to Cæsar,
And challenge better terms.

Syph.   Alas! he's lost!
He's lost, Sempronius; all his thoughts are full
Of Cato's virtues. But I'll try once more
(For every instant I expect him here)
If yet I can subdue those stubborn principles
Of faith and honour, and I know not what,
That have corrupted his Numidian temper,
And struck the infection into all his soul.

Sem. Be sure to press upon him every motive.
Juba's surrender, since his father's death,
Would give up Afric into Cæsar's hands,
And make him lord of half the burning zone.

Syph. But is it true, Sempronius, that your senate
Is called together? Gods! thou must be cautious;
Cato has piercing eyes, and will discern
Our frauds, unless they're covered thick with art.

Sem. Let me alone, good Syphax; I'll conceal
My thoughts in passion ('tis the surest way);
I'll bellow out for Rome, and for my country,
And mouth at Cæsar, till I shake the senate.
Your cold hypocrisy's a stale device,
A worn-out trick: would'st thou be thought in earnest,
Clothe thy feign'd zeal in rage, in fire, in fury!

Syph. In troth, thou'rt able to instruct grey hairs,
And teach the wily African deceit.

Sem. Once more be sure to try thy skill on Juba.
Meanwhile I'll hasten to my Roman soldiers,
Inflame the mutiny, and underhand
Blow up their discontents, till they break out
Unlooked for, and discharge themselves on Cato.
Remember, Syphax, we must work in haste;
Oh, think what anxious moments pass between
The birth of plots, and their last fatal periods!
Oh, 'tis a dreadful interval of time,
Fill'd up with horror all, and big with death!
Destruction hangs on every word we speak,
On every thought, till the concluding stroke
Determines all, and closes our design.   (*Exit.*

Syph. (*solus*). I'll try if yet I can reduce to reason
This headstrong youth, and make him spurn at Cato.
The time is short; Cæsar comes rushing on us——
But hold! young Juba sees me, and approaches!

SCENE IV

JUBA, SYPHAX

Jub. Syphax, I joy to meet thee thus alone.
I have observed of late thy looks are fall'n,
O'ercast with gloomy cares and discontent;
Then tell me, Syphax, I conjure thee, tell me,
What are the thoughts that knit thy brow in frowns,
And turn thine eye thus coldly on thy prince?

Syph. 'Tis not my talent to conceal my thoughts,
Or carry smiles and sunshines in my face,
When discontent sits heavy at my heart:
I have not yet so much the Roman in me.

Jub. Why dost thou cast out such ungenerous terms
Against the lords and sovereigns of the world?
Dost thou not see mankind fall down before them,
And own the force of their superior virtue?
Is there a nation in the wilds of Afric,
Amidst our barren rocks, and burning sands,
That does not tremble at the Roman name?

Syph. Gods! where's the worth that sets this people up
Above your own Numidia's tawny sons?
Do they with tougher sinews bend the bow?
Or flies the javelin swifter to its mark,
Launched from the vigour of a Roman arm?
Who like our active African instructs
The fiery steed, and trains him to his hand?
Or guides in troops the embattled elephant
Loaden with war? These, these are arts, my prince,
In which your Zama does not stoop to Rome.

Jub. These are all virtues of a meaner rank:
Perfections that are placed in bones and nerves.
A Roman soul is bent on higher views:
To civilise the rude unpolished world,
And lay it under the restraint of laws;
To make man mild and sociable to man;
To cultivate the wild licentious savage
With wisdom, discipline, and liberal arts—
The embellishments of life; virtues like these
Make human nature shine, reform the soul,
And break our fierce barbarians into men.

   Syph. Patience, kind heavens!—excuse an old man's warmth,
What are these wondrous civilising arts,
This Roman polish, and this smooth behaviour,
That render man thus tractable and tame?
Are they not wholly to disguise our passions,
To set our looks at variance with our thoughts,
To check the starts and sallies of the soul,
And break off all its commerce with the tongue;
In short, to change us into other creatures
Than what our nature and the gods designed us?

   Jub. To strike thee dumb, turn up thy eyes to Cato!
There mayest thou see to what a godlike height
The Roman virtues lift up mortal man,
While good, and just, and anxious for his friends,
He's still severely bent against himself;
Renouncing sleep, and rest, and food, and ease,
He strives with thirst and hunger, toil and heat;
And when his fortune sets before him all
The pomps and pleasures that his soul can wish,
His rigid virtue will accept of none.

   Syph. Believe me, Prince, there's not an African
That traverses our vast Numidian deserts
In quest of prey, and lives upon his bow,
But better practises those boasted virtues.
Coarse are his meals, the fortune of the chase;
Amidst the running stream he slakes his thirst;
Toils all the day, and at the approach of night,
On the first friendly bank he throws him down,
Or rests his head upon a rock till morn;
Then rises fresh, pursues his wonted game,
And if the following day he chance to find
A new repast, or an untasted spring,
Blesses his stars, and thinks it luxury.

   Jub. Thy prejudices, Syphax, won't discern
What virtues grow from ignorance and choice,
Nor how the hero differs from the brute.
But grant that others could with equal glory
Look down on pleasures, and the baits of sense;

Where shall we find the man that bears affliction,
Great and majestic in his griefs, like Cato?
Heavens, with what strength, what steadiness of mind,
He triumphs in the midst of all his sufferings!
How does he rise against a load of woes,
And thank the gods that throw the weight upon him!
 Syph. 'Tis pride, rank pride, and haughtiness of soul;
I think the Romans call it stoicism.
Had not your royal father thought so highly
Of Roman virtue, and of Cato's cause,
He had not fallen by a slave's hand inglorious;
Nor would his slaughtered army now have lain
On Afric's sands, disfigured with their wounds,
To gorge the wolves and vultures of Numidia.
 Jub. Why dost thou call my sorrows up afresh?
My father's name brings tears into my eyes.
 Syph. O that you'd profit by your father's ills!
 Jub. What wouldst thou have me do?
 Syph.   Abandon Cato.
 Jub. Syphax, I should be more than twice an orphan
By such a loss.
 Syph.   Aye, there's the tie that binds you!
You long to call him father. Marcia's charms
Work in your heart unseen, and plead for Cato.
No wonder you are deaf to all I say.
 Jub. Syphax, your zeal becomes importunate;
I've hitherto permitted it to rave,
And talk at large; but learn to keep it in,
Lest it should take more freedom than I'll give it.
 Syph. Sir, your great father never used me thus.
Alas, he's dead! but can you e'er forget
The tender sorrows, and the pangs of nature,
The fond embraces, and repeated blessings
Which you drew from him in your last farewell?
Still must I cherish the dear sad remembrance,
At once to torture and to please my soul.
The good old king, at parting, wrung my hand
(His eyes brimful of tears), then sighing cried,
Prithee be careful of my son!—His grief
Swelled up so high, he could not utter more.
 Jub. Alas! thy story melts away my soul!
That best of fathers! how shall I discharge
The gratitude and duty which I owe him?
 Syph. By laying up his counsels in your heart.
 Jub. His counsels bade me yield to thy directions:
Then, Syphax, chide me in severest terms,
Vent all thy passion, and I'll stand its shock,
Calm and unruffled as a summer sea,
When not a breath of wind flies o'er its surface.

Syph. Alas! my prince, I'd guide you to your safety.
Jub. I do believe thou wouldst; but tell me how?
Syph. Fly from the fate that follows Cæsar's foes.
Jub. My father scorn'd to do it.
Syph.   And therefore died.
Jub. Better to die ten thousand thousand deaths,
Than wound my honour.
Syph.   Rather say, your love.
Jub. Syphax, I've promised to preserve my temper.
Why wilt thou urge me to confess a flame
I long have stifled, and would fain conceal?
Syph. Believe me, prince, 'tis hard to conquer love,
But easy to divert and break its force.
Absence might cure it, or a second mistress
Light up another flame, and put out this.
The glowing dames of Zama's royal court
Have faces flush'd with more exalted charms;
The sun that rolls his chariot o'er their heads,
Works up more fire and colour in their cheeks:
Were you with these, my prince, you'd soon forget
The pale, unripened beauties of the north.
Jub. 'Tis not a set of features, or complexion,
The tincture of a skin, that I admire:
Beauty soon grows familiar to the lover,
Fades in his eye, and palls upon the sense.
The virtuous Marcia towers above her sex:
True, she is fair (oh, how divinely fair!),
But still the lovely maid improves her charms
With inward greatness, unaffected wisdom,
And sanctity of manners; Cato's soul
Shines out in everything she acts or speaks.
While winning mildness and attractive smiles
Dwell in her looks, and with becoming grace,
Soften the rigour of her father's virtues.
Syph. How does your tongue grow wanton in her praise!
But on my knees, I beg you would consider——

Enter MARCIA *and* LUCIA

Jub. Ha! Syphax, is't not she?—She moves this way;
And with her Lucia, Lucius's fair daughter.
My heart beats thick—I prithee, Syphax, leave me.
Syph. Ten thousand curses fasten on them both!
Now will this woman, with a single glance,
Undo what I've been lab'ring all this while.   (*Exit.*

JUBA, MARCIA, LUCIA

Jub. Hail, charming maid! How does thy beauty smooth
The face of war, and make even horror smile!
At sight of thee my heart shakes off its sorrows;

I feel a dawn of joy break in upon me,
And for a while forget the approach of Cæsar.

   Mar. I should be grieved, young prince, to think my presence
Unbent your thoughts, and slackened 'em to arms,
While, warm with slaughter, our victorious foe,
Threatens aloud, and calls you to the field.

   Jub. Oh, Marcia, let me hope thy kind concerns
And gentle wishes follow me to battle!
The thought will give new vigour to my arm,
Add strength and weight to my descending sword,
And drive it in a tempest on the foe.

   Mar. My prayers and wishes always shall attend
The friends of Rome, the glorious cause of virtue,
And men approved of by the gods and Cato.

   Jub. That Juba may deserve thy pious cares,
I'll gaze for ever on thy godlike father,
Transplanting one by one, into my life,
His bright perfections, till I shine like him.

   Mar. My father never, at a time like this,
Would lay out his great soul in words, and waste
Such precious moments.

   Jub.   Thy reproofs are just,
Thou virtuous maid; I'll hasten to my troops,
And fire their languid souls with Cato's virtue.
If e'er I lead them to the field, when all
The war shall stand ranged in its just array,
And dreadful pomp. then will I think on thee;
Oh, lovely maid! then will I think on thee;
And in the shock of charging hosts, remember
What glorious deeds should grace the man who hopes
For Marcia's love.   (*Exit.*

   Lucia.   Marcia, you're too severe;
How could you chide the young good-natured prince,
And drive him from you with so stern an air,
A prince that loves, and dotes on you to death?

   Mar. 'Tis therefore, Lucia, that I chide him from me:
His air, his voice, his looks, and honest soul,
Speak all so movingly in his behalf,
I dare not trust myself to hear him talk.

   Lucia. Why will you fight against so sweet a passion,
And steel your heart to such a world of charms?

   Mar. How, Lucia! wouldst thou have me sink away
In pleasing dreams, and lose myself in love,
When every moment Cato's life's at stake?
Cæsar comes armed with terror and revenge,
And aims his thunder at my father's head.
Should not the sad occasion swallow up
My other cares and draw them all into it?

   Lucia. Why have not I this constancy of mind,

Who have so many griefs to try its force?
Sure, Nature formed me of her softest mould,
Enfeebled all my soul with tender passions,
And sunk me even below my own weak sex:
Pity and love, by turns, oppress my heart.
  Mar. Lucia, disburden all thy cares on me,
And let me share thy most retired distress.
Tell me, who raises up this conflict in thee?
  Lucia. I need not blush to name them, when I tell thee
They're Marcia's brothers, and the sons of Cato.
  Mar. They both behold thee with their sister's eyes,
And often have revealed their passion to me.
But tell me whose address thou favourest most;
I long to know and yet I dread to hear it.
  Lucia. Which is it Marcia wishes for?
  Mar.   For neither—
And yet for both; the youths have equal share
In Marcia's wishes, and divide their sister:
But tell me which of them is Lucia's choice.
  Lucia. Marcia, they both are high in my esteem;
But in my love—why wilt thou make me name him?
Thou know'st it is a blind and foolish passion,
Pleased and disgusted with it knows not what——
  Mar. Oh, Lucia, I'm perplexed. Oh, tell me which
I must hereafter call my happy brother.
  Lucia. Suppose 'twere Portius, could you blame my choice?—
Oh, Portius, thou hast stolen away my soul!
With what a graceful tenderness he loves!
And breathes the softest, the sincerest vows!
Complacency, and truth, and manly sweetness
Dwell ever on his tongue and smooth his thoughts.
Marcus is over-warm, his fond complaints
Have so much earnestness and passion in them,
I hear him with a secret kind of horror,
And tremble at his vehemence of temper.
  Mar. Alas, poor youth! How canst thou throw him from thee?
Lucia, thou know'st not half the love he bears thee;
Whene'er he speaks of thee, his heart's in flames,
He sends out all his soul in every word,
And thinks, and talks, and looks like one transported.
Unhappy youth! How will thy coldness raise
Tempests and storms in his afflicted bosom!
I dread the consequence.
  Lucia.   You seem to plead
Against your brother Portius.
  Mar.   Heaven forbid!
Had Portius been the unsuccessful lover,
The same compassion would have fallen on him.
  Lucia. Was ever virgin love distressed like mine!

Portius himself oft falls in tears before me,
As if he mourned his rival's ill success;
Then bids me hide the motions of my heart,
Nor show which way it turns. So much he fears
The sad effects that it would have on Marcus.

Mar. He knows too well how easily he's fired,
And would not plunge his brother in despair,
But waits for happier times, and kinder moments.

Lucia. Alas! Too late I find myself involved
In endless griefs and labyrinths of woe,
Born to afflict my Marcia's family,
And sow dissension in the hearts of brothers.
Tormenting thought! It cuts into my soul.

Mar. Let us not, Lucia, aggravate our sorrows,
But to the gods permit the events of things.
Our lives, discolour'd with our present woes,
May still grow white, and smile with happier hours.

So the pure limpid stream, when foul with stains
Of rushing torrents, and descending rains,
Works itself clear, and, as it runs, refines,
Till, by degrees, the floating mirror shines,
Reflects each flower that on the border grows,
And a new heaven in its fair bosom shows.   (*Exeunt.*

ACT II

SCENE I.—*The Senate* [sitting]

Sem. Rome still survives in this assembled senate!
Let us remember we are Cato's friends,
And act like men who claim that glorious title.

Luc. Cato will soon be here, and open to us
The occasion of our meeting. Hark! He comes!
                                [*A sound of trumpets.*
May all the guardian gods of Rome direct him!

Enter CATO

Cato. Fathers, we once again are met in council;
Cæsar's approach has summoned us together,
And Rome attends her fate from our resolves.
How shall we treat this bold aspiring man?
Success still follows him, and backs his crimes;
Pharsalia gave him Rome, Egypt has since
Received his yoke, and the whole Nile is Cæsar's.
Why should I mention Juba's overthrow,
And Scipio's death? Numidia's burning sands

Still smoke with blood. 'Tis time we should decree
What course to take. Our foe advances on us,
And envies us even Libya's sultry deserts.
Fathers, pronounce your thoughts: are they still fixed
To hold it out, and fight it to the last?
Or are your hearts subdued at length, and wrought,
By time and ill success, to a submission?
Sempronius, speak.
    Sem.   My voice is still for war.
Gods! can a Roman senate long debate
Which of the two to choose, slavery or death!
No; let us rise at once, gird on our swords,
And, at the head of our remaining troops,
Attack the foe, break through the thick array
Of his thronged legions, and charge home upon him.
Perhaps some arm, more lucky than the rest,
May reach his heart, and free the world from bondage.
Rise, fathers, rise! 'tis Rome demands your help;
Rise, and revenge her slaughtered citizens,
Or share their fate. The corps of half her senate
Manure the fields of Thessaly, while we
Sit here, deliberating in cold debates,
If we should sacrifice our lives to honour,
Or wear them out in servitude and chains.
Rouse up, for shame! Our brothers of Pharsalia
Point at their wounds, and cry aloud—To battle!
Great Pompey's shade complains that we are slow;
And Scipio's ghost walks unrevenged amongst us.
    Cato. Let not a torrent of impetuous zeal
Transport thee thus beyond the bounds of reason;
True fortitude is seen in great exploits,
That justice warrants, and that wisdom guides;
All else is towering frenzy and distraction.
Are not the lives of those who draw the sword
In Rome's defence entrusted to our care?
Should we thus lead them to a field of slaughter,
Might not the impartial world with reason say
We lavished at our deaths the blood of thousands,
To grace our fall and make our ruin glorious?
Lucius, we next would know what's your opinion.
    Luc. My thoughts, I must confess, are turned on peace.
Already have our quarrels filled the world
With widows and with orphans: Scythia mourns
Our guilty wars, and earth's remotest regions
Lie half unpeopled by the feuds of Rome:
'Tis time to sheathe the sword, and spare mankind.
It is not Cæsar, but the gods, my fathers,
The gods declare against us, and repel
Our vain attempts. To urge the foe to battle

(Prompted by blind revenge and wild despair)
Were to refuse the awards of Providence,
And not to rest in heaven's determination.
Already we have shown our love to Rome,
Now let us show submission to the gods.
We took up arms, not to revenge ourselves,
But free the commonwealth; when this end fails,
Arms have no further use. Our country's cause,
That drew our swords, now wrests them from our hands,
And bids us not delight in Roman blood,
Unprofitably shed. What men could do,
Is done already: Heaven and earth will witness,
If Rome must fall, that we are innocent.

Sem. This smooth discourse and mild behaviour oft
Conceal a traitor—something whispers me
All is not right—Cato, beware of Lucius.   [*Aside to Cato.*

Cato. Let us appear nor rash nor diffident;
Immod'rate valour swells into a fault;
And fear, admitted into public councils,
Betrays like treason. Let us shun 'em both.
Fathers, I cannot see that our affairs
Are grown thus desperate: we have bulwarks round us;
Within our walls are troops inur'd to toil
In Afric's heat, and season'd to the sun;
Numidia's spacious kingdom l'es behind us,
Ready to rise at its young prince's call.
While there is hope, do not distrust the gods;
But wait, at least, till Cæsar's near approach
Force us to yield. 'Twill never be too late
To sue for chains, and own a conqueror.
Why should Rome fall a moment ere her time?
No, let us draw her term of freedom out
In its full length, and spin it to the last,
So shall we gain still one day's liberty:
And let me perish, but, in Cato's judgment,
A day, an hour, of virtuous liberty
Is worth a whole eternity in bondage.

Enter MARCUS

Marc. Fathers, this moment, as I watch'd the gate,
Lodged on my post, a herald is arrived
From Cæsar's camp, and with him comes old Decius,
The Roman knight: he carries in his looks
Impatience, and demands to speak with Cato.

Cato. By your permission, fathers—bid him enter.
                                        (*Exit* MARCUS.
Decius was once my friend, but other prospects
Have loosed those ties, and bound him fast to Cæsar.
His message may determine our resolves.

Enter DECIUS

Dec. Cæsar sends health to Cato——
Cato.   Could he send it
To Cato's slaughtered friends, it would be welcome.
Are not your orders to address the senate?
   Dec. My business is with Cato; Cæsar sees
The straits to which you're driven; and, as he knows
Cato's high worth, is anxious for your life.
   Cato. My life is grafted on the fate of Rome.
Would he save Cato, bid him spare his country.
Tell your dictator this; and tell him, Cato
Disdains a life which he has power to offer.
   Dec. Rome and her senators submit to Cæsar;
Her gen'rals and her consuls are no more,
Who checked his conquests and denied his triumphs.
Why will not Cato be this Cæsar's friend?
   Cato. Those very reasons, thou hast urged, forbid it.
   Dec. Cato, I've orders to expostulate
And reason with you, as from friend to friend:
Think on the storm that gathers o'er your head,
And threatens every hour to burst upon it;
Still may you stand high in your country's honours,
Do but comply, and make your peace with Cæsar,
Rome will rejoice, and cast its eyes on Cato,
As on the second of mankind.
   Cato.   No more;
I must not think of life on such conditions.
   Dec. Cæsar is well acquainted with your virtues,
And therefore sets this value on your life.
Let him but know the price of Cato's friendship,
And name your terms.
   Cato.   Bid him disband his legions,
Restore the commonwealth to liberty,
Submit his actions to the public censure,
And stand the judgment of a Roman senate.
Bid him do this, and Cato is his friend.
   Dec. Cato, the world talks loudly of your wisdom——
   Cato. Nay, more, though Cato's voice was ne'er employed
To clear the guilty, and to varnish crimes,
Myself will mount the rostrum in his favour,
And strive to gain his pardon from the people.
   Dec. A style like this becomes a conqueror.
   Cato. Decius, a style like this becomes a Roman.
   Dec. What is a Roman, that is Cæsar's foe?
   Cato. Greater than Cæsar: he's a friend to virtue.
   Dec. Consider, Cato, you're in Utica,
And at the head of your own little senate:
You don't now thunder in the capitol,

With all the mouths of Rome to second you.

Cato. Let him consider that, who drives us hither.
'Tis Cæsar's sword has made Rome's senate little,
And thinn'd its ranks. Alas! thy dazzled eye
Beholds this man in a false glaring light,
Which conquest and success have thrown upon him;
Didst thou but view him right, thou'dst see him black
With murder, treason, sacrilege, and crimes,
That strike my soul with horror but to name 'em.
I know thou lookst on me as on a wretch
Beset with ills, and covered with misfortunes;
But, by the gods I swear, millions of worlds
Should never buy me to be like that Cæsar.

Dec. Does Cato send this answer back to Cæsar,
For all his gen'rous cares and proffer'd friendship?

Cato. His cares for me are insolent and vain:
Presumptuous man! the gods take care of Cato.
Would Cæsar show the greatness of his soul,
Bid him employ his care for these my friends,
And make good use of his ill-gotten power,
By sheltering men much better than himself.

Dec. Your high, unconquered heart makes you forget
You are a man. You rush on your destruction.
But I have done. When I relate hereafter
The tale of this unhappy embassy,
All Rome will be in tears.   *(Exit.*

Sem.   Cato, we thank thee.
The mighty genius of immortal Rome
Speaks in thy voice; thy soul breathes liberty.
Cæsar will shrink to hear the words thou utterest,
And shudder in the midst of all his conquests.

Luc. The senate owns its gratitude to Cato,
Who with so great a soul consults its safety,
And guards our lives, while he neglects his own.

Sem. Sempronius gives no thanks on this account.
Lucius seems fond of life; but what is life?
'Tis not to stalk about, and draw fresh air
From time to time, or gaze upon the sun;
'Tis to be free. When liberty is gone,
Life grows insipid, and has lost its relish.
Oh, could my dying hand but lodge a sword
In Cæsar's bosom, and revenge my country,
By heavens, I could enjoy the pangs of death,
And smile in agony.

Luc.   Others perhaps
May serve their country with as warm a zeal,
Though 'tis not kindled into so much rage.

Sem. This sober conduct is a mighty virtue
In lukewarm patriots.

    Cato.   Come! no more, Sempronius.
All here are friends to Rome, and to each other.
Let us not weaken still the weaker side
By our divisions.
    Sem.   Cato, my resentments
Are sacrificed to Rome—I stand reproved.
    Cato. Fathers, 'tis time you come to a resolve.
    Luc. Cato, we all go in to your opinion;
Cæsar's behaviour has convinced the senate,
We ought to hold it out till terms arrive.
    Sem. We ought to hold it out till death; but, Cato,
My private voice is drowned amid the senate's.
    Cato. Then let us rise, my friends, and strive to fill
This little interval, this pause of life
(While yet our liberty and fates are doubtful),
With resolution, friendship, Roman bravery,
And all the virtues we can crowd into it;
That Heaven may say, it ought to be prolonged.
Fathers, farewell—the young Numidian prince
Comes forward, and expects to know our counsels.
                            (*Exeunt* SENATORS.

Enter JUBA

    Cato. Juba, the Roman senate has resolved,
Till time give better prospects, still to keep
The sword unsheathed, and turn its edge on Cæsar.
    Jub. The resolution fits a Roman senate.
But, Cato, lend me for a while thy patience,
And condescend to hear a young man speak.
My father, when, some days before his death,
He ordered me to march for Utica
(Alas! I thought not then his death so near!),
Wept o'er me, pressed me in his aged arms,
And, as his griefs gave way, "My son," said he,
"Whatever fortune shall befall thy father,
Be Cato's friend; he'll train thee up to great
And virtuous deeds; do but observe him well,
Thou'lt shun misfortunes, or thou'lt learn to bear 'em."
    Cato. Juba, thy father was a worthy prince,
And merited, alas! a better fate;
But Heaven thought otherwise.
    Jub.   My father's fate,
In spite of all the fortitude that shines
Before my face, in Cato's great example,
Subdues my soul, and fills my eyes with tears.
    Cato. It is an honest sorrow, and becomes thee.
    Jub. My father drew respect from foreign climes!
The kings of Afric sought him for their friend;
Kings far remote, that rule, as fame reports,

Behind the hidden sources of the Nile,
In distant worlds, on t'other side the sun;
Oft have their black ambassadors appeared,
Loaden with gifts, and filled the courts of Zama.
 Cato. I am no stranger to thy father's greatness.
 Jub. I would not boast the greatness of my father,
But point out new alliances to Cato.
Had we not better leave this Utica,
To arm Numidia in our cause, and court
The assistance of my father's powerful friends?
Did they know Cato, our remotest kings
Would pour embattled multitudes about him;
Their swarthy hosts would darken all our plains,
Doubling the native horror of the war,
And making death more grim.
 Cato.   And canst thou think
Cato will fly before the sword of Cæsar!
Reduced, like Hannibal, to seek relief
From court to court, and wander up and down
A vagabond in Afric?
 Jub.   Cato, perhaps
I'm too officious; but my forward cares
Would fain preserve a life of so much value.
My heart is wounded when I see such virtue
Afflicted by the weight of such misfortunes.
 Cato. Thy nobleness of soul obliges me.
But know, young prince, that valour soars above
What the world calls misfortune and affliction.
These are not ills; else would they never fall
On Heaven's first favourites, and the best of men.
The gods, in bounty, work up storms about us,
That give mankind occasion to exert
Their hidden strength, and throw out into practice
Virtues, which shun the day, and lie concealed
In the smooth seasons and the calms of life.
 Jub. I'm charmed whene'er thou talk'st; I pant for virtue;
And all my soul endeavours at perfection.
 Cato. Dost thou love watchings, abstinence, and toil,
Laborious virtues all? Learn them from Cato:
Success and fortune must thou learn from Cæsar.
 Jub. The best good fortune that can fall on Juba,
The whole success at which my heart aspires,
Depends on Cato.
 Cato.   What does Juba say?
Thy words confound me.
 Jub.   I would fain retract them.
Give 'em me back again: they aimed at nothing.
 Cato. Tell me thy wish, young prince; make not my ear
A stranger to thy thoughts.

Jub.   Oh! they're extravagant;
Still let me hide them.
    Cato.   What can Juba ask
That Cato will refuse?
    Juba.   I fear to name it.
Marcia—inherits all her father's virtues.
    Cato. What wouldst thou say?
    Jub.   Cato, thou hast a daughter.
    Cato. Adieu, young prince; I would not hear a word
Should lessen thee in my esteem. Remember,
The hand of fate is over us, and Heaven
Exacts severity from all our thoughts.
It is not now a time to talk of aught
But chains, or conquest; liberty, or death.   (*Exit.*

Enter SYPHAX

    Syph. How's this, my prince? What, covered with confusion?
You look as if yon stern philosopher
Had just now chid you.
    Jub.   Syphax, I'm undone!
    Syph. I know it well.
    Jub.   Cato thinks meanly of me.
    Syph. And so will all mankind.
    Jub.   I've opened to him
The weakness of my soul, my love for Marcia.
    Syph. Cato's a proper person to entrust
A love tale with!
    Jub.   Oh, I could pierce my heart,
My foolish heart! Was ever wretch like Juba?
    Syph. Alas, my prince, how are you changed of late!
I've known young Juba rise before the sun,
To beat the thicket, where the tiger slept,
Or seek the lion in his dreadful haunts:
How did the colour mount into your cheeks,
When first you roused him to the chase!
I've seen you,
Even in the Libyan dog-days, hunt him down,
Then charge him close, provoke him to the rage
Of fangs and claws, and stooping from your horse
Rivet the panting savage to the ground.
    Jub.   Prithee, no more.
    Syph. How would the old king smile,
To see you weigh the paws, when tipped with gold,
And throw the shaggy spoils about your shoulders!
    Jub. Syphax, this old man's talk, though honey flowed
In every word, would now lose all its sweetness.
Cato's displeased, and Marcia lost for ever.
    Syph. Young prince, I yet could give you good advice;
Marcia might still be yours.

Jub.   What say'st thou, Syphax?
By heavens, thou turnest me all into attention.
  Syph. Marcia might still be yours.
  Jub.   As how, dear Syphax?
  Syph. Juba commands Numidia's hardy troops,
Mounted on steeds unused to the restraint
Of curbs or bits, and fleeter than the winds:
Give but the word, we snatch this damsel up,
And bear her off.
  Jub.   Can such dishonest thoughts
Rise up in man? Wouldst thou seduce my youth
To do an act that would destroy mine honour?
  Syph. Gods, I could tear my beard to hear you talk!
Honour's a fine imaginary notion,
That draws in raw and inexperienced men
To real mischiefs, while they hunt a shadow.
  Jub. Wouldst thou degrade thy prince into a ruffian?
  Syph. The boasted ancestors of these great men,
Whose virtues you admire, were all such ruffians.
This dread of nations, this almighty Rome,
That comprehends in her wide empire's bounds
All under heaven, was founded on a rape;
Your Scipios, Cæsars, Pompeys, and your Catos
(These gods on earth) are all the spurious brood
Of violated maids, of ravish'd Sabines.
  Jub. Syphax, I fear that hoary head of thine
Abounds too much in our Numidian wiles.
  Syph. Indeed, my prince, you want to know the world;
You have not read mankind; your youth admires
The throws and swellings of a Roman soul,
Cato's bold flights, the extravagance of virtue.
  Jub. If knowledge of the world makes men perfidious,
May Juba ever live in ignorance!
  Syph. Go, go; you're young.
  Jub.   Gods, must I tamely bear
This arrogance unanswered! thou'rt a traitor,
A false old traitor.
  Syph.   I have gone too far.   (*Aside*
  Jub. Cato shall know the baseness of thy soul.
  Syph. I must appease this storm, or perish in it.   (*Aside.*
Young prince, behold these locks, that are grown white
Beneath a helmet in your father's battles.
  Jub. Those locks shall ne'er protect thy insolence.
  Syph. Must one rash word, the infirmity of age,
Throw down the merit of my better years?
This the reward of a whole life of service!
Curse on the boy! how steadily he hears me!   (*Aside.*
  Jub. Is it because the throne of my forefathers
Still stands unfilled, and that Numidia's crown

Hangs doubtful yet whose head it shall enclose,
Thou thus presum'st to treat thy prince with scorn?

Syph. Why will you rive my heart with such expressions?
Does not old Syphax follow you to war?
What are his aims? Why does he load with darts
His trembling hand, and crush beneath a casque
His wrinkled brows? What is it he aspires to?
Is it not this, to shed the slow remains,
His last poor ebb of blood, in your defence?

Jub. Syphax, no more! I would not hear you talk.

Syph. Not hear me talk! what, when my faith to Juba,
My royal master's son, is called in question?
My prince may strike me dead, and I'll be dumb;
But whilst I live I must not hold my tongue,
And languish out old age in his displeasure.

Jub. Thou know'st the way too well into my heart.
I do believe thee loyal to thy prince.

Syph. What greater instance can I give? I've offer'd
To do an action which my soul abhors,
And gain you whom you love, at any price.

Jub. Was this thy motive? I have been too hasty.

Syph. And 'tis for this my prince has called me traitor.

Jub. Sure thou mistakest; I did not call thee so.

Syph. You did, indeed, my prince, you called me traitor.
Nay, further, threatened you'd complain to Cato.
Of what, my prince, would you complain to Cato?
That Syphax loves you, and would sacrifice
His life, nay more, his honour, in your service?

Jub. Syphax, I know thou lovest me; but indeed
Thy zeal for Juba carried thee too far.
Honour's a sacred tie, the law of kings,
The noble mind's distinguishing perfection,
That aids and strengthens virtue, where it meets her,
And imitates her actions, where she is not;
It ought not to be sported with.

Syph.   By heavens,
I'm ravished when you talk thus, though you chide me!
Alas! I've hitherto been used to think
A blind officious zeal to serve my king
The ruling principle that ought to burn
And quench all others in a subject's heart.
Happy the people who preserve their honour
By the same duties that oblige their prince!

Jub. Syphax, thou now begin'st to speak thyself.
Numidia's grown a scorn among the nations
For breach of public vows. Our Punic faith
Is infamous, and branded to a proverb.
Syphax, we'll join our cares, to purge away
Our country's crimes, and clear her reputation.

Syph. Believe me, prince, you make old Syphax weep
To hear you talk—but 'tis with tears of joy.
If e'er your father's crown adorn your brows,
Numidia will be blest by Cato's lectures.
Jub. Syphax, thy hand; we'll mutually forget
The warmth of youth, and frowardness of age:
Thy prince esteems thy worth, and loves thy person.
If e'er the sceptre comes into my hand,
Syphax shall stand the second in my kingdom.
Syph. Why will you overwhelm my age with kindness?
My joy grows burdensome, I shan't support it.
Jub. Syphax, farewell. I'll hence, and try to find
Some blest occasion that may set me right
In Cato's thoughts. I'd rather have that man
Approve my deeds, than worlds for my admirers. *(Exit.*
Syph. (solus). Young men soon give, and soon forget, affronts;
Old age is slow in both.—A false old traitor!—
Those words, rash boy, may chance to cost thee dear.
My heart had still some foolish fondness for thee,
But hence, 'tis gone! I give it to the winds:
Cæsar, I'm wholly thine.—

Enter SEMPRONIUS

Syph.   All hail, Sempronius!
Well, Cato's senate is resolved to wait
The fury of a siege, before it yields.
Sem. Syphax, we both were on the verge of fate;
Lucius declared for peace, and terms were offer'd
To Cato, by a messenger from Cæsar.
Should they submit, ere our designs are ripe,
We both must perish in the common wreck,
Lost in a general, undistinguished ruin.
Syph. But how stands Cato?
Sem.   Thou hast seen mount Atlas:
Whilst storms and tempests thunder on its brows,
And oceans break their billows at its feet,
It stands unmoved, and glories in its height;
Such is that haughty man; his towering soul,
'Midst all the shocks and injuries of fortune,
Rises superior, and looks down on Cæsar.
Syph. But what's this messenger?
Sem.   I've practised with him,
And found a means to let the victor know
That Syphax and Sempronius are his friends.
But let me now examine in my turn;
Is Juba fixed?
Syph.   Yes—but it is to Cato.
I've tried the force of every reason on him,
Soothed and caressed; been angry, soothed again;

Laid safety, life, and interest in his sight.
But all are vain, he scorns them all for Cato.
   Sem. Come, 'tis no matter; we shall do without him.
He'll make a pretty figure in a triumph,
And serve to trip before the victor's chariot.
Syphax, I now may hope thou hast forsook
Thy Juba's cause, and wishest Marcia mine.
   Syph. May she be thine as fast as thou wouldst have her.
   Sem. Syphax, I love that woman; though I curse
Her and myself, yet, spite of me, I love her.
   Syph. Make Cato sure, and give up Utica,
Cæsar will ne'er refuse thee such a trifle.
But are thy troops prepared for a revolt?
Does the sedition catch from man to man,
And run among the ranks?
   Sem.   All, all is ready;
The factious leaders are our friends, that spread
Murmurs and discontents among the soldiers;
They count their toilsome marches, long fatigues,
Unusual fastings, and will bear no more
This medley of philosophy and war.
Within an hour they'll storm the senate house.
   Syph. Meanwhile I'll draw up my Numidian troops
Within the square, to exercise their arms,
And, as I see occasion, favour thee.
I laugh to think how your unshaken Cato
Will look aghast, while unforeseen destruction
Pours in upon him thus from every side.
So, where our wide Numidian wastes extend,
Sudden the impetuous hurricanes descend,
Wheel through the air, in circling eddies play,
Tear up the sands, and sweep whole plains away.
The helpless traveller, with wild surprise,
Sees the dry desert all around him rise,
And, smothered in the dusty whirlwind, dies.   *(Exeunt.*

ACT III

SCENE I

MARCUS *and* PORTIUS

   Marc. Thanks to my stars, I have not ranged about
The wilds of life, ere I could find a friend;
Nature first pointed out my Portius to me,
And early taught me, by her secret force,
To love thy person, ere I knew thy merit,
Till what was instinct, grew up into friendship.

Por. Marcus, the friendships of the world are oft
Confed'racies in vice, or leagues of pleasure;
Ours has severest virtue for its basis,
And such a friendship ends not but with life.
Marc. Portius, thou know'st my soul in all its weakness;
Then prithee spare me on its tender side;
Indulge me but in love, my other passions
Shall rise and fall by virtue's nicest rules.
Por. When love's well timed, 'tis not a fault to love.
The strong, the brave, the virtuous, and the wise,
Sink in the soft captivity together.
I would not urge thee to dismiss thy passion
(I know 'twere vain), but to suppress its force,
Till better times may make it look more graceful.
Marc. Alas! thou talk'st like one who never felt
The impatient throbs and longings of a soul
That pants and reaches after distant good!
A lover does not live by vulgar time;
Believe me, Portius, in my Lucia's absence
Life hangs upon me, and becomes a burden;
And yet, when I behold the charming maid,
I'm ten times more undone; while hope and fear,
And grief and rage, and love, rise up at once,
And with variety of pain distract me.
Por. What can thy Portius do to give thee help?
Marc. Portius, thou oft enjoy'st the fair one's presence,
Then undertake my cause, and plead it to her
With all the strength and heats of eloquence
Fraternal love and friendship can inspire.
Tell her, thy brother languishes to death,
And fades away, and withers in his bloom;
That he forgets his sleep, and loathes his food;
That youth, and health, and war are joyless to him;
Describe his anxious days, and restless nights,
And all the torments that thou seest me suffer.
Por. Marcus, I beg thee give me not an office
That suits with me so ill. Thou knowest my temper.
Marc. Wilt thou behold me sinking in my woes,
And wilt thou not reach out a friendly arm
To raise me from amidst this plunge of sorrows?
Por. Marcus, thou canst not ask what I'd refuse;
But here, believe me, I've a thousand reasons——
Marc. I know thou'lt say, my passion's out of season,
That Cato's great example and misfortunes
Should both conspire to drive it from my thoughts.
But what's all this to one who loves like me?
Oh, Portius, Portius, from my soul I wish
Thou didst but know thyself what 'tis to love!
Then wouldst thou·pity and assist thy brother.

Por. What should I do? If I disclose my passion,
Our friendship's at an end: if I conceal it,
The world will call me false to a friend and brother.   (*Aside.*

Marc. But see where Lucia, at her wonted hour,
Amid the cool of yon high marble arch,
Enjoys the noonday breeze! Observe her, Portius;
That face, that shape, those eyes, that heaven of beauty!
Observe her well, and blame me if thou canst.

Por. She sees us, and advances——
Marc.   I'll withdraw,
And leave you for a while. Remember, Portius,
Thy brother's life depends upon thy tongue.   (*Exit.*

Enter LUCIA

Lucia. Did not I see your brother Marcus here?
Why did he fly the place, and shun my presence?

Por. Oh, Lucia, language is too faint to show
His rage of love; it preys upon his life;
He pines, he sickens, he despairs, he dies:
His passions and his virtues lie confused,
And mixed together in so wild a tumult,
That the whole man is quite disfigured in him.
Heavens! Would one think 'twere possible for love
To make such ravage in a noble soul!
Oh, Lucia, I'm distressed! My heart bleeds for him;
Ev'n now, while thus I stand blest in thy presence,
A secret damp of grief comes o'er my thoughts,
And I'm unhappy, though thou smil'st upon me.

Lucia. How wilt thou guard thy honour in the shock
Of love and friendship! Think betimes, my Portius,
Think how the nuptial tie, that might ensure
Our mutual bliss, would raise to such a height
Thy brother's griefs, as might perhaps destroy him.

Por. Alas, poor youth! What dost thou think, my Lucia?
His generous, open, undesigning heart
Has begged his rival to solicit for him!
Then do not strike him dead with a denial,
But hold him up in life, and cheer his soul
With the faint glimmering of a doubtful hope;
Perhaps when we have passed these gloomy hours,
And weathered out the storm that beats upon us——

Lucia. No, Portius, no; I see thy sister's tears,
Thy father's anguish, and thy brother's death,
In the pursuit of our ill-fated loves;
And, Portius, here I swear; to Heaven I swear,
To Heaven, and all the powers that judge mankind,
Never to mix my plighted hands with thine,
While such a cloud of mischief hangs upon us,

But to forget our loves, and drive thee out
From all my thoughts—as far as I am able.

Por. What hast thou said? I'm thunderstruck—recall
Those hasty words, or I am lost for ever.

Lucia. Has not the vow already passed my lips?
The gods have heard it, and 'tis sealed in heaven.
May all the vengeance, that was ever poured
On perjured heads, o'erwhelm me, if I break it!

[*After a pause.*

Por. Fixed in astonishment, I gaze upon thee
Like one just blasted by a stroke from Heaven,
Who pants for breath, and stiffens, yet alive,
In dreadful looks, a monument of wrath!

Lucia. At length I've acted my severest part,
I feel the woman breaking in upon me,
And melt about my heart! My tears will flow.
But oh, I'll think no more! The hand of fate
Has torn thee from me, and I must forget thee.

Por. Hard-hearted cruel maid!

Lucia.   Oh, stop those sounds,
Those killing sounds! Why dost thou frown upon me?
My blood runs cold, my heart forgets to heave,
And life itself goes out at thy displeasure.
The gods forbid us to indulge our loves,
But oh! I cannot bear thy hate and live!

Por. Talk not of love, thou never knew'st its force.
I've been deluded, led into a dream
Of fancied bliss. Oh, Lucia, cruel maid!
Thy dreadful vow, loaden with death, still sounds
In my stunned ears. What shall I say or do?
Quick, let us part! Perdition's in thy presence,
And horror dwells about thee! Hah, she faints!
Wretch that I am! What has my rashness done!
Lucia, thou injured innocence! Thou best
And loveliest of thy sex! Awake, my Lucia,
Or Portius rushes on his sword to join thee.
—Her imprecations reach not to the tomb,
They shut not out society in death—
But, hah! She moves! Life wanders up and down
Through all her face, and lights up every charm.

Lucia. Oh, Portius, was this well! To frown on her
That lives upon thy smiles! To call in doubt
The faith of one expiring at thy feet,
That loves thee more than ever woman loved!
—What do I say? My half-recovered sense
Forgets the vow in which my soul is bound.
Destruction stands betwixt us! We must part.

Por. Name not the word, my frighted thoughts run back
And startle into madness at the sound.

Lucia. What wouldst thou have me do? Consider well
The train of ills our love would draw behind it.
Think, Portius, think thou seest thy dying brother
Stabbed at his heart, and all besmeared with blood,
Storming at Heaven and thee! Thy awful sire
Sternly demands the cause, th' accursed cause,
That robs him of his son; poor Marcia trembles,
Then tears her hair, and, frantic in her griefs,
Calls out on Lucia. What could Lucia answer,
Or how stand up in such a scene of sorrow?

Por. To my confusion and eternal grief,
I must approve the sentence that destroys me.
The mist that hung about my mind clears up;
And now athwart the terrors that thy vow
Has planted round thee, thou appearest more fair,
More amiable, and risest in thy charms.
Loveliest of women! Heaven is in thy soul,
Beauty and virtue shine for ever round thee,
Brightening each other! Thou art all divine!

Lucia. Portius, no more; thy words shoot through my heart,
Melt my resolves, and turn me all to love.
Why are those tears of fondness in thy eyes?
Why heaves thy heart? Why swells thy soul with sorrow?
It softens me too much—farewell, my Portius!
Farewell, though death is in the word,—for ever!

Por. Stay, Lucia, stay! What dost thou say? For ever?

Lucia. Have I not sworn? If, Portius, thy success
Must throw thy brother on his fate, farewell—
Oh, how shall I repeat the word?—For ever!

Por. Thus o'er the dying lamp the unsteady flame
Hangs quivering on a point, leaps off by fits,
And falls again, as loth to quit its hold.
Thou must not go; my soul still hovers o'er thee,
And can't get loose.

Lucia.   If the firm Portius shake
To hear of parting, think what Lucia suffers!

Por. 'Tis true, unruffled and serene, I've met
The common accidents of life, but here
Such an unlooked-for storm of ills falls on me,
It beats down all my strength, I cannot bear it.
We must not part.

Lucia.   What dost thou say? Not part!
Hast thou forgot the vow that I have made?
Are not there heavens, and gods, that thunder o'er us!
—But see, thy brother Marcus bends this way;
I sicken at the sight. Once more farewell.
Farewell, and know thou wrong'st me, if thou think'st
Ever was love, or ever grief like mine.   (*Exit.*

Enter MARCUS

Marc. Portius, what hopes? How stands she? Am I doom'd
To life or death?
   Por.   What wouldst thou have me say?
   Marc. What means this pensive posture? Thou appear'st
Like one amazed and terrified.
   Por.   I've reason.
   Marc. Thy downcast looks, and thy disordered thoughts,
Tell me my fate. I ask not the success
My cause has found.
   Por.   I'm grieved I undertook it.
   Marc. What, does the barbarous maid insult my heart,
My aching heart, and triumph in my pains?
That I could cast her from my thoughts for ever!
   Por. Away! you're too suspicious in your griefs;
Lucia, though sworn never to think of love,
Compassionates your pains, and pities you.
   Marc. Compassionates my pains, and pities me!
What is compassion, when 'tis void of love!
Fool that I was, to choose so cold a friend
To urge my cause!—Compassionate my pains!
Prithee what art, what rhetoric didst thou use
To gain this mighty boon?—She pities me!
To one that asks the warm return of love,
Compassion's cruelty, 'tis scorn, 'tis death——
   Por. Marcus, no more; have I deserved this treatment?
   Marc. What have I said? Oh! Portius, oh, forgive me!
A soul, exasperated in ills, falls out
With everything—its friend, itself——But hah!
What means that shout, big with the sounds of war?
What new alarm?
   Por.   A second, louder yet,
Swells in the wind, and comes more full upon us.
   Marc. Oh, for some glorious cause to fall in battle!
Lucia, thou hast undone me: thy disdain
Has broke my heart; 'tis death must give me ease.
   Por. Quick. let us hence. Who knows if Cato's life
Stands sure? Oh, Marcus, I am warmed; my heart
Leaps at the trumpet's voice, and burns for glory.   (*Exeunt.*

Enter SEMPRONIUS, *with the Leaders of the Mutiny*

   Sem. At length the winds are raised, the storm blows high,
Be it your care, my friends, to keep it up
In its full fury, and direct it right,
Till it has spent itself on Cato's head.
Meanwhile, I'll herd among his friends, and seem
One of the number, that, whate'er arrive,
My friends, and fellow-soldiers, may be safe.

First Lead. We all are safe; Sempronius is our friend.
Sempronius is as brave a man as Cato.
But, hark, he enters. Bear up boldly to him;
Be sure you beat him down, and bind him fast.
This day will end our toils and give us rest.
Fear nothing, for Sempronius is our friend.

Enter CATO, LUCIUS, PORTIUS, MARCUS, *etc.*

Cato. Where are those bold, intrepid sons of war,
That greatly turn their backs upon the foe,
And to their general send a brave defiance?
   Sem. Curse on their dastard souls, they stand astonished!
                                               (Aside.

   Cato. Perfidious men! And will you thus dishonour
Your past exploits, and sully all your wars?
Do you confess 'twas not a zeal for Rome,
Nor love of liberty, nor thirst of honour,
Drew you thus far; but hopes to share the spoil
Of conquered towns and plundered provinces?
Fired with such motives you do well to join
With Cato's foes and follow Cæsar's banners.
Why did I 'scape the envenomed aspic's rage,
And all the fiery monsters of the desert,
To see this day? Why could not Cato fall
Without your guilt! Behold, ungrateful men,
Behold my bosom naked to your swords,
And let the man that's injured strike the blow.
Which of you all suspects that he is wronged?
Or thinks he suffers greater ills than Cato?
Am I distinguished from you but by toils,
Superior toils, and heavier weight of cares?
Painful pre-eminence!
   Sem. By heavens, they droop!
Confusion to the villains! all is lost!   *(Aside.*
   Cato. Have you forgotten Libya's burning waste,
Its barren rocks, parched earth, and hills of sand,
Its tainted air, and all its broods of poison?
Who was the first to explore the untrodden path,
When life was hazarded in every step?
Or, fainting in the long laborious march,
When, on the banks of an unlooked-for stream,
You sunk the river with repeated draughts,
Who was the last in all your host that thirsted?
   Sem. If some penurious source by chance appeared,
Scanty of waters, when you scooped it dry,
And offered the full helmet up to Cato,
Did he not dash the untasted moisture from him?
Did he not lead you through the midday sun,

And clouds of dust? Did not his temples glow
In the same sultry winds and scorching heats?

Cato. Hence, worthless men! hence! and complain to Cæsar,
You could not undergo the toil of war,
Nor bear the hardships that your leader bore.

Luc. See, Cato, see the unhappy men; they weep!
Fear, and remorse, and sorrow for their crime,
Appear in every look, and plead for mercy.

Cato. Learn to be honest men, give up your leaders.
And pardon shall descend on all the rest.

Sem. Cato, commit these wretches to my care;
First let 'em each be broken on the rack,
Then, with what life remains, impaled, and left
To writhe at leisure round the bloody stake,
There let 'em hang, and taint the southern wind.
The partners of their crime will learn obedience,
When they look up and see their fellow-traitors
Stuck on a fork, and blackening in the sun.

Luc. Sempronius, why, why wilt thou urge the fate
Of wretched men?

Sem.   How! Wouldst thou clear rebellion?
Lucius (good man) pities the poor offenders,
That would imbrue their hands in Cato's blood.

Cato. Forbear, Sempronius!—see they suffer death,
But in their deaths remember they are men;
Strain not the laws, to make their tortures grievous.
Lucius, the base, degenerate age requires
Severity, and justice in its rigour;
This awes an impious, bold, offending world,
Commands obedience and gives force to laws.
When by just vengeance guilty mortals perish,
The gods behold their punishment with pleasure,
And lay the uplifted thunderbolt aside.

Sem. Cato, I execute thy will with pleasure.

Cato. Meanwhile we'll sacrifice to liberty.
Remember, O my friends! the laws, the rights,
The generous plan of power delivered down
From age to age by your renowned forefathers
(So dearly bought, the price of so much blood):
Oh, let it never perish in your hands!
But piously transmit it to your children.
Do thou, great Liberty, inspire our souls,
And make our lives in thy possession happy,
Or our deaths glorious in thy just defence.   (*Exeunt* CATO, *etc.*

First Lead. Sempronius, you have acted like yourself.
One would have thought you had been half in earnest.

Sem. Villain, stand off; base, grov'ling, worthless wretches,
Mongrels in faction, poor faint-hearted traitors!

Second Lead. Nay, now you carry it too far, Sempronius!

Throw off the mask, there are none here but friends.

Sem. Know, villains, when such paltry slaves presume
To mix in treason, if the plot succeeds,
They're thrown neglected by; but, if it fails,
They're sure to die like dogs, as you shall do.
Here, take these factious monsters, drag 'em forth
To sudden death.   [*Enter Guards.*

First Lead.   Nay, since it comes to this——

Sem. Dispatch 'em quick, but first pluck out their tongues,
Lest with their dying breath they sow sedition.

(Exeunt Guards, with the Leaders.)

Enter SYPHAX

Syph. Our first design, my friend, has proved abortive:
Still there remains an after-game to play;
My troops are mounted; their Numidian steeds
Snuff up the wind and long to scour the desert:
Let but Sempronius head us in our flight,
We'll force the gate, where Marcus keeps his guard,
And hew down all that would oppose our passage.
A day will bring us into Cæsar's camp.

Sem. Confusion! I have failed of half my purpose:
Marcia, the charming Marcia's left behind!

Syph. How! will Sempronius turn a woman's slave?

Sem. Think not thy friend can ever feel the soft
Unmanly warmth and tenderness of love.
Syphax, I long to clasp that haughty maid
And bend her stubborn virtue to my passion:
When I have gone thus far, I'd cast her off.

Syph. Well said! that's spoken like thyself, Sempronius!
What hinders, then, but that thou find her out,
And hurry her away by manly force?

Sem. But how to gain admission? For access
Is given to none but Juba, and her brothers.

Syph. Thou shalt have Juba's dress and Juba's guards,
The doors will open when Numidia's prince
Seems to appear before the slaves that watch them.

Sem. Heavens, what a thought is there! Marcia's my own!
How will my bosom swell with anxious joy
When I behold her struggling in my arms,
With glowing beauty and disordered charms,
While fear and anger, with alternate grace,
Pant in her breast, and vary in her face!
So Pluto, seized of Proserpine, conveyed
To hell's tremendous gloom the affrighted maid,
There grimly smiled, pleased with the beauteous prize,
Nor envied Jove his sunshine and his skies.   *(Exeunt.*

ACT IV

SCENE I

LUCIA *and* MARCIA

Lucia. Now tell me, Marcia, tell me from thy soul,
If thou believ'st 'tis possible for woman
To suffer greater ills than Lucia suffers?

Mar. Oh, Lucia, Lucia, might my big swol'n heart
Vent all its griefs, and give a loose to sorrow,
Marcia could answer thee in sighs, keep pace
With all thy woes, and count out tear for tear.

Lucia. I know thou'rt doomed alike to be belov'd
By Juba, and thy father's friend, Sempronius:
But which of these has power to charm like Portius?

Mar. Still, I must beg thee not to name Sempronius.
Lucia, I like not that loud, boisterous man;
Juba, to all the bravery of a hero,
Adds softest love, and more than female sweetness;
Juba might make the proudest of our sex,
Any of womankind, but Marcia, happy.

Lucia. And why not Marcia? Come, you strive in vain
To hide your thoughts from one who knows too well
The inward glowings of a heart in love.

Mar. While Cato lives, his daughter has no right
To love or hate, but as his choice directs.

Lucia. But should this father give you to Sempronius?

Mar. I dare not think he will; but if he should—
Why wilt thou add to all the griefs I suffer
Imaginary ills, and fancied tortures?
I hear the sound of feet! They march this way!
Let us retire, and try if we can drown
Each softer thought in sense of present danger:
When love once pleads admission to our hearts,
In spite of all the virtue we can boast,
The woman that deliberates is lost.   (*Exeunt.*

Enter SEMPRONIUS, *dressed like* JUBA, *with Numidian
Guards*

Sem. The deer is lodg'd, I've tracked her to her covert.
Be sure you mind the word, and when I give it,
Rush in at once, and seize upon your prey.
Let not her cries or tears have force to move you.
How will the young Numidian rave to see
His mistress lost! If aught could glad my soul
Beyond the enjoyment of so bright a prize,
'Twould be to torture that young, gay barbarian.

—But, hark! what noise! Death to my hopes! 'tis he,
'Tis Juba's self! There is but one way left—
He must be murdered and a passage cut
Through those his guards.—Hah! dastards, do you tremble!
Or act like men, or by yon azure heaven——

Enter JUBA

Jub. What do I see? Who's this, that dare usurp
The guards and habit of Numidia's prince?
Sem. One that was born to scourge thy arrogance,
Presumptuous youth!
Jub. What can this mean? Sempronius!
Sem. My sword shall answer thee. Have at thy heart.
Jub. Nay, then, beware thy own, proud, barbarous man.
(SEMPRONIUS *falls; his Guards surrender.*
Sem. Curse my stars! Am I then doomed to fall
By a boy's hand, disfigured in a vile
Numidian dress, and for a worthless woman?
Gods, I'm distracted! this my close of life!
O for a peal of thunder that would make
Earth, sea, and air, and Heaven, and Cato tremble!   (*Dies.*
Jub. With what a spring his furious soul broke loose
And left the limbs still quivering on the ground!
Hence, let us carry off those slaves to Cato,
That we may there at length unravel all
This dark design, this mystery of fate.
(*Exit Juba with Prisoners, etc.*

Enter LUCIA *and* MARCIA

Lucia. Sure 'twas the clash of swords; my troubled heart
Is so cast down, and sunk amidst its sorrows,
It throbs with fear, and aches at every sound.
Oh, Marcia, should thy brothers, for my sake—
I die away with horror at the thought!
Mar. See, Lucia, see! here's blood! here's blood and murder!
Ha! a Numidian! Heavens preserve the prince!
The face lies muffled up within the garment;
But ah! death to my sight! a diadem,
And purple robes! O gods! 'tis he, 'tis he!
Juba, the loveliest youth that ever warmed
A virgin's heart, Juba, lies dead before us!
Lucia. Now, Marcia now, call up to thy assistance,
Thy wonted strength and constancy of mind,
Thou canst not put it to a greater trial.
Mar. Lucia, look there, and wonder at my patience;
Have I not cause to rave, and beat my breast,
To rend my heart with grief, and run distracted?
Lucia. What can I think, or say, to give thee comfort?

Mar. Talk not of comfort, 'tis for lighter ills:
Behold a sight that strikes all comfort dead.

Enter JUBA, *listening*

I will indulge my sorrows, and give way
To all the pangs and fury of despair;
That man, that best of men, deserved it from me.
    Jub. What do I hear? And was the false Sempronius
That best of men? Oh, had I fallen like him,
And could have thus been mourned, I had been happy.
    Lucia. Here will I stand companion in thy woes
And help thee with my tears! When I behold
A loss like thine I half forget my own.
    Mar. 'Tis not in fate to ease my tortured breast.
This empty world, to me a joyless desert,
Has nothing left to make poor Marcia happy.
    Jub. I'm on the rack! Was he so near her heart?
    Mar. Oh, he was all made up of love and charms!
Whatever maid could wish, or man admire:
Delight of every eye; when he appeared,
A secret pleasure gladdened all that saw him;
But when he talked, the proudest Roman blushed
To hear his virtues, and old age grew wise.
    Jub. I shall run mad!
    Mar.   Oh, Juba! Juba! Juba!
    Jub. What means that voice? Did she not call on Juba?
    Mar. Why do I think on what he was? He's dead!
He's dead, and never knew how much I loved him!
Lucia, who knows but his poor, bleeding heart,
Amidst its agonies, remembered Marcia,
And the last words he uttered called me cruel!
Alas! he knew not, hapless youth, he knew not
Marcia's whole soul was full of love and Juba!
    Jub. Where am I? Do I live: or am indeed
What Marcia thinks? All is Elysium round me!
    Mar. Ye dear remains of the most loved of men,
Nor modesty nor virtue here forbid
A last embrace, while thus——
    Jub.   See, Marcia, see,
The happy Juba lives! he lives to catch
That dear embrace, and to return it too,
With mutual warmth, and eagerness of love.
    Mar. With pleasure and amaze I stand transported!
Sure 'tis a dream! dead and alive at once!
If thou art Juba, who lies there?
    Jub.   A wretch,
Disguised like Juba on a cursed design.
The tale is long, nor have I heard it out;
Thy father knows it all. I could not bear

To leave thee in the neighbourhood of death,
But flew, in all the haste of love, to find thee;
I found thee weeping, and confess this once,
Am rapt with joy to see my Marcia's tears.

  Mar. I've been surprised in an unguarded hour,
But must not now go back; the love, that lay
Half smothered in my breast, has broke through all
Its weak restraints, and burns in its full lustre.
I cannot, if I would, conceal it from thee.

  Jub. I'm lost in ecstasy! And dost thou love,
Thou charming maid?

  Mar.   And dost thou live to ask it?

  Jub. This, this is life indeed! Life worth preserving,
Such life as Juba never felt till now.

  Mar. Believe me, prince, before I thought thee dead,
I did not know myself how much I loved thee.

  Jub. O fortunate mistake!

  Mar.   O happy Marcia!

  Jub. My joy! my best beloved, my only wish!
How shall I speak the transport of my soul!

  Mar. Lucia, thy arm! Oh, let me rest upon it—
The vital blood, that had forsook my heart,
Returns again in such tumultuous tide,
It quite o'ercomes me. Lead to my apartment.
Oh, prince! I blush to think what I have said,
But fate has wrested the confession from me;
Go on, and prosper in the paths of honour.
Thy virtue will excuse my passion for thee.
And make the gods propitious to our love.

                      (*Exeunt* LUCIA *and* MARCIA.

  Jub. I am so blest, I fear 'tis all a dream.
Fortune, thou now hast made amends for all
Thy past unkindness: I absolve my stars.
What though Numidia add her conquered towns
And provinces to swell the victor's triumph,
Juba will never at his fate repine:
Let Cæsar have the world, if Marcia's mine.   (*Exit.*

          A march at a distance.

       Enter CATO *and* LUCIUS

  Luc. I stand astonished! What, the bold Sempronius,
That still broke foremost through the crowd of patriots,
As with a hurricane of zeal transported,
And virtuous even to madness——

  Cato.   Trust me, Lucius,
Our civil discords have produced such crimes,
Such monstrous crimes, I am surprised at nothing.

—Oh, Lucius, I am sick of this bad world!
The daylight and the sun grow painful to me.

Enter PORTIUS

But see where Portius comes: what means this haste?
Why are thy looks thus changed?
 Por.   My heart is grieved,
I bring such news as will afflict my father.
 Cato. Has Cæsar shed more Roman blood?
 Por.   Not so.
The traitor Syphax, as within the square
He exercised his troops, the signal given,
Flew off at once with his Numidian horse
To the south gate, where Marcus holds the watch;
I saw, and called to stop him, but in vain:
He tossed his arm aloft, and proudly told me
He would not stay, and perish, like Sempronius.
 Cato. Perfidious men! But haste, my son, and see
Thy brother Marcus acts a Roman's part. (*Exit* PORTIUS.
—Lucius, the torrent bears too hard upon me:
Justice gives way to force: the conquered world
Is Cæsar's! Cato has no business in it.
 Luc. While pride, oppression, and injustice reign,
The world will still demand her Cato's presence.
In pity to mankind submit to Cæsar,
And reconcile thy mighty soul to life.
 Cato. Would Lucius have me live to swell the number
Of Cæsar's slaves, or by a base submission
Give up the cause of Rome, and own a tyrant?
 Luc. The victor never will impose on Cato
Ungenerous terms. His enemies confess
The virtues of humanity are Cæsar's.
 Cato. Curse on his virtues! they've undone his country.
Such popular humanity is treason——
But see young Juba; the good youth appears
Full of the guilt of his perfidious subjects!
 Luc. Alas, poor prince! his fate deserves compassion.

Enter JUBA

 Jub. I blush, and am confounded to appear
Before thy presence, Cato.
 Cato.   What's thy crime?
 Jub. I'm a Numidian.
 Cato. And a brave one, too. Thou hast a Roman soul.
 Jub. Hast thou not heard of my false countrymen?
 Cato. Alas, young prince!
Falsehood and fraud shoot up in every soil,
The product of all climes—Rome has its Cæsars.

Jub. 'Tis generous thus to comfort the distressed.
Cato. 'Tis just to give applause where 'tis deserved:
Thy virtue, prince, has stood the test of fortune,
Like purest gold, that, tortured in the furnace,
Comes out more bright, and brings forth all its weight.
Jub. What shall I answer thee? My ravished heart
O'erflows with secret joy: I'd rather gain
Thy praise, O Cato! than Numidia's empire.

Enter PORTIUS *hastily*

Por. Misfortune on misfortune! grief on grief!
My brother Marcus——
Cato.   Ha! what has he done?
Has he forsook his post? Has he given way?
Did he look tamely on, and let 'em pass?
Por. Scarce had I left my father, but I met him
Borne on the shields of his surviving soldiers,
Breathless and pale, and covered o'er with wounds.
Long, at the head of his few faithful friends,
He stood the shock of a whole host of foes,
Till, obstinately brave, and bent on death,
Oppress'd with multitudes, he greatly fell.
Cato. I'm satisfied.
Por.   Nor did he fall before
His sword had pierced through the false heart of Syphax.
Yonder he lies. I saw the hoary traitor
Grin in the pangs of death, and bite the ground.
Cato. Thanks to the gods, my boy has done his duty.
—Portius, when I am dead, be sure thou place
His urn near mine.
Por.   Long may they keep asunder!
Luc. Oh, Cato, arm thy soul with all its patience;
See where the corpse of thy dead son approaches!
The citizens and senators, alarmed,
Have gathered round it, and attend it weeping.

CATO *meeting the Corpse*

Cato. Welcome, my son! Here lay him down, my friends
Full in my sight, that I may view at leisure
The bloody corpse, and count these glorious wounds.
—How beautiful is death when earned by virtue!
Who would not be that youth? What pity is it,
That we can die but once to serve our country!
—Why sits this sadness on your brows, my friends?
I should have blushed, if Cato's house had stood
Secure, and flourished in a civil war.
Portius, behold thy brother, and remember,
Thy life is not thine own when Rome demands it.

Jub. Was ever man like this! *(Aside.*

Cato.   Alas! my friends,
Why mourn you thus? Let not a private loss
Afflict your hearts. 'Tis Rome requires our tears,
The mistress of the world, the seat of empire,
The nurse of heroes, the delight of gods,
That humbled the proud tyrants of the earth,
And set the nations free; Rome is no more.
Oh, liberty! Oh, virtue! Oh, my country!

Jub. Behold that upright man! Rome fills his eyes
With tears, that flowed not o'er his own dead son. *(Aside.*

Cato. Whate'er the Roman virtue has subdued,
The sun's whole course, the day and year, are Cæsar's:
For him the self-devoted Decii died,
The Fabii fell, and the great Scipios conquered:
Even Pompey fought for Cæsar. Oh, my friends,
How is the toil of fate, the work of ages,
The Roman empire, fallen! Oh, cursed ambition!
Fallen into Cæsar's hands! Our great forefathers
Had left him naught to conquer but his country.

Jub. While Cato lives, Cæsar will blush to see
Mankind enslaved, and be ashamed of empire.

Cato. Cæsar ashamed! Has not he seen Pharsalia!

Luc. Cato, 'tis time thou save thyself and us.

Cato. Lose not a thought on me; I'm out of danger;
Heaven will not leave me in the victor's hand.
Cæsar shall never say, I conquered Cato.
But oh, my friends! your safety fills my heart
With anxious thoughts; a thousand secret terrors
Rise in my soul. How shall I save my friends?
'Tis now, O Cæsar, I begin to fear thee!

Luc. Cæsar has mercy, if we ask of him.

Cato. Then ask it, I conjure you; let him know,
Whate'er was done against him, Cato did it.
Add, if you please, that I request it of him,—
That I myself, with tears, request it of him,—
The virtue of my friends may pass unpunished.
Juba, my heart is troubled for thy sake.
Should I advise thee to regain Numidia,
Or seek the conqueror?

Jub.   If I forsake thee
Whilst I have life, may Heaven abandon Juba!

Cato. Thy virtues, prince, if I foresee aright,
Will one day make thee great; at Rome, hereafter,
'Twill be no crime to have been Cato's friend.
Portius, draw near: my son, thou oft hast seen
Thy sire engaged in a corrupted state,
Wrestling with vice and faction: now thou seest me
Spent, overpowered, despairing of success;

Let me advise thee to retreat betimes
To thy paternal seat, the Sabine field;
Where the great Censor toiled with his own hands,
And all our frugal ancestors were blessed
In humble virtues, and a rural life;
There live retired, pray for the peace of Rome;
Content thyself to be obscurely good.
When vice prevails, and impious men bear sway,
The post of honour is a private station.
   Por. I hope my father does not recommend
A life to Portius that he scorns himself.
   Cato. Farewell, my friends! If there be any of you
Who dare not trust the victor's clemency,
Know there are ships prepared, by my command,
Their sails already opening to the winds,
That shall convey you to the wished-for port.
Is there aught else, my friends, I can do for you?
The conqueror draws near. Once more, farewell!
If e'er we meet hereafter, we shall meet
In happier climes, and on a safer shore,
Where Cæsar never shall approach us more.
There, the brave youth, with love of virtue fired,
              (*Pointing to the body of his dead son.*)
Who greatly in his country's cause expired,
Shall know he conquered. The firm patriot there,
Who made the welfare of mankind his care,
Though still by faction, vice, and fortune crossed,
Shall find the generous labour was not lost.

ACT V

SCENE I

CATO, *solus, sitting in a thoughtful posture ; in his hand, Plato's
book on the Immortality of the Soul. A drawn sword on the
table by him*

It must be so—Plato, thou reasonest well—
Else whence this pleasing hope, this fond desire,
This longing after immortality?
Or whence this secret dread, and inward horror
Of falling into naught? Why shrinks the soul
Back on herself, and startles at destruction?
'Tis the divinity that stirs within us;
'Tis Heaven itself that points out an hereafter,
And intimates eternity to man.
Eternity! thou pleasing, dreadful thought!

Through what variety of untried being,
Through what new scenes and changes must we pass?
The wide, the unbounded prospect lies before me;
But shadows, clouds, and darkness, rest upon it.
Here will I hold. If there's a Power above us
(And that there is, all nature cries aloud
Through all her works), he must delight in virtue;
And that which he delights in, must be happy.
But when, or where?—This world was made for Cæsar:
I'm weary of conjectures—this must end 'em.
                                   (*Laying his hand on his sword.*
Thus am I doubly armed: my death and life,
My bane and antidote are both before me.
This in a moment brings me to an end;
But this informs me I shall never die.
The soul, secured in her existence, smiles
At the drawn dagger, and defies its point.
The stars shall fade away, the sun himself
Grow dim with age, and nature sink in years,
But thou shalt flourish in immortal youth,
Unhurt amidst the wars of elements,
The wrecks of matter, and the crush of worlds.
What means this heaviness that hangs upon me?
This lethargy that creeps through all my senses?
Nature, oppressed and harassed out with care,
Sinks down to rest. This once I'll favour her,
That my awakened soul may take her flight,
Renewed in all her strength, and fresh with life,
An offering fit for Heaven. Let guilt or fear
Disturb man's rest, Cato knows neither of 'em,
Indifferent in his choice to sleep or die.

Enter PORTIUS

But, hah! how's this? my son! Why this intrusion?
Were not my orders that I would be private?
Why am I disobeyed?
    Por.   Alas! my father!
What means this sword, this instrument of death?
Let me convey it hence.
    Cato.   Rash youth, forbear!
    Por. Oh, let the prayers, the entreaties of your friends,
Their tears, their common danger, wrest it from you!
    Cato. Wouldst thou betray me? Would'st thou give me up
A slave, a captive, into Cæsar's hands?
Retire, and learn obedience to a father,
Or know, young man!——
    Por.   Look not thus sternly on me;
You know I'd rather die than disobey you.
    Cato. 'Tis well! again I'm master of myself.

Now, Cæsar, let thy troops beset our gates,
And bar each avenue; thy gathering fleets
O'erspread the sea, and stop up every port;
Cato shall open to himself a passage,
And mock thy hopes.——
    Por.   Oh, sir! forgive your son,
Whose grief hangs heavy on him. Oh, my father!
How am I sure it is not the last time
I e'er shall call you so? Be not displeased,
Oh, be not angry with me whilst I weep,
And, in the anguish of my heart, beseech you
To quit the dreadful purpose of your soul!
    Cato. Thou hast been ever good and dutiful.
                                      (*Embracing him.*
Weep not, my son, all will be well again;
The righteous gods, whom I have sought to please,
Will succour Cato, and preserve his children.
    Por. Your words give comfort to my drooping heart.
    Cato. Portius, thou mayest rely upon my conduct:
Thy father will not act what misbecomes him.
But go, my son, and see if aught be wanting
Among thy father's friends; see them embarked,
And tell me if the winds and seas befriend them.
My soul is quite weighed down with care, and asks
The soft refreshment of a moment's sleep.   (*Exit.*
    Por. My thoughts are more at ease, my heart revives—

Enter MARCIA

Oh, Marcia! Oh, my sister, still there's hope
Our father will not cast away a life
So needful to us all, and to his country.
He is retired to rest, and seems to cherish
Thoughts full of peace.—He has dispatched me hence
With orders that bespeak a mind composed,
And studious for the safety of his friends.
Marcia, take care that none disturb his slumbers.   (*Exit.*
    Mar. Oh, ye immortal powers that guard the just,
Watch round his couch, and soften his repose,
Banish his sorrows, and becalm his soul
With easy dreams; remember all his virtues,
And show mankind that goodness is your care!

Enter LUCIA

    Lucia. Where is your father, Marcia, where is Cato?
    Mar. Lucia, speak low, he is retired to rest.
Lucia, I feel a gently dawning hope
Rise in my soul We shall be happy still.
    Lucia. Alas, I tremble when I think on Cato!

In every view, in every thought, I tremble!
Cato is stern and awful as a god;
He knows not how to wink at human frailty,
Or pardon weakness that he never felt.
   Mar. Though stern and awful to the foes of Rome,
He is all goodness, Lucia, always mild;
Compassionate and gentle to his friends:
Filled with domestic tenderness, the best,
The kindest father; I have ever found him
Easy and good, and bounteous to my wishes.
   Lucia. 'Tis his consent alone can make us blest.
Marcia, we both are equally involved
In the same intricate, perplexed distress.
The cruel hand of fate, that has destroyed
Thy brother Marcus, whom we both lament——
   Mar. And ever shall lament; unhappy youth!
   Lucia. Has set my soul at large, and now I stand
Loose of my vow. But who knows Cato's thoughts?
Who knows how yet he may dispose of Portius,
Or how he has determined of thyself?
   Mar. Let him but live, commit the rest to Heaven.

Enter LUCIUS

   Luc. Sweet are the slumbers of the virtuous man!
Oh, Marcia, I have seen thy godlike father
Some power invisible supports his soul,
And bears it up, in all its wonted greatness.
A kind, refreshing sleep is fallen upon him:
I saw him stretched at ease; his fancy lost
In pleasing dreams; as I drew near his couch,
He smiled, and cried, "Cæsar, thou canst not hurt me."
   Mar. His mind still labours with some dreadful thought.
   Luc. Lucia, why all this grief, these floods of sorrow?
Dry up thy tears, my child, we all are safe
While Cato lives—his presence will protect us.

Enter JUBA

   Jub. Lucius, the horsemen are returned from viewing
The number, strength, and posture of our foes,
Who now encamp within a short hour's march;
On the high point of yon bright western tower
We ken them from afar; the setting sun
Plays on their shining arms and burnished helmets,
And covers all the field with gleams of fire.
   Luc. Marcia, 'tis time we should awake thy father.
Cæsar is still disposed to give us terms,
And waits at distance, till he hears from Cato.

Enter PORTIUS

Portius, thy looks speak somewhat of importance.
What tidings dost thou bring? Methinks I see
Unusual gladness sparkling in thy eyes.
 Por. As I was hasting to the port, where now
My father's friends, impatient for a passage,
Accuse the lingering winds, a sail arrived
From Pompey's son, who, through the realms of Spain,
Calls out for vengeance on his father's death,
And rouses the whole nation up to arms.
Were Cato at their head, once more might Rome
Assert her rights, and claim her liberty.
But, hark! what means that groan!—Oh, give me way,
And let me fly into my father's presence!   (*Exit.*
 Luc. Cato, amidst his slumbers, thinks on Rome,
And, in the wild disorder of his soul,
Mourns o'er his country.—Ah! a second groan—
Heaven guard us all!
 Mar.   Alas! 'tis not the voice
Of one who sleeps; 'tis agonising pain—
'Tis death is in that sound——

Re-enter PORTIUS

 Por.   Oh, sight of woe!
Oh, Marcia, what we feared, is come to pass!—
Cato is fallen upon his sword——
 Luc.   Oh, Portius!
Hide all the horrors of thy mournful tale,
And let us guess the rest.
 Por.   I've raised him up,
And placed him in his chair; where, pale and faint,
He gasps for breath, and, as his life flows from him,
Demands to see his friends. His servants, weeping,
Obsequious to his orders, bear him hither!——
    (*The back scene opens and discovers* CATO.
 Mar. Oh, Heaven! assist me in this dreadful hour,
To pay the last sad duties to my father!
 Jub. These are thy triumphs, thy exploits, O Cæsar!
 Luc. Now is Rome fallen indeed!
    (CATO *brought forward in his chair.*
Cato.   Here set me down——
Portius, come near me. Are my friends embarked?
Can anything be thought of for their service?
Whilst I yet live, let me not live in vain——
Oh, Lucius, art thou here? Thou art too good.
Let this our friendship live between our children—
Make Portius happy in thy daughter Lucia——
Alas! poor man, he weeps. Marcia, my daughter—

Oh, bend me forward!—Juba loves thee, Marcia—
A senator of Rome, while Rome survived,
Would not have matched his daughter with a king—
But Cæsar's arms have thrown down all distinction—
I'm sick to death——Oh, when shall I get loose
From this vain world, the abode of guilt and sorrow!
And yet, methinks, a beam of light breaks in
On my departing soul——Alas, I fear
I've been too hasty!——Oh, ye powers that search
The heart of man, and weigh his inmost thoughts,
If I have done amiss, impute it not—
The best may err, but you are good, and——Oh!—   (*Dies.*

   Luc. There fled the greatest soul that ever warmed
A Roman breast. O Cato! O my friend!
Thy will shall be religiously observed.
But let us bear this awful corpse to Cæsar,
And lay it in his sight, that it may stand
A fence betwixt us and the victor's wrath;
Cato, though dead, shall still protect his friends.
From hence, let fierce contending nations know
What dire effects from civil discord flow:
'Tis this that shakes our country with alarms,
And gives up Rome a prey to Roman arms;
Produces fraud, and cruelty, and strife,
And robs the guilty world of Cato's life.

                                   (*Exeunt Omnes.*

EPILOGUE

By Dr. Garth

SPOKEN BY MRS. PORTER

WHAT odd fantastic things we women do!
Who would not listen when young lovers woo?
But die a maid, yet have the choice of two!
Ladies are often cruel to their cost;
To give you pain themselves they punish most.
Vows of virginity should well be weighed;
Too oft they're cancelled though in convents made.
Would you revenge such rash resolves—you may:
Be spiteful—and believe the thing we say;
We hate you when you're easily said nay.
How needless, if you knew us, were your fears!
Let Love have eyes and Beauty will have ears.
Our hearts are formed, as you yourselves would choose,
Too proud to ask, too humble to refuse:
We give to merit and to wealth we sell;
He sighs with most success that settles well.
The woes of wedlock with the joys we mix;
'Tis best repenting in a coach and six.
Blame not our conduct, since we but pursue
Those lively lessons we have learned from you:
Your breasts no more the fire of beauty warms,
But wicked wealth usurps the power of charms;
What pains to get the gaudy thing you hate,
To swell in show and be a wretch in state!
At plays you ogle, at the ring you bow;
Even churches are no sanctuaries now.
There, golden idols all your vows receive;
She is no goddess that has naught to give.
Oh, may once more the happy age appear
When words were artless and the thoughts sincere;
When gold and grandeur were unenvied things,
And courts less coveted than groves and springs.
Love then shall only mourn when Truth complains,
And Constancy feel transport in its chains.
Sighs with success their own soft anguish tell,
And eyes shall utter what the lips conceal:
Virtue again to its bright station climb,
And Beauty fear no enemy but Time.
The fair shall listen to desert alone,
And every Lucia find a Cato's son.

THE
TRAGEDY OF JANE SHORE

Nicholas Rowe, born at Little Barford, Bedfordshire, in 1674, was the son of a serjeant-at-law who intended the boy to follow his own profession, and removed him at fifteen from Westminster School to the Inner Temple. But like many another English writer he soon deserted law for literature, a change justified by the immediate success of his first play, a blank-verse tragedy called *The Ambitious Stepmother* which was acted in 1700. His success brought him the friendship of the leading men of letters of the time: a lasting social popularity, due to his geniality, high spirits and charming manner; and the patronage of that Duke of Queensberry to whose son *Jane Shore* is dedicated. Like Addison, he was a Whig, and he held a series of political posts, including that of Poet Laureate, to which he was appointed on the accession of George I. He was well read, not only in the classics, but in French, Spanish and Italian literature; his translation of Lucan's *Pharsalia*—a posthumous publication—was much esteemed; and he was the first systematic editor and biographer of Shakespeare, whose works he published in octavo in 1709.

He died in 1718, and was buried in Westminster Abbey.

THE
TRAGEDY
OF
JANE SHORE.

Written in IMITATION of

Shakespear's Style.

By N. ROWE, Esq;.

———*Conjux ubi pristinus illi*
Respondet Curis.   Virg.

LONDON:

Printed for BERNARD LINTOT, at the *Cross-keys*, between the *Two Temple-Gates*, in *Fleet-street*.

TO HIS GRACE THE DUKE OF QUEENSBERRY AND DOVER, MARQUIS OF BEVERLY, ETC.

My Lord,

I have long lain under the greatest obligations to your Grace's family, and nothing has been more in my wishes, than that I might be able to discharge some part, at least, of so large a debt. But your noble birth and fortune, the power, number, and goodness of those friends you have already, have placed you in such an independency on the rest of the world, that the services I am able to render to your Grace can never be advantageous, I am sure not necessary, to you in any part of your life. However, the next piece of gratitude, and the only one I am capable of, is the acknowledgment of what I owe: and as this is the most public, and indeed the only way I have of doing it, your Grace will pardon me if I take this opportunity to let the world know the duty and honour I had for your illustrious father. It is, I must confess, a very tender point to touch upon; and at the first sight may seem an ill-chosen compliment, to renew the memory of such a loss, especially to a disposition so sweet and gentle, and to a heart so sensible of filial piety as your Grace's has been, even from your earliest childhood. But perhaps this is one of those griefs by which the heart may be made better; and if the remembrance of his death bring heaviness along with it, the honour that is paid to his memory by all good men, shall wipe away those tears, and the example of his life set before your eyes shall be of the greatest advantage to your Grace in the conduct and future disposition of your own.

In a character so amiable as that of the Duke of Queensberry was, there can be no part so proper to begin with as that which was in him, and is in all good men, the foundation of all other virtues, either religious or civil, I mean good-nature: good-nature, which is friendship between man and man, good-breeding in courts, charity in religion, and the true spring of all beneficence in general. This was a quality he possessed in as great a measure as any gentleman I ever had the honour to know. It was this natural sweetness of temper which made him the best man in the world to live with, in any kind of relation. It was this made him a good master to his servants, a good friend to his friends, and the tenderest father to his children. For the last, I can give no better voucher than your Grace; and for the rest, I may appeal to all that have had the honour to know him. There was a spirit and pleasure in his conversation which always enlivened the company he was in; which, together with a certain easiness and frankness in his disposition, that did not at all derogate from the dignity of his birth and character, rendered him infinitely agreeable. And as no man had a more delicate taste of natural wit, his conversations always abounded in good-humour.

For those parts of his character which related to the public, as he was a nobleman of the first rank, and a Minister of State, they will be best known by the great employments he passed through; all which he discharged worthily as to himself, justly to the princes who employed him, and advantageously for his country. There is no occasion to enumerate his several employments, as Secretary of State, for Scotland in particular, for Britain in general, or Lord High Commissioner of Scotland; which last office he bore more than once; but at no time more honourably, and (as I hope) more happily, both for the present age, and for posterity, than when he laid the foundation for the British Union. The constancy and address which he manifested on that occasion are still fresh in everybody's memory; and perhaps when our children shall reap those benefits from that work, which some people do not foresee and hope for now, they may remember the Duke of Queensberry with that gratitude which such a piece of service done to his country deserves.

He showed upon all occasions a strict and immediate attachment to the Crown, in the legal service of which no man could exert himself more dutifully nor more strenuously: and at the same time no man gave more bold and more generous evidences of the love he bore to his country. Of the latter, there can be no better proof than the share he had in the late happy Revolution; nor of the former, than that dutiful respect, and unshaken fidelity, which he preserved for her present Majesty, even to his last moments.

With so many good and great qualities, it is not at all strange that he possessed so large a share, as he was known to have, in the esteem of the queen, and her immediate predecessor; nor that those great princes should repose the highest confidence in him: and at the same time, what a pattern has he left behind him for the nobility in general, and for your Grace in particular, to copy after!

Your Grace will forgive me, if my zeal for your welfare and honour (which nobody has more at heart than myself) shall press you with some more than ordinary warmth to the imitation of your noble father's virtues. You have, my lord, many great advantages, which may encourage you to go on in pursuit of this reputation; it has pleased God to give you naturally that sweetness of temper which, as I have before hinted, is the foundation of all good inclinations. You have the honour to be born, not only of the greatest, but of the best parents; of a gentleman generally beloved, and generally lamented; and of a lady adorned with all virtues that enter into the character of a good wife, an admirable friend, and a most indulgent mother. The natural advantages of your mind have been cultivated by the most proper arts and manners of education. You have the care of many noble friends, and especially of an excellent uncle, to watch over you in the tenderness of your youth. You set out amongst the first of mankind, and I doubt not but your virtues will be equal to the dignity of your rank.

That I may live to see your Grace eminent for the love of your country, for your service and duty to your prince, and, in convenient time, adorned with all the honours that have ever been conferred upon your noble family; that you may be distinguished to posterity, as the bravest, greatest and best man of the age you live in, is the hearty wish and prayer of,

My Lord,
Your Grace's most obedient, and
most faithful, humble servant,
N. Rowe.

PROLOGUE

SPOKEN BY MR. WILKS

To-NIGHT, if you have brought your good old taste,
We'll treat you with a downright English feast.
A tale, which told long since in homely wise,
Hath never failed of melting gentle eyes.
Let no nice sir despise our hapless dame,
Because recording ballads chant her name;
Those venerable ancient song-inditers
Soared many a pitch above our modern writers:
They caterwauled in no romantic ditty,
Sighing for Phillis's, or Chloe's pity.
Justly they drew the fair, and spoke her plain,
And sung her by her Christian name—'twas Jane.
Our numbers may be more refined than those,
But what we've gained in verse, we've lost in prose.
Their words no shuffling, double-meaning knew,
Their speech was homely, but their hearts were true.
In such an age, immortal Shakespeare wrote,
By no quaint rules, nor hampering critics taught;
With rough majestic force he moved the heart,
And strength and nature made amends for Art.
Our humble author does his steps pursue,
He owns he had the mighty bard in view;
And in these scenes has made it more his care
To rouse the passions, than to charm the ear.
Yet for those gentle beaux who love the chime,
The ends of acts still jingle into rhyme.
The ladies, too, he hopes, will not complain,
Here are some subjects for a softer strain,   }
A nymph forsaken, and a perjured swain.
What most he fears is, lest the dames should frown,
The dames of wit and pleasure about to   }
To see our picture drawn, unlike their own.
But lest that error should provoke to fury
The hospitable hundreds of Old Drury,
He bid me say, in our Jane Shore's defence,
She doled about the charitable pence,
Built hospitals, turned saint, and died long since.   }

For her example, whatsoe'er we make it,
They have their choice to let alone, or take it.
Tho' few, as I conceive, will think it meet
To weep so sorely for a sin so sweet:
Or mourn and mortify the pleasant sense,
To rise in tragedy two ages hence.

[In the first edition the Epilogue is printed after the Prologue.]

DRAMATIS PERSONÆ

MEN

DUKE OF GLOSTER	Mr. Cibber
LORD HASTINGS	Mr. Booth
CATESBY	Mr. Husbands
SIR RICHARD RATCLIFFE	Mr. Bowman
BELLMOUR	Mr. Mills
DUMONT	Mr. Wilks

WOMEN

ALICIA	Mrs. Porter
JANE SHORE	Mrs. Oldfield

Several Lords of the Council, Guards, and Attendants.

SCENE—London.

THE TRAGEDY OF JANE SHORE

ACT I., SCENE I.

Scene, The Tower

Enter the DUKE OF GLOSTER, SIR RICHARD RATCLIFFE,
and CATESBY

Gloster. Thus far success attends upon our counsels,
And each event has answered to my wish;
The Queen and all her upstart race are quelled;
Dorset is banished, and her brother Rivers
Ere this lies shorter by the head at Pomfret.
The nobles have with joint concurrence named me
Protector of the Realm: my brother's children,
Young Edward and the little York, are lodged
Here, safe within the Tower. How say you, sirs,
Does not this business wear a lucky face?
The sceptre and the golden wreath of royalty
Seem hung within my reach.
    Ratcliffe.   Then take 'em to you,
And wear 'em and long worthily; you are
The last remaining male of princely York
(For Edward's boys, the State esteems not of 'em),
And therefore on your sovereignty and rule
The commonweal does her dependance make,
And leans upon your Highness' able hand.
    Catesby. And yet to-morrow does the Council meet
To fix a day for Edward's coronation.
Who can expound this riddle?
    Gloster.   That can I.
Those lords are each one my approved good friends,
Of special trust and nearness to my bosom;
And howsoever busy they may seem,
And diligent to bustle in the State,
Their zeal goes on no farther than we lead,
And at our bidding stays.
    Catesby.   Yet there is one,
And he amongst the foremost in his power,
Of whom I wish your Highness were assured:
For me, perhaps it is my nature's fault,
I own I doubt of his inclining much.

63

Gloster. I guess the man at whom your words would point:
Hastings——
    Catesby.   The same.
    Gloster.   He bears me great good will.
    Catesby. 'Tis true, to you, as to the Lord Protector,
And Gloster's duke, he bows with lowly service:
But were he bid to cry, God save King Richard,
Then tell me in what terms he would reply.
Believe me, I have proved the man, and found him:
I know he bears a most religious reverence
To his dead master Edward's royal memory,
And whither that may lead him, is most plain.
Yet more—One of that stubborn sort he is,
Who, if they once grow fond of an opinion,
They call it Honour, Honesty, and Faith,
And sooner part with life than let it go.
    Gloster. And yet this tough impracticable heart
Is governed by a dainty-fingered girl;
Such flaws are found in the most worthy natures;
A laughing, toying, wheedling, whimpering she,
Shall make him amble on a gossip's message,
And take the distaff with a hand as patient
As e'er did Hercules.
    Ratcliffe.   The fair Alicia,
Of noble birth and exquisite of feature,
Has held him long a vassal to her beauty.
    Catesby. I fear he fails in his allegiance there;
Or my intelligence is false, or else
The dame has been too lavish of her feast,
And fed him 'till he loathes.
    Gloster. No more, he comes.

Enter LORD HASTINGS

    Hastings. Health and happiness of many days
Attend upon your Grace.
    Gloster.   My good Lord Chamberlain!
W'are much beholden to your gentle friendship.
    Hastings. My lord, I come an humble suitor to you.
    Gloster. In right good time. Speak out your pleasure freely.
    Hastings. I am to move your Highness in behalf
Of Shore's unhappy wife.
    Gloster.   Say you, of Shore?
    Hastings. Once a bright star that held her place on high;
The first and fairest of our English dames,
While royal Edward held the sovereign rule.
Now sunk in grief and pining with despair,
Her waning form no longer shall incite
Envy in woman, or desire in man.

She never sees the sun but thro' her tears,
And wakes to sigh the live-long night away.

   Gloster. Marry! the times are badly changed with her
From Edward's days to these. Then all was jollity,
Feasting and mirth, light wantonness and laughter,
Piping and playing, minstrelsy and masking;
Till life fled from us like an idle dream,
A show of mummery without a meaning.
My brother, rest and pardon to his soul,
Is gone to his account; for this his minion,
The revel-rout is done——But you were speaking
Concerning her—I have been told that you
Are frequent in your visitation to her.

   Hastings. No farther, my good lord, than friendly pity,
And tender-hearted charity allow.

   Gloster. Go to: I did not mean to chide you for it.
For, sooth to say, I hold it noble in you
To cherish the distressed.—On with your tale.

   Hastings. Thus it is, gracious sir, that certain officers,
Using the warrant of your mighty name,
With insolence unjust, and lawless power,
Have seized upon the lands which late she held
By grant from her great master Edward's bounty.

   Gloster. Somewhat of this, but slightly, have I heard;
And though some counsellors of forward zeal,
Some of most ceremonious sanctity,
And bearded wisdom, often have provoked
The hand of justice to fall heavy on her;
Yet still in kind compassion of her weakness,
And tender memory of Edward's love,
I have withheld the merciless stern law
From doing outrage on her helpless beauty.

   Hastings. Good Heaven, who renders mercy back for mercy,
With open-handed bounty shall repay you:
This gentle deed shall fairly be set foremost,
To screen the wild escapes of lawless passion,
And the long train of frailties flesh is heir to.

   Gloster. Thus far the voice of pity pleaded only,
Our farther and more full extent of grace
Is given to your request. Let her attend,
And to ourself deliver up her griefs.
She shall be heard with patience, and each wrong
At full redrest. But I have other news
Which much import us both, for still my fortunes
Go hand in hand with yours: our common foes,
The Queen's relations, our new-fangled gentry,
Have fallen their haughty crests—that for your privacy.

                                     (*Exeunt.*

SCENE II.—*An Apartment in* JANE SHORE'S *House*

Enter BELLMOUR *and* DUMONT

Bellmour. How she has lived you've heard my tale already,
The rest your own attendance in her family,
Where I have found the means this day to place you,
And nearer observation, best will tell you.
See with what sad and sober cheer she comes.

Enter JANE SHORE

Sure, or I read her visage much amiss,
Or grief besets her hard. Save you, fair lady,
The blessings of the cheerful morn be on you,
And greet your beauty with its opening sweets.
    Jane Shore. My gentle neighbour! your good wishes still
Pursue my hapless fortunes. Ah, good Bellmour!
How few, like thee, inquire the wretched out,
And court the offices of soft humanity!
Like thee reserve their raiment for the naked,
Reach out their bread to feed the crying orphan,
Or mix their pitying tears with those that weep!
Thy praise deserves a better tongue than mine
To speak and bless thy name. Is this the gentleman
Whose friendly service you commended to me?
    Bellmour. Madam! it is.
    Jane Shore (aside).   A venerable aspect!
Age sits with decent grace upon his visage,
And worthily becomes his silver locks;
He wears the marks of many years well spent,
Of virtue, truth well tried, and wise experience;
A friend like this would suit my sorrows well.
    (*To* DUMONT.) Fortune, I fear me, sir, has meant you ill,
Who pays your merit with that scanty pittance
Which my poor hand and humble roof can give.
But to supply these golden vantages,
Which elsewhere you might find, expect to meet
A just regard and value for your worth,
The welcome of a friend, and the free partnership
Of all that little good the world al'ows me.
    Dumont. You overrate me much; and all my answer
Must be my future truth; let that speak for me,
And make up my deserving.
    Jane Shore.   Are you of England?
    Dumont. No, gracious lady, Flanders claims my birth.
At Antwerp has my constant biding been,
Where sometimes I have known more plenteous days
Than those which now my failing age affords.

Jane Shore. Alas! at Antwerp!—Oh, forgive my tears!

(*Weeping.*

They fall for my offences—and must fall
Long, long, e'er they shall wash my stains away.
You knew perhaps—oh grief! oh shame!—my husband.

Dumont. I knew him well—but stay this flood of anguish,
The senseless grave feels not your pious sorrows:
Three years and more are past since I was bid,
With many of our common friends, to wait him
To his last peaceful mansion. I attended,
Sprinkled his clay-cold corpse with holy drops,
According to our Church's reverend rite,
And saw him laid in hallowed ground, to rest.

Jane Shore. Oh! that my soul had known no joy but him,
That I had lived within his guiltless arms,
And dying slept in innocence beside him!
But now his honest dust abhors the fellowship,
And scorns to mix with mine.

Enter a Servant

Servant.   The Lady Alicia
Attends your leisure.

Jane Shore.   I wish to see her.   (*Exit Servant.*
Please, gentle sir, one moment to retire,
I'll wait you on the instant; and inform you
Of each unhappy circumstance in which
Your friendly aid and counsel much may stead me.

(*Exeunt* BELLMOUR *and* DUMONT.

Enter ALICIA

Alicia. Still, my fair friend, still shall I find you thus?
Still shall these sighs heave after one another,
These trickling drops chase one another still,
As if the posting messengers of grief
Could overtake the hours fled far away,
And make old time come back?

Jane Shore.   No, my Alicia,
Heaven and his saints be witness to my thoughts,
There is no hour of all my life o'erpast
That I could wish should take its turn again.

Alicia. And yet some of those days my friend has known,
Some of those years might pass for golden ones,
At least, if womankind can judge of happiness.
What could we wish, we who delight in empire,
Whose beauty is our sovereign good, and gives us
Our reasons to rebel, and power to reign.
What could we more than to behold a monarch,
Lovely, renowned, a conqueror, and young,
Bound in our chains, and sighing at our feet?

Jane Shore. 'Tis true the royal Edward was a wonder,
The goodly pride of all our English youth;
He was the very joy of all that saw him,
Formed to delight, to love, and to persuade.
Impassive spirits and angelic natures
Might have been charmed, like yielding human weakness,
Stooped from their heaven, and listened to his talking.
But what had I to do with kings and courts?
My humble lot had cast me far beneath him;
And that he was the first of all mankind,
The bravest and most lovely, was my curse.

Alicia. Sure, something more than fortune joined your loves;
Nor could his greatness, and his gracious form,
Be elsewhere matched so well, as to the sweetness
And beauty of my friend.

Jane Shore.   Name him no more:
He was the bane and ruin of my peace.
This anguish and these tears, these are the legacies
His fatal love has left me. Thou wilt see me,
Believe me, my Alicia, thou wilt see me,
Ere yet a few short days pass o'er my head,
Abandoned to the very utmost wretchedness.
The hand of power has seized almost the whole
Of what was left for needy life's support;
Shortly thou wilt behold me poor, and kneeling
Before thy charitable door for bread.

Alicia. Joy of my life, my dearest Shore, forbear
To wound my heart with thy foreboding sorrows.
Raise thy sad soul to better hopes than these,
Lift up thy eyes, and let 'em shine once more,
Bright as the morning sun above the mists.
Exert thy charms, seek out the stern Protector,
And soothe his savage temper with thy beauty:
Spite of his deadly unrelenting nature,
He shall be moved to pity and redress thee.

Jane Shore. My form, alas! has long forgot to please;
The scene of beauty and delight is changed,
No roses bloom upon my fading cheek,
Nor laughing graces wanton in my eyes;
But haggard grief, lean-looking sallow care,
And pining discontent, a rueful train,
Dwell on my brow, all hideous and forlorn.
One only shadow of a hope is left me;
The noble-minded Hastings, of his goodness,
Has kindly underta'en to be my advocate,
And move my humble suit to angry Gloster.

Alicia. Does Hastings undertake to plead your cause?
But wherefore should he not? Hastings has eyes;
The gentle lord has a right tender heart,

Melting and easy yielding to impression,
And catching the soft flame from each new beauty;
But yours shall charm him long.
    Jane Shore.   Away, you flatterer!
Nor charge his generous meaning with a weakness
Which his great soul and virtue must disdain.
Too much of love thy hapless friend has proved,
Too many giddy foolish hours are gone,
And in fantastic measures danced away:
May the remaining few know only friendship.
So thou, my dearest, truest, best Alicia,
Vouchsafe to lodge me in thy gentle heart,
A partner there; I will give up mankind,
Forget the transports of increasing passion,
And all the pangs we feel for its decay.
    Alicia. Live! live and reign for ever in my bosom.
                                     (Embracing.
Safe and unrivalled there possess thy own;
And you, ye brightest of the stars above,
Ye saints that once were women here below,
Be witness of the truth, the holy friendship,
Which here to this my other self I vow.
If I not hold her nearer to my soul,
Then every other joy the world can give,
Let poverty, deformity and shame,
Distraction and despair seize me on earth,
Let not my faithless ghost have peace hereafter,
Nor taste the bliss of your celestial fellowship.
    Jane Shore. Yes, thou art true, and only thou art true;
Therefore these jewels, once the lavish bounty
Of royal Edward's love, I trust to thee;   *(Giving a casket.*
Receive this all, that I can call my own,
And let it rest unknown and safe with thee:
That if the State's injustice should oppress me,
Strip me of all, and turn me out a wanderer,
My wretchedness may find relief from thee,
And shelter from the storm.
    Alicia.   My all is thine;
One common hazard shall attend us both,
And both be fortunate, or both be wretched.
But let thy fearful doubting heart be still,
The saints and angels have thee in their charge,
And all things shall be well. Think not the good,
The gentle deeds of mercy thou hast done,
Shall die forgotten all; the poor, the pris'ner,
The fatherless, the friendless, and the widow,
Who daily own the bounty of thy hand,
Shall cry to Heaven, and pull a blessing on thee;
Even man, the merciless insulter man,

Man, who rejoices in our sex's weakness,
Shall pity thee, and with unwonted goodness,
Forget thy failings, and record thy praise.
　Jane Shore. Why should I think that man will do for me
What yet he never did for wretches like me?
Mark by what partial justice we are judged:
Such is the fate unhappy women find,
And such the curse entailed upon our kind,
That man, the lawless libertine, may rove
Free and unquestioned through the wilds of love;
While woman, sense and nature's easy fool,
If poor weak woman swerve from virtue's rule,
If, strongly charmed, she leave the thorny way,
And in the softer paths of pleasure stray;
Ruin ensues, reproach and endless shame,
And one false step entirely damns her fame.
In vain with tears the loss she may deplore,
In vain look back to what she was before,
She sets, like stars that fall, to rise no more.

　　　　　　　　　　　　　　　　　(Exeunt.

ACT II., SCENE I.

Scene continues

Enter ALICIA, *speaking to* JANE SHORE *as entering.*

　Alicia, No farther, gentle friend; good angels guard you,
And spread their gracious wings about your slumbers.
The drowsy night grows on the world, and now
The busy craftsman and the o'erlaboured hind
Forget the travail of the day in sleep:
Care only wakes, and moping pensiveness;
With meagre discontented looks they sit,
And watch the wasting of the midnight taper.
Such vigils must I keep, so wakes my soul,
Restless and self-tormented! Oh, false Hastings!
Thou hast destroyed my peace.　　　*(Knocking without.*
What noise is that?
What visitor is this, who with bold freedom
Breaks in upon the peaceful night and rest
With such a rude approach?

Enter a Servant

　Servant.　　　　　　One from the Court,
Lord Hastings (as I think) demands my lady.
　Alicia. Hastings! Be still, my heart, and try to meet him
With his own arts: with falsehood.—But he comes.

Enter LORD HASTINGS. *Speaks to a servant at entering.*

Hastings. Dismiss my train, and wait alone without.
Alicia here! Unfortunate encounter!
But be it as it may.
    Alicia.   When humbly, thus,
The great descend to visit the afflicted,
When thus unmindful of their rest they come
To soothe the sorrows of the midnight mourner:
Comfort comes with them, like the golden sun,
Dispels the sullen shades with her sweet influence,
And cheers the melancholy house of care.
    Hastings. 'Tis true I would not overrate a courtesy,
Nor let the coldness of delay hang on it,
To nip and blast its favour like a frost;
But rather chose, at this late hour, to come,
That your fair friend may know I have prevailed;
The Lord Protector has received her suit,
And means to show her grace.
    Alicia.   My friend! my lord.
    Hastings. Yes, lady, yours: none has a right more ample
To task my power than you.
    Alicia.   I want the words,
To pay you back a compliment so courtly;
But my heart guesses at the friendly meaning,
And wo'not die your debtor.
    Hastings.   'Tis well, madam.
But I would see your friend,
    Alicia.   O thou false lord!
I would be mistress of my heaving heart,
Stifle this rising rage, and learn from thee
To dress my face in easy dull indifference:
But 'two' not be, my wrongs will tear their way,
And rush at once upon thee.
    Hastings.   Are you wise?
Have you the use of reason? Do you wake?
What means this raving? this transporting passion?
    Alicia. O thou cool traitor! thou insulting tyrant!
Dost thou behold my poor distracted heart,
Thus rent with agonising love and rage,
And ask me what it means? Art thou not false?
Am I not scorned, forsaken and abandoned,
Left, like a common wretch, to shame and infamy,
Given up to be the sport of villains' tongues,
Of laughing parasites, and lewd buffoons;
And all because my soul has doted on thee
With love, with truth, and tenderness unutterable?
    Hastings. Are these the proofs of tenderness and love?

These endless quarrels, discontents, and jealousies,
These never-ceasing wailings and complainings,
These furious starts, these whirlwinds of the soul,
Which every other moment rise to madness?

    Alicia. What proof, alas! have I not given of love?
What have I not abandoned to thy arms?
Have I not set at naught my noble birth,
A spotless fame, and an unblemished race,
The peace of innocence, and pride of virtue?
My prodigality has given thee all;
And now I have nothing left me to bestow,
You hate the wretched bankrupt you have made.

    Hastings. Why am I thus pursued from place to place,
Kept in the view, and crossed at every turn?
In vain I fly, and like a hunted deer,
Scud o'er the lawns, and hasten to the covert;
Ere I can reach my safety, you o'ertake me
With the swift malice of some keen reproach,
And drive the winged shaft deep in my heart.

    Alicia. Hither you fly, and here you seek repose;
Spite of the poor deceit, your arts are known,
Your pious, charitable, midnight visits.

    Hastings. If you are wise, and prize your peace of mind,
Yet take the friendly counsel of my love;
Believe me true, nor listen to your jealousy,
Let not that devil, which undoes your sex,
That cursed curiosity seduce you,
To hunt for needless secrets, which neglected,
Shall never hurt your quiet, but once known,
Shall sit upon your heart, pinch it with pain,
And banish the sweet sleep for ever from you.
Go to—be yet advised——

    Alicia.   Dost thou in scorn,
Preach patience to my rage? And bid me tamely
Sit like a poor contented idiot down,
Nor dare to think thou'st wronged me? Ruin seize thee,
And swift perdition overtake thy treachery!
Have I the least remaining cause to doubt?
Hast thou endeavoured once to hide thy falsehood?
To hide it, might have spoke some little tenderness,
And shown thee half unwilling to undo me:
But thou disdainest the weakness of humanity,
Thy words, and all thy actions, have confessed it;
Even now thy eyes avow it, now they speak,
And insolently own the glorious villainy.

    Hastings. Well then, I own my heart has broke your chains.
Patient I bore the painful bondage long,
At length my generous love disdains your tyranny;
The bitterness and stings of taunting jealousy,

Vexatious days, and jarring joyless nights,
Have driven him forth to seek some safer shelter,
Where he may rest his weary wings in peace.
   Alicia. You triumph! do! And with gigantic pride,
Defy impending vengeance. Heaven shall wink;
No more his arm shall roll the dreadful thunder,
Nor send his lightnings forth. No more his justice
Shall visit the presuming sons of men,
But perjury, like thine, shall dwell in safety.
   Hastings. Whate'er my fate decrees for me hereafter,
Be present to me now my better angel!
Preserve me from the storm which threatens now,
And if I have beyond atonement sinned,
Let any other kind of plague o'ertake me,
So I escape the fury of that tongue.
   Alicia. Thy prayer is heard—I go—but know, proud lord,
Howe'er thou scornest the weakness of my sex,
This feeble hand may find the means to reach thee,
Howe'er sublime in power and greatness placed,
With royal favour guarded round, and graced,
On eagle's wings my rage shall urge her flight,
And hurl thee headlong from thy topmost height;
Then like thy fate, superior will I sit,
And view thee fallen, and grovelling at my feet;
See thy last breath with indignation go,
And tread thee sinking to the shades below.   (*Exit* ALICIA.
   Hastings. How fierce a fiend is passion. With what wildness,
What tyranny untamed, it reigns in woman!
Unhappy sex! whose easy yielding temper
Gives way to every appetite alike:
Each gust of inclination, uncontrolled,
Sweeps through their souls, and sets them in an uproar;
Each motion of the heart rises to fury,
And love in their weak bosoms is a rage
As terrible as hate, and as destructive.
So the wind roars o'er the wide senseless ocean,
And heaves the billows of the boiling deep,
Alike from North, from South, from East, and West;
With equal force the tempest blows by turns
From every corner of the seaman's compass.
But soft ye now—for here comes one disclaims
Strife, and her wrangling train; of equal elements,
Without one jarring atom was she formed,
And gentleness and joy make up her being.

Enter JANE SHORE

Forgive me, fair one, if officious friendship
Intrudes on your repose, and comes thus late,
To greet you with the tidings of success.

The princely Gloster has vouchsafed you hearing,
To-morrow he expects you at the Court;
There plead your cause with never-failing beauty,
Speak all your griefs, and find a full redress.

   Jane Shore. Thus humbly let your lowly servant bend,

(Kneeling.

Thus let me bow my grateful knee to earth,
And bless your noble nature for this goodness.

   Hastings. Rise, gentle dame, you wrong my meaning much,
Think me not guilty of a thought so vain,
To sell my courtesy for thanks like these.

   Jane Shore. 'Tis true, your bounty is beyond my speaking:
But though my mouth be dumb, my heart shall thank you;
And when it melts before the throne of mercy,
Mourning and bleeding for my past offences,
My fervent soul shall breathe one prayer for you,
If prayers of such a wretch are heard on high,
That Heaven will pay you back, when most you need,
The grace and goodness you have shown to me.

   Hastings. If there be aught of merit in my service,
Impute it there where most 'tis due—to love;
Be kind, my gentle mistress, to my wishes,
And satisfy my panting heart with beauty.

   Jane Shore. Alas! my lord——

   Hastings.   Why bend thy eyes to earth?
Wherefore these looks of heaviness and sorrow?
Why breathes that sigh, my love? And wherefore falls
This trickling shower of tears to stain thy sweetness?

   Jane Shore. If pity dwells within your noble breast
(As sure it does), oh, speak not to me thus.

   Hastings. Can I behold thee, and not speak of love?
Even now, thus sadly as thou standest before me,
Thus desolate, dejected, and forlorn,
Thy softness steals upon my yielding senses,
Till my soul faints, and sickens with desire;
How canst thou give this motion to my heart,
And bid my tongue be still?

   Jane Shore.   Cast round your eyes
Upon the high-born beauties of the Court;
Behold, like opening roses, where they bloom,
Sweet to the sense, unsullied all and spotless;
There choose some worthy partner of your heart,
To fill your arms, and bless your virtuous bed;
Nor turn your eyes this way, where sin and misery,
Like loathsome weeds, have overrun the soil,
And the destroyer shame has laid all waste.

   Hastings. What means this peevish, this fantastic change?
Where is thy wonted pleasantness of face?
Thy wonted graces, and thy dimpled smiles?

Where hast thou lost thy wit and sportive mirth?
That cheerful heart, which used to dance for ever,
And cast a day of gladness all around thee?

   Jane Shore. Yes, I will own I merit the reproach;
And for those foolish days of wanton pride,
My soul is justly humbled to the dust:
All tongues, like yours, are licensed to upbraid me,
Still to repeat my guilt, to urge my infamy,
And treat me like that abject thing I have been.
Yet let the saints be witness to this truth,
That now, though late, I look with horror back,
That I detest my wretched self, and curse
My past-polluted life. All-judging Heaven,
Who knows my crimes, has seen my sorrow for them.

   Hastings. No more of this dull stuff. 'Tis time enough
To whine and mortify thyself with penance,
When the decaying sense is palled with pleasure,
And weary Nature tires in her last stage:
Then weep and tell thy beads, when alt'ring rheums
Have stained the lustre of thy starry eyes,
And failing palsies shake thy withered hand.
The present moments claim more generous use;
Thy beauty, night and solitude reproach me,
For having talked thus long. Come let me press thee,
                         (*Laying hold on her.*
Pant on thy bosom, sink into thy arms,
And lose myself in the luxurious fold.

   Jane Shore. Never! by those chaste lights above, I swear
My soul shall never know pollution more.
Forbear, my lord!—Here let me rather die,   (*Kneeling.*
Let quick destruction overtake me here,
And end my sorrows and my shame for ever.

   Hastings. Away with this perverseness, 'tis too much;
Nay, if you strive—'tis monstrous affectation.   (*Striving.*

   Jane Shore. Retire! I beg you leave me——

   Hastings.   Thus to coy it!—
With one who knows you too.

   Jane Shore.   For mercy's sake——

   Hastings. Ungrateful woman! Is it thus you pay
My services?——

   Jane Shore.   Abandon me to ruin,
Rather than urge me——

   Hastings.   This way to your chamber, (*Pulling her.*
There, if you struggle——

   Jane Shore.   Help! O gracious Heaven!
Help! Save me! Help!   (*Crying out.*

         Enter DUMONT; *he interposes.*

   Dumont.   My lord! for honour's sake——

Hastings. Ha! What art thou? Begone

Dumont.   My duty calls me
To my attendance on my mistress here.

Jane Shore. For pity let me go——

Hastings.   Avaunt! base groom——
At distance wait, and know thy office better.

Dumont. Forgo your hold, my lord! 'tis most unmanly,
This violence——

Hastings.   Avoid the room this moment,
Or I will tread thy soul out.

Dumont. No, my lord—
The common ties of manhood call me now,
And bid me thus stand up in the defence
Of an oppressed, unhappy, helpless woman.

Hastings. And dost thou know me, slave?

Dumont.   Yes, thou proud lord!
I know thee well, know thee with each advantage
Which wealth, or power, or noble birth can give thee.
I know thee too for one who stains those honours,
And blots a long illustrious line of ancestry,
By poorly daring thus to wrong a woman.

Hastings. 'Tis wondrous well! I see, my saint-like dame,
You stand provided of your braves and ruffians
To man your cause, and bluster in your brothel.

Dumont. Take back the foul reproach, unmannered railer;
Nor urge my rage too far, lest thou shouldst find
I have as daring spirits in my blood
As thou, or any of thy race e'er boasted;
And though no gaudy titles graced my birth,
Titles, the servile courtier's lean reward,
Sometimes the pay of virtue, but more oft
The hire which greatness gives to slaves and sycophants,
Yet Heaven that made me honest, made me more
Than ever king did, when he made a lord.

Hastings. Insolent villain! Henceforth let this teach thee
                              (*Draws and strikes him.*
The distance 'twixt a peasant and a prince.

Dumont. Nay then, my lord! (*Drawing.*) Learn you by this
              how well
An arm resolved can guard its master's life.   (*They fight.*

Jane Shore. Oh, my distracting fears! Hold, for sweet Heaven.
                    (*They fight,* DUMONT *disarms* LORD HASTINGS.

Hastings. Confusion! baffled by a base-born hind!

Dumont. Now, haughty sir, where is our difference now?
Your life is in my hand, and did not honour,
The gentleness of blood and inborn virtue
(Howe'er unworthy I may seem to you)
Plead in my bosom, I should take the forfeit.
But wear your sword again; and know, a lord

Opposed against a man is but a man.
   Hastings. Curse on my failing hand! Your better fortune
Has given you vantage o'er me; but perhaps
Your triumph may be bought with dear repentance.   *(Exit.*
   Jane Shore. Alas! what have you done! Know you the power,
The mightiness that waits upon this lord?
   Dumont. Fear not, my worthiest mistress; 'tis a cause
In which Heaven's guard shall wait you. Oh, pursue,
Pursue the sacred counsels of your soul,
Which urge you on to virtue; let not danger
Nor the encumb'ring world make faint your purpose.
Assisting angels shall conduct your steps,
Bring you to bliss, and crown your end with peace.
   Jane Shore. Oh that my head were laid, my sad eyes closed,
And my cold corpse wound in my shroud to rest;
My painful heart will never cease to beat,
Will never know a moment's peace till then.
   Dumont. Would you be happy? Leave this fatal place,
Fly from the Court's pernicious neighbourhood;
Where innocence is shamed, and blushing modesty
Is made the scorner's jest; where hate, deceit,
And deadly ruin wear the masks of beauty,
And draw deluded fools with shows of pleasure.
   Jane Shore. Where should I fly, thus helpless and forlorn,
Of friends and all the means of life bereft?
   Dumont. Bellmour, whose friendly care still wakes to serve you,
Has found you out a little peaceful refuge,
Far from the Court and the tumultuous city.
Within an ancient forest's ample verge
There stands a lonely, but a healthful dwelling,
Built for convenience, and the use of life:
Around it fallows, meads, and pastures fair,
A little garden, and a limpid brook,
By Nature's own contrivance seem disposed;
No neighbours but a few poor simple clowns,
Honest and true, with a well-meaning priest:
No faction, or domestic fury's rage,
Did e'er disturb the quiet of that place,
When the contending nobles shook the land
With York and Lancaster's disputed sway.
Your virtue there may find a safe retreat
From the insulting powers of wicked greatness.
   Jane Shore. Can there be so much happiness in store!
A cell like that is all my hopes aspire to.
Haste then, and thither let us wing our flight,
Ere the clouds gather, and the wintry sky
Descends in storms to intercept our passage.
   Dumont. Will you then go? You glad my very soul!
Banish your fears, cast all your cares on me;

Plenty and ease and peace of mind shall wait you,
And make your latter days of life most happy.
Oh, lady! but I must not, cannot tell you,
How anxious I have been for all your dangers,
And how my heart rejoices at your safety.
So when the spring renews the flowery field,
And warns the pregnant nightingale to build,
She seeks the safest shelter of the wood,
Where she may trust her little tuneful brood;
Where no rude swains her shady cell may know,
No serpents climb, nor blasting winds may blow;
Fond of the chosen place, she views it o'er,
Sits there, and wanders through the grove no more:
Warbling she charms it each returning night,
And loves it with a mother's dear delight.   (*Exeunt.*

ACT III., SCENE I.

Scene.—The Court

Enter ALICIA, *with a paper.*

Alicia. This paper to the great Protector's hand
With care and secrecy must be conveyed;
His bold ambition now avows its aim,
To pluck the crown from Edward's infant brow,
And fix it on his own. I know he holds
My faithless Hastings adverse to his hopes,
And much devoted to the orphan king;
On that I build: This paper meets his doubts,
And marks my hated rival as the cause
Of Hastings' zeal for his dead master's sons.
O jealousy! thou bane of pleasing friendship,
Thou worst invader of our tender bosoms;
How does thy rancour poison all our softness,
See turn our gentle natures into bitterness!
And where she comes! Once my heart's dearest blessing,
Now my changed eyes are blasted with her beauty,
Loathe that known face, and sicken to behold her.

Enter JANE SHORE

Jane Shore. Now whither shall I fly to find relief?
What charitable hand will aid me now?
Will stay my failing steps, support my ruins,
And heal my wounded mind with balmy comfort?
Oh, my Alicia!
    Alicia.   What new grief is this?

What unforeseen misfortune has surprised thee,
That racks thy tender heart thus?
 Jane Shore.   Oh! Dumont!
 Alicia. Say! What of him?
 Jane Shore.   That friendly, honest man,
Whom Bellmour brought of late to my assistance,
On whose kind cares, whose diligence and faith,
My surest trust was built, this very morn
Was seized on by the cruel hand of power,
Forced from my house, and borne away to prison.
 Alicia. To prison, said you! Can you guess the cause?
 Jane Shore. Too well, I fear. His bold defence of me
Has drawn the vengeance of Lord Hastings on him.
 Alicia. Lord Hastings! Ha!
 Jane Shore.   Some fitter time must tell thee
The tale of my hard hap. Upon the present
Hang all my poor, my last remaining hopes.
Within this paper is my suit contained;
Here, as the princely Gloster passes forth,
I wait to give it on my humble knees,
And move him for redress.
    (She gives the paper to ALICIA, *who opens and seems*
       to read it.
 Alicia (aside).   Now for a wile
To sting my thoughtless rival to the heart;
To blast her fatal beauties, and divide her
For ever from my perjured Hastings' eyes:
The wanderer may then look back to me,
And turn to his forsaken home again:
Their fashions are the same, it cannot fail.
       (Pulling out the other paper.
 Jane Shore. But see, the great Protector comes this way,
Attended by a train of waiting courtiers.
Give me the paper, friend.
 Alicia (aside).   For love and vengeance!
       (She gives her the other paper.

Enter the DUKE OF GLOSTER, SIR RICHARD RATCLIFFE, CATESBY,
   Courtiers, and other Attendants

 Jane Shore (kneeling). O noble Gloster, turn thy gracious eye,
Incline thy pitying ear to my complaint,
A poor, undone, forsaken, helpless woman
Entreats a little bread for charity,
To feed her wants, and save her life from perishing.
 Gloster. Arise, fair dame, and dry your watery eyes.
    (Receiving the paper, and raising her.
Beshrew me, but 'twere pity of his heart
That could refuse a boon to such a suitress.

Y'have got a noble friend to be your advocate;
A worthy and right gentle lord he is,
And to his trust most true. This present, now,
Some matters of the State detain our leisure;
Those once dispatched, we'll call for you anon,
And give your griefs redress. Go to! be comforted.

   Jane Shore. Good Heavens repay your Highness for this pity,
And shower down blessings on your princely head.
Come, my Alicia, reach thy friendly arm,
And help me to support this feeble frame,
That nodding totters with oppressive woe,
And sinks beneath its load.   (*Exeunt* JANE SHORE *and* ALICIA.

   Gloster.   Now by my holidom!
Heavy of heart she seems, and sore afflicted.
But thus it is when rude calamity
Lays its strong gripe upon these mincing minions;
The dainty gew-gaw forms dissolve at once,
And shiver at the shock. What says her paper? (*Seeming to read.*
Ha! What is this? Come nearer, Ratcliffe! Catesby!
Mark the contents, and then divine the meaning.   (*He reads.*
Wonder not, princely Gloster, at the notice
This paper brings you from a friend unknown;
Lord Hastings is inclined to call you master,
And kneel to Richard as to England's King;
But Shore's bewitching wife misleads his heart,
And draws his service to King Edward's sons.
Drive her away, you break the charm that holds him,
And he, and all his powers, attend on you.

   Ratcliffe. 'Tis wonderful!
   Catesby.   The means by which it came,
Yet stranger too!

   Gloster.   You saw it given but now.
   Ratcliffe. She could not know the purport.
   Gloster.   No, 'tis plain—
She knows it not, it levels at her life;
Should she presume to prate of such high matters,
The meddling harlot! dear she should abide it.

   Catesby. What hand soe'er it comes from, be assured,
It means your Highness well——

   Gloster.   Upon the instant
Lord Hastings will be here; this morn I mean
To prove him to the quick; then if he flinch,
No more but this, away with him at once;
He must be mine or nothing.—But he comes!
Draw nearer this way, and observe me well.   (*They whisper.*

Enter LORD HASTINGS

   Hastings. This foolish woman hangs about my heart,
Lingers and wanders in my fancy still;

This coyness is put on, 'tis art and cunning,
And worn to urge desire—I must possess her.
The groom who lift his saucy hand against me,
Ere this, is humbled, and repents his daring.
Perhaps ev'n she may profit by the example,
And teach her beauty not to scorn my power.
 Gloster. This do, and wait me ere the Council sits.
(Exeunt RATCLIFFE and CATESBY.

My lord, y'are well encountered here has been:
A fair petitioner this morning with us;
Believe me, she has won me much to pity her:
Alas! her gentle nature was not made
To buffet with adversity. I told her
How worthily her cause you had befriended,
How much for your good sake we meant to do;
That you had spoke, and all things should be well.
 Hastings. Your Highness binds me ever to your service.
 Gloster. You know your friendship is most potent with us,
And shares our power. But of this enough,
For we have other matters for your ear:
The State is out of tune; distracting fears
And jealous doubts jar in our public counsels;
Amidst the wealthy city, murmurs rise,
Lewd railings, and reproach, on those that rule,
With open scorn of government; hence credit
And public trust 'twixt man and man are broke.
The golden streams of commerce are withheld,
Which fed the wants of needy hinds and artisans,
Who therefore curse the great, and threat rebellion.
 Hastings. The resty knaves are overrun with ease,
As plenty ever is the nurse of faction.
If in good days, like these, the headstrong herd
Grow madly wanton and repine, it is
Because the reins of power are held too slack,
And reverend authority of late
Has worn a face of mercy more than justice.
 Gloster. Beshrew my heart! but you have well divined
The source of these disorders. Who can wonder
If riot and misrule o'erturn the realm,
When the crown sits upon a baby brow?
Plainly to speak; hence comes the general cry
And sum of all complaint: 'Twill ne'er be well
With England (thus they talk) while children govern.
 Hastings. 'Tis true the king is young; but what of that?
We feel no want of Edward's riper years
While Gloster's valour, and most princely wisdom,
So well support our infant sovereign's place,
His youth's support, and guardian of his throne.
 Gloster. The Council (much I'm bound to thank 'em for it)

Have placed a pageant sceptre in my hand,
Barren of power, and subject to control;
Scorned by my foes, and useless to my friends.
Oh, worthy lord! were mine the rule indeed,
I think I should not suffer rank offence
At large to lord it in the commonweal;
Nor would the realm be rent by discord thus,
Thus fear and doubt betwixt disputed titles.

    Hastings. Of this I am to learn; as not supposing
A doubt like this——

    Gloster.   Ay, marry, but there is—
And that of much concern. Have you not heard
How, on a late occasion, Doctor Shaw
Has moved the people much about the lawfulness
Of Edward's issue? By right grave authority
Of learning and religion, plainly proving
A bastard scion never should be grafted
Upon a royal stock; from thence, at full
Discoursing on my brother's former contract
To Lady Elizabeth Lucy, long before
His jolly match with that same buxom widow,
The queen he left behind him——

    Hastings.   Ill befall
Such meddling priests, who kindle up confusion,
And vex the quiet world with their vain scruples;
By Heaven, 'tis done in perfect spite to peace.
Did not the king,
Our royal master Edward, in concurrence
With his estates assembled, well determine
What course the sovereign rule should take henceforward?
When shall the deadly hate of faction cease,
When shall our long divided land have rest,
If every peevish, moody malcontent
Shall set the senseless rabble in an uproar?
Fright them with dangers, and perplex their brains
Each day with some fantastic giddy change?

    Gloster. What if some patriot for the public good
Should vary from your scheme, new-mould the State?

    Hastings. Curse on the innovating hand attempts it!
Remember him, the villain, righteous Heaven,
In thy great day of vengeance! Blast the traitor
And his pernicious counsels, who for wealth,
For power, the pride of greatness, or revenge,
Would plunge his native land in civil wars!

    Gloster. You go too far, my lord,

    Hastings.   Your Highness's pardon—
Have we so soon forgot those days of ruin,
When York and Lancaster drew forth the battles;
When, like a matron butchered by her sons,

And cast beside some common way, a spectacle
Of horror and affright to passers-by,
Our groaning country bled at every vein,
When murders, rapes, and massacres prevailed;
When churches, palaces, and cities blazed;
When insolence and barbarism triumphed,
And swept away distinction; peasants trod
Upon the necks of nobles; low were laid
The reverend crosier and the holy mitre,
And desolation covered all the land:
Who can remember this, and not, like me,
Here vow to sheathe a dagger in his heart,
Whose damn'd ambition would renew those horrors,
And set, once more, that scene of blood before us?

   Gloster. How now! So hot!
   Hastings.   So brave, and so resolved.
   Gloster. Is then our friendship of so little moment
That you could arm your hand against my life?
   Hastings. I hope your Highness does not think I meant it;
No, Heaven forefend that e'er your princely person
Should come within the scope of my resentment.
   Gloster. Oh! noble Hastings! Nay, I must embrace you;
                             (Embraces him.

By holy Paul! y'are a right honest man;
The time is full of danger and distrust,
And warns us to be wary. Hold me not
Too apt for jealousy and light surmise,
If when I meant to lodge you next my heart,
I put your truth to trial. Keep your loyalty,
And live your king and country's best support:
For me, I ask no more than honour gives,
To think me yours, and rank me with your friends.
   Hastings. Accept what thanks a grateful heart should pay.
Oh! princely Gloster! judge me not ungentle,
Of manners rude, and insolent of speech,
If, when the public safety is in question,
My zeal flows warm and eager from my tongue.
   Gloster. Enough of this: to deal in wordy compliment
Is much against the plainness of my nature;
I judge you by myself, a clear true spirit,
And, as such, once more join you to my bosom.
Farewell, and be my friend.   *(Exit Gloster.*
   Hastings.   I am not read,
Not skilled and practised in the arts of greatness,
To kindle thus, and give a scope to passion.
The duke is surely noble; but he touched me
Even on the tenderest point, the master-string
That makes most harmony or discord to me.
I own the glorious subject fires my breast,

And my soul's darling passion stands confessed;
Beyond or love's or friendship's sacred band,
Beyond myself, I prize my native land;
On this foundation would I build my fame,
And emulate the Greek and Roman name;
Think England's peace bought cheaply with my blood,
And die with pleasure for my country's good. (*Exit.*

ACT IV

Scene I. continues

Enter DUKE OF GLOSTER, RATCLIFFE, *and* CATESBY

Gloster. This was the sum of all; that he would brook
No alteration in the present State.
Marry! at last the testy gentleman
Was almost moved to bid us bold defiance;
But there I dropped the argument, and changing
The first design and purport of my speech,
I praised his good affection to young Edward,
And left him to believe my thoughts like his.
Proceed we then in this forementioned matter,
As nothing bound or trusting to his friendship.
Ratcliffe. Ill does it thus befall. I could have wished
This lord had stood with us. His friends are wealthy,
Thereto his own possessions large and mighty;
The vassals and dependants on his power
Firm in adherence, ready, bold and many;
His name had been of vantage to your Highness,
And stood our present purpose much in stead.
Gloster. This wayward and perverse declining from us
Has warranted at full the friendly notice
Which we this morn received. I hold it certain,
This puling, whining harlot rules his reason,
And prompts his zeal for Edward's bastard brood.
Catesby. If she have such dominion o'er his heart,
And turn it at her will, you rule her fate
And should, by inference and apt deduction,
Be arbiter of his. Is not her bread,
The very means immediate to her being,
The bounty of your hand? Why does she live,
If not to yield obedience to your pleasure,
To speak, to act, to think as you command?
Ratcliffe. Let her instruct her tongue to bear your message;
Teach every grace to smile in your behalf,
And her deluding eyes to gloat for you;

His ductile reason will be wound about,
Be led and turned again, say and unsay,
Receive the yoke, and yield exact obedience.

　Gloster. Your counsel likes me well, it shall be followed;
She waits without, attending on her suit.
Go, call her in, and leave us here alone.

　　　　　　　　　　　(Exeunt RATCLIFFE *and* CATESBY.

How poor a thing is he, how worthy scorn,
Who leaves the guidance of imperial manhood
To such a paltry piece of stuff as this is!
A moppet made of prettiness and pride;
That oftener does her giddy fancies change,
Than glittering dewdrops in the sun do colours—
Now shame upon it! Was our reason given
For such a use? To be thus puffed about
Like a dry leaf, an idle straw, a feather,
The sport of every whistling blast that blows?
Beshrew my heart, but it is wondrous strange;
Sure there is something more than witchcraft in them,
That masters even the wisest of us all.

Enter JANE SHORE

Oh! you are come most fitly. We have pondered
On this your grievance: and though some there are,
Nay, and those great ones too, who would enforce
The rigour of our power to afflict you,
And bear a heavy hand, yet fear not you,
We've ta'en you to our favour; our protection
Shall stand between, and shield you from mishap.

　Jane Shore. The blessings of a heart with anguish broken,
And rescued from despair, attend your Highness.
Alas! my gracious lord! what have I done
To kindle such relentless wrath against me?
If in the days of all my past offences,
When most my heart was lifted with delight,
If I withheld my morsel from the hungry,
Forgot the widow's want, and orphan's cry;
If I have known a good I have not shared,
Nor called the poor to take his portion with me,
Let my worst enemies stand forth and now
Deny the succour which I gave not then.

　Gloster. Marry, there are, though I believe them not,
Who say you meddle in affairs of State:
That you presume to prattle, like a busybody,
Give your advice, and teach the lords of the Council
What fits the order of the commonweal.

　Jane Shore. Oh that the busy world, at least in this,
Would take example from a wretch like me!
None then would waste their hours in foreign thoughts,

Forget themselves, and what concerns their peace,
To tread the mazes of fantastic falsehood,
To haunt her idle sounds and flying tales,
Through all the giddy noisy courts of rumour;
Malicious slander never would have leisure
To search with prying eyes for faults abroad,
If all, like me, considered their own hearts,
And wept the sorrows which they found at home.
    Gloster. Go to! I know your power, and though I trust not
To every breath of fame, I am not to learn
That Hastings is professed your loving vassal.
But fair befall your beauty: use it wisely,
And it may stand your fortunes much in stead;
Give back your forfeit land with large increase,
And place you high in safety and in honour:
Nay, I could point a way, the which pursuing,
You shall not only bring yourself advantage,
But give the realm much worthy cause to thank you.
    Jane Shore. Oh! where or how?—Can my unworthy hand
Become an instrument of good to any?
Instruct your lowly slave, and let me fly
To yield obedience to your dread command.
    Gloster. Why that's well said. Thus then—observe me well.
The State, for many high and potent reasons,
Deeming my brother Edward's sons unfit
For the imperial weight of England's Crown——
    Jane Shore. Alas! for pity.   (*Aside.*
    Gloster.   Therefore have resolved
To set aside their unavailing infancy,
And vest the sovereign rule in abler hands.
This, though of great importance to the public,
Hastings, for very peevishness and spleen,
Does stubbornly oppose.
    Jane Shore.   Does he? Does Hastings?
    Gloster. Ay, Hastings.
    Jane Shore. Reward him for the noble deed, just Heavens:
For this one action, guard him and distinguish him
With signal mercies and with great deliverance;
Save him from wrong, adversity and shame;
Let never-fading honours flourish round him,
And consecrate his name even to time's end:
Let him know nothing else but good on earth,
And everlasting blessedness hereafter.
    Gloster. How now!
    Jane Shore.   The poor, forsaken, royal little ones!
Shall they be left a prey to savage power?
Can they lift up their harmless hands in vain,
Or cry to Heaven for help, and not be heard?
Impossible! O gallant, generous Hastings,

Go on, pursue! Assert the sacred cause:
Stand forth, thou proxy of all-ruling Providence,
And save the friendless infants from oppression.
Saints shall assist thee with prevailing prayers,
And warring angels combat on thy side.

Gloster. You're passing rich in this same heavenly speech,
And spend it at your pleasure. Nay, but mark me!
My favour is not bought with words like these.
Go to—you'll teach your tongue another tale.

Jane Shore. No, though the royal Edward has undone me,
He was my king, my gracious master still;
He loved me too, though 'twas a guilty flame,
And fatal to my peace, yet still he loved me;
With fondness and with tenderness he doted,
Dwelt in my eyes, and lived but in my smiles.
And can I—Oh, my heart abhors the thought!—
Stand by and see his children robbed of right?

Gloster. Dare not, even for thy soul, to thwart me further;
None of your arts, your feigning, and your foolery,
Your dainty, squeamish coying it to me.
Go—to your lord, your paramour, begone;
Lisp in his ear, hang wanton on his neck,
And play your monkey gambols o'er to him:
You know my purpose, look that you pursue it,
And make him yield obedience to my will.
Do it—or woe upon thy harlot's head.

Jane Shore. Oh that my tongue had every grace of speech,
Great and commanding as the breath of kings,
Sweet as the poet's numbers, and prevailing
As soft persuasion to a love-sick maid!
That I had art and eloquence divine,
To pay my duty to my master's ashes,
And plead till death the cause of injured innocence!

Gloster. Ha! Dost thou brave me, minion! Dost thou know
How vile, how very a wretch, my power can make thee;
That I can let loose fear, distress and famine
To hunt thy heels, like hell-hounds, through the world;
That I can place thee in such abject state,
As help shall never find thee; where repining,
Thou shalt sit down and gnaw the earth for anguish,
Groan to the pitiless winds without return,
Howl like the midnight wolf amidst the desert,
And curse thy life in bitterness and misery?

Jane Shore. Let me be branded for the public scorn,
Turned forth, and driven to wander like a vagabond,
Be friendless and forsaken, seek my bread
Upon the barren, wild and desolate wastes,
Feed on my sighs, and drink my falling tears;
Ere I consent to teach my lips injustice,

Or wrong the orphan, who has none to save him.
   Gloster. 'Tis well—we'll try the temper of your heart,
What whoa! Who waits without!

Enter RATCLIFFE, CATESBY, *and Attendants*

   Ratcliffe.   Your Highness' pleasure——
   Gloster. Go, some of you, and turn this strumpet forth;
Spurn her into the street, there let her perish,
And rot upon a dunghill. Through the city
See it proclaimed, that none, on pain of death,
Presume to give her comfort, food, or harbour;
Who ministers the smallest comfort, dies.
Her house, her costly furniture and wealth,
The purchase of her loose luxurious life,
We seize on, for the profit of the State.
Away! Begone!
   Jane Shore. O thou most righteous Judge—
Humbly behold, I bow myself to Thee,
And own Thy justice in this hard decree:
No longer then my ripe offences spare,
But what I merit, let me learn to bear!
Yet since 'tis all my wretchedness can give,
For my past crimes my forfeit life receive;
No pity for my sufferings here I crave,
And only hope forgiveness in the grave.
          (*Exit* JANE SHORE, *guarded by* CATESBY *and others.*
   Gloster. So much for this. Your project's at an end.
                        (*To* RATCLIFFE.
This idle toy, this hilding scorns my power,
And sets us all at naught. See that a guard
Be ready at my call——
   Ratcliffe.   The Council waits
Upon your Highness' leisure.
   Gloster.   Bid 'em enter.

Enter the DUKE OF BUCKINGHAM, EARL OF DERBY, BISHOP OF
ELY, LORD HASTINGS *and others, as to the Council. The*
DUKE OF GLOSTER *takes his place at the upper end, then the*
rest sit

   Derby. In happy time are we assembled here,
To point the day, and fix the solemn pomp,
For placing England's crown with all due rites
Upon our sovereign Edward's youthful brow.
   Hastings. Some busy meddling knaves, 'tis said there are,
As such will still be prating, who presume
To carp and cavil at his royal right;
Therefore I hold it fitting, with the soonest,
To appoint the order of the coronation;
So to approve our duty to the king,

And stay the babbling of such vain gainsayers.
   Derby. We all attend to know your Highness' pleasure.
                              (To GLOSTER.

   Gloster. My lords! A set of worthy men you are,
Prudent and just, and careful for the State:
Therefore to your most grave determination
I yield myself in all things; and demand
What punishment your wisdom shall think meet
To inflict upon those damnable contrivers
Who shall with potions, charms, and witching drugs,
Practise against our person and our life.
   Hastings. So much I hold the king your Highness' debtor,
So precious are you to the commonweal,
That I presume, not only for myself,
But in behalf of these my noble brothers,
To say, whoe'er they be, they merit death.
   Gloster. Then judge yourselves, convince your eyes of truth;
Behold my arm thus blasted, dry and withered,
                         (Pulling up his sleeve

Shrunk like a foul abortion, and decayed,
Like some untimely product of the seasons,
Robbed of its properties of strength and office.
This is the sorcery of Edward's wife,
Who in conjunction with that harlot Shore,
And other like confederate midnight hags,
By force of potent spells, of bloody characters,
And conjurations horrible to hear,
Call fiends and spectres from the yawning deep,
And set the ministers of hell at work,
To torture and despoil me of my life.
   Hastings. If they have done this deed——
   Gloster.   If they have done it!
Talkest thou to me of If's, audacious traitor!
Thou art that strumpet-witch's chief abettor,
The patron and complotter of her mischiefs,
And joined in this contrivance for my death.
Nay, start not, lords.—What ho! a guard there, sirs!

Enter Guard

Lord Hastings, I arrest thee of high treason.
Seize him, and bear him instantly away.
He shall not live an hour. By holy Paul!
I will not dine before his head be brought me:
Ratcliffe, stay you and see that it be done.
The rest that love me, rise and follow me.
          (Exeunt GLOSTER, *and Lords following. Manent*
               LORD HASTINGS, RATCLIFFE *and Guard.*
   Hastings. What! and no more but this—how, to the scaffold!
Oh, gentle Ratcliffe! tell me, do I hold thee?

Or if I dream, what shall I do to wake,
To break, to struggle through this dread confusion?
For surely death itself is not so painful
As is this sudden horror and surprise.
   Ratcliffe. You heard, the duke's commands to me were
        absolute,
Therefore, my lord, address you to your shrift
With all good speed you may. Summon your courage,
And be yourself; for you must die this instant.
   Hastings. Yes, Ratcliffe, I will take thy friendly counsel,
And die as a man should; 'tis somewhat hard
To call my scattered spirits home at once:
But since what must be, must be—let necessity
Supply the place of time and preparation,
And arm me for the blow. 'Tis but to die,
'Tis but to venture on that common hazard
Which many a time in battle I have run;
'Tis but to do what, at that very moment,
In many nations of the peopled earth,
A thousand and a thousand shall do with me:
'Tis but to close my eyes and shut out daylight,
To view no more the wicked ways of men,
No longer to behold the tyrant Gloster,
And be a weeping witness of the woes,
The desolation, slaughter and calamities,
Which he shall bring on this unhappy land.

Enter ALICIA

   Alicia. Stand off! and let me pass—I will, I must,
Catch him once more in these despairing arms,
And hold him to my heart.—Oh, Hastings, Hastings!
   Hastings. Alas! Why com'st thou at this dreadful moment,
To fill me with new terrors, new distractions,
To turn me wild with thy distempered rage,
And shock the peace of my departing soul?
Away! I prithee leave me!
   Alicia.   Stop a minute,
Till my full griefs find passage.—Oh, the tyrant!
Perdition fall on Gloster's head and mine.
   Hastings. What means thy frantic grief?
   Alicia.   I cannot speak—
But I have murdered thee—Oh, I would tell thee!
   Hastings. Speak and give ease to thy conflicting passions.
Be quick, nor keep me longer in suspense,
Time presses, and a thousand crowding thoughts
Break in at once; this way and that they snatch,
They tear my hurried soul: all claim attention,
And yet not one is heard. Oh, speak and leave me,

For I have business would employ an age,
And but a minute's time to get it done in.

Alicia. That, that's my grief—'tis I that urge thee on,
Thus hunt thee to the toil, sweep thee from earth,
And drive thee down this precipice of fate.

Hastings. Thy reason is grown wild. Could thy weak hand
Bring on this mighty ruin? If it could,
What have I done so grievous to thy soul,
So deadly, so beyond the reach of pardon,
That nothing but my life can make atonement?

Alicia. Thy cruel scorn had stung me to the heart,
And set my burning bosom all in flames:
Raving and mad I flew to my revenge,
And writ I know not what—told the Protector
That Shore's detested wife by wiles had won thee,
To plot against his greatness. He believed it
(Oh dire event of my pernicious counsel,)!
And while I meant destruction on her head,
He has turned it all on thine.

Hastings.   Accursed jealousy!
O merciless, wild and unforgiving fiend!
Blindfold it runs to undistinguished mischief,
And murders all it meets. Cursed be its rage,
For there is none so deadly; doubly cursed
Be all those easy fools who give it harbour:
Who turn a monster loose among mankind,
Fiercer than famine, war, or spotted pestilence;
Baneful as death, and horrible as hell.

Alicia. If thou wilt curse, curse rather thine own falsehood;
Curse the lewd maxims of thy perjured sex,
Which taught thee first to laugh at faith and justice,
To scorn the solemn sanctity of oaths,
And make a jest of a poor woman's ruin:
Curse thy proud heart and thy insulting tongue,
That raised this fatal fury in my soul,
And urged my vengeance to undo us both.

Hastings. Oh thou inhuman! turn thy eyes away,
And blast me not with their destructive beams:
Why should I curse thee with my dying breath?
Begone! and let me sigh it out in peace.

Alicia. Canst thou, oh cruel Hastings, leave me thus!
Hear me, I beg thee—I conjure thee, hear me!
While with an agonising heart I swear,
By all the pangs I feel, by all the sorrows,
The terrors and despair thy loss shall give me,
My hate was on my rival bent alone.
Oh! had I once divined, false as thou art,
A danger to thy life, I would have died,
I would have met it for thee, and made bare

My ready faithful breast to save thee from it.

Hastings. Now mark! and tremble at Heaven's just award.
While thy insatiate wrath and fell revenge
Pursued the innocence which never wronged thee,
Behold! the mischief falls on thee and me;
Remorse and heaviness of heart shall wait thee,
And everlasting anguish be thy portion:
For me, the snares of death are wound about me,
And now, in one poor moment, I am gone.
Oh! if thou hast one tender thought remaining,
Fly to thy closet, fall upon thy knee,
And recommend my parting soul to mercy.

Alicia. Oh! yet, before I go for ever from thee,
Turn thee in gentleness and pity to me,   (*Kneeling.*
And in compassion of my strong affliction,
Say, is it possible you can forgive
The fatal rashness of ungoverned love?
For oh! 'tis certain, if I had not loved thee
Beyond my peace, my reason, fame and life,
Desired to death, and doted to distraction,
This day of horror never should have known us.

Hastings. Oh! rise, and let me hush thy stormy sorrows,
                                                            (*Raising her.*
Assuage thy tears, for I will chide no more,
No more upbraid thee, thou unhappy fair one.
I see the hand of Heaven is armed against me,
And, in mysterious providence, decrees
To punish me by thy mistaking hand.
Most righteous doom! for, oh! while I behold thee,
Thy wrongs rise up in terrible array,
And charge thy ruin on me; thy fair fame,
Thy spotless beauty, innocence and youth,
Dishonoured, blasted and betrayed by me.

Alicia. And does thy heart relent for my undoing?
Oh! that inhuman Gloster could be moved
But half so easily as I can pardon!

Hastings. Here then exchange we mutually forgiveness.
So may the guilt of all my broken vows,
My perjuries to thee be all forgotten,
As here my soul acquits thee of my death,
As here I part without one angry thought,
As here I leave [thee] with the softest tenderness,
Mourning the chance of our disastrous loves,
And begging Heaven to bless and to support thee.

Ratcliffe. My lord, dispatch; the duke has sent to chide me
For loitering in my duty——

Hastings.   I obey.

Alicia. Insatiate, savage monster! Is a moment
So tedious to thy malice? Oh! repay him,

Thou great Avenger, give him blood for blood:
Guilt haunt him! Fiends pursue him! Lightning blast him,
Some horrid, cursèd kind of death o'ertake him,
Sudden, and in the fullness of his sins!
That he may know how terrible it is
To want that moment he denies thee now.

   Hastings. 'Tis all in vain, this rage that tears thy bosom,
Like a poor bird that flutters in its cage,
Thou beatest thyself to death. Retire, I beg thee;
To see thee thus, thou knowest not how it wounds me,
Thy agonies are added to my own,
And make the burden more than I can bear.
Farewell! Good angels visit thy afflictions,
And bring thee peace and comfort from above.

   Alicia. Oh! stab me to the heart, some pitying hand,
Now strike me dead——

   Hastings.   One thing I had forgot—
I charge thee by our present common miseries,
By our past loves, if yet they have a name,
By all thy hopes of peace here and hereafter,
Let not the rancour of thy hate pursue
The innocence of thy unhappy friend:
Thou know'st who 'tis I mean. Oh! shouldst thou wrong her,
Just Heaven shall double all thy woes upon thee,
And make 'em know no end. Remember this
As the last warning of a dying man.
Farewell for ever!   *(The Guards carry* HASTINGS *off.*

   Alicia.   For ever? Oh! For ever!
Oh! who can bear to be a wretch for ever!
My rival too! His last thoughts hung on her:
And, as he parted, left a blessing for her.
Shall she be blest, and I be cursed, for ever!
No; since her fatal beauty was the cause
Of all my sufferings, let her share my pains:
Let her, like me, of every joy forlorn,
Devote the hour when such a wretch was born;
Like me to deserts and to darkness run,
Abhor the day, and curse the golden sun;
Cast every good and every hope behind;
Detest the works of nature, loathe mankind:
Like me, with cries distracted fill the air;
Tear her poor bosom, rend her frantic hair;   *(Exit.*
And prove the torments of the last despair.

ACT V

SCENE I.—*The Street*

BELLMOUR *and* DUMONT *or* SHORE

Shore. You saw her then?
Bellmour.   I met her as returning
In solemn penance from the public cross:
Before her certain rascal officers,
Slaves in authority, the knaves of justice,
Proclaimed the tyrant Gloster's cruel orders.
On either side her marched an ill-looked priest,
Who with severe, with horrid haggard eyes,
Did ever and anon by turns upbraid her,
And thunder in her trembling ear damnation.
Around her, numberless the rabble flowed,
Shrouding each other, crowding for a view,
Gaping and gazing, taunting and reviling;
Some pitying, but those, alas! how few!
The most, such iron hearts we are, and such
The base barbarity of human kind,
With insolence and lewd reproach pursued her,
Hooting and railing, and with villainous hands
Gathering the filth from out the common ways,
To hurl upon her head.
Shore.   Inhuman dogs!
How did she bear it?
Bellmour.   With the gentlest patience.
Submissive, sad, and lowly was her look;
A burning taper in her hand she bore,
And on her shoulders carelessly confused
With loose neglect her lovely tresses hung;
Upon her cheek a faintish flush was spread,
Feeble she seemed, and sorely smit with pain,
While barefoot as she trod the flinty pavement,
Her footsteps all along were marked with blood.
Yet silent still she passed and unrepining;
Her streaming eyes bent ever on the earth,
Except when in some bitter pang of sorrow,
To Heaven she seemed in fervent zeal to raise,
And beg that mercy man denied her here.
Shore. When was this piteous sight?
Bellmour.   These last two days.
You know my care was wholly bent on you,
To find the happy means of your deliverance,
Which but for Hastings' death I had not gained.

During that time, although I have not seen her,
Yet divers trusty messengers I've sent
To wait about, and watch a fit convenience
To give her some relief; but all in vain:
A churlish guard attends upon her steps,
Who menace those with death that bring her comfort,
And drive all succour from her.
    Shore.   Let 'em threaten;
Let proud oppression prove its fiercest malice;
So Heaven befriend my soul, as here I vow
To give her help, and share one fortune with her.
    Bellmour. Mean you to see her thus, in your own form?
    Shore. I do.
    Bellmour. And have you thought upon the consequence?
    Shore. What is there I should fear?
    Bellmour.   Have you examined
Into your inmost heart, and tried at leisure
The several secret springs that move the passions?
Has mercy fixed her empire there so sure,
That wrath and vengeance never may return?
Can you resume a husband's name, and bid
That wakeful dragon, fierce resentment, sleep?
    Shore. Why dost thou search so deep, and urge my memory?
To conjure up my wrongs to life again?
I have long laboured to forget myself,
To think on all time, backward, like a space,
Idle and void, where nothing e'er had being;
But thou hast peopled it again; revenge
And jealousy renew their horrid forms,
Shoot all their fires, and drive me to distraction.
    Bellmour. Far be the thought from me! My care was only
To arm you for the meeting: better were it
Never to see her, than to let that name
Recall forgotten rage, and make the husband
Destroy the generous pity of Dumont.
    Shore. Oh! thou hast set my busy brain at work,
And now she musters up a train of images,
Which to preserve my peace I had cast aside,
And sunk in deep oblivion.—Oh! that form!
That angel-face on which my dotage hung!
How have I gazed upon her! till my soul
With very eagerness went forth towards her,
And issued at my eyes. Was there a gem
Which the sun ripens in the Indian mine,
Or the rich bosom of the ocean yields,
What was there art could make, or wealth could buy,
Which I have left unsought to deck her beauty?
What could her king do more?—And yet she fled.
    Bellmour. Away with that sad fancy.

Shore.   Oh! that day!
The thought of it must live for ever with me.
I met her, Bellmour, when the royal spoiler
Bore her in triumph from my widowed home!
Within his chariot by his side she sat,
And listened to his talk with downward looks;
Till sudden as she chanced aside to glance,
Her eyes encountered mine—Oh! then, my friend!
Oh! who can paint my grief and her amazement!
As at the stroke of death, twice turned she pale,
And twice a burning crimson blushed all o'er her;
Then with a shriek heart-wounding loud she cried,
While down her cheeks gushing torrents ran
Fast falling on her hands, which thus she wrung.
Moved at her grief, the tyrant ravisher
With courteous action wooed her oft to turn;
Earnest he seemed to plead; but all in vain;
Even to the last she bent her sight towards me,
And followed me—till I had lost myself.

Bellmour. Alas! for pity! Oh! those speaking tears!
Could they be false? Did she not suffer with you?
For though the king by force possessed her person,
Her unconsenting heart dwelt still with you:
If all her former woes were not enough,
Look on her now, behold her where she wanders,
Hunted to death, distressed on every side,
With no one hand to help; and tell me then,
If ever misery were known like hers?

Shore. And can she bear it? Can that delicate frame
Endure the beating of a storm so rude?
Can she, for whom the various seasons changed,
To court her appetite, and crown her board,
For whom the foreign vintages were pressed,
For whom the merchant spread his silken stores,
Can she—
Entreat for bread, and want the needful raiment,
To wrap her shivering bosom from the weather?
When she was mine, no care came ever nigh her.
I thought the gentlest breeze that wakes the spring,
Too rough to breathe upon her; cheerfulness
Danced all the day before her; and at night
Soft slumbers waited on her downy pillow—
Now, sad and shelterless, perhaps, she lies
Where piercing winds blow sharp, and the chill rain
Drops from some pent-house on her wretched head,
Drenches her locks, and kills her with the cold.
It is too much—Hence with her past offences,
They are atoned at full.—Why stay we then?
Oh! let us haste, my friend, and find her out.

Bellmour. Somewhere about this quarter of the town
I hear the poor abandoned creature lingers:
Her guard, though set with strictest watch to keep
All food and friendship from her, yet permit her
To wander in the streets, there choose her bed,
And rest her head on what cold stone she pleases.
  Shore. Here let us then divide; each in his round
To search her sorrows out; whose hap it is
First to behold her, this way let him lead
Her fainting steps, and meet we here together.   *(Exeun*

Enter JANE SHORE, *her hair hanging loose on her shoulders, and*
barefooted

  Jane Shore. Yet, yet endure, nor murmur, oh! my soul!
For are not thy transgressions great and numberless?
Do they not cover thee like rising floods,
And press thee like a weight of waters down?
Does not the hand of righteousness afflict thee?
And who shall plead against it? Who shall say
To Power Almighty: Thou hast done enough?
Or bid His dreadful rod of vengeance stay?
Wait then with patience, till the circling hours
Shall bring the time of thy appointed rest,
And lay thee down in death. The hireling thus
With labour drudges out the painful day,
And often looks with long-expecting eyes
To see the shadows rise and be dismissed.
And hark! methinks the roar that late pursued me,
Sinks, like the murmurs of a falling wind,
And softens into silence. Does revenge
And malice then grow weary and forsake me?
My guard too, that observed me still so close,
Tire in the task of their inhuman office,
And loiter far behind. Alas! I faint,
My spirits fail at once.—This is the door
Of my Alicia—blessèd opportunity!
I'll steal a little succour from her goodness,
Now, while no eye observes me.   *(She knocks at the door.*

Enter a Servant
                    Is your lady,
My gentle friend, at home? Oh! bring me to her.   *(Going in.*
  Servant. Hold, mistress, whither would you?
                              (Putting her back.
  Jane Shore.   Do you not know me?
  Servant. I know you well, and know my orders too.
You must not enter here——

Jane Shore.   Tell my Alicia
'Tis I would see her.
    Servant.   She is ill at ease,
And will admit no visitor.
    Jane Shore.   But tell her
'Tis I, her friend, the partner of her heart,
Wait at the door and beg——
    Servant.   'Tis all in vain—
Go hence, and howl to those that will regard you.
                    (Shuts the door, and exit.

    Jane Shore. It was not always thus; the time has been
When this unfriendly door, that bars my passage,
Flew wide and almost leaped from off its hinges
To give me entrance here; when this good house
Has poured forth all its dwellers to receive me;
When my approach has made a little holy-day,
And every face was dressed in smiles to meet me:
But now 'tis otherwise; and those who blessed me,
Now curse me to my face. Why should I wander,
Stray farther on, for I can die even here!
                    (She sits down at the door.

    Enter ALICIA *in disorder, two Servants following*

    Alicia. What wretch art thou? whose misery and baseness
Hangs on my door; whose hateful whine of woe
Breaks in upon my sorrows, and distracts
My jarring senses with thy beggar's cry?
    Jane Shore. A very beggar, and a wretch indeed;
One driven by strong calamity to seek
For succour here; one perishing for want;
Whose hunger has not tasted food these three days;
And humbly asks, for charity's dear sake,
A draught of water and a little bread.
    Alicia. And dost thou come to me, to me, for bread?
I know thee not. Go—hunt for it abroad,
Where wanton hands upon the earth have scattered it,
Or cast it on the waters. Mark the eagle,
And hungry vulture, where they wind the prey;
Watch where the ravens of the valley feed,
And seek thy food with them.—I know thee not.
    Jane Shore. And yet there was a time when my Alicia
Has thought unhappy Shore her dearest blessing;
And mourned that live-long day she passed without me,
When, paired like turtles, we were still together;
When often as we prattled arm in arm,
Inclining fondly to me she has sworn
She loved me more than all the world beside.
    Alicia. Ha! sayest thou! Let me look upon thee well.
'Tis true—I know thee now. A mischief on thee!

Thou art that fatal fair, that cursed she,
That set my brain a-madding. Thou hast robbed me;
Thou hast undone me! Murder! Oh, my Hastings!
See his pale bloody head shoots glaring by me!
Give him me back again, thou soft deluder,
Thou beauteous witch——

    Jane Shore.   Alas! I never wronged you—
Oh! then be good to me; have pity on me:
Thou never knew'st the bitterness of want,
And may'st thou never know it. Oh! bestow
Some poor remain, the voiding of thy table,
A morsel to support my famished soul.

    Alicia. Avaunt! and come not near me——

    Jane Shore.   To thy hand
I trusted all, gave my whole store to thee;
Nor do I ask it back, allow me but
The smallest pittance, give me but to eat,
Lest I fall down and perish here before thee.

    Alicia. Nay! tell me not! Where is thy king, thy Edward,
And all the smiling, cringing train of courtiers
That bent the knee before thee?

    Jane Shore.   Oh! for mercy!

    Alicia. Mercy! I know it not—for I am miserable.
I'll give thee misery, for here she dwells;
This is her house, where the sun never dawns,
The bird of night sits screaming o'er the roof,
Grim spectres sweep along the horrid gloom,
And naught is heard but wailings and lamentings.
Hark! something cracks above! it shakes, it totters!
And see the nodding ruin falls to crush me!
'Tis fallen, 'tis here! I feel it on my brain!

    First Servant. This sight disorders her——

    Second Servant.   Retire, dear lady,
And leave this woman——

    Alicia.   Let her take my counsel!
Why shouldst thou be a wretch? Stab, tear thy heart,
And rid thyself of this detested being,
I wo'not linger long behind thee here.
A waving flood of bluish fire swells o'er me;
And now 'tis out, and I am drowned in blood.
Ha! what art thou! thou horrid headless trunk?
It is my Hastings! See! he wafts me on!
Away! I go! I fly! I follow thee.
But come not thou with mischief-making beauty
To interpose between us, look not on him,
Give thy fond arts and thy delusions o'er;
For thou shalt never, never part us more.

                 (*She runs off, her Servants following.*

    Jane Shore. Alas! she raves; her brain, I fear, is turned.

In mercy look upon her, gracious Heaven,
Nor visit her for any wrong to me.
Sure I am near upon my journey's end;
My head runs round, my eyes begin to fail,
And dancing shadows swim before my sight:
I can no more (*Lies down.*); receive me, thou cold earth,
Thou common parent, take me to thy bosom,
And let me rest with thee.

Enter BELLMOUR

Bellmour.   Upon the ground!
Thy miseries can never lay thee lower.
Look up, thou poor afflicted one! thou mourner
Whom none has comforted! Where are thy friends,
The dear companions of thy joyful days,
Whose hearts thy warm prosperity made glad,
Whose arms were taught to grow like ivy round thee,
And bind thee to their bosoms? Thus with thee,
Thus let us live, and let us die, they said,
For sure thou art the sister of our loves,
And nothing shall divide us. Now where are they?

Jane Shore. Ah! Bellmour, where indeed? They stand aloof,
And view my desolation from afar;
When they pass by, they shake their heads in scorn,
And cry, Behold the harlot and her end!
And yet their goodness turns aside to pity me.
Alas! there may be danger, get thee gone!
Let me not pull a ruin on thy head,
Leave me to die alone, for I am fal'en
Never to rise, and all relief is vain.

Bellmour. Yet raise thy drooping head; for I am come
To chase away despair. Behold! where yonder
That honest man, that faithful brave Dumont,
Is hasting to thy aid——

Jane Shore.   Dumont! Ha! Where?
                    (*Raising herself and looking about.*
Then Heaven has heard my prayer; his very name
Renews the springs of life, and cheers my soul.
Has he then 'scaped the snare?

Bellmour. He has; but see——
He comes unlike to that Dumont you knew,
For now he wears your better angel's form,
And comes to visit you with peace and pardon.

Enter SHORE

Jane Shore. Speak, tell me! Which is he? And oh! what would
This dreadful vision! See, it comes upon me—
It is my husband—Ah!   (*She swoons.*
Shore.   She faints! Support her!

Sustain her head, while I infuse this cordial
Into her dying lips—from spicy drugs,
Rich herbs and flowers the potent juice is drawn;
With wondrous force it strikes the lazy spirits,
Drives 'em around, and wakens life anew.
    Bellmour. Her weakness could not bear the strong surprise.
But see, she stirs! and the returning blood
Faintly begins to blush again, and kindle
Upon her ashy cheek——
    Shore.   So—gently raise her—— (*Raising her up.*
    Jane Shore. Ha! What art thou? Bellmour!
    Bellmour.   How fare you, lady?
    Jane Shore. My heart is thrilled with horror——
    Bellmour.   Be of courage—
Your husband lives! 'Tis he, my worthiest friend——
    Jane Shore. Still art thou there!—still dost thou hover round me!
Oh, save me, Bellmour, from his angry shade!
    Bellmour. 'Tis he himself!—he lives!—look up——
    Jane Shore.   I dare not!
Oh that my eyes could shut him out for ever——
    Shore. Am I so hateful then, so deadly to thee,
To blast thy eyes with horror? Since I'm grown
A burden to the world, myself and thee,
Would I had ne'er survived to see thee more.
    Jane Shore. Oh thou most injured—dost thou live indeed!
Fall then, ye mountains, on my guilty head;
Hide me, ye rocks, within your secret caverns;
Cast thy black veil upon my shame, O night,
And shield me with thy sable wing for ever!
    Shore. Why dost thou turn away? Why tremble thus?
Why thus indulge thy fears? And in despair,
Abandon thy distracted soul to horror?
Cast every black and guilty thought behind thee,
And let 'em never vex thy quiet more.
My arms, my heart are open to receive thee,
To bring thee back to thy forsaken home,
With tender joy, with fond forgiving love,
And all the longings of my first desires.
    Jane Shore. No, arm thy brow with vengeance; and appear
The minister of Heaven's inquiring justice.
Array thyself all terrible for judgment,
Wrath in thy eyes, and thunder in thy voice;
Pronounce my sentence, and if yet there be
A woe I have not felt, inflict it on me.
    Shore. The measure of thy sorrows is complete;
And I am come to snatch thee from injustice.
The hand of power no more shall crush thy weakness,
Nor proud oppression grind thy humble soul.
    Jane Shore. Art thou not risen by miracle from death?

Thy shroud is fallen from off thee, and the grave
Was bid to give thee up, that thou mightest come,
The messenger of grace and goodness to me,
To seal my peace, and bless me ere I go.
Oh, let me then fall down beneath thy feet,
And weep my gratitude for ever there;
Give me your drops, ye soft descending rains,
Give me your streams, ye never-ceasing springs,
That my sad eyes may still supply my duty,
And feed an everlasting flood of sorrow!

   Shore. Waste not thy feeble spirits—I have long
Beheld, unknown, thy mourning and repentance;
Therefore my heart has set aside the past,
And holds thee white as unoffending innocence:
Therefore in spite of cruel Gloster's rage,
Soon as my friend had broke my prison-doors,
I flew to thy assistance. Let us haste
Now while occasion seems to smile upon us,
Forsake this place of shame, and find a shelter.

   Jane Shore. What shall I say to you? But I obey——
   Shore. Lean on my arm——
   Jane Shore.   Alas! I am wondrous faint:
But that's not strange, I have not eat these three days.

   Shore. Oh merciless! Look here, my love, I've brought thee
Some rich conserves——
   Jane Shore.   How can you be so good?
But you were ever thus; I well remember
With what fond care, what diligence of love,
You lavished out your wealth to buy me pleasures,
Preventing every wish. Have you forgot
The costly string of pearl you brought me home,
And tied about my neck?—How could I leave you?

   Shore. Taste some of this, or this——
   Jane Shore.   You're strangely altered—
Say, gentle Bellmour, is he not? How pale
Your visage is become! Your eyes are hollow;
Nay, you are wrinkled too. Alas the day!
My wretchedness has cost you many a tear,
And many a bitter pang, since last we parted.

   Shore. No more of that—thou talkest, but dost not eat.
   Jane Shore. My feeble jaws forget their common office,
My tasteless tongue cleaves to the clammy roof,
And now a general loathing grows upon me—
Oh, I am sick at heart!——
   Shore.   Thou murd'rous sorrow!
Wo't thou still drink her blood, pursue her still!
Must she then die! Oh, my poor penitent,
Speak peace to thy sad heart. She hears me not;
Grief masters every sense—help me to hold her——

Enter CATESBY, *with a Guard*

Catesby. Seize on 'em both, as traitors to the State——
Bellmour. What means this violence!——

> (*Guards lay hold on* SHORE *and* BELLMOUR.

Catesby.   Have we not found you,
In scorn of the Protector's strict command,
Assisting this base woman, and abetting
Her infamy?
    Shore.   Infamy on thy head!
Thou tool of power, thou pander to authority!
I tell thee, knave, thou knowest of none so virtuous,
And she that bore thee was an Ethiop to her.
    Catesby. You'll answer this at full.—Away with 'em.
    Shore. Is charity grown treason to your Court?
What honest man would live beneath such rulers?
I am content that we shall die together——
    Catesby. Convey the men to prison; but for her,
Leave her to hunt her fortune as she may.
    Jane Shore. I will not part with him—for me!—for me!
Oh! must he die for me?

> (*Following him as he is carried off—she falls.*

    Shore.   Inhuman villains! (*Breaks from the Guard.*
Stand off! the agonies of death are on her—
She pulls, she gripes me hard with her cold hand.
    Jane Shore. Was this blow wanting to complete my ruin!
Oh, let him go, ye ministers of terror;
He shall offend no more, for I will die,
And yield obedience to your cruel master.
Tarry a little, but a little longer,
And take my last breath with you.
    Shore.   Oh my love!
Why have I lived to see this bitter moment,
This grief by far surpassing all my former?
Why dost thou fix thy dying eyes upon me
With such an earnest, such a piteous look,
As if thy heart were full of some sad meaning
Thou couldst not speak?
    Jane Shore.   Forgive me!—but forgive me!
    Shore. Be witness for me, ye celestial host,
Such mercy and such pardon as my soul
Accords to thee, and begs of Heaven to show thee,
May such befall me at my latest hour,
And make my portion blest or cursed for ever.
    Jane Shore. Then all is well, and I shall sleep in peace——
'Tis very dark, and I have lost you now——
Was there not something I would have bequeathed you?
But I have nothing left me to bestow,
Nothing but one sad sigh. Oh, mercy, Heaven!   (*Dies.*

Bellmour. There fled the soul,
And left her load of misery behind.

Shore. Oh my heart's treasure! Is this pale sad visage
All that remains of thee? Are these dead eyes
The light that cheer my soul? Oh heavy hour!
But I will fix my trembling lips to thine,
Till I am cold and senseless quite, as thou art.
What, must we part then?—will you——

　　　　　　　　　　　(*To the Guards taking him away.*
Fare thee well——　　　　　　　　　　　(*Kissing her.*
Now execute your tyrant's will, and lead me
To bonds, or death, 'tis equally indifferent.

Bellmour. Let those, who view this sad example, know
What fate attends the broken marriage-vow;
And teach their children in succeeding times,
No common vengeance waits upon these crimes;
When such severe repentance could not save
From want, from shame, and an untimely grave.　　　　(*Exeunt.*

EPILOGUE

SPOKEN BY MRS. OLDFIELD

YE modest matrons all, ye virtuous wives,
Who lead with horrid husbands decent lives;
You, who for all you are in such a taking,
To see your spouses drinking, gaming, raking,
Yet make a conscience still of cuckold-making;
What can we say your pardon to obtain?
This matter here was proved against poor Jane:
She never once denied it, but in short,
Whimpered—and cried: Sweet sir, I'm sorry for't.
'Twas well she met a kind, good-natured soul,
We are not all so easy to control:
I fancy one might find in this good town
Some would have told the gentleman his own;
Have answered smart: To what do you pretend,
Blockhead?—As if I must not see a friend:
Tell me of hackney-coaches—jaunts to the city—
Where should I buy my china—Faith, I'll fit ye—
Our wife was of a milder, meeker spirit;
You!—lords and masters!—was not that some merit?
Don't you allow it to be virtuous bearing,
When we submit thus to your domineering?
Well, peace be with her, she did wrong most surely;
But so do many more who look demurely.
Nor should our mourning madam weep alone,
There are more ways of wickedness than one.
If the reforming stage should fall to shaming
Ill-nature, pride, hypocrisy, and gaming;
The poets frequently might move compassion,
And with she-tragedies o'errun the nation.
Then judge the fair offender with good-nature,
And let your fellow-feeling curb your satire.
What if our neighbours have some little failing,
Must we needs fall to damning and to railing?
For her excuse too, be it understood,
That if the woman was not quite so good,
Her lover was a king, she flesh and blood.
And since she has dearly paid the sinful score,
Be kind at last, and pity poor Jane Shore.

105

THE BEGGAR'S OPERA

JOHN GAY began life less fortunately than his two prede-
cessors in this volume, but like them he found his last resting-
place at Westminster, mourned by a circle of wits and poets,
among whom he was the most "artless and best beloved of all."
Born of an impoverished family at Barnstaple, in 1685, Gay was
left an orphan at ten, and before long found himself unhappily
apprenticed to a silk-mercer in London. But he soon apprenticed himself to literature, and after the publication in 1708 of
his first work, a blank-verse poem called *Wine*, his numerous
poems and plays brought him increasing fame, a fair measure
of fortune, the generous patronage of the Queensberrys and
others, and many friends. He was indolent and luxurious,

> "Of manners gentle, of affections mild;
> In wit, a man; simplicity, a child,"

and his health was bad; probably it was fortunate for him that
he was denied the political preferment for which he hankered.

The Shepherd's Week, a mock-pastoral, appeared in 1714, and
secured popularity by its humorous pictures of country life.
Trivia, or the Art of Walking the Streets of London (1716), presented
a vivid panorama of the city life of the time; and these successes
were followed by many lively (and often licentious) fables,
epistles and ballads—of which only *Black-eyed Susan* has survived
in popular memory. *Poems on Several Occasions* (1720) brought
Gay over £1000, and though to his despair he lost it all in the
same year, when the South Sea Bubble burst, his patrons saved
him from want, and the extraordinary success of *The Beggar's
Opera* and *Polly* brought him renewed fortune a few years later.

He died suddenly of fever in 1732, and the Duke and Duchess
of Queensberry inscribed upon the costly monument which they
erected in Westminster Abbey, his own lines:

> "Life is a jest, and all things show it:
> I thought so once, and now I know it."

THE

BEGGAR's

OPERA.

As it is Acted at the

THEATRE-ROYAL

IN

LINCOLNS-INN-FIELDS.

Written by Mr. *GAY*.

Nos hæc novimus esse nihil.   Mart.

To which is Added,

The MUSICK *Engrav'd on* COPPER——

PLATES

LONDON:

Printed for John Watts, at the Printing-Office
in *Wild-Court*, near *Lincoln's-Inn-Fields.*
MDCCXXVIII
[Price 1s. 6d.]

DRAMATIS PERSONÆ

MEN

PEACHUM	Mr. Hippesley
LOCKIT	Mr. Hall
MACHEATH	Mr. Walker
FILCH	Mr. Clark
JEMMY TWITCHER	Mr. H. Bullock
CROOK-FINGERED JACK	Mr. Houghton
WAT DREARY	Mr. Smith
ROBIN OF BAGSHOT	*Macheath's* Mr. Lacy
NIMMING NED	*Gang* Mr. Pit
HARRY PADDINGTON	Mr. Eaton
MAT OF THE MINT	Mr. Spiller
BEN BUDGE	Mr. Morgan
BEGGAR	Mr. Chapman
PLAYER	Mr. Milward

Constables, Drawer, Turnkey, etc.

WOMEN

MRS. PEACHUM	Mrs. Martin
POLLY PEACHUM	Miss Fenton
LUCY LOCKIT	Mrs. Egleton
DIANA TRAPES	Mrs. Martin
MRS. COAXER	Mrs. Holiday
DOLLY TRULL	Mrs. Lacy
MRS. VIXEN	Mrs. Rice
BETTY DOXY	*Women of* Mrs. Rogers
JENNY DIVER	*the Town* Mrs. Clarke
MRS. SLAMMEKIN	Mrs. Morgan
SUKY TAWDRY	Mrs. Palin
MOLLY BRAZEN	Mrs. Sallee

THE BEGGAR'S OPERA

INTRODUCTION

BEGGAR, PLAYER

Beggar. If poverty be a title to poetry, I am sure nobody can dispute mine. I own myself of the company of beggars; and I make one at their weekly festivals at St. Giles's; I have a small yearly salary for my catches, and am welcome to a dinner there whenever I please, which is more than most poets can say.

Player. As we live by the Muses, it is but gratitude in us to encourage poetical merit wherever we find it. The Muses, contrary to all other ladies, pay no distinction to dress, and never partially mistake the pertness of embroidery for wit, nor the modesty of want for dullness. Be the author who he will, we push his play as far as it will go. So, though you are in want, I wish you success heartily.

Beggar. This piece I own was originally writ for the celebrating the marriage of James Chanter and Moll Lay, two most excellent ballad-singers. I have introduced the similes that are in all your celebrated operas; the Swallow, the Moth, the Bee, the Ship, the Flower, etc. Besides, I have a prison scene, which the ladies always reckon charmingly pathetic. As to the parts, I have observed such a nice impartiality to our two ladies, that it is impossible for either of them to take offence. I hope I may be forgiven that I have not made my opera throughout unnatural, like those in vogue; for I have no recitative; excepting this, as I have consented to have neither Prologue nor Epilogue, it must be allowed an opera in all its forms. The piece indeed hath been heretofore frequently represented by ourselves in our great room at St. Giles's, so that I cannot too often acknowledge your charity in bringing it now on the stage.

Player. But I see 'tis time for us to withdraw; the actors are preparing to begin. Play away the overture. *(Exeunt.*

ACT I. SCENE I

Scene, PEACHUM'S *House*

PEACHUM *sitting at a table, with a large book of accounts before him*

AIR I.—" An old woman, clothed in grey."

Through all the employments of life,
  Each neighbour abuses his brother ;
Whore and rogue, they call husband and wife :
  All professions be-rogue one another.
The priest calls the lawyer a cheat :
  The lawyer be-knaves the divine :
And the statesman, because he's so great,
  Thinks his trade as honest as mine.

A lawyer is an honest employment, so is mine. Like me too, he acts in a double capacity, both against rogues, and for 'em; for 'tis but fitting that we should protect and encourage cheats, since we live by them.

SCENE II

PEACHUM, FILCH

Filch. Sir, Black Moll hath sent word her trial comes on in the afternoon, and she hopes you will order matters so as to bring her off.

Peach. Why, she may plead her belly at worst; to my knowledge she hath taken care of that security. But, as the wench is very active and industrious, you may satisfy her that I'll soften the evidence.

Filch. Tom Gagg, sir, is found guilty.

Peach. A lazy dog! When I took him the time before, I told him what he would come to, if he did not mend his hand. This is death, without reprieve. I may venture to book him; (*Writes.*) for Tom Gagg, forty pounds. Let Betty Sly know that I'll save her from transportation, for I can get more by her staying in England.

Filch. Betty hath brought more goods into our lock to-year than any five of the gang; and, in truth, 'tis a pity to lose so good a customer.

Peach. If none of the gang take her off, she may, in the common course of business, live a twelvemonth longer. I love to let women 'scape. A good sportsman always lets the hen-partridges fly, because the breed of the game depends upon them. Besides, here the law allows us no reward: there is nothing to be got by the death of women—except our wives.

Filch. Without dispute, she is a fine woman! 'Twas to her I was obliged for my education, and (to say a bold word) she hath trained up more young fellows to the business than the gaming-table.

Peach. Truly, Filch, thy observation is right. We and the surgeons are more beholden to women than all the professions besides.

AIR II.—"The bonny grey-eyed morn," etc.

Filch. 'Tis woman that seduces all mankind;
By her we first were taught the wheedling arts;
Her very eyes can cheat; when most she's kind,
She tricks us of our money, with our hearts.
For her, like wolves by night, we roam for prey,
And practise every fraud to bribe her charms;
For suits of love, like law, are won by pay,
And beauty must be fee'd into our arms.

Peach. But make haste to Newgate, boy, and let my friends know what I intend; for I love to make them easy, one way or other.

Filch. When a gentleman is long kept in suspense, penitence may break his spirit ever after. Besides, certainty gives a man a good air upon his trial, and makes him risk another without fear or scruple. But I'll away, for 'tis a pleasure to be the messenger of comfort to friends in affliction.

SCENE III

PEACHUM

[*Peach.*] But 'tis now high time to look about me for a decent execution against next sessions. I hate a lazy rogue, by whom one can get nothing till he is hanged. A register of the gang. (*Reading.*) "Crook-fingered Jack"—a year and a half in the service—let me see how much the stock owes to his industry: One, two, three, four, five gold watches, and seven silver ones—a mighty, clean-handed fellow!—sixteen snuff-boxes, five of them of true gold, six dozen of handkerchiefs, four silver-hilted swords, half a dozen of shirts, three tie-periwigs, and a piece of broadcloth. Considering these are only the fruits of his leisure hours, I don't know a prettier fellow; for no man alive hath a more engaging presence of mind upon the road. "Wat Dreary, alias Brown Will"—an irregular dog! who hath an underhand way of disposing of his goods; I'll try him only for a sessions or two longer, upon his good behaviour. "Harry Paddington"—a poor, petty-larceny rascal, without the least genius! that fellow, though he were to live these six months, will never come to the gallows with any credit. "Slippery Sam"—he goes off the next sessions; for the villain hath the impudence to have views of following his trade as a tailor, which he calls an honest employment. "Mat of the Mint"—listed not above a month ago; a promising, sturdy fellow, and diligent in his way; somewhat too bold and hasty, and may raise good contributions on the public, if he does not cut himself short by murder. "Tom Tipple"—a guzzling, soaking sot, who is always too drunk to stand himself, or to make others stand; a cart is absolutely necessary for him. "Robin of Bagshot, alias Gorgon, alias Bluff Bob, alias Carbuncle, alias Bob Booty——"

SCENE IV

PEACHUM, MRS. PEACHUM

Mrs. P. What of Bob Booty, husband? I hope nothing bad hath betided him. You know, my dear, he's a favourite customer of mine—'twas he, made me a present of this ring.

Peach. I have set his name down in the black list, that's all, my dear; he spends his life among women, and, as soon as his money is gone, one or other of the ladies will hang him for the reward, and there's forty pound lost to us for ever!

Mrs. P. You know, my dear, I never meddle in matters of death; I always leave those affairs to you. Women, indeed, are bitter bad judges in these cases; for they are so partial to the brave, that they think every man handsome who is going to the camp, or the gallows.

AIR III.—"Cold and raw," etc.

If any wench Venus's girdle wear,
  Though she be never so ugly :
Lilies and roses will quickly appear
  And her face look wondrous smugly.
Beneath the left ear so fit but a cord
  (A rope so charming a zone is !),
The youth in his cart hath the air of a lord,
  And we cry, There dies an Adonis !

But, really, husband, you should not be too hard-hearted, for you never had a finer, braver set of men than at present. We have not had a murder among them all these seven months; and truly, my dear, that is a great blessing.

Peach. What a dickens is the woman always whimpering about murder for? No gentleman is ever looked upon the worse for killing a man in his own defence; and if business cannot be carried on without it, what would you have a gentleman do?

Mrs. P. If I am in the wrong, my dear, you must excuse me, for nobody can help the frailty of an over-scrupulous conscience.

Peach. Murder is as fashionable a crime as a man can be guilty of. How many fine gentlemen have we in Newgate every year, purely upon that article? If they have wherewithal to persuade the jury to bring in manslaughter, what are they the worse for it? So, my dear, have done upon this subject. Was Captain Macheath here this morning, for the banknotes he left with you last week?

Mrs. P. Yes, my dear; and though the bank hath stopped payment, he was so cheerful, and so agreeable! Sure, there is not a finer gentleman upon the road than the captain! If he comes from Bagshot at any reasonable hour, he hath promised to make one this evening with Polly and me, and Bob Booty, at a party of quadrille. Pray, my dear, is the captain rich?

Peach. The captain keeps too good company ever to grow rich. Marybone, and the chocolate-houses, are his undoing. The man that proposes to get money by play should have the education of a fine gentleman, and be trained up to it from his youth.

Mrs. P. Really, I am sorry, upon Polly's account, the captain hath not more discretion. What business hath he to keep company with lords and gentlemen? He should leave them to prey upon one another.

Peach. Upon Polly's account! What a plague does the woman mean?—Upon Polly's account!

Mrs. P. Captain Macheath is very fond of the girl.

Peach. And what then?

Mrs. P. If I have any skill in the ways of women, I am sure Polly thinks him a very pretty man.

Peach. And what then? You would not be so mad to have the wench marry him! Gamesters and highwaymen are, generally, very good to their whores, but they are very devils to their wives.

Mrs. P. But if Polly should be in love, how should we help her, or how can she help herself? Poor girl, I'm in the utmost concern about her!

AIR IV.—"Why is your faithful slave disdained?" etc.

> *If love the virgin's heart invade,*
> *How, like a moth, the simple maid*
> *Still plays about the flame!*
> *If soon she be not made a wife,*
> *Her honour's singed, and then for life*
> *She's—what I dare not name.*

Peach. Lookye, wife, a handsome wench in our way of business is as profitable as at the bar of a Temple coffee-house, who looks upon it as her livelihood to grant every liberty but one.

You see I would indulge the girl as far as prudently we can. In anything but marriage! After that, my dear, how shall we be safe? Are we not then in her husband's power? For a husband hath the absolute power over all a wife's secrets but her own. If the girl had the discretion of a court lady, who can have a dozen young fellows at her ear without complying with one, I should not matter it; but Polly is tinder, and a spark will at once set her on a flame. Married! If the wench does not know her own profit, sure she knows her own pleasure better than to make herself a property! My daughter, to me, should be like a court lady to a minister of state, a key to the whole gang. Married! if the affair is not already done, I'll terrify her from it by the example of our neighbours.

Mrs. P. Mayhap, my dear, you may injure the girl: she loves to imitate the fine ladies, and she may only allow the captain liberties in the view of interest.

Peach. But 'tis your duty, my dear, to warn the girl against her ruin, and to instruct her how to make the most of her beauty. I'll go to her this moment, and sift her. In the meantime, wife, rip out the coronets and marks of these dozen of cambric handkerchiefs, for I can dispose of them this afternoon to a chap in the city.

SCENE V

MRS. PEACHUM

[*Mrs. P.*] Never was a man more out of the way in an argument than my husband. Why must our Polly, forsooth, differ from her sex, and love only her husband? and why must our Polly's marriage, contrary to all observation, make her the less followed by other men? All men are thieves in love, and like a woman the better for being another's property.

AIR V.—"Of all the simple things we do," etc.

A maid is like the golden ore,
   Which hath guineas intrinsical in't,
Whose worth is never known, before
   It is tried and impressed in the mint.
A wife's like a guinea in gold,
   Stamped with the name of her spouse ;
Now here, now there ; is bought or is sold ;
   And is current in every house.

SCENE VI

MRS. PEACHUM, FILCH

Mrs. P. Come hither, Filch.—I am as fond of this child as though my mind misgave me he were my own. He hath as fine a hand at picking a pocket as a woman, and is as nimble-fingered as a juggler. If an unlucky session does not cut the rope of thy life, I pronounce, boy, thou wilt be a great man in history. Where was your post last night, my boy?

Filch. I plied at the opera, madam; and, considering 'twas neither dark nor rainy, so that there was no great hurry in getting chairs and coaches, made a tolerable hand on't—these seven handkerchiefs, madam.

Mrs. P. Coloured ones, I see. They are of sure sale from our warehouse at Redriff, among the seamen.

Filch. And this snuff-box.

Mrs. P. Set in gold! A pretty encouragement, this, to a young beginner!

Filch. I had a fair tug at a charming gold watch. Pox take the tailors for making the fobs so deep and narrow!—it stuck by the way, and I was forced to make my escape under a coach. Really, madam, I fear I shall be cut off in the flower of my youth, so that, every now and then, since I was pumped, I have thoughts of taking up and going to sea.

Mrs. P. You should go to Hockley-in-the-Hole, and to Marybone, child, to learn valour; these are the schools that have bred so many brave men. I thought, boy, by this time, thou hadst lost fear as well as shame. Poor lad! how little does he know yet of the Old Bailey! For the first fact, I'll ensure thee from being hanged; and going to sea, Filch, will come time enough, upon a sentence of transportation. But now, since you have nothing better to do, even go to your book, and learn your catechism: for, really, a man makes but an ill figure in the ordinary's paper who cannot give a satisfactory answer to his questions. But, hark you, my lad, don't tell me a lie; for you know I hate a liar:—Do you know of anything that hath passed between Captain Macheath and our Polly?

Filch. I beg you, madam, don't ask me; for I must either tell a lie to you or to Miss Polly; for I promised her I would not tell.

Mrs. P. But when the honour of our family is concerned——

Filch. I shall lead a sad life with Miss Polly, if ever she come to know I told you. Besides, I would not willingly forfeit my own honour, by betraying anybody.

Mrs. P. Yonder comes my husband and Polly. Come, Filch, you shall go with me into my own room, and tell me the whole story. I'll give thee a glass of a most delicious cordial that I keep for my own drinking.

SCENE VII

PEACHUM, POLLY

Polly. I know as well as any of the fine ladies how to make the most of myself and of my man too. A woman knows how to be mercenary, though she hath never been in a court or at an assembly. We have it in our natures, papa. If I allow Captain Macheath some trifling liberties, I have this watch and other visible marks of his favour to show for it. A girl who cannot grant some things, and refuse what is most material, will make a poor hand of her beauty, and soon be thrown upon the common.

AIR VI.—"What shall I do to show how much I love her?" etc.

> Virgins are like the fair flower in its lustre,
>   Which in the garden enamels the ground,
> Near it the bees in play flutter and cluster,
>   And gaudy butterflies frolic around :
>
> But when once plucked 'tis no longer alluring,
>   To Covent Garden 'tis sent (as yet sweet),
> There fades, and shrinks, and grows past all enduring,
>   Rots, stinks, and dies, and is trod under feet.

Peach. You know, Polly, I am not against your toying and trifling with a customer, in the way of business, or to get out a secret or so; but if I find out that you have played the fool, and are married, you jade you, I'll cut your throat, hussy. Now, you know my mind.

SCENE VIII

PEACHUM, POLLY, MRS. PEACHUM

AIR VII.—"O London is a fine town."

Mrs. P (in a very great passion).

> Our Polly is a sad slut ! nor heeds what we have taught her,
> I wonder any man alive will ever rear a daughter !
> For she must have both hoods and gowns, and hoops to swell her
>   pride,
> With scarves and stays, and gloves and lace, and she will have
>   men beside :
> And when she's dressed with care and cost, all tempting, fine and gay,
> As men should serve a cowcumber, she flings herself away.

You baggage! you hussy! you inconsiderate jade! had you been hanged it would not have vexed me; for that might have been your misfortune; but to do such a mad thing by choice!—The wench is married, husband.

Peach. Married! the captain is a bold man, and will risk anything for money: to be sure he believes her a fortune. Do you think your mother and I should have lived comfortably so long together if ever we had been married? Baggage!

Mrs. P. I knew she was always a proud slut, and now the wench hath played the fool and married, because, forsooth, she would do like the gentry! Can you support the expense of a husband, hussy, in gaming, drinking and whoring? Have you money enough to carry on the daily quarrels of man and wife about who shall squander most? There are not many husbands and wives who can bear the charges of plaguing one another in a handsome way. If you must be married, could you introduce nobody into our family but a highwayman! Why, thou foolish jade, thou wilt be as ill-used and as much neglected as if thou hadst married a lord!

Peach. Let not your anger, my dear, break through the rules of decency; for the captain looks upon himself in the military capacity as a gentleman by his profession. Besides what he hath already, I know he is in a fair way of getting or of dying; and both these ways, let me tell you, are most excellent chances for a wife. Tell me, hussy, are you ruined or no?

Mrs. P. With Polly's fortune she might very well have gone off to a person of distinction: yes, that you might, you pouting slut.

Peach. What! is the wench dumb? Speak, or I'll make you plead by squeezing out an answer from you. Are you really bound wife to him, or are you only upon liking?   (*Pinches her.*

Polly. Oh!   (*Screaming.*

Mrs. P. How the mother is to be pitied who hath handsome daughters! Locks, bolts, bars, and lectures of morality, are nothing to them; they break through them all; they have as much pleasure in cheating a father and mother as in cheating at cards.

Peach. Why, Polly, I shall soon know if you are married, by Macheath's keeping from our house.

AIR VIII.—"Grim king of the ghosts," etc.

Polly.   *Can love be controlled by advice?*
            Will Cupid our mothers obey?
            Though my heart were as frozen as ice,
            At his flame 'twould have melted away.
            When he kissed me, so closely he pressed,
            'Twas so sweet that I must have complied,
            So I thought it both safest and best
            To marry, for fear you should chide.

Mrs. P. Then all the hopes of our family are gone for ever and ever!

Peach. And Macheath may hang his father- and mother-in-law, in hope to get into their daughter's fortune.

Polly. I did not marry him (as 'tis the fashion) coolly and deliberately, for honour or money—but I love him.

Mrs. P. Love him! worse and worse! I thought the girl had been better bred. Oh, husband! husband! her folly makes me mad! my head swims! I'm distracted! I can't support myself——Oh!   (*Faints.*

Peach. See, wench, to what a condition you have reduced your poor mother! A glass of cordial this instant! How the poor woman takes it to heart! (POLLY *goes out, and returns with it.*) Ah, hussy, now this is the only comfort your mother has left.

Polly. Give her another glass, sir; my mamma drinks double the quantity whenever she is out of order. This you see fetches her.

Mrs. P. The girl shows such a readiness, and so much concern, that I could almost find in my heart to forgive her.

AIR IX.—"O Jenny, O Jenny, where hast thou been?"

[*Mrs. P.*]   *O Polly, you might have toyed and kissed ;*
     By keeping men off you keep them on.
Polly.   *But he so teased me,*
      And he so pleased me,
    What I did you must have done.

Mrs. P. Not with a highwayman—you sorry slut.

Peach. A word with you, wife. 'Tis no new thing for a wench to take man without consent of parents. You know 'tis the frailty of woman, my dear!

Mrs. P. Yes, indeed, the sex is frail; but the first time a woman is frail, she should be somewhat nice methinks, for then or never is the time to make her fortune: after that she hath nothing to do but to guard herself from being found out, and she may do what she pleases.

Peach. Make yourself a little easy; I have a thought shall soon set all matters again to rights. Why so melancholy, Polly? Since what is done cannot be undone, we must all endeavour to make the best of it.

Mrs. P. Well, Polly, as far as one woman can forgive another, I forgive thee. Your father is too fond of you, hussy.

Polly. Then all my sorrows are at an end.

Mrs. P. A mighty likely speech in troth for a wench who is just married!

AIR X.—"Thomas, I cannot," etc.

Polly.   *I like a ship in storms was tossed,*
    Yet afraid to put into land,
   For seized in the port the vessel's lost
    Whose treasure is contraband.
     The waves are laid,
     My duty's paid ;
    O joy beyond expression !
     Thus safe ashore
     I ask no more ;
    My all is in my possession.

Peach. I hear customers in t'other room; go talk with 'em, Polly; but come to us again as soon as they are gone.—But hark ye, child, if 'tis the gentleman who was here yesterday about the repeating watch, say you believe we can't get intelligence of it till to-morrow, for I lent it to Sukey Straddle, to make a figure with to-night at a tavern in Drury Lane. If t'other gentleman calls for the silver-hilted sword, you know beetle-browed Jemmy hath it on, and he doth not come from Tunbridge till Tuesday night, so that it cannot be had till then.

SCENE IX

PEACHUM, MRS. PEACHUM

Peach. Dear wife! be a little pacified; don't let your passion run away with your senses: Polly, I grant you, has done a rash thing.

Mrs. P. If she had had only an intrigue with the fellow, why the very best families have excused and huddled up a frailty of that sort. 'Tis marriage, husband, that makes it a blemish.

Peach. But money, wife, is the true fuller's earth for reputations; there is not a spot or stain but what it can take out. A rich rogue nowadays is fit company for any gentleman; and the world, my dear, hath not such a contempt for roguery as you imagine. I tell you, wife, I can make this match turn to our advantage.

Mrs. P. I am very sensible, husband, that Captain Macheath is worth money, but I am in doubt whether he hath not two or three wives already, and then if he should die in a session or two, Polly's dower would come into dispute.

Peach. That indeed is a point which ought to be considered.

AIR XI.—"A soldier and a sailor."

> *A fox may steal your hens, sir,*
> *A whore your health and pence, sir,*
> *Your daughter rob your chest, sir,*
> *Your wife may steal your rest, sir,*
> *A thief your goods and plate.*
> *But this is all for picking,*
> *With rest, pence, chest and chicken;*
> *It ever was decreed, sir,*
> *If lawyer's hand is fee'd, sir,*
> *He steals your whole estate.*

The lawyers are bitter enemies to those in our way; they don't care that anybody should get a clandestine livelihood but themselves.

SCENE X

MRS. PEACHUM, PEACHUM, POLLY

Polly. 'Twas only Nimming Ned: he brought in a damask window-curtain, a hoop-petticoat, a pair of silver candlesticks, a periwig, and one silk stocking, from the fire that happened last night.

Peach. There is not a fellow that is cleverer in his way, and saves more goods out of the fire, than Ned. But now, Polly, to your affair; for matters must not be left as they are. You are married then, it seems?

Polly. Yes, sir.

Peach. And how do you propose to live, child?

Polly. Like other women, sir; upon the industry of my husband.

Mrs. P. What! is the wench turned fool? A highwayman's wife, like a soldier's, hath as little of his pay as of his company.

Peach. And had not you the common views of a gentle-woman in your marriage, Polly?

Polly. I don't know what you mean, sir.

Peach. Of a jointure, and of being a widow.

Polly. But I love him, sir: how then could I have thoughts of parting with him?

Peach. Parting with him! why that is the whole scheme and intention of all marriage articles. The comfortable estate of widowhood is the only hope that keeps up a wife's spirits. Where is the woman who would scruple to be a wife, if she had it in her power to be a widow whenever she pleased? If you have any views of this sort, Polly, I shall think the match not so very unreasonable.

Polly. How I dread to hear your advice! Yet I must beg you to explain yourself.

Peach. Secure what he hath got, have him peached the next sessions, and then at once you are made a rich widow.

Polly. What! murder the man I love! The blood runs cold at my heart with the very thought of it.

Peach. Fie, Polly! what hath murder to do in the affair? Since the thing sooner or later must happen, I dare say that the captain himself would like that we should get the reward for his death sooner than a stranger. Why, Polly, the captain knows that as 'tis his employment to rob, so 'tis ours to take robbers; every man in his business: so that there is no malice in the case.

Mrs. P. Ay, husband, now you have nicked the matter. To have him peached is the only thing could ever make me forgive her.

AIR XII.—"Now ponder well, ye parents dear."

Polly.   *Oh ponder well! be not severe;*
                So save a wretched wife,
            For on the rope that hangs my dear
                Depends poor Polly's life.

Mrs. P. But your duty to your parents, hussy, obliges you to hang him. What would many a wife give for such an opportunity!

Polly. What is a jointure, what is widowhood, to me? I know my heart; I cannot survive him.

AIR XIII.—"Le printemps rappelle aux armes."

        The turtle thus with plaintive crying,
            Her lover dying,
        The turtle thus with plaintive crying
            Laments her dove.
        Down she drops quite spent with sighing,
            Paired in death, as paired in love.

Thus, sir, it will happen to your poor Polly.

Mrs. P. What! is the fool in love in earnest then? I hate thee for being particular. Why, wench, thou art a shame to thy very sex!

Polly. But hear me, mother—if you ever loved——

Mrs. P. Those cursed play-books she reads have been her ruin! One word more, hussy, and I shall knock your brains out, if you have any.

Peach. Keep out of the way, Polly, for fear of mischief, and consider of what is proposed to you.

Mrs. P. Away, hussy! Hang your husband, and be dutiful.

SCENE XI

MRS. PEACHUM, PEACHUM

(POLLY *listening.*

Mrs. P. The thing, husband, must and shall be done. For the sake of intelligence we must take other measures and have him peached the next session without her consent. If she will not know her duty, we know ours.

Peach. But really, my dear! it grieves one's heart to take off a great man. When I consider his personal bravery, his fine stratagems, how much we have already got by him, and how much more we may get, methinks I can't find in my heart to have a hand in his death: I wish you could have made Polly undertake it.

Mrs. P. But in a case of necessity—our own lives are in danger.

Peach. Then indeed we must comply with the customs of the world, and make gratitude give way to interest.—He shall be taken off.

Mrs. P. I'll undertake to manage Polly.

Peach. And I'll prepare matters for the Old Bailey.

SCENE XII

POLLY

Polly. Now I'm a wretch indeed!—Methinks I see him already in the cart, sweeter and more lovely than the nosegay in his hand!—I hear the crowd extolling his resolution and intrepidity! —What volleys of sighs are sent from the windows of Holborn, that so comely a youth should be brought to disgrace! I see him at the tree! the whole circle are in tears! Even butchers weep! —Jack Ketch himself hesitates to perform his duty and would be glad to lose his fee by a reprieve.—What then will become of Polly?—As yet I may inform him of their design, and aid him in his escape.—It shall be so.—But then he flies, absents himself, and I bar myself from his dear, dear conversation! That too will distract me.—If he keeps out of the way my papa and mamma may in time relent, and we may be happy.—If he stays, he is hanged, and then he is lost for ever!—He intended to lie concealed in my room till the dusk of the evening. If they are abroad I'll this instant let him out, lest some accident should prevent him.   (*Exit, and returns.*

SCENE XIII

POLLY, MACHEATH

AIR XIV.—"Pretty parrot, say," etc.

Mac.	*Pretty Polly, say,*
	When I was away,
	Did your fancy never stray
	To some newer lover ?
Polly.	*Without disguise,*
	Heaving sighs,
	Doting eyes,
	My constant heart discover,
	Fondly let me loll !
Mac.	*O pretty, pretty Poll !*

Polly. And are you as fond as ever, my dear?

Mac. Suspect my honour, my courage, suspect anything but my love. May my pistols miss fire, and my mare slip her shoulder while I am pursued, if I ever forsake thee!

Polly. Nay, my dear! I have no reason to doubt you, for I find in the romance you lent me, none of the great heroes were ever false in love.

AIR XV.—"Pray, fair one, be kind."

Mac.
> *My heart was so free,*
> *It roved like the bee,*
> *Till Polly my passion requited :*
> *I sipped each flower,*
> *I changed every hour,*
> *But here every flower is united.*

Polly. Were you sentenced to transportation, sure, my dear, you could not leave me behind you—could you?

Mac. Is there any power, any force, that could tear me from thee? You might sooner tear a pension out of the hands of a courtier, a fee from a lawyer, a pretty woman from a looking-glass, or any woman from quadrille. But to tear me from thee is impossible!

AIR XVI.—"Over the hills, and far away."

> *Were I laid on Greenland's coast,*
> > *And in my arms embraced my lass,*
> *Warm amidst eternal frost,*
> > *Too soon the half-year's night would pass.*

Polly.
> *Were I sold on Indian soil,*
> > *Soon as the burning day was closed,*
> *I could mock the sultry toil*
> > *When on my charmer's breast reposed.*

Mac.   *And I would love you all the day,*
Polly.   *Every night would kiss and play,*
Mac.   *If with me you'd fondly stray*
Polly.   *Over the hills, and far away.*

Polly. Yes, I would go with thee. But oh!—how shall I speak it? I must be torn from thee! We must part!

Mac. How! part!

Polly. We must, we must! My papa and mamma are set against thy life: they now, even now, are in search after thee: they are preparing evidence against thee; thy life depends upon a moment!

AIR XVII.—"Gin thou wert mine awn thing."

> *O, what pain it is to part !*
> > *Can I leave thee, can I leave thee ?*
> *O, what pain it is to part !*
> > *Can thy Polly ever leave thee ?*

But lest death my love should thwart,
And bring thee to the fatal cart,
Thus I tear thee from my bleeding heart.
Fly hence, and let me leave thee.

One kiss, and then!—one kiss!—Begone!—Farewell!

Mac. My hand, my heart, my dear, is so riveted to thine, that I cannot unloose my hold!

Polly. But my papa may intercept thee, and then I should lose the very glimmering of hope. A few weeks, perhaps, may reconcile us all. Shall thy Polly hear from thee?

Mac. Must I then go?

Polly. And will not absence change your love?

Mac. If you doubt it, let me stay—and be hanged.

Polly. Oh, how I fear! how I tremble! Go—but, when safety will give you leave, you will be sure to see me again; for, till then, Polly is wretched.

AIR XVIII.—"O the broom," etc.

Mac.   *The miser thus a shilling sees,*
Which he's obliged to pay,
With sighs resigns it by degrees,
And fears 'tis gone for ay.

(*Parting and looking back at each other with fondness : he at one door, she at another.*

Polly.   *The boy thus, when his sparrow's flown,*
The bird in silence eyes :
But soon as out of sight 'tis gone,
Whines, whimpers, sobs, and cries.

ACT II. SCENE I

A Tavern near Newgate

JEMMY TWITCHER, CROOK-FINGERED JACK, WAT DREARY, ROBIN OF BAGSHOT, NIMMING NED, HENRY PADDINGTON, MAT OF THE MINT, BEN BUDGE, *and the rest of the Gang, at the table, with wine, brandy, and tobacco*

Ben. But prithee, Mat, what is become of thy brother Tom? I have not seen him since my return from transportation.

Mat. Poor brother Tom had an accident, this time twelve-month, and so clever made a fellow he was, I could not save him from these fleaing rascals, the surgeons; and now, poor man, he is among the otamies at Surgeons' Hall.

Ben. So, it seems, his time was come.

Jemmy. But the present time is ours, and nobody alive hath more. Why are the laws levelled at us? Are we more dishonest than the rest of mankind? What we win, gentlemen, is our own, by the law of arms and the right of conquest.

Crook. Where shall we find such another set of practical philosophers, who, to a man, are above the fear of death?

Wat. Sound men, and true!

Robin. Of tried courage, and indefatigable industry!

Ned. Who is there here that would not die for his friend?

Harry. Who is there here that would betray him for his interest?

Mat. Show me a gang of courtiers that can say as much.

Ben. We are for a just partition of the world; for every man hath a right to enjoy life.

Mat. We retrench the superfluities of mankind. The world is avaricious, and I hate avarice. A covetous fellow, like a jackdaw, steals what he was never made to enjoy, for the sake of hiding it. These are the robbers of mankind; for money was made for the free-hearted and generous: and where is the injury of taking from another what he hath not the heart to make use of?

Jemmy. Our several stations for the day are fixed. Good luck attend us all! Fill the glasses!

AIR I.—"Fill ev'ry glass," etc.

Mat.   Fill ev'ry glass, for wine inspires us,
                    And fires us
              With courage, love, and joy.
              Women and wine should life employ;
                Is there aught else on earth desirous?

Chorus.   Fill ev'ry glass, etc.

SCENE II

To them enter MACHEATH

Mac. Gentlemen, well met; my heart hath been with you this hour, but an unexpected affair hath detained me. No ceremony, I beg you!

Mat. We were just breaking up, to go upon duty. Am I to have the honour of taking the air with you, sir, this evening, upon the heath? I drink a dram, now and then, with the stage-coachmen, in the way of friendship and intelligence; and I know that, about this time, there will be passengers, upon the western road, who are worth speaking with.

Mac. I was to have been of that party—but——

Mat. But what, sir?

Mac. Is there any man who suspects my courage?

Mat. We have all been witnesses of it.

Mac. My honour and truth to the gang?

Mat. I'll be answerable for it.

Mac. In the division of our booty, have I ever shown the least marks of avarice or injustice?

Mat. By these questions, something seems to have ruffled you. Are any of us suspected?

Mac. I have a fixed confidence, gentlemen, in you all, as men of honour, and as such I value and respect you. Peachum is a man that is useful to us.

Mat. Is he about to play us any foul play? I'll shoot him through the head.

Mac. I beg you, gentlemen, act with conduct and discretion. A pistol is your last resort.

Mat. He knows nothing of this meeting.

Mac. Business cannot go on without him: he is a man who knows the world, and is a necessary agent to us. We have had a slight difference, and, till it is accommodated, I shall be obliged to keep out of his way. Any private dispute of mine shall be of no ill consequence to my friends. You must continue to act under his direction; for, the moment we break loose from him, our gang is ruined.

Mat. As a bawd to a whore I grant you he is, to us, of great convenience.

Mac. Make him believe I have quitted the gang, which I can never do but with life. At our private quarters I will continue to meet you. A week, or so, will probably reconcile us.

Mat. Your instructions shall be observed. 'Tis now high time for us to repair to our several duties; so, till the evening, at our quarters in Moorfields, we bid you farewell.

Mac. I shall wish myself with you. Success attend you.

(*Sits down, melancholy, at the table.*

AIR II.—March in Rinaldo, with drums and trumpets.

Mat.   Let us take the road :
        Hark ! I hear the sound of coaches,
        The hour of attack approaches,
        To your arms, brave boys, and load.
        See the ball I hold !
        Let the chemists toil like asses,
        Our fire their fire surpasses,
        And turns all our lead to gold.

(*The Gang, ranged in front of the stage, load their pistols, and stick them under their girdles, then go off, singing the first part in chorus.*

SCENE III

MACHEATH, DRAWER

Mac. What a fool is a fond wench! Polly is most confoundedly bit. I love the sex; and a man who loves money might as well be contented with one guinea, as I with one woman. The town, perhaps, hath been as much obliged to me for recruiting it with free-hearted ladies, as to any recruiting-officer in the army. If it were not for us, and the other gentlemen of the sword, Drury Lane would be uninhabited.

AIR III.—"Would you have a young virgin," etc.

> *If the heart of a man is depressed with cares,*
> *The mist is dispelled when a woman appears,*
> *Like the notes of a fiddle, she sweetly, sweetly,*
> *Raises the spirits, and charms our ears.*
> *Roses and lilies her cheeks disclose,*
> *But her ripe lips are more sweet than those;*
> > *Press her,*
> > *Caress her,*
> > *With blisses,*
> > *Her kisses*
> *Dissolve us in pleasure and soft repose.*

I must have women—there is nothing unbends the mind like them: money is not so strong a cordial for the time. Drawer!

Enter DRAWER

Is the porter gone for all the ladies, according to my directions?

Drawer. I expect him back every minute; but you know, sir, you sent him as far as Hockley-in-the-Hole for three of the ladies; for one in Vinegar Yard, and for the rest of them some-where about Lewkner's Lane. Sure some of them are below, for I hear the bar bell. As they come, I will show them up. Coming! coming!

SCENE IV

MACHEATH, MRS. COAXER, DOLLY TRULL, MRS. VIXEN, BETTY DOXY, JENNY DIVER, MRS. SLAMMEKIN, SUKEY TAWDRY, *and* MOLLY BRAZEN

Mac. Dear Mrs. Coaxer, you are welcome! you look charm-ingly to-day: I hope you don't want the repairs of quality, and lay on paint.—Dolly Trull! kiss me, you slut! are you as amorous as ever, hussy? You are always so taken up with stealing hearts, that you don't allow yourself time to steal anything else. Ah, Dolly! thou wilt ever be a coquette.—Mrs. Vixen, I'm yours!

I always loved a woman of wit and spirit; they make charming mistresses, but plaguy wives.—Betty Doxy! come hither, hussy: do you drink as hard as ever? You had better stick to good whole-some beer, for, in troth, Betty, strong waters will, in time, ruin your constitution: you should leave those to your betters.—What, and my pretty Jenny Diver too! as prim and demure as ever! There is not any prude, though ever so high bred, hath a more sanctified look, with a more mischievous heart: ah, thou art a dear, artful hypocrite!—Mrs. Slammekin! as careless and genteel as ever! All you fine ladies, who know your own beauty, affect an undress.—But see! here's Sukey Tawdry come to contradict what I was saying. Everything she gets one way, she lays out upon her back. Why, Sukey, you must keep at least a dozen tally-men.—Molly Brazen! (*She kisses him.*) That's well done: I love a free-hearted wench: thou hast a most agreeable assur-ance, girl, and art as willing as a turtle.—But hark! I hear music! The harper is at the door. "If music be the food of love, play on!" Ere you seat yourselves, ladies, what think you of a dance? Come in.

Enter HARPER

Play the French tune that Mrs. Slammekin was so fond of.

> (*A dance à la ronde in the French manner: near the end of it this Song and Chorus.*

AIR IV.—Cotillion.

> Youth's the season made for joys,
>   Love is then our duty:
> She alone who that employs,
>   Well deserves her beauty.
>   Let's be gay
>   While we may,
> Beauty's a flower despised in decay.

Chorus.   *Youth's the season, etc.*

> Let us drink and sport to-day,
>   Ours is not to-morrow:
> Love with youth flies swift away,
>   Age is naught but sorrow.
>   Dance and sing,
>   Time's on the wing,
> Life never knows the return of spring.

Chorus.   *Let us drink, etc.*

Mac. Now, pray, ladies, take your places. Here, fellow. (*Pays the Harper.*) Bid the drawer bring us more wine. (*Exit Harper.*)

If any of the ladies choose gin, I hope they will be so free as to call for it.

Jenny. You look as if you meant me. Wine is strong enough for me. Indeed, sir, I never drink strong waters but when I have the colic.

Mac. Just the excuse of the fine ladies! why, a lady of quality is never without colic. I hope, Mrs. Coaxer, you have had good success of late in your visits among the mercers?

Mrs. C. We have so many interlopers. Yet with industry, one may still have a little picking. I carried a silver-flowered lutestring and a piece of black padesoy to Mr. Peachum's Lock but last week.

Mrs. V. There's Molly Brazen hath the ogle of a rattlesnake. She riveted a linen-draper's eye so fast upon her, that he was nicked of three pieces of cambric before he could look off.

Braz. O dear madam! But sure nothing can come up to your handling of laces! And then you have such a sweet deluding tongue! To cheat a man is nothing; but the woman must have the fine parts indeed who cheats a woman!

Mrs. V. Lace, madam, lies in a small compass, and is of easy conveyance. But you are apt, madam, to think too well of your friends.

Mrs. C. If any woman hath more art than another, to be sure 'tis Jenny Diver. Though her fellow be never so agreeable, she can pick his pocket as coolly as if money were her only pleasure. Now that is a command of the passions uncommon in a woman!

Jenny. I never go to a tavern with a man but in the view of business. I have other hours, and other sort of men, for my pleasure. But had I your address, madam——

Mac. Have done with your compliments, ladies, and drink about. You are not so fond of me, Jenny, as you used to be.

Jenny. 'Tis not convenient, sir, to show my fondness among so many rivals. 'Tis your own choice, and not the warmth of my inclination, that will determine you.

AIR V.—" All in a misty morning," etc.

> Before the barn-door crowing,
> The Cock by hens attended,
> His eyes around him throwing,
> Stands for a while suspended ;
> Then one he singles from the crew,
> And cheers the happy hen :
> With how do you do, and how do you do,
> And how do you do again.

Mac. Ah, Jenny! thou art a dear slut.

Trull. Pray, madam, were you ever in keeping?

Tawd. I hope, madam, I han't been so long upon the town but I have met with some good fortune as well as my neighbours.

Trull. Pardon me, madam, I meant no harm by the question: 'twas only in the way of conversation.

Tawd. Indeed, madam, if I had not been a fool, I might have lived very handsomely with my last friend. But upon his missing five guineas, he turned me off. Now I never suspected he had counted them.

Mrs. S. Who do you look upon, madam, as your best sort of keepers?

Trull. That, madam, is thereafter as they be.

Mrs. S. Madam was once kept by a Jew; and bating their religion, to women they are a good sort of people.

Tawd. Now for my own part, I own I like an old fellow: for we always make them pay for what they can't do.

Mrs. V. A spruce 'prentice, let me tell you, ladies, is no ill thing; they bleed freely. I have sent at least two or three dozen of them, in my time, to the Plantations.

Jenny. But to be sure, sir, with so much good fortune as you have had upon the road, you must be grown immensely rich.

Mac. The road, indeed, hath done me justice, but the gaming-table hath been my ruin.

AIR VI.—"When once I lay with another man's wife."

Jenny.　　　The gamesters and lawyers are jugglers alike :
　　　　　　　　If they meddle, your all is in danger ;
　　　　　　　　Like gipsies, if once they can finger a souse,
　　　　　　　　Your pockets they pick, and they pilfer your house,
　　　　　　　　And give your estate to a stranger.

These are the tools of a man of honour. Cards and dice are only fit for cowardly cheats, who prey upon their friends.

　　　　　　　　(*She takes up his pistol.* TAWDRY *takes up the other.*

Tawd. This, sir, is fitter for your hand. Besides your loss of money, 'tis a loss to the ladies. Gaming takes you off from women. How fond could I be of you! but before company, 'tis ill-bred.

Mac. Wanton hussies!

Jenny. I must and will have a kiss to give my wine a zest.

　　　　　　　　(*They take him about the neck, and make signs to* PEACHUM *and Constables : who rush in upon him.*

SCENE V

To them PEACHUM and Constables

Peach. I seize you, sir, as my prisoner.

Mac. Was this well done, Jenny? Women are decoy ducks; who can trust them! Beasts, jades, jilts, harpies, furies, whores!

Peach. Your case, Mr. Macheath, is not particular. The greatest heroes have been ruined by women. But, to do them justice, I must own they are a pretty sort of creatures, if we could trust them. You must now, sir, take your leave of the ladies: and, if they have a mind to make you a visit, they will be sure to find you at home. The gentleman, ladies, lodges in Newgate. Constables, wait upon the captain to his lodgings.

AIR VII.—"When first I laid siege to my Chloris," etc.

Mac.　　　*At the tree I shall suffer with pleasure,*
　　　　　At the tree I shall suffer with pleasure,
　　　　　　Let me go where I will,
　　　　　　In all kinds of ill,
　　　　I shall find no such furies as these are.

Peach. Ladies, I'll take care the reckoning shall be discharged.
　　　　　(*Exit* MACHEATH, *guarded, with* PEACHUM *and
　　　　　Constables.*

SCENE VI
The Women remain

Mrs. V. Look, Mrs. Jenny, though Mr. Peachum may have made a private bargain with you and Sukey Tawdry for betraying the captain, as we were all assisting, we ought all to share alike.

Mrs. C. I think Mr. Peachum, after so long an acquaintance, might have trusted me as well as Jenny Diver.

Mrs. S. I am sure at least three men of his hanging, and in a year's time, too (if he did me justice), should be set down to my account.

Trull. Mrs. Slammekin, that is not fair. For you know one of them was taken in bed with me.

Jenny. As far as a bowl of punch or a treat, I believe Mrs. Sukey will join with me. As for anything else, ladies, you cannot in conscience expect it.

Mrs. S. Dear madam——
Trull. I would not for the world——
Mrs. S. 'Tis impossible for me——
Trull. As I hope to be saved, madam——
Mrs. S. Nay, then I must stay here all night——
Trull. Since you command me.　　(*Exeunt with great ceremony.*

SCENE VII
Newgate

LOCKIT, *Turnkeys*, MACHEATH, *Constables.*

Lockit. Noble captain, you are welcome! you have not been a lodger of mine this year and half. You know the custom, sir; garnish, captain, garnish. Hand me down those fetters there.

Mac. Those, Mr. Lockit, seem to be the heaviest of the whole set. With your leave, I should like the farther pair better.

Lockit. Lookye, captain, we know what is fittest for our prisoners. When a gentleman uses me with civility, I always do the best I can to please him.—Hand them down, I say.— We have them of all prices, from one guinea to ten; and 'tis fitting every gentleman should please himself.

Mac. I understand you, sir. (*Gives money.*) The fees here are so many, and so exorbitant, that few fortunes can bear the expense of getting off handsomely, or of dying like a gentleman.

Lockit. Those, I see, will fit the captain better. Take down the farther pair. Do but examine them, sir—never was better work—how genteelly they are made! They will fit as easy as a glove, and the nicest man in England might not be ashamed to wear them. (*He puts on the chains.*) If I had the best gentleman in the land in my custody, I could not equip him more handsomely. And so, sir, I now leave you to your private meditations.

SCENE VIII

MACHEATH

AIR. VIII.—"Courtiers, courtiers, think it no harm," etc.

[*Mac.*]   *Man may escape from rope and gun,*
      Nay, some have outlived the doctor's pill :
    Who takes a woman, must be undone,
      That basilisk is sure to kill.
    The fly that sips treacle is lost in the sweets,
      So he that tastes woman, woman, woman,
    He that tastes woman, ruin meets.

To what a woeful plight have I brought myself! Here must I (all day long, till I am hanged) be confined to hear the reproaches of a wench who lays her ruin at my door. I am in the custody of her father; and, to be sure, if he knows of the matter, I shall have a fine time on't betwixt this and my execution.— But I promised the wench marriage. What signifies a promise to a woman? does not man, in marriage itself, promise a hundred things that he never means to perform? Do all we can, women will believe us: for they look upon a promise as an excuse for following their own inclinations. But here comes Lucy, and I cannot get from her—would I were deaf!

SCENE IX

MACHEATH, LUCY

Lucy. You base man, you!—how can you look me in the face, after what hath passed between us? See here, perfidious wretch, how I am forced to bear about the load of infamy you have laid upon me. Oh, Macheath! thou hast robbed me of my quiet —to see thee tortured would give me pleasure.

AIR IX.—"A lovely lass to a friar came," etc.

Thus when a good housewife sees a rat
In her trap in the morning taken,
With pleasure her heart goes pit-a-pat,
In revenge for her loss of bacon,
 Then she throws him
 To the dog or cat,
To be worried, crushed, and shaken.

Mac. Have you no bowels, no tenderness, my dear Lucy, to see a husband in these circumstances?

Lucy. A husband!

Mac. In every respect but the form, and that, my dear, may be said over us at any time. Friends should not insist upon ceremonies. From a man of honour his word is as good as his bond.

Lucy. It is the pleasure of all you fine men to insult the women you have ruined.

AIR X.—"'Twas when the sea was roaring," etc.

How cruel are the traitors,
 Who lie and swear in jest,
To cheat unguarded creatures
 Of virtue, fame, and rest !
Whoever steals a shilling
 Through shame the guilt conceals :
In love the perjured villain
 With boasts the theft reveals.

Mac. The very first opportunity, my dear, (but have patience) you shall be my wife in whatever manner you please.

Lucy. Insinuating monster! And so you think I know nothing of the affair of Miss Polly Peachum? I could tear thy eyes out.

Mac. Sure, Lucy, you can't be such a fool as to be jealous of Polly!

Lucy. Are you not married to her, you brute, you?

Mac. Married! very good. The wench gives it out only to vex thee, and to ruin me in thy good opinion. 'Tis true I go to the house, I chat with the girl, I kiss her, I say a thousand things to her (as all gentlemen do) that mean nothing, to divert myself; and now the silly jade hath set it about that I am married to her, to let me know what she would be at. Indeed, my dear Lucy, these violent passions may be of ill consequence to a woman in your condition.

Lucy. Come, come, captain, for all your assurance, you know that Miss Polly hath put it out of your power to do me the justice you promised me.

Mac. A jealous woman believes everything her passion suggests. To convince you of my sincerity, if we can find the ordinary, I shall have no scruples of making you my wife; and I know the consequence of having two at a time.

Lucy. That you are only to be hanged, and so get rid of them both.

Mac. I am ready, my dear Lucy, to give you satisfaction— if you think there is any in marriage. What can a man of honour say more?

Lucy. So then it seems you are not married to Miss Polly?

Mac. You know, Lucy, the girl is prodigiously conceited: no man can say a civil thing to her but (like other fine ladies) her vanity makes her think he's her own for ever and ever.

AIR XI.—"The Sun hath loosed his weary teams," etc.

> *The first time at the looking-glass*
> *The mother sets her daughter,*
> *The image strikes the smiling lass*
> *With self-love ever after.*
> *Each time she looks, she, fonder grown,*
> *Thinks every charm grows stronger;*
> *But alas, vain maid! all eyes but your own*
> *Can see you are not younger.*

When women consider their own beauties, they are all alike unreasonable in their demands; for they expect their lovers should like them as long as they like themselves.

Lucy. Yonder is my father. Perhaps this way we may light upon the ordinary, who shall try if you will be as good as your word—for I long to be made an honest woman.

SCENE X

PEACHUM, LOCKIT *with an account book.*

Lockit. In this last affair, brother Peachum, we are agreed. You have consented to go halves in Macheath.

Peach. We shall never fall out about an execution. But as to that article, pray how stands our last year's account?

Lockit. If you will run your eye over it, you'll find 'tis fair and clearly stated.

Peach. This long arrear of the Government is very hard upon us. Can it be expected that we should hang our acquaintances for nothing, when our betters will hardly save theirs without being paid for it? Unless the people in employment pay better, I promise them for the future I shall let other rogues live beside their own.

Lockit. Perhaps, brother, they are afraid these matters may be carried too far. We are treated, too, by them with contempt, as if our profession were not reputable.

Peach. In one respect indeed our employment may be reckoned dishonest, because, like great statesmen, we encourage those who betray their friends.

Lockit. Such language, brother, anywhere else might turn to your prejudice. Learn to be more guarded, I beg you.

AIR XII.—"How happy are we," etc.

> *When you censure the age,*
> *Be cautious and sage,*
> *Lest the courtiers offended should be :*
> *If you mention vice or bribe,*
> *'Tis so pat to all the tribe,*
> *Each cries—That was levelled at me.*

Peach. Here's poor Ned Clincher's name I see: sure, brother Lockit, there was a little unfair proceeding in Ned's case: for he told me in the condemned hold, that for value received you had promised him a session or two longer without molestation.

Lockit. Mr. Peachum, this is the first time my honour was ever called in question.

Peach. Business is at an end, if once we act dishonourably.

Lockit. Who accuses me?

Peach. You are warm, brother.

Lockit. He that attacks my honour, attacks my livelihood— and this usage, sir, is not to be borne.

Peach. Since you provoke me to speak, I must tell you, too, that Mrs. Coaxer charges you with defrauding her of her information money for the apprehending of Curlpated Hugh. Indeed, indeed, brother, we must punctually pay our spies, or we shall have no information.

Lockit. Is this language to me, sirrah—who have saved you from the gallows, sirrah!   *(Collaring each other.*

Peach. If I am hanged, it shall be for ridding the world of an arrant rascal.

Lockit. This hand shall do the office of the halter you deserve, and throttle you—you dog!

Peach. Brother, brother, we are both in the wrong—we shall be both losers in the dispute—for you know we have it in our power to hang each other. You should not be so passionate.

Lockit. Nor you so provoking.

Peach. 'Tis our mutual interest, 'tis for the interest of the world, we should agree. If I said anything, brother, to the prejudice of your character, I ask pardon.

Lockit. Brother Peachum, I can forgive as well as resent. Give me your hand: suspicion does not become a friend.

Peach. I only meant to give you occasion to justify yourself. But I must now step home, for I expect the gentleman about this snuff-box that Filch nimmed two nights ago in the park. I appointed him at this hour.

SCENE XI

Lockit, Lucy

Lockit. Whence come you, hussy?

Lucy. My tears might answer that question.

Lockit. You have then been whimpering and fondling like a spaniel over the fellow that hath abused you.

Lucy. One can't help love; one can't cure it. 'Tis not in my power to obey you and hate him.

Lockit. Learn to bear your husband's death like a reasonable woman; 'tis not the fashion nowadays so much as to affect sorrow upon these occasions. No woman would ever marry, if she had not the chance of mortality for a release. Act like a woman of spirit, hussy, and thank your father for what he is doing.

AIR XIII.—"Of a noble race was Shenkin."

Lucy.   *Is then his fate decreed, sir,*
            Such a man can I think of quitting?
        When first we met, so moves me yet,
            O see how my heart is splitting!

Lockit. Lookye, Lucy, there is no saving him, so I think you must even do like other widows—buy yourself weeds, and be cheerful.

AIR XIV

You'll think, ere many days ensue,
    This sentence not severe;
I hang your husband, child, 'tis true,
    But with him hang your care.
    Twang dang dillo dee.

Like a good wife, go moan over your dying husband; that, child, is your duty. Consider, girl, you can't have the man and the money, too—so make yourself as easy as you can, by getting all you can from him.

SCENE XII

Lucy, Macheath

Lucy. Though the ordinary was out of the way to-day, I hope, my dear, you will upon the first opportunity quiet my scruples. Oh, sir! my father's hard heart is not to be softened, and I am in the utmost despair.

Mac. But if I could raise a small sum—would not twenty guineas, think you, move him? Of all the arguments in the way of business, the perquisite is the most prevailing. Your father's perquisites for the escape of prisoners must amount to a considerable sum in the year. Money, well timed, and properly applied, will do anything.

AIR XV.—"London Ladies."

If you at an office solicit your due,
And would not have matters neglected,
You must quicken the clerk with a perquisite, too,
To do what his duty directed.
Or would you the frowns of a lady prevent,
She too has this palpable failing,
The perquisite softens her into consent ;
That reason with all is prevailing.

Lucy. What love or money can do, shall be done; for all my comfort depends upon your safety.

SCENE XIII

LUCY, MACHEATH, POLLY

Polly. Where is my dear husband? Was a rope ever intended for this neck! Oh, let me throw my arms about it, and throttle thee with love! Why dost thou turn away from me?—'tis thy Polly—'tis thy wife.

Mac. Was ever such an unfortunate rascal as I am!

Lucy. Was there ever such another villain!

Polly. Oh, Macheath! was it for this we parted? Taken! imprisoned! tried! hanged! Cruel reflection! I'll stay with thee till death—no force shall tear thy dear wife from thee now. What means my love?—not one kind word! not one kind look! Think what thy Polly suffers to see thee in this condition.

AIR XVI.—"All in the Downs," etc.

Thus when the swallow, seeking prey,
Within the sash is closely pent,
His consort with bemoaning lay
Without sits pining for the event.
Her chattering lovers ali around her skim ;
She heeds them not, poor bird, her soul's with him.

Mac. I must disown her. (*Aside.*) The wench is distracted!

Lucy. Am I then bilked of my virtue? Can I have no

reparation? Sure men were born to lie, and women to believe them! Oh, villain! villain!

Polly. Am I not thy wife? Thy neglect of me, thy aversion to me, too severely proves it. Look on me—tell me, am I not thy wife?

Lucy. Perfidious wretch!

Polly. Barbarous husband!

Lucy. Hadst thou been hanged five months ago, I had been happy.

Polly. And I, too. If you had been kind to me till death, it would not have vexed me—and that's no very unreasonable request (though from a wife) to a man who hath not above seven or eight days to live.

Lucy. Art thou, then, married to another? Hast thou two wives, monster?

Mac. If women's tongues can cease for an answer—hear me.

Lucy. I won't. Flesh and blood can't bear my usage!

Polly. Shall not I claim my own? Justice bids me speak.

AIR XVII.—"Have you heard of a frolicsome ditty," etc.

Mac.   *How happy could I be with either,*
                 Were t'other dear charmer away !
                 But, while ye thus tease me together,
                 To neither a word will I say ;
                      But toll de roll, etc.

Polly. Sure, my dear, there ought to be some preference shown to a wife—at least, she may claim the appearance of it. He must be distracted with misfortunes, or he could not use me thus.

Lucy. Oh, villain! villain! thou hast deceived me! I could even inform against thee with pleasure. Not a prude wishes more heartily to have facts against her intimate acquaintance than I now wish to have facts against thee. I would have her satisfaction, and they should all out.

AIR XVIII.—"Irish trot."

Polly. I'm bubbled.
Lucy.   I'm bubbled.
Polly.   Oh, how I'm troubled !
Lucy. Bamboozled and bit !
Polly.   My distresses are doubled.
Lucy. When you come to the tree, should the hangman refuse,
        These fingers, with pleasure, could fasten the noose.
Polly. I'm bubbled, etc.

Mac. Be pacified, my dear Lucy—this is all a fetch of Polly's to make me desperate with you, in case I get off. If I am hanged, she would fain have the credit of being thought my widow.

Really, Polly, this is no time for a dispute of this sort; for when-ever you are talking of marriage, I am thinking of hanging.

Polly. And hast thou the heart to persist in disowning me?

Mac. And hast thou the heart to persist in persuading me that I am married? Why, Polly, dost thou seek to aggravate my misfortunes?

Lucy. Really, Miss Peachum, you but expose yourself; besides, 'tis barbarous in you to worry a gentleman in his circumstances.

AIR XIX

Polly.

> *Cease your funning,*
> *Force or cunning,*
> *Never shall my heart trepan ;*
> *All these sallies*
> *Are but malice,*
> *To seduce my constant man.*

> *'Tis most certain,*
> *By their flirting,*
> *Women oft have envy shown ;*
> *Pleased to ruin*
> *Others' wooing,*
> *Never happy in their own !*

Decency, madam, methinks, might teach you to behave yourself with some reserve with the husband while his wife is present.

Mac. But, seriously, Polly, this is carrying the joke a little too far.

Lucy. If you are determined, madam, to raise a disturbance in the prison, I shall be obliged to send for the turnkey to show you the door. I am sorry, madam, you force me to be so ill-bred.

Polly. Give me leave to tell you, madam, these forward airs don't become you in the least, madam; and my duty, madam, obliges me to stay with my husband, madam.

AIR XX.—"Good morrow, Gossip Joan."

Lucy.

> *Why, how now, Madam Flirt ?*
> *If you thus must chatter,*
> *And are for flinging dirt,*
> *Let's try, who best can spatter,*
> > *Madam Flirt !*

Polly.

> *Why, how now, saucy jade ?*
> *Sure, the wench is tipsy !*
> *How can you see me made*   (To him.
> *The scoff of such a gipsy ?*
> > *Saucy jade !*   (To her.

SCENE XIV

LUCY, MACHEATH, POLLY, PEACHUM

Peach. Where's my wench? Ah, hussy, hussy! Come home, you slut! and when your fellow is hanged, hang yourself, to make your family some amends.

Polly. Dear, dear father! do not tear me from him. I must speak—I have more to say to him. Oh, twist thy fetters about me, that he may not haul me from thee!

Peach. Sure, all women are alike! if ever they commit the folly, they are sure to commit another, by exposing themselves. Away—not a word more! You are my prisoner now, hussy.

AIR XXI.—"Irish howl."

Polly.
> *No power on earth can e'er divide*
> *The knot that sacred love hath tied.*
> *When parents draw against our mind,*
> *The true love's knot they faster bind.*
> > *Oh, oh, ray, oh Amborah—Oh, oh, etc.*

(*Holding* MACHEATH, PEACHUM *pulling her.*

SCENE XV

LUCY, MACHEATH

Mac. I am naturally compassionate, wife, so that I could not use the wench as she deserved, which made you, at first, suspect there was something in what she said.

Lucy. Indeed, my dear, I was strangely puzzled!

Mac. If that had been the case, her father would never have brought me into this circumstance. No, Lucy, I had rather die than be false to thee!

Lucy. How happy am I, if you say this from your heart! for I love thee so, that I could sooner bear to see thee hanged than in the arms of another.

Mac. But couldst thou bear to see me hanged?

Lucy. Oh, Macheath! I could never live to see that day!

Mac. You see, Lucy, in the account of love, you are in my debt. And you must now be convinced that I rather choose to die than be another's. Make me, if possible, love thee more, and let me owe my life to thee. If you refuse to assist me, Peachum and your father will immediately put me beyond all means of escape.

Lucy. My father, I know, hath been drinking hard with the prisoners, and, I fancy, he is now taking his nap in his own room. If I can procure the keys, shall I go off with thee, my dear?

Mac. If we are together, 'twill be impossible to lie concealed. As soon as the search begins to be a little cool, I will send to thee; till then, my heart is thy prisoner.

Lucy. Come, then, my dear husband, owe thy life to me; and, though you love me not, be grateful. But that Polly runs in my head strangely.

Mac. A moment of time may make us unhappy for ever.

Air XXII.—"The Lass of Patie's Mill."

Lucy.
> *I like the fox shall grieve,*
>   *Whose mate hath left her side;*
> *Whom hounds, from morn to eve,*
>   *Chase o'er the country wide.*

> *Where can my lover hide?*
>   *Where cheat the wary pack?*
> *If love be not his guide,*
>   *He never will come back.*

ACT III. SCENE I.

SCENE—Newgate

Lockit, Lucy

Lockit. To be sure, wench, you must have been aiding and abetting to help him to this escape?

Lucy. Sir, here hath been Peachum and his daughter Polly, and, to be sure, they know the ways of Newgate as well as if they had been born and bred in the place all their lives. Why must all your suspicion light upon me?

Lockit. Lucy, Lucy, I will have none of these shuffling answers!

Lucy. Well, then, if I know anything of him, I wish I may be burned!

Lockit. Keep your temper, Lucy, or I shall pronounce you guilty.

Lucy. Keep yours, sir—I do wish I may be burned, I do, and what can I say more to convince you?

Lockit. Did he tip handsomely? How much did he come down with? Come, hussy, don't cheat your father, and I shall not be angry with you. Perhaps you have made a better bargain with him than I could have done. How much, my good girl?

Lucy. You know, sir, I am fond of him, and would have given money to have kept him with me.

Lockit. Ah, Lucy! thy education might have put thee more upon thy guard: for a girl in the bar of an ale-house is always besieged.

Lucy. Dear sir, mention not my education, for 'twas to that I owe my ruin.

Air I.—"If love's a sweet passion," etc.

> *When young at the bar you first taught me to score*
> *And bid me be free with my lips, and no more ;*
> *I was kissed by the parson, the squire, and the sot ;*
> *When the guest was departed, the kiss was forgot.*
> *But his kiss was so sweet, and so closely he pressed,*
> *That I languished and pined till I granted the rest.*

If you can forgive me, sir, I will make a fair confession; for, to be sure, he hath been a most barbarous villain to me!

Lockit. And so you have let him escape, hussy—have you?

Lucy. When a woman loves, a kind look, a tender word, can persuade her to anything, and I could ask no other bribe.

Lockit. Thou wilt always be a vulgar slut, Lucy. If you would not be looked upon as a fool, you should never do anything but upon the foot of interest. Those that act otherwise are their own bubbles.

Lucy. But love, sir, is a misfortune that may happen to the most discreet woman, and in love we are all fools alike. Notwithstanding all he swore, I am now fully convinced that Polly Peachum is actually his wife. Did I let him escape, fool that I was! to go to her? Polly will wheedle herself into his money; and then Peachum will hang him, and cheat us both.

Lockit. So I am to be ruined because, forsooth, you must be in love! A very pretty excuse!

Lucy. I could murder that impudent, happy strumpet! I gave him his life, and that creature enjoys the sweets of it. Ungrateful Macheath!

Air II.—"South Sea Ballad."

> *My love is all madness and folly ;*
>   *Alone I lie,*
>   *Toss, tumble, and cry,*
> *What a happy creature is Polly !*
> *Was e'er such a wretch as I ?*
> *With rage I redden like scarlet,*
> *That my dear inconstant varlet,*
>   *Stark blind to my charms,*
>   *Is lost in the arms*
> *Of that jilt, that inveigling harlot !*
>   *Stark blind to my charms,*
>   *Is lost in the arms*
> *Of that jilt, that inveigling harlot !*
> *This, this my resentment alarms.*

Lockit. And so, after all this mischief, I must stay here to be entertained with your caterwauling, Mistress Puss! Out of my sight, wanton strumpet! You shall fast, and mortify yourself into reason, with, now and then, a little handsome discipline, to bring you to your senses. Go!

SCENE II

LOCKIT

Peachum then intends to outwit me in this affair; but I'll be even with him. The dog is leaky in his liquor, so I'll ply him that way, get the secret from him, and turn this affair to my own advantage. Lions, wolves, and vultures don't live together in herds, droves or flocks. Of all animals of prey, man is the only sociable one. Every one of us preys upon his neighbour, and yet we herd together. Peachum is my companion my friend—according to the custom of the world, indeed, he may quote thousands of precedents for cheating me—and shall not I make use of the privilege of friendship to make him a return?

AIR III.—"Packington's Pound."

Thus gamesters united in friendship are found,
    Though they know that their industry all is a cheat;
They flock to their prey at the dice-box's sound,
    And join to promote one another's deceit.
        But if by mishap
        They fail of a chap,
To keep in their hands, they each other entrap.
Like pikes, lank with hunger, who miss of their ends,
They bite their companions, and prey on their friends.

Now, Peachum, you and I, like honest tradesmen, are to have a fair trial which of us two can overreach the other. Lucy!

Enter LUCY

Are there any of Peachum's people now in the house?
Lucy. Filch, sir, is drinking a quartern of strong waters in the next room with Black Moll.
Lockit. Bid him come to me.

SCENE III

LOCKIT, FILCH

Lockit. Why, boy, thou lookest as if thou wert half starved; like a shotten herring.
Filch. One had need have the constitution of a horse to go through the business. Since the favourite child-getter was dis-

abled by a mishap, I have picked up a little money by helping
the ladies to a pregnancy against their being called down to
sentence. But if a man cannot get an honest livelihood any
easier way, I am sure 'tis what I can't undertake for another
session.

Lockit. Truly, if that great man should tip off, 'twould be
an irreparable loss. The vigour and prowess of a knight-errant
never saved half the ladies in distress that he hath done. But,
boy, canst thou tell me where thy master is to be found?

Filch. At his Lock ¹, sir, at the Crooked Billet.

Lockit. Very well. I have nothing more with you. (*Exit* FILCH.)
I'll go to him there, for I have many important affairs to settle
with him; and in the way of those transactions, I'll artfully
get into his secret. So that Macheath shall not remain a day
longer out of my clutches.

SCENE IV.—*A Gaming-House*

MACHEATH, *in a fine tarnished coat,* BEN BUDGE, MAT OF THE MINT

Mac. I am sorry, gentlemen, the road was so barren of money.
When my friends are in difficulties, I am always glad that my
fortune can be serviceable to them. (*Gives them money.*) You see,
gentlemen, I am not a mere Court friend, who professes everything and will do nothing.

AIR IV.—"Lillibulero."

The modes of the Court so common are grown,
  That a true friend can hardly be met ;
Friendship for interest is but a loan,
  Which they let out for what they can get.
    'Tis true, you find
    Some friends so kind,
Who will give you good counsel themselves to defend.
    In sorrowful ditty,
    They promise, they pity,
But shift you for money from friend to friend.

But we, gentlemen, have still honour enough to break through
the corruptions of the world. And while I can serve you, you may
command me.

Ben. It grieves my heart that so generous a man should be
involved in such difficulties as oblige him to live with such ill
company and herd with gamesters.

Mat. See the partiality of mankind! One man may steal a
horse better than another look over a hedge. Of all mechanics,
of all servile handicrafts, a gamester is the vilest. But yet, as
many of the quality are of the profession, he is admitted amongst
the politest company, I wonder we are not more respected.

¹ A cant word, signifying a warehouse where stolen goods are deposited.

Mac. There will be deep play to-night at Marybone, and consequently money may be picked up upon the road. Meet me there, and I'll give you the hint who is worth setting.

Mat. The fellow with a brown coat with a narrow gold binding, I am told, is never without money.

Mac. What do you mean, Mat? Sure you will not think of meddling with him! He's a good honest kind of a fellow and one of us.

Ben. To be sure, sir, we will put ourselves under your direction.

Mac. Have an eye upon the money-lenders. A rouleau or two would prove a pretty sort of an expedition. I hate extortion.

Mat. Those rouleaux are very pretty things. I hate your bank bills—there is such a hazard in putting them off.

Mac. There is a certain man of distinction who in his time has nicked me out of a great deal of the ready. He is in my cash, Ben; I'll point him out to you this evening, and you shall draw upon him for the debt. The company are met; I hear the dice-box in the other room. So, gentlemen, your servant. You'll meet me at Marybone.

SCENE V.—*Peachum's Lock*

A table with wine, brandy, pipes and tobacco

PEACHUM, LOCKIT

Lockit. The Coronation account, brother Peachum, is of so intricate a nature, that I believe it will never be settled.

Peach. It consists indeed of a great variety of articles. It was worth to our people, in fees of different kinds, above ten instalments. This is part of the account, brother, that lies open before us.

Lockit. A lady's tail of rich brocade—that I see is disposed of.

Peach. To Mrs. Diana Trapes, the tally-woman, and she will make a good hand on't in shoes and slippers, to trick out young ladies upon their going into keeping.

Lockit. But I don't see any article of the jewels.

Peach. Those are so well known that they must be sent abroad —you'll find them entered under the article of exportation. As for the snuff-boxes, watches, swords, etc., I thought it best to enter them under their several heads.

Lockit. Seven and twenty women's pockets complete; with the several things therein contained; all sealed, numbered and entered.

Peach. But, brother, it is impossible for us now to enter upon this affair. We should have the whole day before us. Besides, the account of the last half-year's plate is in a book by itself, which lies at the other office.

Lockit. Bring us then more liquor. To-day shall be for pleasure —to-morrow for business. Ah, brother, those daughters of ours are two slippery hussies—keep a watchful eye upon Polly, and Macheath in a day or two shall be our own again.

Lockit.   *What gudgeons are we men !*
     Every woman's easy prey.
Though we have felt the hook, agen
     We bite, and they betray.

     The bird that has been trapped,
       When he hears his calling mate,
     To her he flies, again he's clipped
       Within the wiry grate.

Peach. But what signifies catching the bird, if your daughter Lucy will set open the door of the cage?

Lockit. If men were answerable for the follies and frailties of their wives and daughters, no friends could keep a good correspondence together for two days. This is unkind of you, brother; for among good friends, what they say or do goes for nothing.

Enter a Servant.

Serv. Sir, here's Mrs. Diana Trapes wants to speak with you.

Peach. Shall we admit her, brother Lockit?

Lockit. By all means—she's a good customer, and a fine-spoken woman, and a woman who drinks and talks so freely will enliven the conversation.

Peach. Desire her to walk in.   (*Exit Servant.*

SCENE VI

PEACHUM, LOCKIT, MRS. TRAPES

Peach. Dear Mrs. Dye, your servant—one may know by your kiss that your gin is excellent.

Mrs. T. I was always very curious in my liquors.

Lockit. There is no perfumed breath like it—I have been long acquainted with the flavour of those lips—han't I, Mrs. Dye?

Mrs. T. Fill it up. I take as large draughts of liquor as I did of love. I hate a flincher in either.

In the days of my youth I could bill like a dove,
     fa, la, la, etc.
Like a sparrow at all times was ready for love,
     fa, la, la, etc.
The life of all mortals in kissing should pass,
Lip to lip while we're young—then the lip to the glass,
     fa, la, la, etc.

But now, Mr. Peachum, to our business. If you have blacks of
any kind, brought in of late, mantoes, velvet scarfs, petticoats,
let it be what it will, I am your chap, for all my ladies are very
fond of mourning.

Peach. Why, look, Mrs. Dye, you deal so hard with us that
we can afford to give the gentlemen who venture their lives for
the goods little or nothing.

Mrs. T. The hard times oblige me to go very near in my
dealing. To be sure, of late years I have been a great sufferer by
the Parliament. Three thousand pounds would hardly make me
amends. The Act for destroying the mint was a severe cut upon
our business—till then, if a customer stepped out of the way,
we knew where to have her. No doubt, you know Mrs. Coaxer—
there's a wench now (till to-day) with a good suit of clothes
of mine upon her back, and I could never set eyes upon her for
three months together. Since the Act too against imprisonment
for small sums, my loss there, too, has been very considerable,
and it must be so, when a lady can borrow a handsome petticoat, or a clean gown, and I not have the least hank upon her!
And o' my conscience, nowadays most ladies take a delight in
cheating, when they can do it with safety.

Peach. Madam, you had a handsome gold watch of us t'other
day for seven guineas. Considering we must have our profit, to
a gentleman upon the road, a gold watch will be scarce worth
the taking.

Mrs. T. Consider, Mr. Peachum, that watch was remarkable,
and not of very safe sale. If you have any black velvet scarfs,
they are a handsome winter wear, and take with most gentlemen who deal with my customers. 'Tis I that put the ladies upon
a good foot. 'Tis not youth or beauty that fixes the price. The
gentlemen always pay according to their dress, from half a
crown to two guineas; and yet those hussies make nothing of
bilking me. Then, too, allowing for accidents, I have eleven fine
customers now down under the surgeon's hands; what with
fees and other expenses, there are great goings-out and no
comings-in, and not a farthing to pay for at least a month's
clothing. We run great risks, great risks indeed.

Peach. As I remember, you said something just now of Mrs.
Coaxer.

Mrs. T. Yes, sir—to be sure, I stripped her of a suit of my own
clothes about two hours ago; and have left her as she should be,
in her shift, with a lover of hers at my house. She called him
upstairs as he was going to Marybone in a hackney-coach. And
I hope for her own sake and mine, she will persuade the captain
to redeem her, for the captain is very generous to the ladies.

Lockit. What captain?

Mrs. T. He thought I did not know him. An intimate acquaintance of yours, Mr. Peachum—only Captain Macheath—as fine as
a lord.

Peach. To-morrow, dear Mrs. Dye, you shall set your own price upon any of the goods you like—we have at least half a dozen velvet scarfs and all at your service. Will you give me leave to make you a present of this suit of night-clothes for your own wearing? But are you sure it is Captain Macheath?

Mrs. T. Though he thinks I have forgot him, nobody knows him better. I have taken a great deal of the captain's money in my time at second-hand, for he always loved to have his ladies well dressed.

Peach. Mr. Lockit and I have a little business with the captain; you understand me—and we will satisfy you for Mrs. Coaxer's debt.

Lockit. Depend upon it—we will deal like men of honour.

Mrs. T. I don't inquire after your affairs—so whatever happens, I wash my hands on it. It has always been my maxim, that one friend should assist another. But if you please, I'll take one of the scarfs home with me, 'tis always good to have something in hand.

SCENE VII.—*Newgate*

Lucy

Jealousy, rage, love, and fear, are at once tearing me to pieces. How am I weather-beaten and shattered with distresses!

AIR VII.—"One evening having lost my way," etc.

> *I'm like a skiff on the ocean tossed,*
> *Now high, now low, with each billow borne,*
> *With her rudder broke and her anchor lost,*
> *Deserted and all forlorn.*
> *While thus I lie rolling and tossing all night,*
> *That Polly lies sporting on seas of delight!*
> *Revenge, revenge, revenge,*
> *Shall appease my restless sprite.*

I have the ratsbane ready—I run no risk; for I can lay her death upon the gin, and so many die of that naturally, that I shall never be called in question. But say I were to be hanged —I never could be hanged for anything that would give me greater comfort than the poisoning that slut.

Enter FILCH

Filch. Madam, here's our Miss Polly come to wait upon you.
Lucy. Show her in.

SCENE VIII

LUCY, POLLY

Lucy. Dear madam! your servant. I hope you will pardon my passion when I was so happy to see you last—I was so overrun with the spleen, that I was perfectly out of myself; and really when one hath the spleen, everything is to be excused by a friend.

AIR VIII.—"Now, Roger, I'll tell thee, because thou'rt my son.'

> *When a wife's in her pout*
> *(As she's sometimes, no doubt),*
> *The good husband, as meek as a lamb,*
> *Her vapours to still,*
> *First grants her her will,*
> *And the quieting draught is a dram ;*
> *Poor man ! and the quieting draught is a dram.*

—I wish all our quarrels might have so comfortable a reconciliation.

Polly. I have no excuse for my own behaviour, madam, but my misfortunes—and really, madam, I suffer too upon your account.

Lucy. But, Miss Polly, in the way of friendship, will you give me leave to propose a glass of cordial to you?

Polly. Strong waters are apt to give me the headache. I hope, madam, you will excuse me?

Lucy. Not the greatest lady in the land could have better in her closet for her own private drinking. You seem mighty low in spirits, my dear!

Polly. I am sorry, madam, my health will not allow me to accept of your offer. I should not have left you in the rude manner I did when we met last, madam, had not my papa hauled me away so unexpectedly. I was indeed somewhat provoked, and perhaps might use some expressions that were disrespectful—but really, madam, the captain treated me with so much contempt and cruelty, that I deserved your pity rather than your resentment.

Lucy. But since his escape, no doubt, all matters are made up again. Ah, Polly! Polly! 'tis I am the unhappy wife, and he loves you as if you were only his mistress.

Polly. Sure, madam, you cannot think me so happy as to be the object of your jealousy. A man is always afraid of a woman who loves him too well. So that I must expect to be neglected and avoided.

Lucy. Then our cases, my dear Polly, are exactly alike. Both of us indeed have been too fond.

AIR IX.—"O Bessy Bell."

Polly.	*A curse attends that woman's love*
	Who always would be pleasing.
Lucy.	*The pertness of the billing dove,*
	Like tickling is but teasing.
Polly.	*What then in love can woman do?*
Lucy.	*If we grow fond they shun us.*
Polly.	*And when we fly them, they pursue:*
Lucy.	*But leave us when they've won us.*

Lucy. Love is so very whimsical in both sexes, that it is impossible to be lasting. But my heart is particular, and contradicts my own observation.

Polly. But really, mistress Lucy, by his last behaviour I think I ought to envy you. When I was forced from him he did not show the least tenderness. But perhaps he hath a heart not capable of it.

AIR X.—"Would fate to me Belinda give."

Among the men coquets we find,
Who court by turns all womankind:
And we grant all their hearts desired
When they are flattered and admired.

The coquets of both sexes are self-lovers, and that is a love no other whatever can dispossess. I fear, my dear Lucy, our husband is one of those.

Lucy. Away with these melancholy reflections! Indeed, my dear Polly, we are both of us a cup too low; let me prevail upon you to accept of my offer.

AIR XI.—"Come, sweet lass."

Come, sweet lass,
Let's banish sorrow
Till to-morrow:
Come, sweet lass,
Let's take a chirping glass.
Wine can clear
The vapours of despair,
And make us light as air;
Then drink and banish care.

I can't bear, child, to see you in such low spirits—and I must persuade you to what I know will do you good.—I shall now soon be even with the hypocritical strumpet.   (*Aside.*

SCENE IX

POLLY

Polly. All this wheedling of Lucy cannot be for nothing—at this time too, when I know she hates me! The dissembling of a woman is always the forerunner of mischief. By pouring strong waters down my throat she thinks to pump some secrets out of me. I'll be upon my guard, and won't taste a drop of her liquor, I'm resolved.

SCENE X

LUCY, *with strong waters.* POLLY

Lucy. Come, Miss Polly.

Polly. Indeed, child, you have given yourself trouble to no purpose. You must, my dear, excuse me.

Lucy. Really, Miss Polly, you are so squeamishly affected about taking a cup of strong waters as a lady before company. I vow, Polly, I shall take it monstrously ill if you refuse me. Brandy and men, though women love them never so well, are always taken by us with some reluctance—unless 'tis in private.

Polly. I protest, madam, it goes against me——What do I see! Macheath again in custody! Now every glimmering of happiness is lost!   (*Drops the glass of liquor on the ground.*

Lucy. Since things are thus, I am glad the wench hath escaped, for by this event 'tis plain she was not happy enough to deserve to be poisoned.   (*Aside.*

SCENE XI

LOCKIT, MACHEATH, PEACHUM, LUCY, POLLY

Lockit. Set your heart at rest, captain. You have neither the chance of love nor money for another escape, for you are ordered to be called down upon your trial immediately.

Peach. Away, hussies! This is not a time for a man to be hampered with his wives—you see the gentleman is in chains already.

Lucy. O husband, husband! my heart longed to see thee, but to see thee thus distracts me!

Polly. Will not my dear husband look upon his Polly? Why hadst thou not flown to me for protection? With me thou hadst been safe.

AIR XII.—"The last time I went o'er the moor."

Polly.	*Hither, dear husband, turn your eyes !*
Lucy.	*Bestow one glance to cheer me.*
Polly.	*Think, with that look, thy Polly dies.*
Lucy.	*Oh, shun me not, but hear me !*

Polly.	'Tis Polly sues.
Lucy.	'Tis Lucy speaks.
Polly.	Is thus true love requited?
Lucy.	My heart is bursting.
Polly.	Mine, too, breaks.
Lucy.	Must I——
Polly.	Must I be slighted?

Mac. What would you have me say, ladies? You see, this affair will soon be at an end, without my disobliging either of you.

Peach. But the settling of this point, captain, might prevent a lawsuit between your two widows.

AIR XIII.—"Tom Tinker's my true love."

Mac. Which way shall I turn me? how can I decide?
Wives, the day of our death, are as fond as a bride.
One wife is too much for most husbands to hear,
But two at a time there's no mortal can bear.
This way, and that way, and which way I will,
What would comfort the one, t'other wife would take ill.

Polly. But, if his own misfortunes have made him insensible to mine, a father, sure, will be more compassionate!—Dear, dear, sir! sink the material evidence, and bring him off at his trial—Polly, upon her knees, begs it of you.

AIR XIV.—"I am a poor shepherd, undone."

When my hero in court appears,
And stands arraigned for his life,
Then think of poor Polly's tears,
For, ah! poor Polly's his wife.
Like the sailor, he holds up his hand,
Distressed, on the dashing wave;
To die a dry death at land,
Is as bad as a watery grave.
And alas, poor Polly!
Alack, and well-a-day!
Before I was in love,
Oh! every month was May.

Lucy. If Peachum's heart is hardened, sure, sir, you will have more compassion on a daughter. I know the evidence is in your power. How, then, can you be a tyrant to me?   (*Kneeling.*

AIR XV.—"Ianthe the lovely," etc.

When he holds up his hand arraigned for his life,
O think of your daughter, and think I'm his wife!

What are cannons, or bombs, or clashing of swords ?
For death is more certain by witnesses' words.
Then nail up their lips ; that dread thunder allay ;
And each month of my life will hereafter be May.

Lockit. Macheath's time is come, Lucy. We know our own
affairs, therefore let us have no more whimpering or whining.

AIR XVI.—"A cobbler there was," etc.

Ourselves, like the great, to secure a retreat,
When matters require it, must give up our gang :
    And good reason why,
    Or, instead of the fry,
    Even Peachum and I,
Like poor petty rascals, might hang, hang ;
Like poor petty rascals, might hang.

Peach. Set your heart at rest, Polly—your husband is to die
to-day; therefore, if you are not already provided, 'tis high time
to look about for another. There's comfort for you, you slut!

Lockit. We are ready, sir, to conduct you to the Old Bailey.

AIR XVII.—"Bonny Dundee."

Mac.   *The charge is prepared, the lawyers are met,*
      The judges all ranged (a terrible show !).
    I go undismayed, for death is a debt—
      A debt on demand, so take what I owe.
    Then farewell, my love—dear charmers, adieu !
    Contented I die—'tis the better for you.
    Here ends all dispute for the rest of our lives,
    For this way, at once, I please all my wives.

Now, gentlemen, I am ready to attend you.

SCENE XII

LUCY, POLLY, FILCH

Polly. Follow them, Filch, to the court. And when the trial
is over, bring me a particular account of his behaviour, and of
everything that happened. You'll find me here with Miss Lucy.
(*Exit* FILCH.) But why is all this music ?

Lucy. The prisoners whose trials are put off till next session
are diverting themselves.

Polly. Sure there is nothing so charming as music ! I'm fond
of it to distraction. But alas ! now all mirth seems an insult upon
my affliction. Let us retire, my dear Lucy, and indulge our
sorrows. The noisy crew you see are coming upon us.   (*Exeunt.*

A dance of prisoners in chains, etc.

SCENE XIII.—*The Condemned Hold*
MACHEATH, *in a melancholy posture*

AIR XVIII.—"Happy Groves."
Oh, cruel, cruel, cruel case!
Must I suffer this disgrace?

AIR XIX.—"Of all the girls that are so smart."
Of all the friends in time of grief,
  When threatening death looks grimmer,
Not one so sure can bring relief
  As this best friend, a brimmer.   (*Drinks.*

AIR XX.—"Britons, strike home."
Since I must swing—I scorn, I scorn to wince or whine.
                                        (*Rises.*

AIR XXI.—"Chevy Chace."
But now again my spirits sink,
I'll raise them high with wine.
                    (*Drinks a glass of wine.*

AIR XXII.—"To old Sir Simon, the king."
But valour the stronger grows,
  The stronger liquor we're drinking,
And how can we feel our woes,
  When we've lost the trouble of thinking?
                                        (*Drinks.*

AIR XXIII.—"Joy to great Cæsar."
If thus, a man can die
Much bolder with brandy.
          (*Pours out a bumper of brandy.*

AIR XXIV.—"There was an old woman."
So I take off this bumper—and now I can stand the test,
And my comrades shall see that I die as brave as the best.
                                        (*Drinks.*

AIR XXV.—"Did you ever hear of a gallant sailor?"
But can I leave my pretty hussies,
Without one tear, or tender sigh?

AIR XXVI.—"Why are mine eyes still flowing?"
Their eyes, their lips, their busses,
Recall my love—Ah! must I die?

AIR XXVII.—"Green Sleeves."

Since laws were made, for every degree,
To curb vice in others, as well as me,
I wonder we han't better company
Upon Tyburn tree.
But gold from law can take out the sting ;
And if rich men, like us, were to swing,
'Twould thin the land, such numbers to string
Upon Tyburn tree.

Jailer. Some friends of yours, captain, desire to be admitted —I leave you together.

SCENE XIV

MACHEATH, BEN BUDGE, MAT OF THE MINT

Mac. For my having broke prison, you see, gentlemen, I am ordered immediate execution. The sheriff's officers, I believe, are now at the door. That Jemmy Twitcher should 'peach me, I own, surprised me. 'Tis a plain proof that the world is all alike, and that even our gang can no more trust one another than other people; therefore, I beg you, gentlemen, to look well to yourselves, for, in all probability, you may live some months longer.

Mat. We are heartily sorry, captain, for your misfortune, but 'tis what we must all come to.

Mac. Peachum and Lockit, you know, are infamous scoundrels —their lives are as much in your power, as yours are in theirs. Remember your dying friend—'tis my last request. Bring those villains to the gallows before you, and I am satisfied.

Mat. We'll do it.

Jailer. Miss Polly and Miss Lucy entreat a word with you.

Mac. Gentlemen, adieu!

SCENE XV

LUCY, MACHEATH, POLLY

Mac. My dear Lucy! my dear Polly! whatsoever hath passed between us is now at an end. If you are fond of marrying again, the best advice I can give you is to ship yourselves off for the West Indies, where you'll have a fair chance of getting a husband apiece; or by good luck, two or three, as you like best.

Polly. How can I support this sight!

Lucy. There is nothing moves one so much as a great man in distress.

AIR XXVIII.—"All you that must take a leap," etc.

Lucy. '*Would I might be hanged!*
Polly.   *And I would so too!*
Lucy. *To be hanged with you,*
Polly.   *My dear, with you.*
Mac. *Oh, leave me to thought! I fear, I doubt!*
      I tremble—I droop!—See, my courage is out!
                                    (*Turns up the empty bottle.*
Polly. *No token of love?*
Mac.   *See, my courage is out!*
                                    (*Turns up the empty pot.*
Lucy. *No token of love?*
Polly.   *Adieu!*
Lucy.   *Farewell!*
Mac. *But hark! I hear the toll of the bell.*
Chorus.   *Tol de rol lol, etc.*

Jailer. Four women more, captain, with a child apiece. See, here they come!

Enter Women and Children

Mac. What! four wives more! this is too much. Here, tell the sheriff's officers I am ready.   (*Exit* MACHEATH, *guarded.*

SCENE XVI

To them enter PLAYER and BEGGAR

Player. But, honest friend, I hope you don't intend that Macheath shall be really executed.

Beggar. Most certainly, sir. To make the piece perfect, I was for doing strict poetical justice. Macheath is to be hanged; and for the other personages of the drama, the audience must have supposed they were all either hanged or transported.

Player. Why then, friend, this is a downright deep tragedy. The catastrophe is manifestly wrong, for an opera must end happily.

Beggar. Your objection, sir, is very just; and is easily removed. For you must allow that, in this kind of drama, 'tis no matter how absurdly things are brought about—so—you rabble there—run and cry a reprieve—let the prisoner be brought back to his wives in triumph.

Player. All this we must do, to comply with the taste of the town.

Beggar. Through the whole piece you may observe such a similitude of manners in high and low life, that it is difficult to determine whether (in the fashionable vices) the fine gentlemen imitate the gentlemen of the road, or the gentlemen of the road the fine gentlemen. Had the play remained as I at first intended, it would have carried a most excellent moral. 'Twould have shown that the lower sort of people have their vices in a degree as well as the rich: and that they are punished for them.

SCENE XVII

To them MACHEATH, *with rabble, etc.*

Mac. So, it seems, I am not left to my choice, but must have a wife at last. Lookye, my dears, we will have no controversy now. Let us give this day to mirth, and I am sure, she who thinks herself my wife will testify her joy by a dance.

All. Come, a dance! a dance!

Mac. Ladies, I hope you will give me leave to present a partner to each of you; and (if I may without offence) for this time, I take Polly for mine—and for life, you slut, for we were really married. As for the rest——But, at present, keep your own secret. (*To* POLLY.

A DANCE

AIR XXIX.—"Lumps of Pudding," etc.

Thus I stand like a Turk, with his doxies around,
From all sides their glances his passion confound ;
For black, brown, and fair, his inconstancy burns,
And the different beauties subdue him by turns :
Each calls forth her charms to provoke his desires,
Though willing to all, with but one he retires :
But think of this maxim, and put off your sorrow,
The wretch of to-day, may be happy to-morrow.

CHORUS

But think of this maxim, etc.

THE TRAGEDY OF TRAGEDIES

OR

TOM THUMB THE GREAT

HENRY FIELDING, the great novelist, was born at Sharpham Park, near Glastonbury, in 1707, the son of General Edmund Fielding. After some years at Eton and a youthful love-affair, Fielding was sent to Leyden to study law, but by 1728 he was back in London, a tall, handsome youth, energetic and generous, with no money and a taste for the coarser pleasures of the town. His plays were written to make money, and most of them, unlike *The Tragedy of Tragedies*, are hasty work of poor quality.

About 1735 he married the beautiful Charlotte Craddock, and soon afterwards became manager of the Little Theatre in the Haymarket, but abandoned the drama for law, and was called to the Bar in 1740.

Two years later appeared the first of those novels by which we know him best—*Joseph Andrews*. This was begun as a burlesque of Richardson's *Pamela* and, to a lesser extent, of Cibber's *Apology*, but it grew under his hand until it became a "comic Epic-Poem in Prose," and "inaugurated a new method in fiction"—the method of the modern novel. His *Miscellanies* (1743) included *Jonathan Wild*, a masterpiece of irony; but his greatest and most popular novel, *Tom Jones*, did not appear until 1749. *Amelia* was published two years later, and the *Journal of a Voyage to Lisbon*, posthumously, in 1755.

During this period of his greatest literary activity, Fielding suffered much from poverty, ill-health, and sorrow at the death of his wife. In 1748 he was made a Justice of the Peace for Westminster and carried out his duties with an honesty, devotion and ability which make his work a turning-point in the social history of London. Worn out at last, suffering from jaundice, dropsy and asthma, he took the voyage to Lisbon in quest of health and died there in 1754, at the age of forty-eight.

THE

TRAGEDY

OF

TRAGEDIES;

OR THE

LIFE *and* DEATH

OF

TOM THUMB *the Great.*

As it is Acted at the

THEATRE in the *Hay-Market.*

With the ANNOTATIONS of

H. SCRIBLERUS SECUNDUS

LONDON,

Printed; And Sold by *J. Roberts* in *Warwick-Lane*

M DCC XXXI.

Price One Shilling.

[The title-page is that of the first edition, but the text is printed from the third edition (1737) which differs from the first only in very trivial details, chiefly corrections of misprints, and has the advantage that it marks footnotes with figures instead of the more disfiguring letters.

The most important critics mentioned in the footnotes are B[entle]y, D[enni]s, T[heobal]d, S[almo]n, and W[elsted].]

The first, third and later editions have frontispiece by Hogarth, which represents Huncamunca holding the candle so that she can examine Glumdalca's "beauty," with a very diminutive Tom Thumb standing by (Act II. sc. vii.). Austin Dobson points out that this frontispiece "constitutes the earliest reference to the friendship with the painter, of which so many traces are to be found in Fielding's works."

H. SCRIBLERUS SECUNDUS;

HIS PREFACE

THE town hath seldom been more divided in its opinion than concerning the merit of the following scenes. Whilst some publicly affirmed, That no author could produce so fine a piece but Mr. P[ope], others have with as much vehemence insisted, That no one could write anything so bad but Mr. F[ielding].

Nor can we wonder at this dissension about its merit, when the learned world have not unanimously decided even the very nature of this tragedy. For though most of the universities in Europe have honoured it with the name of *egregium et maximi pretii opus, Tragœdiis tam antiquis quàm novis longe anteponendum*; nay, Dr. B—— hath pronounced, *Citiùs Mœvii Æneadem quam Scribleri istius tragœdiam hanc crediderim, cujus autorem Senecam ipsum tradidisse haud dubitârim*"; and the great Professor Burman hath styled Tom Thumb, *Heroum omnium tragicorum facile principem*. Nay, though it hath, among other languages, been translated into Dutch, and celebrated with great applause at Amsterdam (where burlesque never came) by the title of *Mynheer Vander Thumb*, the burgomasters receiving it with that reverent and silent attention which becometh an audience at a deep tragedy: notwithstanding all this, there have not been wanting some who have represented these scenes in a ludicrous light; and Mr. D—— hath been heard to say, with some concern, That he wondered a tragical and Christian nation would permit a representation on its theatre, so visibly designed to ridicule and extirpate everything that is great and solemn among us.

This learned critic and his followers were led into so great an error by that surreptitious and piratical copy which stole last year into the world; with what injustice and prejudice to our author will be acknowledged, I hope, by everyone who shall happily peruse this genuine and original copy. Nor can I help remarking, to the great praise of our author, that however imperfect the former was, even that faint resemblance of the true *Tom Thumb* contained sufficient beauties to give it a run of upwards of forty nights to the politest audiences. But, notwithstanding that applause which it received from all the best judges, it was as severely censured by some few bad ones, and, I believe rather maliciously than ignorantly, reported to have been intended a burlesque on the loftiest parts of tragedy, and designed to banish what we generally call fine things from the stage.

Now, if I can set my country right in an affair of this import- ance, I shall lightly esteem any labour which it may cost. And this I the rather undertake, first, as it is indeed in some measure incumbent on me to vindicate myself from that surreptitious copy before mentioned, published by some ill-meaning people under my name: secondly, as knowing myself more capable of doing justice to our author than any other man, as I have given myself more pains to arrive at a thorough understanding of this little piece, having for ten years together read nothing else; in which time, I think I may modestly presume, with the help of my English dictionary, to comprehend all the meanings of every word in it.

But should any error of my pen awaken Clariss. Bentleium to enlighten the world with his annotations on our author, I shall not think that the least reward or happiness arising to me from these my endeavours.

I shall waive at present what hath caused such feuds in the learned world, whether this piece was originally written by Shakespeare, though certainly that, were it true, must add a considerable share to its merit; especially with such who are so generous as to buy and to commend what they never read, from an implicit faith in the author only: a faith which our age abounds in as much as it can be called deficient in any other.

Let it suffice, that *The Tragedy of Tragedies, or The Life and Death of Tom Thumb* was written in the reign of Queen Elizabeth. Nor can the objection made by Mr. D——, that the tragedy must then have been antecedent to the history, have any weight, when we consider, that though the *History of Tom Thumb*, printed by and for Edward M——r, at the Looking-Glass on London Bridge, be of a later date, still must we suppose this history to have been transcribed from some other, unless we suppose the writer thereof to be inspired: a gift very faintly contended for by the writers of our age. As to this history not bearing the stamp of second, third, or fourth edition, I see but little in that objection; editions being very uncertain lights to judge of books by: and perhaps Mr. M——r may have joined twenty editions in one, as Mr. C——l hath ere now divided one into twenty.

Nor doth the other argument, drawn from the little care our author hath taken to keep up to the letter of the history, carry any greater force. Are there not instances of plays wherein the history is so perverted, that we can know the heroes whom they celebrate by no other marks than their names: nay, do we not find the same character placed by different poets in such different lights, that we can discover not the least sameness or even likeness in the features? The Sophonisba of Mairet, and of Lee, is a tender, passionate, amorous mistress of Masinissa;

Corneille and Mr. Thomson give her no other passion but the love of her country, and make her as cool in her affection to Masinissa as to Syphax. In the two latter, she resembles the character of Queen Elizabeth; in the two former she is the picture of Mary Queen of Scotland. In short, the one Sophonisba is as different from the other as the Brutus of Voltaire is from the Marius Jun. of Otway; or as the Minerva is from the Venus of the Ancients.

Let us now proceed to a regular examination of the tragedy before us, in which I shall treat separately of the Fable, the Moral, the Characters, the Sentiments, and the Diction. And first of the *Fable*, which I take to be the most simple imaginable; and, to use the words of an eminent author, "One, regular, and uniform, not charged with a multiplicity of incidents, and yet affording several revolutions of fortune; by which the passions may be excited, varied, and driven to their full tumult of emotion." Nor is the action of this tragedy less great than uniform. The spring of all is the love of Tom Thumb for Huncamunca, which causeth the quarrel between their Majesties in the first act; the passion of Lord Grizzle in the second; the rebellion, fall of Lord Grizzle and Glumdalca, devouring of Tom Thumb by the cow, and that bloody catastrophe in the third.

Nor is the *Moral* of this excellent tragedy less noble than the *Fable*; it teaches these two instructive lessons, viz. That human happiness is exceeding transient, and, That death is the certain end of all men; the former whereof is inculcated by the fatal end of Tom Thumb; the latter by that of all the other personages.

The *Characters* are, I think, sufficiently described in the Dramatis Personæ; and I believe we shall find few plays where greater care is taken to maintain them throughout, and to preserve in every speech that characteristical mark which distinguishes them from each other, "But," says Mr. D——, "how well doth the character of Tom Thumb, whom we must call the hero of this tragedy, if it hath any hero, agree with the precepts of Aristotle, who defineth 'Tragedy' to be the imitation of a short, but perfect action, containing a just greatness in itself, etc. What greatness can be in a fellow whom history relateth to have been no higher than a span?" This gentleman seemeth to think, with Sergeant Kite, that the greatness of a man's soul is in proportion to that of his body, the contrary of which is affirmed by our English physiognominical writers. Besides, if I understand Aristotle right, he speaketh only of the greatness of the action, and not of the person.

As for the *Sentiments* and the *Diction*, which now only remain to be spoken to; I thought I could afford them no stronger justification than by producing parallel passages out of the best of our English writers. Whether this sameness of thought and expression, which I have quoted from them, proceeded from an agreement in their way of thinking, or whether they have borrowed from our author, I leave the reader to determine. I shall adventure to affirm this of the *Sentiments* of our author: that they are generally the most familiar which I have ever met with, and at the same time delivered with the highest dignity of phrase; which brings me to speak of his *Diction*. Here I shall only beg one postulatum, viz. That the greatest perfection of the language of a tragedy is, that it is not to be understood; which granted (as I think it must be) it will necessarily follow, that the only ways to avoid this is by being too high or too low for the understanding, which will comprehend everything within its reach. Those two extremities of style Mr. Dryden illustrates by the familiar image of two inns, which I shall term the Aerial and the Subterrestrial.

Horace goes farther, and showeth when it is proper to call at one of these inns, and when at the other:

> *Telephus & Peleus, cum pauper & exul uterque,*
> *Projicit Ampullas & sesquipedalia verba.*

That he approveth of the *sesquipedalia verba* is plain; for had not Telephus and Peleus used this sort of diction in prosperity. they could not have dropped it in adversity. The Aerial Inn, therefore (says Horace), is proper only to be frequedted dy princes and other great men, in the highest affluence of fortune; the Subterrestrial is appointed for the entertainment of the poorer sort of people only, whom Horace advises:

> —— *dolere sermone pedestri.*

The true meaning of both which citations is, that bombast is the proper language for joy, and doggerel for grief, the latter of which is literally implied in the *sermo pedestris*, as the former is in the *sesquipedalia verba*.

Cicero recommendeth the former of these. *Quid est tam furiosum vel tragicum quām verborum sonitus inanis, nullā subjectā sententia neque scientiā.*" What can be so proper for tragedy as a set of big-sounding words, so contrived together as to convey no meaning? which I shall one day or other prove to be the sublime of Longinus. Ovid declareth absolutely for the latter inn:

> *Omne genus scripti gravitate tragœdia vincit.*

Tragedy hath of all writings the greatest share in the Bathos, which is the profound of Scriblerus.

I shall not presume to determine which of these two styles be properer for tragedy. It sufficeth that our author excelleth in both. He is very rarely within sight through the whole play, either rising higher than the eye of your understanding can soar, or sinking lower than it careth to stoop. But here it may perhaps be observed, that I have given more frequent instances of authora who have imitated him in the sublime, than in the contrary. To which I answer, first, bombast being properly a redundancy of genius, instances of this nature occur in poets whose names do more honour to our author than the writers in the doggerel, which proceeds from a cool, calm, weighty way of thinking. Instances whereof are most frequently to be found in authors of a lower class. Secondly, that the works of such authors are difficultly found at all. Thirdly, that it is a very hard task to read them, in order to extract these flowers from them. And lastly, it is very often difficult to transplant them at all; they being like some flowers of a very nice nature, which will flourish in no soil but their own: for it is easy to transcribe a thought, but not the want of one. The *Earl of Essex*, for instance, is a little garden of choice rarities, whence you can scarce transplant one line so as to preserve its original beauty. This must account to the reader for his missing the names of several of his acquaintance, which he had certainly found here, had I ever read their works; for which, if I have not a just esteem, I can at least say with Cicero, *Quæ non contemno, quippè quæ nunquam legerim*. However, that the reader may meet with due satisfaction in this point, I have a young commentator from the university, who is reading over all the modern tragedies, at five shillings a dozen, and collecting all that they have stole from our author, which shall shortly be added as an appendix to this work.

DRAMATIS PERSONÆ

MEN

KING ARTHUR, a passionate sort of King, husband to Queen Dollallolla, of whom he stands a little in fear; father to Huncamunca, whom he is very fond of; and in love with Glumdalca . . . . Mr. Mullart

TOM THUMB THE GREAT, a little hero with a great soul, something violent in his temper, which is a little abated by his love for Huncamunca . . . . . Young Verhuyck

GHOST OF GAFFER THUMB, a whimsical sort of ghost . . . . Mr. Lacy

LORD GRIZZLE, extremely zealous for the liberty of the subject, very choleric in his temper, and in love with Huncamunca Mr. Jones

MERLIN, a conjurer, and in some sort father to Tom Thumb . . . . . Mr. Hallam

NOODLE } Courtiers in place, and consequently of that party that is
DOODLE } uppermost
{ Mr. Reynolds
{ Mr. Wathan

FOODLE, a Courtier that is out of place, and consequently of that party that is undermost . . . . Mr. Ayres

BAILIFF, } and } Of the party of the Plaintiff
FOLLOWER }
{ Mr. Peterson
{ Mr. Hicks

PARSON, of the side of the Church . . Mr. Watson

WOMEN

QUEEN DOLLALLOLLA, wife to King Arthur,
and mother to Huncamunca, a woman
entirely faultless, saving that she is a little
given to drink; a little too much a virago
towards her husband, and in love with
Tom Thumb　.　　.　　.　　.　　.　　Mrs. Mullart

THE PRINCESS HUNCAMUNCA, daughter to
their Majesties King Arthur and Queen
Dollallolla, of a very sweet, gentle, and
amorous disposition, equally in love with
Lord Grizzle and Tom Thumb, and
desirous to be married to them both　.　Mrs. Jones

GLUMDALCA, of the Giants, a captive queen,
beloved by the King, but in love with
Tom Thumb　.　　.　　.　　.　　.　　Mrs. Dove

CLEORA　　⎫　Maids of Honour, in　⎧　Noodle
MUSTACHA　⎭　　　love with　　　⎩　Doodle

Courtiers, Guards, Rebels, Drums, Trumpets, Thunder and
Lightning.

SCENE.—The Court of King Arthur, and a plain thereabouts.

TOM THUMB THE GREAT

ACT I. SCENE I

Scene—The Palace

DOODLE, NOODLE

Doodle. Sure such a day as this was never seen!
The sun himself, on this auspicious day,
Shines like a beau in a new birthday suit:
This down the seams embroidered, that the beams.
All nature wears one universal grin.[1]
Noodle. This day, O Mr. Doodle, is a day
Indeed!——; A day we never saw before.[2]
The mighty Thomas Thumb[3] victorious comes;

[1] Corneille recommends some very remarkable day wherein to fix the action of a tragedy. This the best of our tragical writers have understood to mean a day remarkable for the serenity of the sky, or what we generally call a fine summer's day. So that, according to this their exposition, the same months are proper for tragedy which are proper for pastoral. Most of our celebrated English tragedies, as *Cato, Mariamne, Tamerlane*, etc., begin with their observations on the morning. Lee seems to have come the nearest to this beautiful description of our author's:

> *The morning dawns with an unwonted crimson,*
> *The flowers all odorous seem, the garden birds*
> *Sing louder, and the laughing sun ascends*
> *The gaudy earth with an unusual brightness,*
> *All nature smiles.*   Cæs. Borg.

Masinissa in the new *Sophonisba* is also a favourite of the sun:

> ——*The sun too seems*
> *As conscious of my joy, with broader eye*
> *To look abroad the world, and all things smile*
> *Like Sophonisba.*

Memnon in the *Persian Princess* makes the sun decline rising, that he may not peep on objects which would profane his brightness.

> ——*The morning rises slow,*
> *And all those ruddy streaks that us'd to paint*
> *The day's approach are lost in clouds, as if*
> *The horrors of the night had sent 'em back,*
> *To warn the sun he should not leave the sea,*
> *To peep,* etc.

[2] This line is highly conformable to the beautiful simplicity of the ancients. It hath been copied by almost every modern:

Not to be is not to be in woe.	State of Innocence.
Love is not sin but where 'tis sinful love.	Don Sebastian.
Nature is nature, Lælius.	Sophonisba.
Men are but men, we did not make ourselves.	Revenge.

[3] Dr. B—y reads: "The mighty Tall-mast Thumb." Mr. D—s: "The mighty thumping Thumb." Mr. T—d reads: "Thundering." I think "Thomas" more agreeable to the great simplicity so apparent in our author.

Millions of giants crowd his chariot wheels,
Giants [1] to whom the giants in Guildhall
Are infant dwarfs. They frown, and foam, and roar,
While Thumb, regardless of their noise, rides on.
So some cock-sparrow, in a farmer's yard,
Hops at the head of an huge flock of turkeys.
    Doodle. When Goody Thumb first brought this Thomas forth,
The genius of our land triumphant reigned;
Then, then, O Arthur! did thy genius reign.
    Noodle. They tell me it is whispered in the books [2]
Of all our sages, that this mighty hero,
By Merlin's art begot, hath not a bone
Within his skin, but is a lump of gristle.
    Doodle. Then 'tis a gristle of no mortal kind;
Some god, my Noodle, stept into the place
Of Gaffer Thumb, and more than half begot

---

[1] That learned historian Mr. S—n, in the third number of his criticism on our author, takes great pains to explode this passage. "It is," says he, "difficult to guess what Giants are here meant, unless the Giant Despair in the *Pilgrim's Progress*, or the Giant Greatness in the *Royal Villain*; for I have heard of no other sort of giants in the reign of King Arthur." Petrus Burmanus makes three Tom Thumbs, one whereof he supposes to have been the same person whom the Greeks called Hercules, and that by these giants are to be understood the centaurs slain by that hero. Another Tom Thumb he contends to have been no other than the Hermes Trismegistus of the ancients. The third Tom Thumb he places under the reign of King Arthur, to which third Tom Thumb, says he, the actions of the other two were attributed. Now, tho' I know that this opinion is supported by an assertion of Justus Lipsius, *Thomam illum Thumbum non alium quàm Herculem fuisse satis constat*, yet shall I venture to oppose one line of Mr. Midwinter against them all:

    In Arthur's Court Tom Thumb did live.

"But then," says Dr. B—y, "if we place Tom Thumb in the Court of King Arthur it will be proper to place that Court out of Britain, where no giants were ever heard of." Spenser, in his *Faërie Queene*, is of another opinion, where describing Albion he says:

    ——*Far within, a savage nation dwelt*
    Of hideous giants.

And in the same canto:

    Then Elfar; who two brethren giants had,
    The one of which had two heads—
    The other three.

Risum teneatis, Amici.

[2] "To whisper in books," says Mr. D—s, "is arrant nonsense." I am afraid this learned man does not sufficiently understand the extensive meaning of the word *whisper*. If he had rightly understood what is meant by the "senses whisp'ring the soul" in the *Persian Princess*, or what "whisp'ring like winds" is in *Aurengzebe*, or like thunder in another author, he would have understood this. Emmeline in Dryden sees a voice, but she was born blind, which is an excuse Panthea cannot plead in *Cyrus*, who hears a sight:

    ——*Your description will surpass*
    All fiction, painting, or dumb show of horror,
    That ever ears yet heard, or eyes beheld.

When Mr. D—s understands these he will understand whispering in books.

This mighty Tom.[1]

 Noodle.   Sure he was sent express
From Heaven to be the pillar of our State.[2]
Though small his body be, so very small
A chairman's leg is more than twice as large,
Yet is his soul like any mountain big,
And as a mountain once brought forth a mouse,
So doth this mouse contain a mighty mountain.[3]

 Doodle. Mountain indeed! So terrible his name,
The giant nurses frighten children with it,[4]
And cry Tom Thumb is come, and if you are
Naughty will surely take the child away.

 Noodle. But hark! these trumpets speak the King's approach.[5]

 Doodle. He comes most luckily for my petition.

             (*Flourish.*

SCENE II

KING, QUEEN, GRIZZLE, NOODLE, DOODLE, FOODLE

 King. Let nothing but a face of joy appear;[6]
The man who frowns this day shall lose his head,
That he may have no face to frown withal.
Smile, Dollallolla—Ha! what wrinkled sorrow

  1   *Some ruffian stepped into his father's place,*
      And more than half begot him.
             Mary Queen of Scots.

  2   *For Ulamar seems sent express from heaven,*
      To civilise this rugged Indian clime.
              Liberty Asserted.

 [3] *Omne majus continet in se minus, sed minus non in se majus continere potest,*" says Scaliger in *Thumbo.*—I suppose he would have cavilled at these beautiful lines in the *Earl of Essex*:

      ————*Thy most inveterate soul,*
      That looks through the foul prison of thy body.

And at those of Dryden:

      The palace is without too well design'd,
      Conduct me in, for I will view thy mind.
              Aurengzebe.

 [4] Mr. Banks has copied this almost verbatim:

      It was enough to say, here's Essex come,
      And nurses stilled their children with the fright.
             Earl of Essex.

 [5] The Trumpet in a tragedy is generally as much as to say " Enter King," which makes Mr. Banks in one of his plays call it the " trumpet's formal sound."

 [6] Phraortes in the *Captives* seems to have been acquainted with King Arthur.

      Proclaim a festival for seven days' space,
      Let the Court shine in all its pomp and lustre,
      Let all our streets resound with shouts of joy ;
      Let music's care-dispelling voice be heard ;
      The sumptuous banquet and the flowing goblet
      Shall warm the cheek, and fill the heart with gladness.
      Astarbe shall sit mistress of the feast.

Hangs, sits, lies, frowns upon thy knitted brow? [1]
Whence flow those tears fast down thy blubbered cheeks,
Like a swoll'n gutter, gushing through the streets?
  Queen. Excess of joy, my lord, I've heard folks say,
Gives tears as certain as excess of grief. [2]
  King. If it be so, let all men cry for joy,
Till my whole Court be drownèd with their tears;
Nay, till they overflow my utmost land,
And leave me nothing but the sea to rule. [3]
  Doodle. My liege, I a petition have here got.
  King. Petition me no petitions, sir, to-day;
Let other hours be set apart for business.
To-day it is our pleasure to be drunk, [4]

1   *Repentance frowns on thy contracted brow.*   Sophonisba.
     Hung on his clouded brow, I mark'd despair.   Ibid.
     ——*A sullen gloom*
    Scowls on his brow.   Busiris.
[2] Plato is of this opinion, and so is Mr. Banks:
    Behold these tears sprung from fresh pain and joy.
                    Earl of Essex.
[3] These floods are very frequent in the tragic authors:
    Near to some murmuring brook I'll lay me down,
    Whose waters, if they should too shallow flow,
    My tears shall swell them up till I will drown.
                  Lee's Sophonisba.

    Pouring forth tears at such a lavish rate,
    That were the world on fire they might have drowned
    The wrath of Heaven, and quenched the mighty ruin.
                  Mithridates.
One author changes the waters of grief to those of joy:
    ——*These tears, that sprung from tides of grief,*
    Are now augmented to a flood of joy.
                  Cyrus the Great.
Another:
    Turns all the streams of hate, and makes them flow
    In pity's channel.   Royal Villain.
One drowns himself:
    ——*Pity like a torrent pours me down,*
    Now I am drowning all within a deluge.
                  Anna Bullen.
Cyrus drowns the whole world:
    Our swelling grief
    Shall melt into a deluge, and the world
    Shall drown in tears.
                  Cyrus the Great.
[4] ""An expression vastly beneath the dignity of tragedy," says
Mr. D——s, yet we find the word he cavils at in the mouth of Mithridates
less properly used, and applied to a more terrible idea:
    I would be drunk with death.   Mithridates.
The author of the new *Sophonisba* taketh hold of this monosyllable
and uses it pretty much to the same purpose:
    The Carthaginian sword with Roman blood
    Was drunk.
I would ask Mr. D——s, which gives him the best idea, a drunken king,
or a drunken sword?
  Mr. Tate dresses up King Arthur's resolution in heroics:
    Merry, my lord, o' th' captain's humour right,
    I am resolved to be dead drunk to-night.
  Lee also uses this charming word:
    Love's the drunkenness of the mind.
                  Gloriana.

And this our Queen shall be as drunk as we.
    Queen. (Though I already half seas over am) [1]
If the capacious goblet overflow
With arrack-punch—'fore George! I'll see it out;
Of rum and brandy I'll not taste a drop.
    King. Though rack, in punch, eight shillings be a quart,
And rum and brandy be no more than six,
Rather than quarrel you shall have your will.   (*Trumpets.*
But, ha! the warrior comes; the Great Tom Thumb,
The little hero, giant-killing boy,
Preserver of my kingdom, is arrived.

SCENE III

    TOM THUMB, *to them with Officers, Prisoners, and Attendants*

    King. Oh! welcome most, most welcome [2] to my arms.
What gratitude can thank away the debt
Your valour lays upon me?
    Queen.   —— Oh! ye gods! [3]   (*Aside.*
    Thumb. When I'm not thanked at all I'm thanked enough,
I've done my duty, and I've done no more. [4]
    Queen. Was ever such a godlike creature seen!   (*Aside.*
    King. Thy modesty's a candle to thy merit, [5]
It shines itself, and shows thy merit too.
But say, my boy, where didst thou leave the giants?
    Thumb. My liege, without the castle gates they stand,
The castle gates too low for their admittance.
    King. What look they like?
    Thumb.   Like nothing but themselves.
    Queen. And sure thou art like nothing but thyself. [6]   (*Aside.*
    King. Enough! the vast idea fills my soul.
I see them, yes, I see them now before me:
The monstrous, ugly, barb'rous sons of whores.
But, ha! what form majestic strikes our eyes?
So perfect, that it seems to have been drawn
By all the gods in council: so fair she is,

---

[1] Dryden has borrowed this, and applied it improperly:
    I'm half seas o'er in death.   Cleomenes.
[2] This figure is in great use among the tragedians:
    'Tis therefore, therefore 'tis.   Victim.
    I long, repent, repent and long again.   Busiris.
[3] A tragical exclamation.
[4] This line is copied verbatim in the *Captives*.
[5] We find a candlestick for this candle in two celebrated authors:
    ——*Each star withdraws*
    His golden head, and burns within the socket.
                              Nero.
    A soul grown old and sunk into the socket.
                              Sebastian.

[6] This simile occurs very frequently among the dramatic writers of
both kinds.

That surely at her birth the council paused,
And then at length cried out, This is a woman![1]
   Thumb. Then were the gods mistaken. She is not
A woman, but a giantess whom we,
With much ado, have made a shift to haul[2]
Within the town; for she is by a foot
Shorter than all her subject giants were.[3]
   Glum. We yesterday were both a queen and wife,[3]
One hundred thousand giants owned our sway,
Twenty whereof were married to ourself.
   Queen. Oh! happy state of giantism—where husbands
Like mushrooms grow, whilst hapless we are forced
To be content, nay, happy thought with one.
   Glum. But then to lose them all in one black day!
That the same sun which, rising, saw me wife
To twenty giants, setting, should behold
Me widowed of them all! My worn out heart,
That ship, leaks fast, and the great heavy lading,
My soul, will quickly sink.[4]
   Queen.   Madam, believe
I view your sorrows with a woman's eye;
But learn to bear them with what strength you may,
To-morrow we will have our grenadiers
Drawn out before you, and you then shall choose
What husbands you think fit.

---

[1] Mr. Lee hath stolen this thought from our author:

> ——*This perfect face, drawn by the gods in council,*
> *Which they were long a-making.*   Lu. Jun. Brut.

> ——*At his birth the heavenly council paused,*
> *And then at last cry'd out, "This is a man!"*

Dryden hath improved this hint to the utmost perfection:

> *So perfect that the very gods, who formed you, wondered*
> *At their own skill, and cried, "A lucky hit*
> *Has mended our design!" Their envy hindered,*
> *Or you had been immortal, and a pattern,*
> *When heaven would work for ostentation sake,*
> *To copy out again.*   All for Love.

Banks prefers the works of Michael Angelo to that of the gods:

> *A pattern for the gods to make a man by,*
> *Or Michael Angelo to form a statue.*

[2] "It is impossible," says Mr. W——, "sufficiently to admire this natural easy line."

[3] This tragedy, which in most points resembles the ancients, differs from them in this, that it assigns the same honour to lowness of stature which they did to height. The gods and heroes in Homer and Virgil are continually described higher by the head than their followers, the contrary of which is observed by our author. In short to exceed on either side is equally admirable, and a man of three foot is as wonderful a sight as a man of nine.

[4]
> *My blood leaks fast, and the great heavy lading*
> *My soul will quickly sink.*   Mithridates.

> *My soul is like a ship.*   Injured Love.

Glum.   Madam, I am
Your most obedient, and most humble servant.[1]
   King. Think, mighty Princess, think this Court your own,
Nor think the landlord me, this house my inn;
Call for whate'er you will, you'll nothing pay.
I feel a sudden pain within my breast,
Nor know I whether it arise from love,
Or only the wind-colic.[2] Time must show.
O Thumb! what do we to thy valour owe?
Ask some reward, great as we can bestow.
   Thumb. I ask not kingdoms, I can conquer those,
I ask not money, money I've enough;
For what I've done, and what I mean to do,
For giants slain, and giants yet unborn,
Which I will slay—if this be called a debt,
Take my receipt in full—I ask but this,[3]
To sun myself in Huncamunca's eyes.[4]
   King. Prodigious bold request! }
   Queen. Be still, my soul![5]   (*Aside.*
   Thumb. My heart is at the threshold of your mouth,
And waits its answer there. Oh! do not frown;
I've tried, to reason's tune, to tune my soul,
But love did overwind and crack the string,
Though Jove in thunder had cried out, You shan't,
I should have loved her still—for oh, strange fate,
Then when I loved her least I loved her most![6]

---

[1] This well-bred line seems to be copied in the *Persian Princess*:

> *To be your humblest, and most faithful slave.*

[2] This doubt of the king puts me in mind of a passage in the *Captives*,
where the noise of feet is mistaken for the rustling of leaves:

> ——*Methinks I hear*
> *The sound of feet ;*
> *No, 'twas the wind that shook yon cypress boughs.*

[3] Mr. Dryden seems to have had this passage in his eye in the first
page of *Love Triumphant*.
[4] Don Carlos in the *Revenge* suns himself in the charms of his mistress:

> *While in the lustre of her charms I lay.*

[5] A tragical phrase much in use.
[6] This speech hath been taken to pieces by several tragical authors,
who seem to have rifled it and shared its beauties among them.

> *My soul waits at the portal of thy breast,*
> *To ravish from thy lips the welcome news.*
>   Anna Bullen.
> *My soul stands list'ning at my ears.*
>   Cyrus the Great.
> *Love to his tune my jarring heart would bring,*
> *But reason overwinds and cracks the string.*
>   Duke of Guise.
> ——*I should have loved,*
> *Though Jove in muttering thunder had forbid it.*
>   New Sophonisba.
> *And when it (my heart) wild resolves to love no more,*
> *Then is the triumph of excessive love.*   Ibidem.

King. It is resolved—the Princess is your own.

Thumb. Oh! happy, happy, happy, happy Thumb.[1]

Queen. Consider, sir, reward your soldier's merit,
But give not Huncamunca to Tom Thumb.

King. Tom Thumb! Odzooks, my wide-extended realm
Knows not a name so glorious as Tom Thumb.
Let Macedonia, Alexander boast,
Let Rome her Cæsars and her Scipios show,
Her Messieurs France, let Holland boast Mynheers,
Ireland her O's, her Macs let Scotland boast,
Let England boast no other than Tom Thumb.

Queen. Though greater yet his boasted merit was,
He shall not have my daughter, that is pos'.

King. Ha! sayst thou, Dollallolla?

Queen.   I say he shan't.

King. Then by our royal self we swear you lie.[2]

Queen. Who but a dog, who but a dog[3]
Would use me as thou dost? Me, who have lain
These twenty years so loving by thy side![4]
But I will be revenged. I'll hang myself,
Then tremble all who did this match persuade,
For riding on a cat from high I'll fall,
And squirt down royal vengeance on you all.[5]

Foodle. Her Majesty the Queen is in a passion.[6]

King. Be she or be she not[7]—I'll to the girl
And pave thy way, O Thumb. Now, by ourself,
We were indeed a pretty king of clouts
To truckle to her will. For when by force
Or art the wife her husband overreaches,
Give him the petticoat, and her the breeches.

Thumb. Whisper, ye winds, that Huncamunca's mine!
Echoes repeat, that Huncamunca's mine!

---

[1] Masinissa is one-fourth less happy than Tom Thumb:
　　　Oh! happy, happy, happy.
　　　　　　　　　　　　　　New Sophonisba.

[2]　　　　　　*No by myself.*　　　　　　Anna Bullen.

[3]　　　　　　　　——*Who caused*
　　This dreadful revolution in my fate?
　　Ulamar. *Who but a dog, who but a dog?*
　　　　　　　　　　　　　　Liberty Asserted.

[4]　　　　　　　——*A bride*
　　Who twenty years lay loving by your side.
　　　　　　　　　　　　　　Banks.

[5]　　*For borne upon a cloud from high I'll fall,*
　　And rain down royal vengeance on you all.
　　　　　　　　　　　　　　Albion Queens.

[6] An information very like this we have in the *Tragedy of Love*,
where Cyrus having stormed in the most violent manner, Cyaxares
observes very calmly:
　　Why, nephew Cyrus—you are moved.

[7]　　　　*'Tis in your choice.*
　　Love me, or love me not.
　　　　　　　　　　　　　　Conquest of Granada.

The dreadful business of the war is o'er,
And beauty, heavenly beauty! crowns my toils;
I've thrown the bloody garment now aside,
And Hymeneal sweets invite my bride.
 So when some chimney-sweeper, all the day,
Hath through dark paths pursued the sooty way,
At night, to wash his hands and face he flies,
And in his t'other shirt with his Brickdusta lies.[1]

SCENE IV

Grizzle, *solus*

Where art thou, Grizzle! where are now thy glories?
Where are the drums that wakened thee to honour?
Greatness is a laced coat from Monmouth Street,
Which fortune lends us for a day to wear,
To-morrow puts it on another's back.
The spiteful sun but yesterday surveyed
His rival high as Saint Paul's cupola;
Now may he see me as Fleet Ditch laid low.[2]

SCENE V

Queen, Grizzle

 Queen. Teach me to scold, prodigious-minded Grizzle,
Mountain of treason, ugly as the devil,
Teach this confounded hateful mouth of mine
To spout forth words malicious as thyself,
Words which might shame all Billingsgate to speak.[3]
 Grizzle. Far be it from my pride to think my tongue
Your royal lips can in that art instruct,
Wherein you so excel. But may I ask,
Without offence, wherefore my queen would scold?
 Queen. Wherefore? Oh! Blood and thunder! han't thou heard
(What ev'ry corner of the Court resounds)
That little Thumb will be a great man made?
 Grizzle. I heard it, I confess—for who, alas!
Can always stop his ears?[4]—but would my teeth,
By grinding knives, had first been set on edge.

---

[1] There is not one beauty in this charming speech but hath been borrowed by almost every tragic writer.

[2] Mr. Banks has (I wish I could not say too servilely) imitated this of Grizzle in his *Earl of Essex*:

  Where art thou, Essex, etc.

[3] The Countess of Nottingham in the *Earl of Essex* is apparently acquainted with Dollallolla.

[4] Grizzle was not probably possessed of that glue of which Mr. Banks speaks in his *Cyrus*:

  I'll glue my ears to every word.

Queen. Would I had heard, at the still noon of night,
The hallaloo of fire in every street!
Odsbobs! I have a mind to hang myself,
To think I should a grandmother be made
By such a rascal. Sure the King forgets,
When in a pudding, by his mother put,
The bastard, by a tinker, on a stile
Was dropped.—O good Lord Grizzle! can I bear
To see him from a pudding mount the throne?
Or can, oh can! my Huncamunca bear
To take a pudding's offspring to her arms?

Grizzle. Oh Horror! Horror! Horror! Cease, my Queen,
Thy voice, like twenty screech-owls, wracks my brain.[1]

Queen. Then rouse thy spirit—we may yet prevent
This hated match.

Grizzle.   We will; not Fate itself,[2]
Should it conspire with Thomas Thumb, should cause it.
I'll swim through seas; I'll ride upon the clouds;
I'll dig the earth; I'll blow out ev'ry fire;
I'll rave; I'll rant; I'll rise; I'll rush; I'll roar;
Fierce as the man whom smiling[3] dolphins bore
From the prosaic to the poetic shore.
I'll tear the scoundrel into twenty pieces.

Queen. Oh, no! prevent the match, but hurt him not;
For, though I would not have him have my daughter,
Yet can we kill the man that killed the giants?

Grizzle. I tell you, madam, it was all a trick.
He made the giants first, and then he killed them;
As fox-hunters bring foxes to the wood,
And then with hounds they drive them out again.

Queen. How! have you seen no giants? Are there not
Now, in the yard, ten thousand proper giants?

Grizzle. Indeed I cannot positively tell,
But firmly do believe there is not one.[4]

---

[1]   *Screech-owls, dark ravens and amphibious monsters*
        Are screaming in that voice.   Mary Queen of Scots.

[2] The reader may see all the beauties of this speech in a late ode called the *Naval Lyric.*

[3] This epithet to a dolphin doth not give one so clear an idea as were to be wished, a smiling fish seeming a little more difficult to be imagined than a flying fish. Mr. Dryden is of opinion, that smiling is the property of reason, and that no irrational creature can smile.

          Smiles not allowed to beasts from reason move.
                              State of Innocence.

[4] These lines are written in the same key with those in the *Earl of Essex:*

          Why sayest thou so? I love thee well, indeed
          I do, and thou shalt find by this, 'tis true.

Or with this in *Cyrus:*

          The most heroic mind that ever was.

And with above half of the modern tragedies.

Queen. Hence! from my sight! thou traitor, hie away!
By all my stars! thou enviest Tom Thumb.
Go, sirrah! go, hie away! hie!—thou art
A setting dog. Begone! [1]
   Grizzle.   Madam, I go.
Tom Thumb shall feel the vengeance you have raised:
So, when two dogs are fighting in the streets,
With a third dog, one of the two dogs meets,
With angry teeth he bites him to the bone,
And this dog smarts for what that dog had done.

SCENE VI

QUEEN, *sola*

And whither shall I go?—Alack-a-day!
I love Tom Thumb—but must not tell him so;
For what's a woman when her virtue's gone?
A coat without its lace; wig out of buckle;
A stocking with a hole in't. I can't live
Without my virtue, or without Tom Thumb.
Then let me weigh them in two equal scales, [2]
In this scale put my virtue, that, Tom Thumb.
Alas! Tom Thumb is heavier than my virtue.
But hold!—perhaps I may be left a widow:
This match prevented, then Tom Thumb is mine:
In that dear hope I will forget my pain,
   So, when some wench to Tothill-Bridewell's sent,
With beating hemp and flogging she's content;
She hopes in time to ease her present pain,
At length is free, and walks the streets again.

---

[1] Aristotle in that excellent work of his, which is very justly styled his masterpiece, earnestly recommends using the terms of art, however coarse or even indecent they may be. Mr. Tate is of the same opinion.

> Bru. *Do not, like young hawks, fetch a course about,*
> *Your game flies fair.*
> Fra. *Do not fear it.*
> *He answers you in your own hawking phrase.*
>
>   Injured Love.

I think these two great authorities are sufficient to justify Dollallolla in the use of the phrase, "Hie away! hie!" when in the same line she says she is speaking to a setting dog.

[2] We meet with such another pair of scales in Dryden's *King Arthur*:

> *Arthur and Oswald, and their different fates*
> *Are weighing now within the scales of Heaven.*

Also in *Sebastian*:

> *This hour my lot is weighing in the scales.*

ACT II. SCENE I

Scene—The Street

BAILIFF, FOLLOWER

Bailiff. Come on, my trusty Follower, come on,
This day discharge thy duty, and at night
A double mug of beer and beer shall glad thee.
Stand here by me, this way must Noodle pass.
    Follower. No more, no more, O Bailiff! every word
Inspires my soul with virtue. Oh! I long
To meet the enemy in the street—and nab him:
To lay arresting hands upon his back,
And drag him trembling to the sponging-house.
    Bailiff. There, when I have him, I will sponge upon him.
O glorious thought! by the sun, moon and stars,
I will enjoy it, though it be in thought!
Yes, yes, my Follower, I will enjoy it.[1]
    Follower. Enjoy it then some other time, for now
Our prey approaches.
    Bailiff.   Let us retire.

SCENE II

TOM THUMB, NOODLE, BAILIFF, FOLLOWER

Thumb. Trust me, my Noodle, I am wondrous sick;
For though I love the gentle Huncamunca,
Yet at the thought of marriage I grow pale;
For oh!—but swear thou'lt keep it ever secret,[2]
I will unfold a tale will make thee stare.
    Noodle. I swear by lovely Huncamunca's charms.
    Thumb. Then know—my grandmamma hath often said,
Tom Thumb, beware of marriage.[3]
    Noodle.   Sir, I blush
To think a warrior, great in arms as you,
Should be affrighted by his grandmamma;

---

[1] Mr. Rowe is generally imagined to have taken some hints from
this scene in his character of Bajazet; but as he, of all the tragic writers,
bears the least resemblance to our author in his diction, I am unwilling
to imagine he would condescend to copy him in this particular.
[2] This method of surprising an audience by raising their expectation
to the highest pitch, and then balking it, hath been practised with
great success by most of our tragical authors.
[3] Almeyda in *Sebastian* is in the same distress:

> *Sometimes methinks I hear the groan of ghosts,*
> *Thin hollow sounds and lamentable screams ;*
> *Then, like a dying echo from afar,*
> *My mother's voice that cries : Wed not, Almeyda !*
> *Forewarned, Almeyda, marriage is thy crime.*

Can an old woman's empty dreams deter
The blooming hero from the virgin's arms?
Think of the joy that will your soul alarm,
When in her fond embraces clasped you lie,
While on her panting breast dissolved in bliss,
You pour out all Tom Thumb in every kiss.

Thumb. O Noodle, thou hast fired my eager soul;
Spite of my grandmother she shall be mine;
I'll hug, caress, I'll eat her up with love:
Whole days, and nights, and years shall be too short
For our enjoyment; every sun shall rise
Blushing, to see us in our bed together.[1]

Noodle. Oh, sir! this purpose of your soul pursue.
Bailiff. Oh, sir! I have an action against you.
Noodle. At whose suit is it?
Bailiff.   At your tailor's, sir.
Your tailor put this warrant in my hands,
And I arrest you, sir, at his commands.

Thumb. Ha! dogs! Arrest my friend before my face!
Think you Tom Thumb will suffer this disgrace!
But let vain cowards threaten by their word,
Tom Thumb shall show his anger by his sword.
                    (*Kills the* BAILIFF *and his* FOLLOWER.

Bailiff. Oh, I am slain!
Follower.   I am murdered also,
And to the shades, the dismal shades below,
My Bailiff's faithful Follower I go.

Noodle. Go then to Hell like rascals as you are,
And give our service to the bailiffs there.[2]

Thumb. Thus perish all the bailiffs in the land,
Till debtors at noonday shall walk the streets,
And no one fear a bailiff or his writ.

---

[1] "As very well he may if he hath any modesty in him," says
Mr. D——s. The author of *Busiris* is extremely zealous to prevent the
sun's blushing at any indecent object; and therefore on all such
occasions he addresses himself to the sun, and desires him to keep out
of the way:

> *Rise never more, O sun! let night prevail,*
> *Eternal darkness close the world's wide scene.*
>   Busiris.

> *Sun, hide thy face, and put the world in mourning.*
>   Ibid.

Mr. Banks makes the sun perform the office of Hymen; and therefore
not likely to be disgusted at such a sight:

> *The sun sets forth like a gay brideman with you.*
>   Mary Queen of Scots.

[2] Neurmahal sends the same message to Heaven:

> *For I would have you, when you upwards move,*
> *Speak kindly of us to our friends above.*
>   Aurengzebe.

We find another to Hell in the *Persian Princess*:

> *Villain, get thee down*
> *To Hell, and tell them that the fray's begun.*

SCENE III.—*The Princess Huncamunca's Apartment.*

HUNCAMUNCA, CLEORA, MUSTACHA

Hunc. Give me some music—see that it be sad.[1]

CLEORA *sings.*

Cupid, ease a love-sick maid,
Bring thy quiver to her aid ;
With equal ardour wound the swain :
Beauty should never sigh in vain.

II

Let him feel the pleasing smart,
Drive thy arrow through his heart ;
When one you wound, you then destroy ;
When both you kill, you kill with joy.

Hunc. Oh, Tom Thumb! Tom Thumb! wherefore art thou Tom Thumb ?[2]
Why hadst thou not been born of royal race?
Why had not mighty Bantam been thy father?
Or else the King of Brentford, Old or New?
Must. I am surprised that your Highness can give yourself a moment's uneasiness about that little insignificant fellow, Tom Thumb the Great [3]—one properer for a plaything than a husband. Were he my husband his horns should be as long as his body. If you had fallen in love with a grenadier, I should not have wondered at it—if you had fallen in love with something; but to fall in love with nothing!
Hunc. Cease, my Mustacha, on thy duty cease.
The zephyr, when in flowery vales it plays,
Is not so soft, so sweet as Thummy's breath.
The dove is not so gentle to its mate.
Must. The dove is every bit as proper for a husband. Alas! madam, there's not a beau about the Court looks so little like a man. He is a perfect butterfly, a thing without substance, and almost without shadow too.
Hunc. This rudeness is unseasonable; desist
Or I shall think this railing comes from love.
Tom Thumb's a creature of that charming form
That no one can abuse, unless they love him.
Must. Madam, the King.

---

[1] Anthony gives the same command in the same words.

[2]   *Oh! Marius, Marius ; wherefore art thou Marius ?*
                                                  Otway's Marius.
[3] Nothing is more common than these seeming contradictions, such as:

Haughty Weakness.   Victim.
Great small world.   Noah's Flood.

SCENE IV

KING, HUNCAMUNCA

King. Let all but Huncamunca leave the room.

                    (*Exeunt* CLEORA *and* MUSTACHA.

Daughter, I have observed of late some grief
Unusual in your countenance—your eyes,
That, like two open windows,[1] used to show
The lovely beauty of the rooms within,
Have now two blinds before them. What is the cause?
Say, have you not enough of meat and drink?
We've given strict orders not to have you stinted.

    Hunc. Alas! my lord, I value not myself,
That once I eat two fowls and half a pig;
Small is that praise: but oh! a maid may want
What she can neither eat nor drink.[2]

    King.   What's that?

    Hunc. Oh! spare my blushes; but I mean a husband.[3]

    King. If that be all, I have provided one,
A husband great in arms, whose warlike sword

---

[1] Lee hath improved this metaphor:

> *Dost thou not view joy peeping from my eyes,*
> *The casements opened wide to gaze on thee?*
> *So Rome's glad citizens to windows rise,*
> *When they some young triumpher fain would see.*
>   Gloriana.

[2] Almahide hath the same contempt for these appetites:

> *To eat and drink can no perfection be.*
>   Conquest of Granada.

The Earl of Essex is of a different opinion, and seems to place the chief happiness of a general therein:

> *Were but commanders half so well rewarded,*
> *Then they might eat.*   Banks's Earl of Essex.

But if we may believe one, who knows more than either, the devil himself, we shall find eating to be an affair of more moment than is generally imagined.

> *Gods are immortal only by their food.*
>   Lucifer in the State of Innocence.

[3] This expression is enough of itself (says Mr. D——s) utterly to destroy the character of Huncamunca; yet we find a woman of no abandoned character in Dryden adventuring farther, and thus excusing herself:

> *To speak our wishes first, forbid it pride.*
> *Forbid it modesty. True, they forbid it,*
> *But nature does not. When we are athirst,*
> *Or hungry, will imperious nature stay,*
> *Nor eat, nor drink, before 'tis bid fall on.*
>   Cleomenes.

Cassandra speaks before she is asked, Huncamunca afterwards. Cassandra speaks her wishes to her lover, Huncamunca only to her father

Streams with the yellow blood of slaughtered giants.
Whose name in Terrâ Incognitâ is known,
Whose valour, wisdom, virtue make a noise
Great as the kettle-drums of twenty armies.
 Hunc. Whom does my royal father mean?
 King.   Tom Thumb.
 Hunc. Is it possible?
 King.   Ha! the window-blinds are gone,
A country-dance of joy is in your face,
Your eyes spit fire, your cheeks grow red as beef.[1]
 Hunc. Oh! there's a magic music in that sound,
Enough to turn me into beef indeed.
Yes, I will own, since licensed by your word,
I'll own Tom Thumb the cause of all my grief.
For him I've sighed, I've wept, I've gnawed my sheets.
 King. Oh! thou shalt gnaw thy tender sheets no more,
A husband thou shalt have to mumble now.
 Hunc. Oh! happy sound! henceforth let no one tell
That Huncamunca shall lead apes in hell.
Oh! I am overjoyed!
 King.   I see thou art.
Joy lightens in thy eyes, and thunders from thy brows;
Transports, like lightning, dart along thy soul,[2]
As small-shot through a hedge.
 Hunc.   Oh! say not small.
 King. This happy news shall on our tongue ride post,
Ourself will bear the happy news to Thumb.
Yet think not, daughter, that your powerful charms
Must still detain the hero from his arms;
Various his duty, various his delight;
Now is his turn to kiss, and now to fight;
And now to kiss again. So mighty Jove,
When with excessive thund'ring tired above,
Comes down to earth, and takes a bit — and then
Flies to his trade of thund'ring back again.[3]

[1]
  Her eyes resistless magic bear,
  Angels I see, and gods are dancing there.
            Lee's Sophonisba.

[2] Mr. Dennis, in that excellent tragedy called *Liberty Asserted*,
which is thought to have given so great a stroke to the late French
king, hath frequent imitations of this beautiful speech of King Arthur:

  Conquest light'ning in his eyes, and thund'ring in his arm.
  Joy lightened in her eyes.
  Joys like lightning dart along my soul.

[3]
  Jove, with excessive thund'ring tired above,
  Comes down for ease, enjoys a nymph, and then
  Mounts dreadful, and to thund'ring goes again.

              Gloriana.

SCENE V

Grizzle, Huncamunca

Grizzle. Oh! Huncamunca, Huncamunca, oh![1]
Thy pouting breasts, like kettle-drums of brass,
Beat everlasting loud alarms of joy;
As bright as brass they are, and oh! as hard;
Oh! Huncamunca, Huncamunca, oh!
  Hunc. Ha! dost thou know me, Princess as I am,
That thus of me you dare to make your game?[2]
  Grizzle. Oh, Huncamunca, well I know that you
A Princess are, and a king's daughter, too;
But love no meanness scorns, no grandeur fears; }
Love often lords into the cellar bears,
And bids the sturdy porter come upstairs.
For what's too high for love, or what's too low?
Oh! Huncamunca, Huncamunca, oh!
  Hunc. But granting all you say of love were true,
My love, alas! is to another due!
In vain to me a-suitoring you come,
For I'm already promised to Tom Thumb.
  Grizzle. And can my Princess such a durgan wed,
One fitter for your pocket than your bed!
Advised by me, the worthless baby shun,
Or you will ne'er be brought to bed of one.
Oh! take me to thy arms, and never flinch,
Who am a man, by Jupiter, ev'ry inch.
Then while in joys together lost we lie,
I'll press thy soul while gods stand wishing by.[3]
  Hunc. If, sir, what you insinuate you prove,
All obstacles of promise you remove;
For all engagements to a man must fall,
Whene'er that man is proved no man at all.
  Grizzle. Oh! let him seek some dwarf, some fairy miss,
Where no joint-stool must lift him to the kiss.

[1] This beautiful line, which ought, says Mr. W——, to be written in gold, is imitated in the new *Sophonisba*:

> *Oh! Sophonisba, Sophonisba, oh!*
> *Oh! Narva, Narva, oh!*

The author of a song called *Duke upon Duke* hath improved it:

> *Alas! O Nick, O Nick, alas!*

Where, by the help of a little false spelling, you have two meanings in the repeated words.

[2] Edith, in the *Bloody Brother*, speaks to her lover in the same familiar language:

> *Your grace is full of game.*

[3]
> *Traverse the glittering chambers of the sky,* }
> *Borne on a cloud in view of fate I'll lie,*
> *And press her soul while gods stand wishing by.*
>   Hannibal.

But by the stars and glory you appear
Much fitter for a Prussian Grenadier;
One globe alone on Atlas' shoulders rests,
Two globes are less than Huncamunca's breasts:
The Milky Way is not so white, that's flat,
And sure thy breasts are full as large as that.
   Hunc. Oh, sir, so strong your eloquence I find,
It is impossible to be unkind.
   Grizzle. Ah! speak that o'er again, and let the sound
From one pole to another pole rebound;
The earth and sky each be a battledoor,
And keep the sound, that shuttlecock, up an hour; [1]
To Doctors Commons for a licence I
Swift as an arrow from a bow will fly.
   Hunc. Oh no! lest some disaster we should meet,
'Twere better to be married at the Fleet.
   Grizzle. Forbid it, all ye powers, a Princess should
By that vile place contaminate her blood;
My quick return shall to my charmer prove,
I travel on the post-horses of love. [2]
   Hunc. Those post-horses to me will seem too slow,
Though they should fly swift as the gods, when they
Ride on behind that post-boy, Opportunity.

SCENE VI

TOM THUMB, HUNCAMUNCA

   Thumb. Where is my Princess, where's my Huncamunca?
Where are those eyes, those cardmatches of love,
That light up all with love my waxen soul? [3]
Where is that face, which artful nature made

[1]
   Let the four winds from distant corners meet,
   And on their wings first bear it into France;
   Then back again to Edina's proud walls,
   Till victim to the sound the aspiring city falls.
                          Albion Queens.

[2] I do not remember any metaphors so frequent in the tragic poets as those borrowed from riding post:

   The gods and opportunity ride post.   Hannibal.

   ——*Let's rush together,*
   For Death rides post.   Duke of Guise.

   Destruction gallops to thy murder post.   Gloriana.

[3] This image too very often occurs:

   ——*Bright as when thy eye*
   First lighted up our loves.   Aurengzebe.

   This not a crown alone lights up my name.   Busiris.

In the same moulds where Venus self was cast? [1]
 Hunc. Oh! what is music to the ear that's deaf,[2]
Or a goose-pie to him that has no taste?
What are these praises now to me, since I
Am promised to another?
 Thumb.   Ha! promised?
 Hunc. Too sure; it's written in the Book of Fate.
 Thumb. Then I will tear away the leaf
Wherein it's writ, or if Fate won't allow
So large a gap within its journal-book,
I'll blot it out at least.[3]

---

[1] There is great dissension among the poets concerning the method of making man. One tells his mistress that the mould she was made in being lost, Heaven cannot form such another. Lucifer, in Dryden, gives a merry description of his own formation:

> *Whom Heaven neglecting, made and scarce designed,*
> *But threw me in for number to the rest.*
>   State of Innocency.

In one place the same poet supposes man to be made of metal:

> *I was formed*
> *Of that coarse metal, which when she was made,*
> *The gods threw by for rubbish.*   All for Love.

In another of dough:

> *When the gods moulded up the paste of man,*
> *Some of their clay was left upon their hands,*
> *And so they made Egyptians.*   Cleomenes.

In another of clay:

> ———*Rubbish of remaining clay.*   Sebastian.

One makes the soul of wax:

> *Her waxen soul begins to melt apace.*   Anna Bullen.

Another of flint:

> *Sure our two souls have somewhere been acquainted*
> *In former beings, or struck out together,*
> *One spark to Afric flew, and one to Portugal.*
>   Sebastian.

To omit the great quantities of iron, brazen and leaden souls which are so plenty in modern authors—I cannot omit the dress of a soul as we find it in Dryden:

> *Souls shirted but with air.*   King Arthur.

Nor can I pass by a particular sort of soul in a particular sort of description in the new *Sophonisba*:

> *Ye mysterious powers,*
> ———*Whether through your gloomy depths I wander,*
> *Or on the mountains walk, give me the calm,*
> *The steady smiling soul, where wisdom sheds*
> *Eternal sunshine, and eternal joy.*

[2] This line Mr. Banks has plundered entire in his *Anna Bullen.*

[3]
> *Good Heaven! the book of fate before me lay,*
> *But to tear out the journal of that day,*
> *Or if the order of the world below,*
> *Will not the gap of one whole day allow,*
> *Give me that minute when she made her vow.*
>   Conquest of Granada.

SCENE VII

GLUMDALCA, TOM THUMB, HUNCAMUNCA

Glum. I need not ask if you are Huncamunca,[1]
Your brandy-nose proclaims——
Hunc.   I am a Princess;
Nor need I ask who you are.
Glum.   A giantess;
The Queen of those who made and unmade queens.
Hunc. The man, whose chief ambition is to be
My sweetheart, hath destroyed these mighty giants.
Glum. Your sweetheart? Dost thou think the man who once
Hath worn my easy chains, will e'er wear thine?
Hunc. Well may your chains be easy, since, if fame
Says true, they have been tried on twenty husbands.
The glove or boot, so many times pulled on,[2]
May well fit easy on the hand or foot.
Glum. I glory in the number, and when I
Sit poorly down, like thee, content with one,
Heaven change this face for one as bad as thine.
Hunc. Let me see nearer what this beauty is,
That captivates the heart of men by scores.

> *(Holds a candle to her face.*

Oh! Heaven, thou art as ugly as the devil.
Glum. You'd give the best of shoes within your shop
To be but half so handsome.
Hunc.   Since you come
To that, I'll put my beauty to the test;[3]
Tom Thumb, I'm yours, if you with me will go.
Glum. Oh! stay, Tom Thumb, and you alone shall fill
That bed where twenty giants used to lie.
Thumb. In the balcony that o'erhangs the stage,

---

[1] I know some of the commentators have imagined that Mr. Dryden, in the altercative scene between Cleopatra and Octavia, a scene which Mr. Addison inveighs against with great bitterness, is much beholden to our author. How just this their observation is I will not presume to determine.

[2] "A cobbling poet indeed," says Mr. D——. And yet I believe we may find as monstrous images in the tragic authors. I'll put down one:
Untie your folded thoughts, and let them dangle loose as a bride's hair.
                                        Injured Love.
Which line seems to have as much title to a milliner's shop as our author's to a shoemaker's.

[3] Mr. L—— takes occasion in this place to commend the great care of our author to preserve the metre of blank verse, in which Shakespeare, Jonson and Fletcher were so notoriously negligent; and the moderns in imitation of our author, so laudably observant:
                    ——*Then does*
        Your majesty believe that he can be
    A traitor!
                                        Earl of Essex.
Every page of *Sophonisba* gives us instances of this excellence.

I've seen a whore two 'prentices engage;
One half a crown does in his fingers hold,
The other shows a little piece of gold;
She the half-guinea wisely does purloin,
And leaves the larger and the baser coin.
   Glum. Left, scorned, and loathed for such a chit as this;
I feel the storm that's rising in my mind,
Tempests and whirlwinds rise, and roll and roar.[1]
I'm all within a hurricane, as if
The world's four winds were pent within my carcass.[2]
Confusion, horror, murder, guts and death.[3]

SCENE VIII

KING, GLUMDALCA

   King. Sure never was so sad a king as I,[4]
My life is worn as ragged as a coat
A beggar wears; a prince should put it off,[5]
To love a captive and a giantess.
O Love! O Love! how great a king art thou!
My tongue's thy trumpet, and thou trumpetest,
Unknown to me, within me.[6] Oh, Glumdalca!
Heaven thee designed a giantess to make,
But an angelic soul was shuffled in.[7]
I am a multitude of walking griefs,[8]
And only on her lips the balm is found,[9]
To spread a plaster that might cure them all.

---

[1]   *Love mounts and rolls about my stormy mind.*
                                        Aurengzebe.

   Tempests and whirlwinds through my bosom move.
                                        Cleomenes.

[2]   *With such a furious tempest on his brow,*
       As if the world's four winds were pent within
       His blustering carcass.   Anna Bullen.

[3] *Verba tragica.*
[4] This speech hath been terribly mauled by the poets.

[5]   ——*My life is worn to rags;*
              Not worth a prince's wearing.
                                        Love Triumph.

[6]   *Must I beg the pity of my slave?*
       Must a king beg! But Love's a greater king,
       A tyrant, nay a devil that possesses me.
       He tunes the organ of my voice and speaks,
          Unknown to me, within me.   Sebastian.

[7]   *When thou wert formed Heaven did a man begin;*
       But a brute soul by chance was shuffled in.
                                        Aurengzebe.

[8]   ——*I am a multitude*
          Of walking griefs.   New Sophonisba.

[9]   *I will take thy scorpion blood,*
       And lay it to my grief till I have ease.
                                        Anna Bullen.

Glum. What do I hear?
King.   What do I see?
Glum.   Oh!
King.   Ah!
Glum. Ah, wretched queen!
King.   Oh! wretched king! [1]
Glum.   Ah!
King.   Oh! [2]

SCENE IX

TOM THUMB, HUNCAMUNCA, PARSON

Parson. Happy's the wooing that's not long a-doing;
For, if I guess aright, Tom Thumb this night
Shall give a being to a new Tom Thumb.
Thumb. It shall be my endeavour so to do.
Hunc. Oh! fie upon you, sir, you make me blush.
Thumb. It is the virgin's sign, and suits you well:
I know not where, nor how, nor what I am; [3]
I'm so transported I have lost myself. [4]

[1] Our author, who everywhere shows his great penetration into
human nature, here outdoes himself; where a less judicious poet would
have raised a long scene of whining love. He, who understood the
passions better, and that so violent an affection as this must be too
big for utterance, chooses rather to send his characters off in this
sullen and doleful manner; in which admirable conduct he is imitated
by the author of the justly celebrated *Eurydice.* Dr. Young seems to
point at this violence of passion:

                    ——*passion chokes*
          Their words, and they're the statues of despair.

And Seneca tells us, *Curæ leves loquuntur, ingentes stupent.* The story
of the Egyptian king in Herodotus is too well known to need to be
inserted. I refer the more curious reader to the excellent Montaigne,
who hath written an essay on this subject.

[2]   *To part is death——*
                    'Tis death to part.
               ——Ah.
               ——Oh.   Don Carlos.

[3]   *Nor know I whether,*
             What am I, who or where.   Busiris.
          I was I know not what, and am I know not how.
                                                   Gloriana.

[4] To understand sufficiently the beauty of this passage it will be
necessary that we comprehend every man to contain two selves.
I shall not attempt to prove this from philosophy, which the poets
make so plainly evident.
One runs away from the other:
          ——*Let me demand your majesty,*
          Why fly you from yourself?   Duke of Guise.
In a second, one self is a guardian to the other:
          Leave me the care of me.   Conquest of Granada.
Again:
          Myself am to myself less near.   Ibid.
In the same, the first self is proud of the second:
          I myself am proud of me.   State of Innocence.

Hunc. Forbid it, all ye stars, for you're so so small,
That were you lost you'd find yourself no more.
So the unhappy sempstress once, they say,
Her needle in a pottle, lost, of hay;
In vain she looked, and looked, and made her moan,
For ah! the needle was for ever gone.

    Parson. Long may they live, and love, and propagate,
Till the whole land be peopled with Tom Thumbs.
So when the Cheshire cheese a maggot breeds,[1]
Another and another still succeeds:
By thousands, and ten thousands they increase,
Till one continued maggot fills the rotten cheese.

SCENE X

NOODLE, *and then* GRIZZLE

    Noodle. Sure Nature means to break her solid chain,
Or else unfix the world, and in a rage
To hurl it from its axle-tree and hinges;[2]
All things are so confused, the King's in love,
Till Queen is drunk, the Princess married is.

In a third, distrustful of him:

> *Fain I would tell, but whisper it in mine ear,*
> *That none besides might hear, nay not myself.*
>   Earl of Essex.

In a fourth, honours him:

> *I honour Rome,*
> *But honour too myself.*   Sophonisba.

In a fifth, at variance with him:

> *Leave me not thus at variance with myself.*
>   Busiris.

Again, in a sixth:

> *I find myself divided from myself.*   Medea.
> *She seemed the sad effigies of herself.*   Banks.
>
> *Assist me, Zulema, if thou wouldst be*
> *The friend thou seemest, assist me against me.*
>   Albion Queens.

From all which it appears that there are two selves; and therefore
Tom Thumb's losing himself is no such solecism as it hath been represented by men, rather ambitious of criticising than qualified to criticise.

    [1] Mr. F—— imagines this parson to have been a Welsh one from
his simile.

    [2] Our author hath been plundered here according to custom:

> *Great Nature break thy chain that links together*
> *The fabric of the world, and make a chaos,*
> *Like that within my soul.*   Love Triumphant.
>
> *——Startle Nature, unfix the globe,*
> *And hurl it from its axle-tree and hinges.*
>   Albion Queens.
>
> *The tottering earth seems sliding off its props.*

Grizzle. Oh! Noodle, hast thou Huncamunca seen?

Noodle. I've seen a thousand sights this day, where none
Are by the wonderful bitch herself outdone,
The King, the Queen, and all the Court are sights.

Grizzle. D—n your delay, you trifler, are you drunk, ha?
I will not hear one word but Huncamunca.[1]

Noodle. By this time she is married to Tom Thumb.

Grizzle. My Huncamunca.[2]

Noodle.   Your Huncamunca,
Tom Thumb's Huncamunca, every man's Huncamunca.

Grizzle. If this be true, all womankind are damned.

Noodle. If it be not, may I be so myself.

Grizzle. See where she comes! I'll not believe a word
Against that face, upon whose ample brow
Sits innocence with majesty enthroned.[3]

GRIZZLE, HUNCAMUNCA

Grizzle. Where has my Huncamunca been? See here
The licence in my hand!

Hunc.   Alas! Tom Thumb.

Grizzle. Why dost thou mention him?

Hunc.   Ah me! Tom Thumb.

Grizzle. What means my lovely Huncamunca?

Hunc.   Hum!

Grizzle. Oh! Speak.

Hunc.   Hum!

Grizzle.   Ha! your every word is Hum:
You force me still to answer you, Tom Thumb.[4]
Tom Thumb, I'm on the rack, I'm in a flame,
Tom Thumb, Tom Thumb, Tom Thumb, you love the name;[5]
So pleasing is that sound, that were you dumb
You still would find a voice to cry, Tom Thumb!

Hunc. Oh! Be not hasty to proclaim my doom,
My ample heart for more than one has room,
A maid, like me, Heaven formed at least for two,

---

[1]   *D—n your delay, ye torturers proceed,*
        I will not hear one word but Almahide.

                        Conquest of Granada.

[2] Mr. Dryden hath imitated this in *All for Love.*

[3] This Miltonic style abounds in the new *Sophonisba*:

                ——*And on her ample brow*
        Sat majesty.

[4]   *Your every answer still so ends in that,*
        You force me still to answer you Morat.

                        Aurengzebe.

[5]   *Morat, Morat, Morat, you love the name.*   Ibid.

I married him, and now I'll marry you.[1]
  Grizzle. Ha! dost thou own thy falsehood to my face?
Think'st thou that I will share thy husband's place,
Since to that office one cannot suffice,
And since you scorn to dine one single dish on,
Go, get your husband put into commission,
Commissioners to discharge (ye gods), it fine is,
The duty of a husband to your Highness;
Yet think not long I will my rival bear,
Or unrevenged the slighted willow wear;
The gloomy, brooding tempest, now confined
Within the hollow caverns of my mind,
In dreadful whirl shall roll along the coasts,
Shall thin the land of all the men it boasts,
And cram up ev'ry chink of hell with ghosts.[2]
So I have seen, in some dark winter's day,
A sudden storm rush down the sky's highway,
Sweep through the streets with terrible ding-dong,
Gush through the spouts, and wash whole crowds along.
The crowded shops the thronging vermin screen,
Together cram the dirty and the clean,
And not one shoe-boy in the street is seen.[3]
  Hunc. Oh! fatal rashness should his fury slay
My hapless bridegroom on his wedding-day;
I, who this morn of two chose which to wed,
May go again this night alone to bed;
So have I seen some wild unsettled fool,
Who had her choice of this and that joint-stool;

[1] " Here is a sentiment for the virtuous Huncamunca," says Mr. D——s.
And yet, with the leave of this great man, the virtuous Panthea in
Cyrus hath an heart every whit as ample:

> *For two I must confess are gods to me,*
> *Which is my Abradatus first, and thee.*
> Cyrus the Great.

Nor is the lady in *Love Triumphant* more reserved, though not so
intelligible:

> ——*I am so divided,*
> *That I grieve most for both, and love both most.*

[2] A ridiculous supposition to anyone who considers the great and
extensive largeness of hell, says a commentator. But not so to those
who consider the great expansion of immaterial substance. Mr. Banks
makes one soul to be so expanded that heaven could not contain it:

> *The heavens are all too narrow for her soul.*
> Virtue Betrayed.

The *Persian Princess* hath a passage not unlike the author of this:

> *We will send such shoals of murdered slaves,*
> *Shall glut hell's empty regions.*

This threatens to fill hell even though it were empty; Lord Grizzle
only to fill up the chinks, supposing the rest already full.

[3] Mr. Addison is generally thought to have had this simile in his eye
when he wrote that beautiful one at the end of the third act of his *Cato.*

To give the preference to either loath,
And fondly coveting to sit on both:
While the two stools her sitting-part confound,
Between 'em both fall squat upon the ground.[1]

ACT III. SCENE I

Scene—King Arthur's Palace

GHOST, *solus* [2]

Hail! ye black horrors of midnight's midnoon!
Ye fairies, goblins, bats and screech-owls, hail!
And oh! ye mortal watchmen, whose hoarse throats
The immortal ghosts dread croakings counterfeit,
All hail!—Ye dancing phantoms, who by day
Are some condemned to fast, some feast in fire;

[1] This beautiful simile is founded on a proverb which does honour to the English language:

Between two stools the breech falls to the ground.

I am not so well pleased with any written remains of the ancients, as with those little aphorisms which verbal tradition hath delivered down to us, under the title of proverbs. It were to be wished that instead of filling their pages with the fabulous theology of the pagans, our modern poets would think it worth their while to enrich their works with the proverbial sayings of their ancestors. Mr. Dryden hath chronicled one in heroic:

Two ifs scarce make one possibility.
                                        Conquest of Granada.

My Lord Bacon is of opinion, that whatever is known of arts and sciences might be proved to have lurked in the Proverbs of Solomon. I am of the same opinion in relation to those above mentioned. At least I am confident that a more perfect system of ethics, as well as economy, might be compiled out of them than is at present extant, either in the works of the ancient philosophers, or those more valuable, as more voluminous, ones of the modern divines.

[2] Of all the particulars in which the modern stage falls short of the ancient, there is none so much to be lamented as the great scarcity of ghosts in the latter. Whence this proceeds I will not presume to determine. Some are of opinion that the moderns are unequal to that sublime language which a ghost ought to speak. One says ludicrously that ghosts are out of fashion; another that they are properer for comedy; forgetting, I suppose, that Aristotle hath told us that a ghost is the soul of tragedy; for so I render the ψυχή ὁ αὖθθ τί τραγωδίας, which M. Dacier, amongst others, hath mistaken; I suppose misled by not understanding the *fabula* of the Latins, which signifies a ghost as well as a fable.

——*Te premet nox, fabulæque manes.*

                                                          Hor.

Of all the ghosts that have ever appeared on the stage, a very learned and judicious foreign critic gives the preference to this of our author. These are his words, speaking of this tragedy: . . . *Nec quidquam in illâ admirabilius quam phasma quoddam horrendum, quod omnibus aliis spectris, quibuscum scatet Anglorum tragœdia, longè (pace D—isii V. Doctiss. dixerim) prœtulerim.*

Now play in churchyards, skipping o'er the graves,
To the loud music of the silent bell.[1]
All hail!

SCENE II

KING and GHOST

King. What noise is this—what villain dares,
At this dread hour, with feet and voice profane,
Disturb our royal walls?
    Ghost.   One who defies
Thy empty power to hurt him; one who dares
Walk in thy bedchamber.[2]
    King.   Presumptuous slave!
Thou diest.
    Ghost. Threaten others with that word,
I am a ghost, and am already dead.[3]
    King. Ye stars! 'tis well; were thy last hour to come
This moment had been it; yet by thy shroud
I'll pull thee backward, squeeze thee to a bladder,
Till thou dost groan thy nothingness away.[4]
Thou fliest! 'Tis well.   (GHOST *retires.*
I thought what was the courage of a ghost![5]

---

[1] We have already given instances of this figure.

[2] Almanzor reasons in the same manner:

      ———A ghost I'll be,
  And from a ghost, you know, no place is free.
                 Conquest of Granada.

[3] "The man who writ this wretched pun," says Mr. D——, "would
have picked your pocket." Which he proceeds to show not only bad
in itself, but doubly so on so solemn an occasion. And yet in that
excellent play of *Liberty Asserted* we find something very much resem-
bling a pun in the mouth of a mistress, who is parting with the lover
she is fond of:

  Ul. *Oh, mortal woe! one kiss, and then farewell.*
  Irene. *The gods have given to others to fare well.*
  O miserably must Irene fare.

Agamemnon, in the *Victim*, is full as facetious on the most solemn
occasion, that of sacrificing his daughter:

  Yes, daughter, yes; you will assist the priest;
  Yes, you must offer up your—vows for Greece.

[4]
  I'll pull thee backwards by thy shroud to light,
  Or else I'll squeeze thee, like a bladder, there,
  And make thee groan thyself away to air.
                 Conquest of Granada.

  Snatch me, ye gods, this moment into nothing.
                 Cyrus the Great.

[5]
  So, art thou gone? Thou canst no conquest boast,
  I thought what was the courage of a ghost.
                 Conquest of Granada.

King Arthur seems to be as brave a fellow as Almanzor, who says
most heroically:

      ———In spite of ghosts I'll on.

Yet dare not, on thy life.—Why say I that,
Since life thou hast not?—Dare not walk again
Within these walls, on pain of the Red Sea.
For, if henceforth I ever find thee here,
As sure, sure as a gun, I'll have thee laid——
   Ghost. Were the Red Sea a sea of Hollands gin,
The liquor (when alive) whose very smell
I did detest, did loathe—yet, for the sake
Of Thomas Thumb, I would be laid therein.
   King. Ha! said you?
   Ghost.   Yes, my liege, I said Tom Thumb,
Whose father's ghost I am—once not unknown
To mighty Arthur. But, I see, 'tis true,
The dearest friend, when dead, we all forget.
   King. 'Tis he, it is the honest Gaffer Thumb!
Oh! let me press thee in my eager arms,
Thou best of ghosts! Thou something more than ghost!
   Ghost. Would I were something more, that we again
Might feel each other in the warm embrace.
But now I have the advantage of my King,
For I feel thee, whilst thou dost not feel me.[1]
   King. But say, thou dearest air,[2] oh! say what dread,
Important business sends thee back to earth?
   Ghost. Oh! then prepare to hear—which but to hear,
Is full enough to send thy spirit hence.
Thy subjects up in arms, by Grizzle led,
Will, ere the rosy-fingered morn shall ope
The shutters of the sky, before the gate
Of this thy royal palace swarming spread:
So have I seen the bees in clusters swarm,
So have I seen the stars in frosty nights,
So have I seen the sand in windy days,
So have I seen the ghosts on Pluto's shore,
So have I seen the flowers in spring arise,
So have I seen the leaves in autumn fall,
So have I seen the fruits in summer smile,
So have I seen the snow in winter frown.[3]
   King. D—n all thou'st seen!—Dost thou, beneath the shape
Of Gaffer Thumb, come hither to abuse me
With similes to keep me on the rack?

---

[1] The ghost of Lausaria in *Cyrus* is a plain copy of this, and is therefore worth reading:

> *Ah, Cyrus!*
> *Thou mayest as well grasp water, or fleet air,*
> *As think of touching my immortal shade.*
>   Cyrus the Great.

[2]   *Thou better part of heavenly air.*
          Conquest of Granada.

[3] "A string of similes," says one, "proper to be hung up in the cabinet of a prince."

Hence—or, by all the torments of thy hell,
I'll run thee through the body, though thou'st none.[1]
Ghost. Arthur, beware; I must this moment hence,
Not frighted by your voice, but by the cocks;
Arthur, beware, beware, beware, beware!
Strive to avert thy yet impending fate;
For if thou'rt killed to-day,
To-morrow all thy care will come too late.

SCENE III

KING, *solus*

King. Oh! stay, and leave me not uncertain thus!
And whilst thou tellest me what's like my fate,
Oh! teach me how I may avert it too!
Curst be the man who first a simile made!
Curst ev'ry bard who writes!—So have I seen
Those whose comparisons are just and true,
And those who liken things not like at all.
The devil is happy that the whole creation
Can furnish out no simile to his fortune.

SCENE IV

KING, QUEEN

Queen. What is the cause, my Arthur, that you steal
Thus silently from Dollallolla's breast?
Why dost thou leave me in the dark alone,[2]
When well thou know'st I am afraid of sprites?
King. Oh, Dollallolla! do not blame my love;
I hoped the fumes of last night's punch had laid
Thy lovely eyelids fast. But, oh! I find
There is no power in drams to quiet wives;
Each morn, as the returning sun, they wake,
And shine upon their husbands.
Queen. Think, oh! think
What a surprise it must be to the sun,
Rising, to find the vanished world away.

---

[1] This passage hath been understood several different ways by the commentators. For my part I find it difficult to understand it at all. Mr. Dryden says:

> *I have heard something how two bodies meet,*
> *But how two souls join I know not.*

So that till the body of a spirit is better understood, it will be difficult to understand how it is possible to run him through it.
[2] Cydaria is of the same fearful temper with Dollallolla:

> *I never durst in darkness be alone.*

Ind. Emp.

What less can be the wretched wife's surprise
When, stretching out her arms to fold thee fast,
She folds her useless bolster in her arms!
Think, think on that—oh! think. think well on that![1]
I do remember also to have read
In Dryden's *Ovid's Metamorphoses*,
That Jove in form inanimate did lie
With beauteous Danae [2]; and trust me, love,
I feared the bolster might have been a Jove.[3]

   King. Come to my arms, most virtuous of thy sex;
Oh, Dollallolla! were all wives like thee,
So many husbands never had worn horns.
Should Huncamunca of thy worth partake,
Tom Thumb indeed were blest.—Oh fatal name!
For didst thou know one quarter what I know,
Then wouldst thou know—alas! what thou wouldst know!

   Queen. What can I gather hence? Why dost thou speak
Like men who carry raree-shows about!
Now you shall see, gentlemen, what you shall see.
O tell me more, or thou hast told too much.

SCENE V

KING, QUEEN, NOODLE

   Noodle. Long life attend your Majesties serene,
Great Arthur, King, and Dollallolla, Queen!
Lord Grizzle, with a bold rebellious crowd,
Advances to the palace, threat'ning loud,
Unless the Princess be delivered straight,
And the victorious Thumb, without his pate,
They are resolved to batter down the gate.

SCENE VI

KING, QUEEN, HUNCAMUNCA, NOODLE

   King. See where the Princess comes! Where is Tom Thumb?
   Hunc. Oh! sir, about an hour and half ago
He sallied out to encounter with the foe,
And swore, unless his fate had him misled,
From Grizzle's shoulders to cut off his head,
And serv't up with your chocolate in bed.

---

[1]   *Think well of this, think that, think every way.*
                                Sophonisba.

[2] These quotations are more usual in the comic than in the tragic writers.

[3] "This distress," says Mr. D——, "I must allow to be extremely beautiful, and tends to heighten the virtuous character of Dollallolla, who is so exceeding delicate, that she is in the highest apprehension from the inanimate embrace of a bolster. An example worthy of imitation from all our writers of tragedy."

King. 'Tis well, I find one devil told us both.
Come, Dollallolla, Huncamunca, come,
Within we'll wait for the victorious Thumb;
In peace and safety we secure may stay,
While to his arm we trust the bloody fray;
Though men and giants should conspire with gods,
He is alone equal to all these odds.[1]

Queen. He is, indeed, a helmet [2] to us all,
While he supports we need not fear to fall;
His arm dispatches all things to our wish,
And serves up ev'ry foe's head in a dish.
Void is the mistress of the house of care,
While the good cook presents the bill of fare;
Whether the cod, that northern king of fish,
Or duck, or goose, or pig, adorn the dish,
No fears the number of her guests afford,
But at her hour she sees the dinner on the board.

SCENE VII.—*A Plain*

LORD GRIZZLE, FOODLE, *and* REBELS

Grizzle. Thus far our arms with victory are crowned;
For though we have not fought, yet we have found

---

[1] *Credat Judæus Apelles.*
"*Non ego——*" says Mr. D——. "For, passing over the absurdity of being equal to odds, can we possibly suppose a little insignificant fellow—I say again, a little insignificant fellow—able to vie with a strength which all the Samsons and Herculeses of antiquity would be unable to encounter?"

I shall refer this incredulous critic to Mr. Dryden's defence of his Almanzor; and lest that should not satisfy him, I shall quote a few lines from the speech of a much braver fellow than Almanzor, Mr. Johnson's Achilles:

> *Though human race rise in embattled hosts,*
> *To force her from my arms—O son of Aireus!*
> *By that immortal power, whose deathless spirit*
> *Informs this earth, I will oppose them all.*
>
> Victim.

[2] "I have heard of being supported by a staff," says Mr. D——, "but never of being supported by a helmet." I believe he never heard of sailing with wings, which he may read in no less a poet than Mr. Dryden:

> *Unless we borrow wings, and sail through air.*
>
> Love Triumph.

What will he say to a kneeling valley?

> ——*I'll stand*
> *Like a safe valley, that low bends the knee*
> *To some aspiring mountain.*
>
> Injured Love.

I am ashamed of so ignorant a carper, who doth not know that an epithet in tragedy is very often no other than an expletive. Do not we read in the new *Sophonisba* of "grinding chains," "blue plagues," "white occasions," and "blue serenity"? Nay, 'tis not the adjective only, but sometimes half a sentence is put by way of expletive, as "Beauty pointed high with spirit," in the same play, and "In the lap of blessing, to be most cursed," in the *Revenge*.

No enemy to fight withal.[1]

Foodle. Yet I,
Methinks, would willingly avoid this day,
This first of April, to engage our foes.[2]

Grizzle. This day, of all the days of the year, I'd choose,
For on this day my grandmother was born.
Gods! I will make Tom Thumb an April fool;
Will teach his wit an errand it ne'er knew,
And send it post to the Elysian shades.[3]

Foodle. I'm glad to find our army is so stout,
Nor does it move my wonder less than joy.

Grizzle. What friends we have, and how we came so strong,
I'll softly tell you as we march along.[4]

SCENE VIII

Thunder and lightning

Tom Thumb, Glumdalca, *cum suis.*

Thumb. Oh, Noodle! hast thou seen a day like this?
The unborn thunder rumbles o'er our heads,[5]
As if the gods meant to unhinge the world;
And heaven and earth in wild confusion hurl;
Yet I will boldly tread the tott'ring ball.[6]

Merl. Tom Thumb!

Thumb.   What voice is this I hear?

Merl.   Tom Thumb!

Thumb. Again it calls.

Merl.   Tom Thumb!

Glum.   It calls again.

Thumb. Appear, whoe'er thou art, I fear thee not.

Merl. Thou hast no cause to fear, I am thy friend,

---

[1] A victory like that of Almanzor:
> *Almanzor is victorious without fight.*
>
>   Conq. of Granada.

[2]
> *Well have we chose an happy day for fight,*
> *For every man in course of time has found,*
> *Some days are lucky, some unfortunate.*
>
>   K. Arthur.

[3] We read of such another in Lee:
> *Teach his rude wit a flight she never made,*
> *And sent her post to the Elysian shade.*
>
>   Gloriana.

[4] These lines are copied verbatim in the *Indian Emperor.*

[5]
> *Unborn thunder rolling in a cloud.*
>
>   Conq. of Granada.

[6]
> *Were heaven and earth in wild confusion hurlea,*
> *Should the rash gods unhinge the rolling world,*
> *Undaunted would I tread the tott'ring ball,*
> *Crushed, but unconquered, in the dreadful fall.*
>
>   Female Warrior.

Merlin by name, a conjurer by trade,
And to my art thou dost thy being owe.
   Thumb. How!
   Merl. Hear then the mystic getting of Tom Thumb.

> *His father was a ploughman plain,*
>   *His mother milked the cow :*
> *And yet the way to get a son,*
>   *This couple knew not how.*
> *Until such time the good old man*
>   *To learnèd Merlin goes,*
> *And there to him, in great distress,*
>   *In secret manner shows,*
> *How in his heart he wished to have*
>   *A child, in time to come,*
> *To be his heir, though it might be*
>   *No bigger than his thumb :*
> *Of which old Merlin was foretold,*
>   *That he his wish should have :*
> *And so a son of stature small,*
>   *The charmer to him gave.*[1]

Thou'st heard the past, look up and see the future.
   Thumb. Lost in amazement's gulf my senses sink; [2]
See there, Glumdalca, see another me! [3]
   Glum. O sight of horror! see, you are devoured
By the expanded jaws of a red cow.
   Merl. Let not these sights deter thy noble mind,
For lo! a sight more glorious courts thy eyes;
See from afar a theatre arise;
There ages yet unborn shall tribute pay
To the heroic actions of this day:
Then buskin tragedy at length shall choose
Thy name the best supporter of her muse. [4]
   Thumb. Enough, let every warlike music sound,
We fall contented, if we fall renowned.

---

[1] See the *History of Tom Thumb*, page 2.

[2]
>   ——*Amazement swallows up my sense,*
> *And in th' impetuous whirl of circling fate*
> *Drinks down my reason.*   Persian Princess.

[3]
>   ——*I have outfaced myself,*
> *What! am I two? Is there another me?*
>   K. Arthur.

[4] The character of Merlin is wonderful throughout, but most so in this prophetic part. We find several of these prophecies in the tragic authors, who frequently take this opportunity to pay a compliment to their country, and sometimes to their prince. None but our author (who seems to have detested the least appearance of flattery) would have passed by such an opportunity of being a political prophet.

SCENE IX

LORD GRIZZLE, FOODLE, REBELS, *on one side.* TOM THUMB, GLUMDALCA, *on the other*

Foodle. At length the enemy advances nigh,
I hear them with my ear, and see them with my eye.[1]
Grizzle. Draw all your swords; for liberty we fight,
And liberty the mustard [2] is of life.
Thumb. Are you the man whom men famed Grizzle name?
Grizzle. Are you the much more famed Tom Thumb? [3]
Thumb. The same.
Grizzle. Come on, our worth upon ourselves we'll prove,
For liberty I fight.
Thumb. And I for love.
    (*A bloody engagement between the two armies here; drums beating, trumpets sounding, thunder and lightning. They fight off and on several times. Some fall.* GRIZZLE *and* GLUMDALCA *remain.*
Glum. Turn, coward, turn, nor from a woman fly.
Grizzle. Away—thou art too ignoble for my arm.
Glum. Have at thy heart.
Grizzle. Nay, then I thrust at thine.
Glum. You push too well, you've run me through the guts,
And I am dead.
Grizzle. Then there's an end of one.
Thumb. When thou art dead, then there's an end of two,
Villain!
Grizzle. Tom Thumb!
Thumb. Rebel!
Grizzle. Tom Thumb!
Thumb. Hell!
Grizzle. Huncamunca![4]

[1]   *I saw the villain, Myron, with these eyes I saw him.*
                                   Busiris.
In both which places it is intimated that it is sometime possible to see with other eyes than your own.
[2] "This mustard," says Mr. D——, "is enough to turn one's stomach. I would be glad to know what idea the author had in his head when he wrote it." This will be, I believe, best explained by a line of Mr. Dennis:
    And gave him liberty, the salt of life.
                              Liberty Asserted.
The understanding that can digest the one, will not rise at the other.
[3]   *Han. Are you the chief whom men famed Scipio call?*
    Scip. Are you the much more famous Hannibal?
                             Hannibal.
[4] Dr. Young seems to have copied this engagement in his *Busiris:*
        Myr. *Villain!*
        Mem. *Myron!*
        Myr. *Rebel!*
        Mem. *Myron!*
        Myr. *Hell!*
        Mem. *Mandane.*

Thumb. Thou hast it there.
Grizzle.   Too sure I feel it.
Thumb. To Hell then, like a rebel as you are,
And give my service to the rebels there.
   Grizzle. Triumph not, Thumb, nor think thou shalt enjoy
Thy Huncamunca undisturbed; I'll send
My ghost to fetch her to the other world;[1]
It shall but bait at Heaven, and then return.[2]
But, ha! I feel Death rumbling in my brains,[3]
Some kinder sprite knocks softly at my soul,[4]
And gently whispers it to haste away:
I come, I come, most willingly I come.
So when some city wife for country air,
To Hampstead or to Highgate does repair;[5]
Her, to make haste, her husband does implore,
And cries, "My dear, the coach is at the door."
With equal wish, desirous to be gone,
She gets into the coach, and then she cries: "Drive on!"
   Thumb. With those last words he vomited his soul,[6]
Which, like whipped cream, the devil will swallow down.[7]
Bear off the body, and cut off the head,
Which I will to the King in triumph lug!
Rebellion's dead, and now I'll go to breakfast.

SCENE X

KING, QUEEN, HUNCAMUNCA, *and Courtiers*

   King. Open the prisons, set the wretched free,
And bid our treasurer disburse six pounds

---

[1] This last speech of my Lord Grizzle hath been of great service to our poets:

> ———*I'll hold it fast*
> *As life, and when life's gone I'll hold this last;*
> *And if thou tak'st it from me when I'm slain,*
> *I'll send my ghost and fetch it back again.*
> Conq. of Granada.

[2]
> *My soul should with such speed obey,*
> *It should not bait at heaven to stop its way.*

Lee seems to have had this last in his eye:

> *'Twas not my purpose, sir, to tarry there,*
> *I would but go to heaven to take the air.*
> Gloriana.

[3]
> *A rising vapour rumbling in my brains.*
> Cleomenes.

[4]
> *Some kind sprite knocks softly at my soul,*
> *To tell me Fate's at hand.*

[5] Mr. Dryden seems to have had this simile in his eye when he says:
> *My soul is packing up, and just on wing.*
> Conq. of Granada.

[6]
> *And in a purple vomit poured his soul.*

[7]
> *The devil swallows vulgar souls*
> *Like whipped cream.*   Sebastian.

To pay their debts. Let no one weep to-day.
Come, Dollallolla; curse that odious name!
It is so long it asks an hour to speak it.
By heavens! I'll change it into Doll, or Loll,
Or any other civil monosyllable
That will not tire my tongue.[1]—Come, sit thee down.
Here seated let us view the dancer's sports;
Bid 'em advance. This is the wedding-day
Of Princess Huncamunca and Tom Thumb;
Tom Thumb! who wins two victories to-day,[2]
And this way marches, bearing Grizzle's head.

A Dance here

　　Noodle. Oh! monstrous, dreadful, terrible! Oh! Oh!
Deaf be my ears, for ever blind my eyes!
Dumb be my tongue! feet lame! all senses lost!
Howl wolves, grunt bears, hiss snakes, shriek all ye ghosts![3]
　　King. What does the blockhead mean?
　　Noodle. I mean, my liege,
Only to grace my tale with decent horror;[4]
Whilst from my garret, twice two stories high,
I looked abroad into the streets below,
I saw Tom Thumb attended by the mob,
Twice twenty shoe-boys, twice two dozen links,
Chairmen and porters, hackney-coachmen, whores;
Aloft he bore the grizly head of Grizzle;
When of a sudden through the streets there came
A cow, of larger than the usual size,
And in a moment—guess, oh! guess the rest!
And in a moment swallowed up Tom Thumb.
　　King. Shut up again the prisons, bid my treasurer
Not give three farthings out—hang all the culprits,
Guilty or not, no matter—ravish virgins.
Go bid the schoolmasters whip all their boys;
Let lawyers, parsons, and physicians loose,
To rob, impose on, and to kill the world.

---

[1]
　　　How I could curse my name of Ptolemy!
　　　It is so long it asks an hour to write it.
　　　By heaven! I'll change it into Jove, or Mars,
　　　Or any other civil monosyllable,
　　　That will not tire my hand.
　　　　　　　　　　　　　　　　　Cleomenes.

[2] Here is a visible conjunction of two days in one, by which our author may have either intended an emblem of a wedding, or to insinuate that men in the honeymoon are apt to imagine time shorter than it is. It brings into my mind a passage in the comedy called the *Coffee-House Politician*:

　　　We will celebrate this day at my house to-morrow.

[3] These beautiful phrases are all to be found in one single speech of King Arthur, or *The British Worthy*.

[4]
　　　I was but teaching him to grace his tale
　　　With decent horror.
　　　　　　　　　　　　　　　　　Cleomenes.

Noodle. Her Majesty the Queen is in a swoon.

Queen. Not so much in a swoon, but I have still
Strength to reward the messenger of ill news. (*Kills* Noodle.

Noodle. Oh! I am slain.

Cle. My lover's killed, I will revenge him so.
(*Kills the* Queen.

Hunc. My mamma killed! vile murderess, beware.
(*Kills* Cleora.

Doodle. This for an old grudge, to thy heart.
(*Kills* Huncamunca.

Must. And this
I drive to thine, O Doodle! for a new one. (*Kills* Doodle.

King. Ha! Murderess vile, take that. (*Kills* Must.
And take thou this. (*Kills himself, and falls.*
So when the child whom nurse from danger guards,
Sends Jack for mustard with a pack of cards;
Kings, queens and knaves throw one another down,
Till the whole pack lies scattered and o'erthrown;
So all our pack upon the floor is cast,
And all I boast is—that I fall the last.[1]   (*Dies.*

---

[1] We may say with Dryden:

> *Death did at length so many slain forget,*
> *And left the tale, and took them by the great.*

I know of no tragedy which comes nearer to this charming and
bloody catastrophe than *Cleomenes*, where the curtain covers five
principal characters dead on the stage. These lines, too,

> *I ask no questions then, of Who killed who ?*
> *The bodies tell the story as they lie,*

seem to have belonged more properly to this scene of our author.—
Nor can I help imagining they were originally his. The *Rival Ladies*,
too, seems beholden to this scene:

> *We're now a chain of lovers linked in death,*
> *Julia goes first, Gonsalvo hangs on her,*
> *And Angelina hangs upon Gonsalvo,*
> *As I on Angelina.*

No scene, I believe, ever received greater honours than this. It was
applauded by several encores, a word very unusual in tragedy—and
it was very difficult for the actors to escape without a second slaughter.
This I take to be a lively assurance of that fierce spirit of liberty
which remains among us, and which Mr. Dryden, in his *Essay on
Dramatic Poetry*, hath observed: "Whether custom," says he, "hath so
insinuated itself into our countrymen, or Nature hath so formed
them to fierceness, I know not, but they will scarcely suffer combats,
and other objects of horror, to be taken from them." And indeed I am
for having them encouraged in this martial disposition. Nor do I believe
our victories over the French have been owing to anything more than
to those bloody spectacles daily exhibited in our tragedies, of which
the French stage is so entirely clear.

THE LONDON MERCHANT

GEORGE LILLO was of Flemish descent, and was born in London in 1693. Little is known of his life. He is believed to have been a jeweller, fairly successful in business, and a dissenter with strong religious views. Contemporary writers speak highly of his character, and the warmest tribute of all was paid by Henry Fielding: He "had the gentlest and honestest manners, and at the same time the most friendly and obliging. . . . He had the spirit of an old Roman, joined to the innocence of a primitive Christian; he was content with his little state of life, in which his excellent temper of mind gave him a happiness beyond the power of riches. . . . In short, he was one of the best of men, and those who knew him best will most regret his loss."

Lillo died in 1739, and was buried in the vault of Shoreditch Church.

THE
London Merchant:

OR, THE

HISTORY

OF

GEORGE BARNWELL.

As it is Acted at the

THEATRE-ROYAL

IN

DRURY-LANE.

By His Majesty's Servants.

By Mr. *LILLO.*

Learn to be wise from others Harm,
And you shall do full well.

Old Ballad of the Lady's Fall.

LONDON:

Printed for J. Gray, at the *Cross-Keys* in the *Poultry;* and
sold by J. Roberts, in *Warwick-Lane.* MDCCXXXI.

[Price One Shilling and Six-pence]

TO SIR JOHN EYLES, Bar.

*Member of Parliament for, and Alderman of the City of London,
and Sub-Governor of the South-Sea Company.*

Sir,

If tragic poetry be, as Mr. Dryden has somewhere said, the
most excellent and most useful kind of writing, the more ex-
tensively useful the moral of any tragedy is, the more excellent
that piece must be of its kind.

I hope I shall not be thought to insinuate that this, to which
I have presumed to prefix your name, is such; that depends on
its fitness to answer the end of tragedy, the exciting of the
passions, in order to the correcting such of them as are criminal,
either in their nature, or through their excess. Whether the
following scenes do this in any tolerable degree, is, with the
deference that becomes one who would not be thought vain,
submitted to your candid and impartial judgment.

What I would infer is this, I think, evident truth; that tragedy
is so far from losing its dignity, by being accommodated to the
circumstances of the generality of mankind, that it is more truly
august in proportion to the extent of its influence, and the
numbers that are properly affected by it. As it is more truly
great to be the instrument of good to many, who stand in need
of our assistance, than to a very small part of that number.

If princes, etc., were alone liable to misfortune, arising from
vice or weakness in themselves or others, there would be good
reason for confining the characters in tragedy to those of superior
rank; but, since the contrary is evident, nothing can be more
reasonable than to proportion the remedy to the disease.

I am far from denying that tragedies, founded on any instructive and extraordinary events in history, or a well-invented
fable, where the persons introduced are of the highest rank,
are without their use, even to the bulk of the audience. The strong
contrast between a Tamerlane and a Bajazet, may have its
weight with an unsteady people, and contribute to the fixing
of them in the interest of a prince of the character of the former,
when through their own levity, or the arts of designing men,
they are rendered factious and uneasy, though they have the
highest reason to be satisfied. The sentiments and example of
a Cato may inspire his spectators with a just sense of the value
of liberty, when they see that honest patriot prefer death to an
obligation from a tyrant who would sacrifice the constitution
of his country, and the liberties of mankind, to his ambition or
revenge. I have attempted, indeed, to enlarge the province of

the graver kind of poetry, and should be glad to see it carried on by some abler hand. Plays founded on moral tales in private life may be of admirable use, by carrying conviction to the mind with such irresistible force as to engage all the faculties and powers of the soul in the cause of virtue, by stifling vice in its first principles. They who imagine this to be too much to be attributed to tragedy, must be strangers to the energy of that noble species of poetry. Shakespeare, who has given such amazing proofs of his genius, in that as well as in comedy, in his *Hamlet* has the following lines:

> "Had he the motive and the cause for passion
> That I have, he would drown the stage with tears
> And cleave the general ear with horrid speech;
> Make mad the guilty, and appal the free,
> Confound the ignorant; and amaze indeed
> The very faculty of eyes and ears."

and farther in the same speech:

> "I've heard that guilty creatures at a play
> Have, by the very cunning of the scene,
> Been so struck to the soul, that presently
> They have proclaimed their malefactions."

Prodigious! yet strictly just. But I shan't take up your valuable time with my remarks; only give me leave just to observe, that he seems so firmly persuaded of the power of a well-wrote piece to produce the effect here ascribed to it, as to make Hamlet venture his soul on the event, and rather trust that than a me senger from the other world, though it assumed, as he expresses it, his noble father's form, and assured him that it was his spirit. "I'll have," says Hamlet, "grounds more relative;

> . . . The Play's the thing,
> Wherein I'll catch the conscience of the King."

Such plays are the best answers to them who deny the lawfulness of the stage.

Considering the novelty of this attempt, I thought it would be expected from me to say something in its excuse; and I was unwilling to lose the opportunity of saying something of the usefulness of tragedy in general, and what may be reasonably expected from the farther improvement of this excellent kind of poetry.

Sir, I hope you will not think I have said too much of an art, a mean specimen of which I am ambitious enough to recommend to your favour and protection. A mind, conscious of superior worth, as much despises flattery as it is above it. Had I found in myself an inclination to so contemptible a vice, I should not have chose Sir JOHN EYLES for my patron. And indeed the best writ panegyric, though strictly true, must place you in a light much inferior to that in which you have long been fixed by the love and esteem of your fellow-citizens; whose choice of you for one of their representatives in Parliament has sufficiently declared their sense of your merit. Nor hath the knowledge of your worth been confined to the city. The proprietors in the South Sea Company, in which are included numbers of persons as considerable for their rank, fortune, and understanding, as any in the kingdom, gave the greatest proof of their confidence in your capacity and probity, when they chose you Sub-Governor of their Company, at a time when their affairs were in the utmost confusion, and their properties in the greatest danger. Nor is the Court insensible of your importance. I shall not, therefore, attempt your character, nor pretend to add anything to a reputation so well established.

Whatever others may think of a Dedication wherein there is so much said of other things, and so little of the person to whom it is addressed, I have reason to believe that you will the more easily pardon it on that very account.

I am, SIR,

Your most obedient

humble servant,

GEORGE LILLO.

PROLOGUE

SPOKEN BY MR. CIBBER, JUN.

THE tragic muse, sublime, delights to show
Princes distressed, and scenes of royal woe;
In awful pomp, majestic, to relate
The fall of nations, or some hero's fate;
That sceptred chiefs may, by example, know
The strange vicissitude of things below;
What dangers on security attend;
How pride and cruelty in ruin end;
Hence, Providence supreme to know, and own
Humanity, adds glory to a throne.
In ev'ry former age, and foreign tongue,
With native grandeur thus the goddess sung.
Upon our stage, indeed, with wished success,
You've sometimes seen her in a humbler dress—
Great only in distress. When she complains
In Southerne's, Rowe's, or Otway's moving strains,
The brilliant drops that fall from each bright eye,
The absent pomp with brighter gems supply.
Forgive us, then, if we attempt to show,
In artless strains, a tale of private woe.
A London 'prentice ruined is our theme,
Drawn from the famed old song that bears his name.
We hope your taste is not so high, to scorn
A moral tale esteemed ere you were born;
Which, for a century of rolling years,
Has filled a thousand, thousand eyes with tears.
If thoughtless youth to warn, and shame the age
From vice destructive, well becomes the stage;
If this example innocence secure,
Prevent our guilt, or by reflection cure;
If Millwood's dreadful guilt, and sad despair,
Commend the virtue of the good and fair;
Though art be wanting, and our numbers fail,
Indulge th' attempt in justice to the tale.

DRAMATIS PERSONÆ

MEN

THOROWGOOD	. Mr. Bridgwater
BARNWELL, Uncle to George . .	. Mr. Roberts
GEORGE BARNWELL	. Mr. Cibber, Jun.
TRUEMAN	. Mr. W. Mills
BLUNT	. Mr. R. Wetherilt

WOMEN

MARIA	. Mrs. Cibber
MILLWOOD	. Mrs. Butler
LUCY	. Mrs. Charke

Officers with their Attendants, Keeper, and Footmen.

SCENE—LONDON, and an adjacent village.

THE LONDON MERCHANT

OR THE

HISTORY OF GEORGE BARNWELL

ACT I

SCENE I.—*A room in Thorowgood's House*

THOROWGOOD *and* TRUEMAN

Trueman. Sir, the packet from Genoa is arrived.

(Gives letters.

Thorowgood. Heaven be praised! The storm that threatened our royal mistress, pure religion, liberty, and laws, is for a time diverted. The haughty and revengeful Spaniard, disappointed of the loan on which he depended from Genoa, must now attend the slow return of wealth from his new world, to supply his empty coffers, ere he can execute his purposed invasion of our happy island. By which means time is gained to make such preparations on our part, as may, Heaven concurring, prevent his malice, or turn the meditated mischief on himself.

True. He must be insensible indeed, who is not affected when the safety of his country is concerned. Sir, may I know by what means? If I am too bold——

Thor. Your curiosity is laudable; and I gratify it with the greater pleasure, because from thence you may learn how honest merchants, as such, may sometimes contribute to the safety of their country, as they do at all times to its happiness; that if hereafter you should be tempted to any action that has the appearance of vice or meanness in it, upon reflecting on the dignity of our profession, you may, with honest scorn, reject whatever is unworthy of it.

True. Should Barnwell, or I, who have the benefit of your example, by our ill-conduct bring any imputation on that honourable name, we must be left without excuse.

Thor. You compliment, young man. (TRUEMAN *bows respectfully*). Nay, I am not offended. As the name of merchant never degrades the gentleman, so by no means does it exclude him; only take heed not to purchase the character of complaisant at the expense of your sincerity. But to answer your question: The bank of Genoa had agreed, at excessive interest, and on

221

good security, to advance the King of Spain a sum of money
sufficient to equip his vast Armada; of which our peerless Elizabeth (more than in name the mother of her people) being well
informed, sent Walsingham, her wise and faithful secretary, to
consult the merchants of this loyal city; who all agreed to direct
their several agents to influence, if possible, the Genoese to
break their contract with the Spanish Court. 'Tis done; the
state and bank of Genoa, having maturely weighed, and rightly
judged of their true interest, prefer the friendship of the merchants of London to that of the monarch who proudly styles
himself King of both Indies.

True. Happy success of prudent counsels! What an expense of
blood and treasure is here saved! Excellent queen! O how
unlike to former princes, who made the danger of foreign enemies
a pretence to oppress their subjects by taxes great and grievous
to be borne.

Thor. Not so our gracious queen, whose richest exchequer is
her people's love, as their happiness her greatest glory.

True. On these terms to defend us, is to make our protection
a benefit worthy her who confers it, and well worth our acceptance. Sir, have you any commands for me at this time?

Thor. Only to look carefully over the files, to see whether
there are any tradesmen's bills unpaid; if there are, to send and
discharge 'em. We must not let artificers lose their time, so useful to the public and their families, in unnecessary attendance.

SCENE II

THOROWGOOD *and* MARIA

Well, Maria, have you given orders for the entertainment? I
would have it in some measure worthy the guests. Let there be
plenty, and of the best, that the courtiers, though they should
deny us citizens politeness, may at least commend our hospitality.

Maria. Sir, I have endeavoured not to wrong your well-
known generosity by an ill-timed parsimony.

Thor. Nay, 'twas a needless caution: I have no cause to doubt
your prudence.

Maria. Sir, I find myself unfit for conversation at present; I
should but increase the number of the company, without adding
to their satisfaction.

Thor. Nay, my child, this melancholy must not be indulged.

Maria. Company will but increase it: I wish you would
dispense with my absence. Solitude best suits my present temper.

Thor. You are not insensible that it is chiefly on your account
these noble lords do me the honour so frequently to grace my
board. Should you be absent, the disappointment may make
them repent their condescension, and think their labour lost.

Maria. He that shall think his time or honour lost in visiting

you, can set no real value on your daughter's company; whose
only merit is, that she is yours. The man of quality who chooses
to converse with a gentleman and merchant of your worth and
character, may confer honour by so doing, but he loses none.

Thor. Come, come, Maria; I need not tell you that a young
gentleman may prefer your conversation to mine, yet intend
me no disrespect at all; for though he may lose no honour in my
company, 'tis very natural for him to expect more pleasure in
yours. I remember the time when the company of the greatest
and wisest man in the kingdom would have been insipid and
tiresome to me, if it had deprived me of an opportunity of
enjoying your mother's.

Maria. Yours, no doubt, was as agreeable to her; for generous
minds know no pleasure in society but where 'tis mutual.

Thor. Thou knowest I have no heir, no child, but thee; the
fruits of many years' successful industry must all be thine. Now
it would give me pleasure, great as my love, to see on whom you
will bestow it. I am daily solicited by men of the greatest rank
and merit for leave to address you; but I have hitherto declined
it, in hopes that, by observation, I should learn which way your
inclination tends; for, as I know love to be essential to happiness
in the marriage state, I had rather my approbation should confirm your choice than direct it.

Maria. What can I say! How shall I answer, as I ought, this
tenderness, so uncommon even in the best of parents! But you
are without example; yet, had you been less indulgent, I had been
most wretched. That I look on the crowd of courtiers that visit
here, with equal esteem, but equal indifference, you have observed,
and I must needs confess; yet, had you asserted your authority,
and insisted on a parent's right to be obeyed, I had submitted,
and to my duty sacrificed my peace.

Thor. From your perfect obedience in every other instance,
I feared as much; and therefore would leave you without a
bias, in an affair wherein your happiness is so immediately
concerned.

Maria. Whether from a want of that just ambition that
would become your daughter, or from some other cause, I know
not; but I find high birth and titles don't recommend the man
who owns them to my affections.

Thor. I would not that they should, unless his merit recommends him more. A noble birth and fortune, though they make
not a bad man good, yet they are a real advantage to a worthy
one, and place his virtues in the fairest light.

Maria. I cannot answer for my inclinations; but they shall
ever be submitted to your wisdom and authority. And as you
will not compel me to marry where I cannot love, so love shall
never make me act contrary to my duty.—Sir, have I your
permission to retire?

Thor. I'll see you to your chamber.

SCENE III.—*A room in Millwood's House*

MILLWOOD, LUCY *waiting*

Mill. How do I look to-day, Lucy?

Lucy. Oh, killingly, madam! A little more red, and you'll be irresistible! But why this more than ordinary care of your dress and complexion? What new conquest are you aiming at?

Mill. A conquest would be new, indeed!

Lucy. Not to you, who make 'em every day—but to me— Well! 'tis what I'm never to expect, unfortunate as I am. But your wit and beauty——

Mill. First made me a wretch, and still continue me so. Men, however generous or sincere to one another, are all selfish hypocrites in their affairs with us; we are no otherwise esteemed or regarded by them, but as we contribute to their satisfaction.

Lucy. You are certainly, madam, on the wrong side in this argument. Is not the expense all theirs? And I am sure it is our own fault, if we han't our share of the pleasure.

Mill. We are but slaves to men.

Lucy. Nay, 'tis they that are slaves, most certainly, for we lay them under contribution.

Mill. Slaves have no property; no, not even in themselves: all is the victor's.

Lucy. You are strangely arbitrary in your principles, madam.

Mill. I would have my conquests complete, like those of the Spaniards in the New World; who first plundered the natives of all the wealth they had, and then condemned the wretches to the mines for life, to work for more.

Lucy. Well, I shall never approve of your scheme of government: I should think it much more politic, as well as just, to find my subjects an easier employment.

Mill. It is a general maxim among the knowing part of mankind, that a woman without virtue, like a man without honour or honesty, is capable of any action, though never so vile. And yet what pains will they not take, what arts not use, to seduce us from our innocence, and make us contemptible and wicked, even, in their own opinion? Then is it not just, the villains to their cost should find us so? But guilt makes them suspicious, and keeps them on their guard; therefore we can take advantage only of the young and innocent part of the sex; who, having never injured women, apprehend no injury from them.

Lucy. Ay, they must be young indeed!

Mill. Such a one, I think, I have found. As I've passed through the city, I have often observed him receiving and paying considerable sums of money; from thence I conclude he is employed in affairs of consequence.

Lucy. Is he handsome?

Mill. Ay, ay, the stripling is well made.

Lucy. About——

Mill. Eighteen.

Lucy. Innocent, handsome, and about eighteen! You'll be vastly happy. Why, if you manage well, you may keep him to yourself these two or three years.

Mill. If I manage well, I shall have done with him much sooner. Having long had a design on him, and meeting him yesterday, I made a full stop, and gazing wishfully on his face, asked him his name. He blushed; and, bowing very low, answered, George Barnwell. I begged his pardon for the freedom I had taken, and told him that he was the person I had long wished to see, and to whom I had an affair of importance to communicate at a proper time and place. He named a tavern; I talked of honour and reputation, and invited him to my house. He swallowed the bait, promised to come, and this is the time I expect him. (*Knocking at the door.*) Somebody knocks—D'ye hear; I am at home to nobody to-day but him.

SCENE IV

MILLWOOD

Mill. Less affairs must give way to those of more consequence; and I am strangely mistaken if this does not prove of great importance to me and him too, before I have done with him. Now, after what manner shall I receive him? Let me consider— what manner of person am I to receive? He is young, innocent, and bashful; therefore I must take care not to shock him at first. But then, if I have any skill in physiognomy, he is amorous, and, with a little assistance, will soon get the better of his modesty. I'll trust to nature, who does wonders in these matters. If to seem what one is not, in order to be the better liked for what one really is; if to speak one thing, and mean the direct contrary, be art in a woman,—I know nothing of nature.

SCENE V

To her BARNWELL, *bowing very low.* LUCY *at a distance*

Mill. Sir! the surprise and joy——

Barn. Madam——

Mill. This is such a favour.   (*Advancing.*

Barn. Pardon me, madam.

Mill. So unhoped for.   (*Still advances.*

          (BARNWELL *salutes her, and retires in confusion.*

To see you here. Excuse the confusion——

Barn. I fear I am too bold.

Mill. Alas, sir! All my apprehensions proceed from my fears

of your thinking me so. Please, sir, to sit. I am as much at a loss
how to receive this honour as I ought, as I am surprised at your
goodness in conferring it.

Barn. I thought you had expected me: I promised to come.

Mill. That is the more surprising; few men are such religious
observers of their word.

Barn. All, who are honest, are.

Mill. To one another; but we silly women are seldom thought
of consequence enough to gain a place in your remembrance.

(Laying her hand on his, as by accident.

Barn. Her disorder is so great, she don't perceive she has
laid her hand on mine. Heaven! how she trembles! What can
this mean?   *(Aside.*

Mill. The interest I have in all that relates to you (the reason
of which you shall know hereafter) excites my curiosity; and
were I sure you would pardon my presumption, I should desire
to know your real sentiments on a very particular affair.

Barn. Madam, you may command my poor thoughts on any
subject. I have none that I would conceal.

Mill. You'll think me bold.

Barn. No, indeed.

Mill. What, then, are your thoughts of love?

Barn. If you mean the love of women, I have not thought
of it [at] all. My youth and circumstances make such thoughts
improper in me yet. But if you mean the general love we owe to
mankind, I think no one has more of it in his temper than
myself. I don't know that person in the world whose happiness
I don't wish, and wouldn't promote were it in my power. In an
especial manner I love my uncle, and my master; but above all,
my friend.

Mill. You have a friend, then, whom you love?

Barn. As he does me, sincerely.

Mill. He is, no doubt, often blessed with your company and
conversation.

Barn. We live in one house together, and both serve the same
worthy merchant.

Mill. Happy, happy youth! Whoe'er thou art, I envy thee,
and so must all who see and know this youth. What have I lost,
by being formed a woman! I hate my sex, my self. Had I been
a man, I might, perhaps, have been as happy in your friendship,
as he who now enjoys it, but as it is—Oh!——

Barn. (*aside*). I never observed women before; or this is,
sure, the most beautiful of her sex. You seem disordered, madam.
May I know the cause?

Mill. Do not ask me—I can never speak it, whatever is the
cause. I wish for things impossible. I would be a servant, bound
to the same master as you are, to live in one house with you.

Barn. (*aside*). How strange, and yet how kind, her words
and actions are! And the effect they have on me is as strange.

I feel desires I never knew before. I must be gone, while I have power to go. Madam, I humbly take my leave.

Mill. You will not, sure, leave me so soon!

Barn. Indeed I must.

Mill. You cannot be so cruel! I have prepared a poor supper, at which I promised myself your company.

Barn. I am sorry I must refuse the honour that you designed me: but my duty to my master calls me hence. I never yet neglected his service. He is so gentle and so good a master, that should I wrong him, though he might forgive me, I never should forgive myself.

Mill. Am I refused by the first man, the second favour I ever stooped to ask? Go, then, thou proud, hard-hearted youth; but know, you are the only man that could be found who would let me sue twice for greater favours.

Barn. What shall I do! How shall I go, or stay!

Mill. Yet do not, do not leave me! I wish my sex's pride would meet your scorn; but when I look upon you, when I behold those eyes——Oh! spare my tongue, and let my blushes speak— this flood of tears to[o], that will force its way, and declare— what woman's modesty should hide.

Barn. Oh, heaven! she loves me, worthless as I am. Her looks, her words, her flowing tears confess it. And can I leave her, then? Oh, never, never!—Madam, dry up those tears: you shall command me always; I will stay here for ever, if you'd have me.

Lucy. So! she has wheedled him out of his virtue of obedience already, and will strip him of all the rest, one after another, till she has left him as few as her ladyship or myself. (*Aside.*

Mill. Now you are kind, indeed! but I mean not to detain you always: I would have you shake off all slavish obedience to your master; but you may serve him still.

Lucy. Serve him still! Ay, or he'll have no opportunity of fingering his cash; and then he'll not serve your end, I'll be sworn. (*Aside.*

SCENE VI

To them BLUNT

Blunt. Madam, supper's on the table.

Mill. Come, sir, you'll excuse all defects. My thoughts were too much employed on my guest to observe the entertainment.

(*Exeunt* MILLWOOD *and* BARNWELL.

SCENE VII

LUCY *and* BLUNT

Blunt. What! is all this preparation, this elegant supper, variety of wines, and music, for the entertainment of that young fellow?

Lucy. So it seems.

Blunt. What! is our mistress turned fool at last! She's in love with him, I suppose.

Lucy. I suppose not. But she designs to make him in love with her, if she can.

Blunt. What will she get by that? He seems under age, and can't be supposed to have much money.

Lucy. But his master has; and that's the same thing, as she'll manage it.

Blunt. I don't like this fooling with a handsome young fellow; while she's endeavouring to ensnare him, she may be caught herself.

Lucy. Nay, were she like me, that would certainly be the consequence; for, I confess, there is something in youth and innocence that moves me mightily.

Blunt. Yes; so does the smoothness and plumpness of a partridge move a mighty desire in the hawk to be the destruction of it.

Lucy. Why, birds are their prey, as men are ours; though, as you observed, we are sometimes caught ourselves. But that, I dare say, will never be the case with our mistress.

Blunt. I wish it may prove so; for you know we all depend upon her. Should she trifle away her time with a young fellow that there's nothing to be got by, we must all starve.

Lucy. There's no danger of that; for I am sure she has no view in this affair but interest.

Blunt. Well, and what hopes are there of success in that?

Lucy. The most promising that can be. 'Tis true the youth has his scruples; but she'll soon teach him to answer them, by stifling his conscience. Oh, the lad is in a hopeful way, depend upon it.

SCENE VIII

BARNWELL *and* MILLWOOD *at an entertainment*

Barn. What can I answer? All that I know is, that you are fair, and I am miserable.

Mill. We are both so; and yet the fault is in ourselves.

Barn. To ease our present anguish, by plunging into guilt, is to buy a moment's pleasure with an age of pain.

Mill. I should have thought the joys of love as lasting as they are great; if ours prove otherwise, 'tis your inconstancy must make them so.

Barn. The law of heaven will not be reversed, and that requires us to govern our passions.

Mill. To give us sense of beauty and desires, and yet forbid us to taste and be happy, is a cruelty to nature. Have we passions only to torment us?

Barn. To hear you talk, though in the cause of vice—to gaze upon your beauty—press your hand—and see your snow-white bosom heave and fall—enflames my wishes. My pulse beats high —my senses all are in a hurry, and I am on the rack of wild desire. Yet, for a moment's guilty pleasure, shall I lose my innocence, my peace of mind, and hopes of solid happiness?

Mill. Chimeras all!—Come on with me and prove
No joy's like woman kind, nor Heaven like love.

Barn. I would not, yet must on—
Reluctant thus, the merchant quits his ease,
And trusts to rocks, and sands, and stormy seas;
In hopes some unknown golden coast to find,
Commits himself, though doubtful, to the wind;
Longs much for joys to come, yet mourns those left behind.

ACT II

SCENE I.—*A room in Thorowgood's House*

BARNWELL

Barn. How strange are all things round me! Like some thief, who treads forbidden ground, fearful I enter each apartment of this well-known house. To guilty love, as if it was too little, already have I added breach of trust. A thief! Can I know myself that wretched thing, and look my honest friend and injured master in the face? Though hypocrisy may awhile conceal my guilt, at length it will be known, and public shame and ruin must ensue. In the meantime, what must be my life? Ever to speak a language foreign to my heart; hourly to add to the number of my crimes, in order to conceal 'em. Sure such was the condition of the grand apostate, when first he lost his purity. Like me, disconsolate, he wandered; and, while yet in heaven, bore all his future hell about him.

SCENE II

BARNWELL *and* TRUEMAN

True. Barnwell, oh, how I rejoice to see you safe! So will our master, and his gentle daughter; who, during your absence, often inquired after you.

Barn. (*aside*). Would he were gone! His officious love will pry into the secrets of my soul.

True. Unless you knew the pain the whole family has felt on your account, you can't conceive how much you are beloved. But why thus cold and silent? When my heart is full of joy for your return, why do you turn away; why thus avoid me? What have I done? How am I altered since you saw me last? Or rather,

what have you done; and why are you thus changed? for I am
still the same.

Barn. (*aside*). What have I done, indeed!

True. Not speak!—nor look upon me!——

Barn. (*aside*). By my face he would discover all I would
conceal; methinks already I begin to hate him.

True. I cannot bear this usage from a friend; one whom till
now I ever found so loving; whom yet I love; though this unkindness strikes at the root of friendship, and might destroy it
in any breast but mine.

Barn. I am not well. (*Turning to him.*) Sleep has been a
stranger to these eyes since you beheld them last.

True. Heavy they look, indeed, and swollen with tears;—
now they o'erflow. Rightly did my sympathising heart forebode
last night, when thou wast absent, something fatal to our peace.

Barn. Your friendship engages you too far. My troubles
whatever they are, are mine alone, you have no interest in them;
nor ought your concern for me give you a moment's pain.

True. You speak as if you knew of friendship nothing but
the name. Before I saw your grief I felt it. Since we parted last
I have slept no more than you, but pensive in my chamber sat
alone, and spent the tedious night in wishes for your safety and
return; e'en now, though ignorant of the cause, your sorrow
wounds me to the heart.

Barn. 'Twill not be always thus. Friendship and all engagements cease, as circumstances and occasions vary; and since
you once may hate me, perhaps it might be better for us both
that now you loved me less.

True. Sure I but dream! Without a cause would Barnwell
use me thus? Ungenerous and ungrateful youth, farewell; I
shall endeavour to follow your advice. (*Going.*) [*Aside.*] Yet stay;
perhaps I am too rash; and angry, when the cause demands
compassion. Some unforeseen calamity may have befallen him,
too great to bear.

Barn. [*aside*]. What part am I reduced to act! 'Tis vile and
base to move his temper thus, the best of friends and men.

True. I am to blame; prithee forgive me, Barnwell. Try to
compose your ruffled mind; and let me know the cause that thus
transports you from yourself. My friendly counsel may restore
your peace.

Barn. All that is possible for man to do for man, your generous
friendship may effect; but here even that's in vain.

True. Something dreadful is labouring in your breast; Oh,
give it vent, and let me share your grief; 'twill ease your pain,
should it admit no cure, and make it lighter by the part I bear.

Barn. Vain supposition! my woes increase by being observed;
should the cause be known, they would exceed all bounds.

True. So well I know thy honest heart, guilt cannot harbour
there.

Barn. (*aside*). Oh, torture insupportable!

True. Then why am I excluded? Have I a thought I would conceal from you?

Barn. If still you urge me on this hated subject, I'll never enter more beneath this roof, nor see your face again.

True. 'Tis strange—but I have done, say but you hate me not.

Barn. Hate you! I am not that monster yet.

True. Shall our friendship still continue?

Barn. It's a blessing I never was worthy of, yet now must stand on terms; and but upon conditions can confirm it.

True. What are they?

Barn. Never hereafter, though you should wonder at my conduct, desire to know more than I am willing to reveal.

True. 'Tis hard; but upon any conditions I must be your friend.

Barn. Then, as much as one lost to himself can be another's, I am yours.   (*Embracing.*

True. Be ever so, and may Heaven restore your peace!

Barn. Will yesterday return? We have heard the glorious sun, that till then incessant rolled, once stopped his rapid course, and once went back. The dead have risen, and parched rocks poured forth a liquid stream to quench a people's thirst; the sea divided, and formed walls of water, while a whole nation passed in safety through its sandy bosom; hungry lions have refused their prey, and men unhurt have walked amidst consuming flames. But never yet did time, once past, return.

True. Though the continued chain of time has never once been broke, nor ever will, but uninterrupted must keep on its course, till lost in eternity it ends there where it first begun: yet, as Heaven can repair whatever evils time can bring upon us, he who trusts Heaven ought never to despair. But business requires our attendance—business, the youth's best preservative from ill, as idleness his worst of snares. Will you go with me?

Barn. I'll take a little time to reflect on what has passed, and follow you.

SCENE III

BARNWELL

Barn. I might have trusted Trueman to have applied to my uncle to have repaired the wrong I have done my master—but what of Millwood? Must I expose her, too? Ungenerous and base! Then Heaven requires it not. But Heaven requires that I forsake her. What! never see her more! Does Heaven require that? I hope I may see her, and Heaven not be offended. Presumptuous hope—dearly already have I proved my frailty; should I once more tempt Heaven, I may be left to fall never to rise again. Yet shall I leave her, for ever leave her, and not let her know the cause? She who loves me with such a boundless passion! Can cruelty be duty? I judge of what she then must feel, by what I now endure. The love of life, and fear of shame, opposed by inclination strong as death or shame, like wind and tide in raging conflict met, when neither can prevail, keep me in doubt. How then can I determine!

SCENE IV

Thorowgood *and* Barnwell

Thor. Without a cause assigned, or notice given, to absent yourself last night was a fault, young man, and I came to chide you for it, but hope I am prevented. That modest blush, the confusion so visible in your face, speak grief and shame. When we have offended Heaven, It requires no more; and shall man, who needs himself to be forgiven, be harder to appease? If my pardon or love be of moment to your peace, look up secure of both.

Barn. (*aside*). This goodness has o'ercome me. Oh, sir, you know not the nature and extent of my offence; and I should abuse your mistaken bounty to receive 'em. Though I had rather die than speak my shame; though racks could not have forced the guilty secret from my breast, your kindness has.

Thor. Enough, enough, whate'er it be; this concern shows you're convinced, and I am satisfied. How painful is the sense of guilt to an ingenuous mind! Some youthful folly, which it were prudent not to inquire into. When we consider the frail condition of humanity, it may raise our pity, not our wonder, that youth should go astray; when reason, weak at the best when opposed to inclination, scarce formed, and wholly unassisted by experience, faintly contends, or willingly becomes the slave of sense. The state of youth is much to be deplored; and the more so, because they see it not; they being then to danger most exposed when they are least prepared for their defence.

Barn. It will be known, and you recall your pardon and abhor me.

Thor. I never will; so Heaven confirm to me the pardon of my offences! Yet be upon your guard in this gay, thoughtless season of your life; now, when the sense of pleasure's quick, and passion high, the voluptuous appetites raging and fierce demand the strongest curb, take heed of a relapse: when vice becomes habitual, the very power of leaving it is lost.

Barn. Hear me, then, on my knees, confess——

Thor. I will not hear a syllable more upon this subject; it were not mercy, but cruelty, to hear what must give you such torment to reveal.

Barn. This generosity amazes and distracts me.

Thor. This remorse makes thee dearer to me than if thou hadst never offended. Whatever is your fault, of this I am certain, 'twas harder for you to offend, than me to pardon.

SCENE V

BARNWELL

Barn. Villain! Villain! Villain! basely to wrong so excellent a man. Should I again return to folly?—Detested thought!— But what of Millwood then?—Why, I renounce her; I give her up. The struggle's over, and virtue has prevailed. Reason may convince, but gratitude compels. This unlooked for generosity has saved me from destruction.   (*Going.*

SCENE VI

To him a Footman

Foot. Sir, two ladies from your uncle in the country desire to see you.

Barn. (*aside*). Who should they be?—Tell them I'll wait upon them.

SCENE VII

BARNWELL

Barn. Methinks I dread to see them. Guilt, what a coward hast thou made me! Now everything alarms me.

SCENE VIII.—*Another room in Thorowgood's House*

MILLWOOD *and* LUCY: *and to them a Footman*

Foot. Ladies, he'll wait upon you immediately.

Mill. 'Tis very well. I thank you.

SCENE IX

BARNWELL, MILLWOOD *and* LUCY

Barn. Confusion! Millwood!

Mill. That angry look tells me that here I'm an unwelcome guest; I feared as much; the unhappy are so everywhere.

Barn. Will nothing but my utter ruin content you?

Mill. Unkind and cruel! Lost myself, your happiness is now my only care.

Barn. How did you gain admission?

Mill. Saying we were desired by your uncle to visit and deliver a message to you, we were received by the family without suspicion, and with much respect directed here.

Barn. Why did you come at all?

Mill. I never shall trouble you more. I'm come to take my leave for ever. Such is the malice of my fate: I go hopeless, despairing ever to return. This hour is all I have left me; one short hour is all I have to bestow on love and you, for whom I thought the longest life too short.

Barn. Then we are met to part for ever?

Mill. It must be so. Yet think not that time or absence ever shall put a period to my grief, or make me love you less. Though I must leave you, yet condemn me not.

Barn. Condemn you! No; I approve your resolution, and rejoice to hear it; 'tis just—'tis necessary—I have well weighed, and found it so.

Lucy (*aside*). I am afraid the young man has more sense than she thought he had.

Barn. Before you came, I had determined never to see you more.

Mill. (*aside*). Confusion!

Lucy (*aside*). Ay, we are all out! This is a turn so unexpected, that I shall make nothing of my part; they must e'en play the scene betwixt themselves.

Mill. It was some relief to think, though absent, you would love me still. But to find, though fortune had been kind, that you, more cruel and inconstant, had resolved to cast me off—this, as I never could expect, I have not learnt to bear.

Barn. I am sorry to hear you blame in me a resolution that so well becomes us both.

Mill. I have reason for what I do, but you have none.

Barn. Can we want a reason for parting, who have so many to wish we never had met?

Mill. Look on me, Barnwell. Am I deformed or old, that satiety so soon succeeds enjoyment? Nay, look again; am I not she whom yesterday you thought the fairest and the kindest of her sex, whose hand, trembling with ecstasy, you pressed and moulded thus, while on my eyes you gazed with such delight as if desire increased by being fed?

Barn. No more; let me repent my former follies, if possible, without remembering what they were.

Mill. Why?

Barn. Such is my frailty, that 'tis dangerous.

Mill. Where is the danger, since we are to part?

Barn. The thought of that already is too painful.

Mill. If it be painful to part, then I may hope, at least, you do not hate me?

Barn. No, no, I never said I did. Oh, my heart!

Mill. Perhaps you pity me?

Barn. I do—I do. Indeed, I do.

Mill. You'll think upon me?

Barn. Doubt it not, while I can think at all.

Mill. You may judge an embrace at parting too great a favour—though it would be the last. (*He draws back.*) A look shall then suffice. Farewell—for ever.

SCENE X

Barnwell

Barn. If to resolve to suffer be to conquer, I have conquered. Painful victory!

SCENE XI

Barnwell, Millwood *and* Lucy

Mill. One thing I had forgot;—I never must return to my own house again. This I thought proper to let you know, lest your mind should change, and you should seek in vain to find me there. Forgive me this second intrusion; I only came to give you this caution, and that, perhaps, was needless.

Barn. I hope it was; yet it is kind, and I must thank you for it.

Mill. (*to Lucy*). My friend, your arm. Now I am gone for ever. (*Going.*

Barn. One more thing. Sure there's no danger in my knowing where you go? If you think otherwise——

Mill. (*weeping*). Alas!

Lucy (*aside*). We are right, I find; that's my cue. Ah, dear sir, she's going she knows not whither; but go she must.

Barn. Humanity obliges me to wish you well; why will you thus expose yourself to needless troubles?

Lucy. Nay, there's no help for it: she must quit the town immediately, and the kingdom as soon as possible. It was no small matter, you may be sure, that could make her resolve to leave you.

Mill. No more, my friend; since he for whose dear sake alone I suffer, and am content to suffer, is kind and pities me; where'er I wander, through wilds and deserts, benighted and forlorn, that thought shall give me comfort.

Barn. For my sake!—Oh, tell me how! which way am I so cursed, as to bring such ruin on thee?

Mill. No matter; I am contented with my lot.

Barn. Leave me not in this uncertainty.

Mill. I have said too much.

Barn. How, how am I the cause of your undoing?

Mill. 'Twill but increase your troubles.

Barn. My troubles can't be greater than they are.

Lucy. Well, well, sir, if she won't satisfy you, I will.

Barn. I am bound to you beyond expression.

Mill. Remember, sir, that I desired you not to hear it.

Barn. Begin, and ease my racking expectation.

Lucy. Why, you must know, my lady here was an only child; but her parents dying while she was young, left her and her fortune (no inconsiderable one, I assure you) to the care of a gentleman who has a good estate of his own.

Mill. Ay, ay, the barbarous man is rich enough; but what are riches when compared to love?

Lucy. For a while he performed the office of a faithful guardian, settled her in a house, hired her servants—But you have seen in what manner she lived, so I need say no more of that.

Mill. How I shall live hereafter, Heaven knows!

Lucy. All things went on as one could wish; till some time ago, his wife dying, he fell violently in love with his charge, and would fain have married her. Now the man is neither old nor ugly, but a good personable sort of a man; but I don't know how it was, she could never endure him. In short, her ill-usage so provoked him, that he brought in an account of his executorship, wherein he makes her debtor to him——

Mill. A trifle in itself, but more than enough to ruin me, whom, by this unjust account, he had stripped of all before.

Lucy. Now, she having neither money nor friend, except me, who am as unfortunate as herself, he compelled her to pass his account, and give bond for the sum he demanded; but still provided handsomely for her, and continued his courtship, till being informed by his spies (truly I suspect some in her own family) that you were entertained at her house, and stayed with her all night, he came this morning raving and storming like a madman, talks no more of marriage (so there's no hopes of making up matters that way) but vows her ruin, unless she'll allow him the same favour that he supposes she granted you.

Barn. Must she be ruined, or find her refuge in another's arms?

Mill. He gave me but an hour to resolve in; that's happily spent with you. And now I go——

Barn. To be exposed to all the rigours of the various seasons; the summer's parching heat, and winter's cold; unhoused, to wander, friendless, through the unhospitable world, in misery and want; attended with fear and danger, and pursued by malice and revenge. Wouldst thou endure all this for me, and can I do nothing, nothing to prevent it?

Lucy. 'Tis really a pity there can be no way found out.

Barn. Oh, where are all my resolutions now? Like early vapours, or the morning dew, chased by the sun's warm beams, they're vanished and lost, as though they had never been.

Lucy. Now, I advised her, sir, to comply with the gentleman; that would not only put an end to her troubles, but make her fortune at once.

Barn. Tormenting fiend, away! I had rather perish, nay, see her perish, than have her saved by him. I will, myself, prevent her ruin, though with my own. A moment's patience; I'll return immediately.

SCENE XII

MILLWOOD *and* LUCY

Lucy. 'Twas well you came; or, by what I can perceive, you had lost him.

Mill. That, I must confess, was a danger I did not foresee; I was only afraid he should have come without money. You know, a house of entertainment, like mine, is not kept with nothing.

Lucy. That's very true; but then you should be reasonable in your demands; 'tis pity to discourage a young man.

SCENE XIII

BARNWELL, MILLWOOD *and* LUCY

Barn. [*aside*]. What am I about to do?—Now you, who boast your reason all-sufficient, suppose yourselves in my condition, and determine for me, whether it's right to let her suffer for my faults, or, by this small addition to my guilt, prevent the ill-effects of what is past.

Lucy. These young sinners think everything in the ways of wickedness so strange! But I could tell him that this is nothing but what's very common; for one vice as naturally begets another, as a father a son. But he'll find out that himself, if he lives long enough.

Barn. Here, take this, and with it purchase your deliverance; return to your house, and live in peace and safety.

Mill. So, I may hope to see you there again?

Barn. Answer me not, but fly; lest, in the agonies of my remorse, I take again what is not mine to give, and abandon thee to want and misery.

Mill. Say but you'll come.

Barn. You are my fate, my heaven or my hell; only leave me now, dispose of me hereafter as you please.

SCENE XIV

BARNWELL

Barn. What have I done! Were my resolutions founded on reason, and sincerely made—why then has Heaven suffered me to fall? I sought not the occasion; and, if my heart deceives me not, compassion and generosity were my motives. Is virtue inconsistent with itself, or are vice and virtue only empty names? Or do they depend on accidents, beyond our power to produce or to prevent—wherein we have no part, and yet must be determined by the event? But why should I attempt to reason? All is confusion, horror and remorse. I find I am lost, cast down from all my late-erected hopes, and plunged again in guilt, yet scarce know how or why:

Such undistinguished horrors make my brain,
Like hell, the seat of darkness and of pain.

ACT III

SCENE I.—[*Thorowgood's House*]

THOROWGOOD *and* TRUEMAN [*discovered, with account books, seated at a table*]

Thor. Methinks I would not have you only learn the method of merchandise, and practise it hereafter, merely as a means of getting wealth. 'Twill be well worth your pains to study it as a science. See how it is founded in reason, and the nature of things; how it has promoted humanity, as it has opened and yet keeps up an intercourse between nations, far remote from one another in situation, customs and religion; promoting arts, industry, peace and plenty; by mutual benefits diffusing mutual love from pole to pole.

True. Something of this I have considered, and hope, by your assistance, to extend my thoughts much farther. I have observed those countries, where trade is promoted and encouraged, do not make discoveries to destroy, but to improve mankind by love and friendship; to tame the fierce and polish the most savage; to teach them the advantages of honest traffic, by taking from them, with their own consent, their useless superfluities, and giving them, in return, what, from their ignorance in manual arts, their situation, or some other accident, they stand in need of.

Thor. 'Tis justly observed: the populous East, luxuriant, abounds with glittering gems, bright pearls, aromatic spices, and health-restoring drugs. The late found Western world glows with unnumbered veins of gold and silver ore. On every climate and on every country, Heaven has bestowed some good peculiar to itself. It is the industrious merchant's business to collect the various blessings of each soil and climate, and, with the product of the whole, to enrich his native country.—Well! I have examined your accounts: they are not only just, as I have always found them, but regularly kept, and fairly entered. I commend your diligence. Method in business is the surest guide. He who neglects it frequently stumbles, and always wanders perplexed, uncertain, and in danger.—Are Barnwell's accounts ready for my inspection? He does not use to be the last on these occasions.

True. Upon receiving your orders he retired, I thought, in some confusion. If you please, I'll go and hasten him. I hope he has not been guilty of any neglect.

Thor. I'm now going to the Exchange; let him know, at my return I expect to find him ready.

SCENE II

MARIA *with a book. Sits and reads*

Maria. How forcible is truth! The weakest mind, inspired with love of that, fixed and collected in itself, with indifference beholds the united force of earth and hell opposing. Such souls are raised above the sense of pain, or so supported that they regard it not. The martyr cheaply purchases his Heaven; small are his sufferings, great is his reward. Not so the wretch who combats love with duty; when the mind, weakened and dissolved by the soft passion, feeble and hopeless, opposes its own desires—what is an hour, a day, a year of pain, to a whole life of tortures such as these?

SCENE III

TRUEMAN *and* MARIA

True. Oh, Barnwell! Oh, my friend! how art thou fallen!

Maria. Ha! Barnwell! What of him? Speak! say, what of Barnwell?

True. 'Tis not to be concealed: I've news to tell of him that will afflict your generous father, yourself, and all who knew him.

Maria. Defend us, Heaven!

True. I cannot speak it. See there.

(Gives a letter, MARIA *reads.*

"Trueman, I know my absence will surprise my honoured master and yourself; and the more, when you shall understand that the reason of my withdrawing is my having embezzled part of the cash with which I was entrusted. After this, 'tis needless to inform you, that I intend never to return again. Though this might have been known by examining my accounts, yet to

prevent that unnecessary trouble, and to cut off all fruitless
expectations of my return, I have left this from the lost
GEORGE BARNWELL.''

True. Lost indeed! Yet how he should be guilty of what he
there charges himself withal, raises my wonder equal to my
grief. Never had youth a higher sense of virtue. Justly he thought,
and as he thought he practised; never was life more regular than
his. An understanding uncommon at his years; an open, generous
manliness of temper; his manners easy, unaffected, and engaging.

Maria. This, and much more, you might have said with
truth. He was the delight of every eye, and joy of every heart
that knew him.

True. Since such he was, and was my friend, can I support
his loss? See, the fairest and happiest maid this wealthy city
boasts, kindly condescends to weep for thy unhappy fate, poor,
ruined Barnwell!

Maria. Trueman, do you think a soul so delicate as his, so
sensible of shame, can e'er submit to live a slave to vice?

True. Never, never. So well I know him, I'm sure this act of
his, so contrary to his nature, must have been caused by some
unavoidable necessity.

Maria. Is there no means yet to preserve him?

True. Oh, that there were! But few men recover reputation
lost, a merchant never. Nor would he, I fear, though I should
find him, ever be brought to look his injured master in the face.

Maria. I fear as much, and therefore would never have my
father know it.

True. That's impossible.

Maria. What's the sum?

True. 'Tis considerable; I've marked it here, to show it, with
the letter, to your father, at his return.

Maria. If I should supply the money, could you so dispose
of that and the account, as to conceal this unhappy mismanage-
ment from my father?

True. Nothing more easy. But can you intend it? Will you
save a helpless wretch from ruin? Oh, 'twere an act worthy
such exalted virtue as Maria's! Sure Heaven, in mercy to my
friend, inspired the generous thought.

Maria. Doubt not but I would purchase so great a happiness
at a much dearer price. But how shall he be found?

True. Trust to my diligence for that. In the meantime, I'll
conceal his absence from your father, or find such excuses for
it, that the real cause shall never be suspected.

Maria. In attempting to save from shame one whom we
hope may yet return to virtue, to Heaven and you, the judges
of this action, I appeal, whether I have done anything mis-
becoming my sex and character.

True. Earth must approve the deed, and Heaven, I doubt
not, will reward it.

Maria. If Heaven succeed it, I am well rewarded. A virgin's fame is sullied by suspicion's slightest breath; and therefore, as this must be a secret from my father and the world for Barnwell's sake, for mine let it be so to him.

SCENE IV.—*Millwood's House*

LUCY *and* BLUNT

Lucy. Well, what do you think of Millwood's conduct now?

Blunt. I own it is surprising. I don't know which to admire most, her feigned or his real passion; though I have sometimes been afraid that her avarice would discover her. But his youth and want of experience make it the easier to impose on him.

Lucy. No, it is his love. To do him justice, notwithstanding his youth, he don't want understanding. But you men are much easier imposed on in these affairs, than your vanity will allow you to believe. Let me see the wisest of you all as much in love with me as Barnwell is with Millwood, and I'll engage to make as great a fool of him.

Blunt. And, all circumstances considered, to make as much money of him too?

Lucy. I can't answer for that. Her artifice, in making him rob his master at first, and the various stratagems by which she has obliged him to continue in that course, astonish even me, who know her so well.

Blunt. But then you are to consider that the money was his master's.

Lucy. There was the difficulty of it. Had it been his own, it had been nothing. Were the world his, she might have it for a smile. But those golden days are done; he's ruined, and Millwood's hopes of further profits there are at an end.

Blunt. That's no more than we all expected.

Lucy. Being called by his master to make up his accounts, he was forced to quit his house and service; and wisely flies to Millwood for relief and entertainment.

Blunt. I have not heard of this before: how did she receive him?

Lucy. As you would expect. She wondered what he meant; was astonished at his impudence; and, with an air of modesty peculiar to herself, swore so heartily that she never saw him before, that she put me out of countenance.

Blunt. That's much indeed! But how did Barnwell behave?

Lucy. He grieved; and at length, enraged at this barbarous treatment, was preparing to be gone, and making toward the door, showed a bag of money which he had stolen from his master, the last he is ever like to have from thence.

Blunt. But then, Millwood?

Lucy. Ay, she, with her usual address, returned to her old

arts of lying, swearing, and dissembling; hung on his neck and
wept, and swore 'twas meant in jest, till the easy fool melted
into tears, threw the money into her lap, and swore he had
rather die than think her false.

Blunt. Strange infatuation!

Lucy. But what followed was stranger still. As doubts and
fears, followed by reconcilement, ever increase love where the
passion is sincere, so in him it caused so wild a transport of
excessive fondness, such joy, such grief, such pleasure, and such
anguish, that nature in him seemed sinking with the weight,
and the charmed soul disposed to quit his breast for hers. Just
then, when every passion with lawless anarchy prevailed, and
reason was in the raging tempest lost, the cruel, artful Millwood
prevailed upon the wretched youth to promise—what I tremble
to but think on.

Blunt. I am amazed! What can it be?

Lucy. You will be more so, to hear it is to attempt the life
of his nearest relation and best benefactor.

Blunt. His uncle! whom we have often heard him speak of,
as a gentleman of a large estate, and fair character, in the
country where he lives!

Lucy. The same. She was no sooner possessed of the last dear
purchase of his ruin, but her avarice, insatiate as the grave,
demands this horrid sacrifice—Barnwell's near relation; and
unsuspected virtue must give too easy means to seize the good
man's treasure, whose blood must seal the dreadful secret, and
prevent the terrors of her guilty fears.

Blunt. Is it possible she could persuade him to do an act like
that? He is, by nature, honest, grateful, compassionate, and
generous; and though his love and her artful persuasions have
wrought him to practise what he most abhors, yet we all can
witness for him with what reluctance he has still complied! So
many tears he shed o'er each offence, as might, if possible,
sanctify theft, and make a merit of a crime.

Lucy. 'Tis true, at the naming the murder of his uncle, he
started into rage; and, breaking from her arms (where she till
then had held him with well-dissembled love, and false endear-
ments), called her cruel monster, devil! and told her she was
born for his destruction. She thought it not for her purpose to
meet his rage with rage, but affected a most passionate fit of
grief, railed at her fate, and cursed her wayward stars, that still
her wants should force her to press him to act such deeds as
she must needs abhor as well as he; but told him necessity had
no law, and love no bounds; that therefore he never truly loved,
but meant, in her necessity, to forsake her; then kneeled and
swore, that since by his refusal he had given her cause to doubt
his love, she never would see him more, unless, to prove it true,
he robbed his uncle to supply her wants, and murdered him to
keep it from discovery.

Blunt. I am astonished! What said he?

Lucy. Speechless he stood; but in his face you might have read that various passions tore his very soul. Oft he in anguish threw his eyes towards Heaven, and then as often bent their beams on her, then wept and groaned, and beat his breast; at length, with horror not to be expressed, he cried, Thou cursèd fair, have I not given dreadful proofs of love? What drew me from my youthful innocence to stain my then unspotted soul, but love? What caused me to rob my gentle master, but cursèd love? What makes me now a fugitive from his service, loathed by myself, and scorned by all the world, but love? What fills my eyes with tears, my soul with torture never felt on this side death before? Why, love, love, love! And why, above all, do I resolve (for, tearing his hair, he cried, I do resolve) to kill my uncle?

Blunt. Was she not moved? It makes me weep to hear the sad relation.

Lucy. Yes—with joy, that she had gained her point. She gave him no time to cool, but urged him to attempt it instantly. He's now gone. If he performs it, and escapes, there's more money for her; if not, he'll ne'er return, and then she's fairly rid of him.

Blunt. 'Tis time the world was rid of such a monster.

Lucy. If we don't do our endeavours to prevent this murder, we are as bad as she.

Blunt. I am afraid it is too late.

Lucy. Perhaps not. Her barbarity to Barnwell makes me hate her. We have run too great a length with her already. I did not think her or myself so wicked, as I find, upon reflection, we are.

Blunt. 'Tis true, we have all been too much so. But there is something so horrid in murder, that all other crimes seem nothing when compared to that; I would not be involved in the guilt of that for all the world.

Lucy. Nor I, Heaven knows. Therefore let us clear ourselves, by doing all that is in our power to prevent it. I have just thought of a way that to me seems probable. Will you join with me to detect this cursèd design?

Blunt. With all my heart. How else shall I clear myself? He who knows of a murder intended to be committed, and does not discover it, in the eye of the law and reason is a murderer.

Lucy. Let us lose no time; I'll acquaint you with the particulars as we go.

SCENE V.—*A walk at some distance from a Country-Seat*

Barnwell

Barn. A dismal gloom obscures the face of day. Either the sun has slipped behind a cloud, or journeys down the west of heaven with more than common speed, to avoid the sight of

what I am doomed to act. Since I set forth on this accursed
design, where'er I tread, methinks the solid earth trembles
beneath my feet. Yonder limpid stream, whose hoary fall has
made a natural cascade, as I passed by, in doleful accents seemed
to murmur "Murder!" The earth, the air and water seem concerned, but that's not strange: the world is punished, and Nature
feels the shock, when Providence permits a good man's fall.
Just Heaven! Then what should I be! For him that was my
father's only brother—and, since his death, has been to me a
father; who took me up an infant and an orphan, reared me
with tenderest care, and still indulged me with most paternal
fondness? Yet here I stand avowed his destined murderer—I
stiffen with horror at my own impiety. 'Tis yet unperformed—
what if I quit my bloody purpose, and fly the place? (*Going,
then stops.*)—But whither, oh, whither shall I fly? My master's
once friendly doors are ever shut against me; and without money
Millwood will never see me more; and life is not to be endured
without her. She's got such firm possession of my heart and
governs there with such despotic sway.—Ay, there's the cause
of all my sin and sorrow: 'tis more than love; 'tis the fever of
the soul and madness of desire. In vain does nature, reason,
conscience, all oppose it; the impetuous passion bears down all
before it, and drives me on to lust, to theft, and murder. Oh,
conscience! feeble guide to virtue! who only shows us when we
go astray, but wants the power to stop us in our course!—Ha!
in yonder shady walk I see my uncle. He's alone. Now for
my disguise. (*Plucks out a visor.*)—This is his hour of private
meditation. Thus daily he prepares his soul for Heaven; whilst I
—But what have I to do with Heaven? Ha! no struggles,
conscience—

> *Hence, hence, remorse, and ev'ry thought that's good:*
> *The storm that lust began must end in blood.*
> > (*Puts on the visor, draws a pistol [and exit].*)

SCENE VI.—*A close walk in a Wood*

UNCLE

[*Uncle.*] If I were superstitious, I should fear some danger
lurked unseen, or death were nigh. A heavy melancholy clouds
my spirits. My imagination is filled with ghastly forms of dreary
graves, and bodies changed by death; when the pale lengthened
visage attracts each weeping eye, and fills the musing soul at
once with grief and horror, pity and aversion.—I will indulge
the thought. The wise man prepares himself for death by making
it familiar to his mind. When strong reflections hold the mirror
near, and the living in the dead behold their future selves, how
does each inordinate passion and desire cease, or sicken at the

view! The mind scarce moves; the blood, curdling and chilled, creeps slowly through the veins: fixed still, and motionless like the solemn object of our thoughts, we are almost at present what we must be hereafter; till curiosity awakes the soul, and sets it on inquiry.

SCENE VII

UNCLE. GEORGE BARNWELL *at a distance*

Uncle. O Death! thou strange mysterious power, seen every day, yet never understood but by the incommunicative dead, what art thou? The extensive mind of man, that with a thought circles the earth's vast globe, sinks to the centre, or ascends above the stars; that worlds exotic finds, or thinks it finds, thy thick clouds attempts to pass in vain, lost and bewildered in the horrid gloom; defeated, she returns more doubtful than before; of nothing certain but of labour lost.

(*During this speech* BARNWELL *sometimes presents the pistol, and draws it back again ; at last he drops it, at which his uncle starts and draws his sword.*

Barn. Oh, 'tis impossible!

Uncle. A man so near me! armed and masked——

Barn. Nay, then there's no retreat.

(*Plucks a poignard from his bosom, and stabs him.*

Uncle. Oh, I am slain! All-gracious Heaven, regard the prayer of thy dying servant; bless, with thy choicest blessings, my dearest nephew; forgive my murderer, and take my fleeting soul to endless mercy.

(BARNWELL *throws off his mask ; runs to him ; and kneeling by him, raises and chafes him.*

Barn. Expiring saint! Oh, murdered, martyred uncle! lift up your dying eyes, and view your nephew in your murderer!——Oh, do not look so tenderly upon me!——Let indignation lighten from your eyes, and blast me ere you die!——By Heaven, he weeps, in pity of my woes!——Tears, tears, for blood!——The murdered, in the agonies of death, weeps for his murderer.——Oh, speak your pious purpose; pronounce my pardon, then, and take me with you!——He would, but cannot.——Oh, why, with such fond affection, do you press my murdering hand?——What! will you kiss me! (*Kisses him. Uncle groans and dies.*) He is gone for ever—and oh! I follow. (*Swoons away upon his uncle's dead body.*) Do I still live to press the suffering bosom of the earth? Do I still breathe, and taint with my infectious breath the wholesome air! Let Heaven from its high throne, in justice or in mercy, now look down on that dear murdered saint, and me the murderer. And, if his vengeance spares, let pity strike and end my wretched being!—— Murder the worst of crimes, and parricide the worst of murders, and this the worst of parricides! Cain, who stands on record from the birth of time, and must to its last final period, as accursed, slew a brother favoured above him. Detested Nero by another's hand dispatched a mother that he feared and hated. But I, with my own hand, have murdered a brother, mother, father, and a friend, most loving and beloved. This execrable act of mine's without a parallel. O may it ever stand alone—the last of murders, as it is the worst!

> The rich man thus, in torment and despair,
> Preferred his vain, but charitable prayer.
> The fool, his own soul lost, would fain be wise
> For others' good ; but Heaven his suit denies.
> By laws and means well known we stand or fall,
> And one eternal rule remains for all.

ACT IV

SCENE I.—[A room in Thorowgood's House]

MARIA

Maria. How falsely do they judge who censure or applaud as we're afflicted or rewarded here! I know I am unhappy, yet cannot charge myself with any crime, more than the common frailties of our kind, that should provoke just Heaven to mark me out for sufferings so uncommon and severe. Falsely to accuse ourselves, Heaven must abhor; then it is just and right that innocence should suffer, for Heaven must be just in all its ways. Perhaps by that they are kept from moral evils much worse than penal, or more improved in virtue; or may not the lesser ills that they sustain be the means of greater good to others? Might all the joyless days and sleepless nights that I have passed but purchase peace for thee—

> Thou dear, dear cause of all my grief and pain,
> Small were the loss, and infinite the gain ;
> Though to the grave in secret love I pine,
> So life, and fame, and happiness were thine.

SCENE II

TRUEMAN and MARIA

Maria. What news of Barnwell?

True. None. I have sought him with the greatest diligence, but all in vain.

Maria. Doth my father yet suspect the cause of his absenting himself?

True. All appeared so just and fair to him, it is not possible he ever should; but his absence will no longer be concealed. Your father's wise; and, though he seems to hearken to the friendly excuses I would make for Barnwell, yet I am afraid he regards them only as such, without suffering them to influence his judgment.

Maria. How does the unhappy youth defeat all our designs to serve him! Yet I can never repent what we have done. Should he return, 'twill make his reconciliation with my father easier, and preserve him from future reproach from a malicious, unforgiving world.

SCENE III

To them THOROWGOOD *and* LUCY

Thor. This woman here has given me a sad and (bating some circumstances) too probable account of Barnwell's defection.

Lucy. I am sorry, sir, that my frank confession of my former unhappy course of life, should cause you to suspect my truth on this occasion.

Thor. It is not that; your confession has in it all the appearance of truth. (*To them.*) Among many other particulars, she informs me that Barnwell has been influenced to break his trust and wrong me at several times of considerable sums of money. Now as I know this to be false, I would fain doubt the whole of her relation; too dreadful to be willingly believed.

Maria. Sir, your pardon; I find myself on a sudden so indisposed that I must retire. (*Aside.*) Providence opposes all attempts to save him. Poor ruined Barnwell! Wretched, lost Maria!

SCENE IV

THOROWGOOD, TRUEMAN, *and* LUCY

Thor. How I am distressed on every side! Pity for that unhappy youth, fear for the life of a much valued friend—and then, my child—the only joy and hope of my declining life!—Her melancholy increases hourly, and gives me painful apprehensions of her loss.—Oh, Trueman, this person informs me that your friend, at the instigation of an impious woman, is gone to rob and murder his venerable uncle.

True. Oh, execrable deed! I am blasted with the horror of the thought!

Lucy. This delay may ruin all.

Thor. What to do or think, I know not. That he ever wronged me, I know is false; the rest may be so too; there's all my hope.

True. Trust not to that; rather suppose all true, than lose a moment's time. Even now the horrid deed may be a-doing—dreadful imagination!—or it may be done, and we are vainly debating on the means to prevent what is already past.

Thor. This earnestness convinces me that he knows more than he has yet discovered. What, ho! without there, who waits?

SCENE V

To them a Servant

Thor. Order the groom to saddle the swiftest horse, and prepare himself to set out with speed!—An affair of life and death demands his diligence.

SCENE VI

THOROWGOOD, TRUEMAN *and* LUCY

Thor. For you, whose behaviour on this occasion I have no time to commend as it deserves, I must engage your farther assistance. Return and observe this Millwood till I come. I have your directions, and will follow you as soon as possible.

SCENE VII

THOROWGOOD *and* TRUEMAN

Thor. Trueman, you I am sure would not be idle on this occasion.

SCENE VIII

TRUEMAN

True. He only who is a friend can judge of my distress.

SCENE IX.—*Millwood's House*

MILLWOOD

Mill. I wish I knew the event of his design. The attempt without success would ruin him. Well what have I to apprehend from that? I fear too much. The mischief being only intended, his friends, in pity of his youth, turn all their rage on me. I should have thought of that before. Suppose the deed done; then, and then only, I shall be secure. Or what if he returns without attempting it at all?

SCENE X

MILLWOOD, *and* BARNWELL, *bloody*

Mill. But he is here, and I have done him wrong. His bloody hands show he has done the deed, but show he wants the prudence to conceal it.

Barn. Where shall I hide me? Whither shall I fly, to avoid the swift unerring hand of justice?

Mill. Dismiss those fears: though thousands had pursued you to the door, yet being entered here, you are safe as innocence. I have such a cavern, by art so cunningly contrived, that the piercing eyes of jealousy and revenge may search in vain nor find the entrance to the safe retreat. There will I hide you, if any danger's near.

Barn. Oh, hide me—from myself, if it be possible; for while I bear my conscience in my bosom, though I were hid where man's eye never saw, nor light e'er dawned, 'twere all in vain. For that inmate, that impartial judge, will try, convict, and sentence me for murder, and execute me with never-ending torments. Behold these hands, all crimsoned o'er with my dear uncle's blood. Here's a sight to make a statue start with horror, or turn a living man into a statue!

Mill. Ridiculous! Then it seems you are afraid of your own shadow; or, what's less than a shadow, your conscience.

Barn. Though to man unknown I did the accursed act, what can we hide from Heaven's omniscient eye?

Mill. No more of this stuff. What advantage have you made of his death; or what advantage may yet be made of it? Did you secure the keys of his treasure? Those, no doubt, were about him? What gold, what jewels, or what else of value have you brought me?

Barn. Think you, I added sacrilege to murder? Oh, had you seen him as his life flowed from him in a crimson flood, and heard him praying for me by the double name of nephew and of murderer; alas, alas! he knew not then that his nephew was his murderer: how would you have wished, as I did, though you had a thousand years of life to come, to have give them all to have lengthened his one hour! But being dead, I fled the sight of what my hands had done; nor could I, to have gained the empire of the world, have violated, by theft, his sacred corpse.

Mill. Whining, preposterous, canting villain! to murder your uncle, rob him of life, nature's first, last, dear prerogative, after which there's no injury, then fear to take what he no longer wanted, and bring to me your penury and guilt. Do you think I'll hazard my reputation, nay, my life, to entertain you?

Barn. Oh, Millwood!—this from thee?—But I have done. If you hate me, if you wish me dead, then you are happy; for, oh, 'tis sure my grief will quickly end me.

Mill [aside]. In his madness he will discover all, and involve me in his ruin. We are on a precipice from whence there's no retreat for both. Then, to preserve myself.—(*Pauses.*)—There is no other way—'tis dreadful, but reflection comes too late when danger's pressing, and there's no room for choice. It must be done. (*Stamps.*

SCENE XI

To them a Servant

Mill. Fetch me an officer, and seize this villain he has confessed himself a murderer. Should I let him escape, I justly might be thought as bad as he.

SCENE XII

MILLWOOD *and* BARNWELL

Barn. O Millwood! sure thou dost not, cannot mean it. Stop the messenger; upon my knees, I beg you call him back. 'Tis fit I die indeed, but not by you. I will this instant deliver myself into the hands of justice, indeed I will; for death is all I wish. But thy ingratitude so tears my wounded soul, 'tis worse ten thousand times than death with torture.

Mill. Call it what you will; I am willing to live, and live secure, which nothing but your death can warrant.

Barn. If there be a pitch of wickedness that seats the author beyond the reach of vengeance, you must be secure. But what remains for me, but a dismal dungeon, hard galling fetters, an awful trial, and ignominious death—justly to fall unpitied and abhorred; after death to be suspended between heaven and earth, a dreadful spectacle, the warning and horror of a gaping crowd. This I could bear, nay, wish not to avoid, had it come from any hand but thine.

SCENE XIII

MILLWOOD, BARNWELL, BLUNT, *Officer and Attendants*

Mill. Heaven defend me! Conceal a murderer! Here, sir; take this youth into your custody. I accuse him of murder, and will appear to make good my charge. (*They seize him.*

Barn. To whom, of what, or how shall I complain? I'll not accuse her: the hand of Heaven is in it, and this the punishment of lust and parricide. Yet Heaven, that justly cuts me off, still suffers her to live, perhaps to punish others. Tremendous mercy! so fiends are cursed with immortality, to be the executioners of Heaven:

Be warned, ye youths, who see my sad despair,
Avoid lewd women, false as they are fair;

> *By reason guided, honest joys pursue ;*
> *The fair, to honour and to virtue true,*
> *Just to herself, will ne'er be false to you.*
> *By my example learn to shun my fate*
> *(How wretched is the man who's wise too late !);*
> *Ere innocence, and fame, and life, be lost,*
> *Here purchase wisdom, cheaply, at my cost !*

> [*Officers take him out.*

SCENE XIV

MILLWOOD *and* BLUNT

Mill. Where is Lucy? Why is she absent at such a time?

Blunt. Would I had been so, too, thou devil!

Mill. Insolent! This to me!

Blunt. The worst that we know of the devil is, that he first seduces to sin and then betrays to punishment.

SCENE XV

MILLWOOD

They disapprove of my conduct, and mean to take this opportunity to set up for themselves. My ruin is resolved. I see my danger, but scorn it and them. I was not born to fall by such weak instruments. (*Going.*

SCENE XVI

THOROWGOOD *and* MILLWOOD

Thor. Where is this scandal of her own sex, and curse of ours?

Mill. What means this insolence? Who do you seek?

Thor. Millwood.

Mill. Well, you have found her then. I am Millwood.

Thor. Then you are the most impious wretch that e'er the sun beheld.

Mill. From your appearance I should have expected wisdom and moderation, but your manners belie your aspect. What is your business here? I know you not.

Thor. Hereafter you may know me better; I am Barnwell's master.

Mill. Then you are master to a villain; which, I think, is not much to your credit.

Thor. Had he been as much above thy arts as my credit is superior to thy malice, I need not blush to own him.

Mill. My arts! I don't understand you, sir. If he has done amiss what's that to me? Was he my servant, or yours? You should have taught him better.

Thor. Why should I wonder to find such uncommon impudence in one arrived to such a height of wickedness! When innocence is banished, modesty soon follows. Know, sorceress, I'm not ignorant of any of your arts by which you first deceived the unwary youth. I know how, step by step, you've led him on, reluctant and unwilling, from crime to crime, to this last horrid act; which you contrived, and by your cursed wiles even forced him to commit, and then betrayed him.

Mill. (*aside*). Ha! Lucy has got the advantage of me, and accused me first. Unless I can turn the accusation, and fix it upon her and Blunt, I am lost.

Thor. Had I known your cruel design sooner, it had been prevented. To see you punished, as the law directs, is all that now remains. Poor satisfaction! for he, innocent as he is compared to you, must suffer too. But Heaven, who knows our frame, and graciously distinguishes between frailty and presumption, will make a difference though man cannot, who sees not the heart, but only judges by the outward action.

Mill. I find, sir, we are both unhappy in our servants. I was surprised at such ill-treatment from a gentleman of your appearance without cause; and therefore too hastily returned it; for which I ask your pardon. I now perceive you have been so far imposed on, as to think me engaged in a former correspondence with your servant, and some way or other accessary to his undoing.

Thor. I charge you as the cause, the sole cause of all his guilt, and all his suffering; of all he now endures, and must endure, till a violent and shameful death shall put a dreadful period to his life and miseries together.

Mill. 'Tis very strange! But who's secure from scandal and detraction? So far from contributing to his ruin, I never spoke to him till since that fatal accident, which I lament as much as you. 'Tis true I have a servant, on whose account he has of late frequented my house. If she has abused my good opinion of her, am I to blame? Hasn't Barnwell done the same by you?

Thor. I hear you; pray go on.

Mill. I have been informed he had a violent passion for her, and she for him: but I always thought it innocent. I know her poor, and given to expensive pleasures. Now, who can tell but she may have influenced the amorous youth to commit this murder to supply her extravagancies?—It must be so. I now recollect a thousand circumstances that confirm it. I'll have her, and a man-servant that I suspect as an accomplice, secured immediately. I hope, sir, you will lay aside your ill-grounded suspicions of me, and join to punish the real contrivers of this bloody deed. (*Offers to go.*

Thor. Madam, you pass not this way: I see your design, but shall protect them from your malice.

Mill. I hope you will not use your influence, and the credit of your name, to screen such guilty wretches. Consider, sir, the wickedness of persuading a thoughtless youth to such a crime.

Thor. I do—and of betraying him when it was done.

Mill. That which you call betraying him may convince you of my innocence. She who loves him, though she contrived the murder, would never have delivered him into the hands of justice, as I, struck with horror at his crimes, have done.

Thor. How should an unexperienced youth escape her snares? The powerful magic of her wit and form might betray the wisest to simple dotage, and fire the blood that age had froze long since. Even I, that with just prejudice came prepared, had by her artful story been deceived, but that my strong conviction of her guilt makes even a doubt impossible! Those whom subtly you would accuse, you know are your accusers; and, what proves unanswerably their innocence and your guilt, they accused you before the deed was done, and did all that was in their power to have prevented it.

Mill. Sir, you are very hard to be convinced; but I have such a proof, which, when produced, will silence all objections.
                                                                    [*Exit.*

SCENE XVII

THOROWGOOD. LUCY, TRUEMAN, BLUNT, *Officers, etc.*

Lucy. Gentlemen, pray place yourselves, some on one side of that door, and some on the other; watch her entrance, and act as your prudence shall direct you. This way (*To* THOROW-GOOD.), and note her behaviour. I have observed her; she's driven to the last extremity, and is forming some desperate resolution. I guess at her design.

SCENE XVIII

To them MILLWOOD *with a pistol.* TRUEMAN *secures her*

True. Here thy power of doing mischief ends; deceitful, cruel, bloody woman!

Mill. Fool, hypocrite, villain; man! thou canst not call me that.

True. To call thee woman were to wrong the sex, thou devil!

Mill. That imaginary being is an emblem of thy cursed sex collected; a mirror wherein each particular man may see his own likeness, and that of all mankind.

True. Think not, by aggravating the fault of others to extenuate thy own, of which the abuse of such uncommon perfections of mind and body is not the least.

Mill. If such I had, well may I curse your barbarous sex, who robbed me of 'em ere I knew their worth; then left me, too late, to count their value by their loss. Another and another spoiler came, and all my gain was poverty and reproach. My soul disdained, and yet disdains, dependence and contempt. Riches, no matter by what means obtained, I saw secured the worst of men from both. I found it, therefore, necessary to be rich, and to that end I summoned all my arts. You call 'em wicked, be it so; they were such as my conversation with your sex had furnished me withal.

Thor. Sure none but the worst of men conversed with thee.

Mill. Men of all degrees, and all professions, I have known, yet found no difference but in their several capacities; all were alike wicked, to the utmost of their power. In pride, contention, avarice, cruelty and revenge, the reverend priesthood were my unerring guides. From suburb-magistrates, who live by ruined reputations, as the unhospitable natives of Cornwall do by shipwrecks, I learned that to charge my innocent neighbours with my crimes, was to merit their protection; for to screen the guilty is the less scandalous when many are suspected, and detraction, like darkness and death, blackens all objects and levels all distinction. Such are your venal magistrates, who favour none but such as, by their office, they are sworn to punish. With them, not to be guilty is the worst of crimes; and large fees privately paid is every needful virtue.

Thor. Your practice has sufficiently discovered your contempt of laws, both human and divine; no wonder then that you should hate the officers of both.

Mill. I hate you all; I know you, and expect no mercy. Nay, I ask for none; I have done nothing that I am sorry for; I followed my inclinations, and that the best of you does every day. All actions are alike natural and indifferent to man and beast, who devour, or are devoured, as they meet with others weaker or stronger than themselves.

Thor. What pity it is, a mind so comprehensive, daring and inquisitive should be a stranger to religion's sweet, but powerful charms.

Mill. I am not fool enough to be an atheist, though I have known enough of men's hypocrisy to make a thousand simple women so. Whatever religion is in itself—as practised by mankind, it has caused the evils you say it was designed to cure. War, plague and famine, has not destroyed so many of the human race as this pretended piety has done, and with such barbarous cruelty—as if the only way to honour Heaven were to turn the present world into hell.

Thor. Truth is truth, though from an enemy and spoke in malice. You bloody, blind, and superstitious bigots, how will you answer this?

Mill. What are your laws, of which you make your boast, but the fool's wisdom, and the coward's valour; the instrument and screen of all your villainies, by which you punish in others what you act yourselves, or would have acted had you been in their circumstances. The judge who condemns the poor man for being a thief, had been a thief himself had he been poor. Thus you go on, deceiving and being deceived, harassing, and plaguing, and destroying one another. But women are your universal prey.

> *Women, by whom you are the source of joy,*
> *With cruel arts you labour to destroy ;*
> *A thousand ways our ruin you pursue,*
> *Yet blame in us those arts first taught by you.*
> *Oh, may from hence each violated maid,*
> *By flattering, faithless, barb'rous man betrayed,*
> *When robbed of innocence and virgin fame,*
> *From your destruction raise a nobler name ;*
> *To right their sex's wrongs devote their mind,*
> *And future Millwoods prove to plague mankind.*

ACT V

SCENE I.—*A room in a Prison*

THOROWGOOD, BLUNT *and* LUCY

Thor. I have recommended to Barnwell a reverend divine, whose judgment and integrity I am well acquainted with. Nor has Millwood been neglected; but she, unhappy woman, still obstinate, refuses his assistance.

Lucy. This pious charity to the afflicted well becomes your character; yet pardon me, sir, if I wonder you were not at their trial.

Thor. I knew it was impossible to save him, and I and my family bear so great a part in his distress, that to have been present would have aggravated our sorrows without relieving his.

Blunt. It was mournful indeed. Barnwell's youth and modest deportment, as he passed, drew tears from every eye: when placed at the bar, and arraigned before the reverend judges, with many tears and interrupting sobs he confessed and aggravated his offences, without accusing or once reflecting on Millwood, the shameless author of his ruin; who dauntless and unconcerned stood by his side, viewing with visible pride and contempt the vast assembly, who all with sympathising sorrow wept for the wretched youth. Millwood, when called upon to answer, loudly insisted upon her innocence, and made an artful and bold defence; but, finding all in vain, the impartial jury and the learned bench concurring to find her guilty, how did she curse herself, poor Barnwell, us, her judges, all mankind! But what could that avail? She was condemned, and is this day to suffer with him.

Thor. The time draws on. I am going to visit Barnwell, as you are Millwood.

Lucy. We have not wronged her, yet I dread this interview. She is proud, impatient, wrathful, and unforgiving. To be the branded instruments of vengeance, to suffer in her shame, and sympathise with her in all she suffers, is the tribute we must pay for our former ill-spent lives, and long confederacy with her in wickedness.

Thor. Happy for you it ended when it did! What you have done against Millwood, I know, proceeded from a just abhorrence of her crimes, free from interest, malice, or revenge. Proselytes to virtue should be encouraged. Pursue your proposed reformation, and know me hereafter for your friend.

Lucy. This is a blessing as unhoped for as unmerited; but Heaven, that snatched us from impending ruin, sure intends you as its instrument to secure us from apostasy.

Thor. With gratitude to impute your deliverance to Heaven is just. Many, less virtuously disposed than Barnwell was, have never fallen in the manner he has done; may not such owe their safety rather to Providence than to themselves? With pity and compassion let us judge him! Great were his faults, but strong was the temptation. Let his ruin learn us diffidence, humanity and circumspection; for we, who wonder at his fate — perhaps, had we like him been tried, like him we had fallen too.

SCENE II.—*A Dungeon. A table and lamp*

THOROWGOOD, BARNWELL *reading*

Thor. See there the bitter fruits of passion's detested reign, and sensual appetite indulged; severe reflections, penitence, and tears.

Barn. My honoured, injured master, whose goodness has covered me a thousand times with shame, forgive this last unwilling disrespect. Indeed I saw you not.

Thor. 'Tis well; I hope you are better employed in viewing of yourself. Your journey's long, your time for preparation almost spent. I sent a reverend divine to teach you to improve it, and should be glad to hear of his success.

Barn. The word of truth, which he recommended for my constant companion in this my sad retirement, has at length removed the doubts I laboured under. From thence I've learned the infinite extent of heavenly mercy; that my offences, though great, are not unpardonable: and that 'tis not my interest only, but my duty, to believe and to rejoice in that hope. So shall Heaven receive the glory, and future penitents the profit of my example.

Thor. Go on! How happy am I who live to see this!

Barn. 'Tis wonderful that words should charm despair, speak peace and pardon to a murderer's conscience; but truth and mercy flow in every sentence, attended with force and energy divine. How shall I describe my present state of mind? I hope in doubt, and trembling I rejoice; I feel my grief increase, even as my fears give way. Joy and gratitude now supply more tears than the horror and anguish of despair before.

Thor. These are the genuine signs of true repentance; the only preparatory, certain way to everlasting peace. O the joy it gives to see a soul formed and prepared for heaven! For this the faithful minister devotes himself to meditation, abstinence and prayer, shunning the vain delights of sensual joys, and daily dies that others may live for ever. For this he turns the sacred volumes o'er, and spends his life in painful search of truth. The love of riches and the lust of power he looks on with just contempt and detestation, who only counts for wealth the souls he wins, and whose highest ambition is to serve mankind. If the reward of all his pains be to preserve one soul from wandering, or turn one from the error of his ways, how does he then rejoice, and own his little labours over-paid!

Barn. What do I owe for all your generous kindness! But though I cannot, Heaven can and will reward you.

Thor. To see thee thus, is joy too great for words. Farewell! —Heaven strengthen thee.—Farewell!

Barn. Oh, sir, there's something I could say, if my sad swelling heart would give me leave.

Thor. Give it vent a while, and try.

Barn. I had a friend—'tis true I am unworthy—yet methinks your generous example might persuade——Could I not see him once before I go from whence there's no return?

Thor. He's coming, and as much thy friend as ever. But I'll not anticipate his sorrow; too soon he'll see the sad effect of this contagious ruin. This torrent of domestic misery bears too hard upon me. I must retire to indulge a weakness I find impossible to overcome. Much loved—and much lamented youth! —Farewell!—Heaven strengthen thee.—Eternally farewell!

Barn. The best of masters and of men—Farewell. While I live, let me not want your prayers.

Thor. Thou shalt not. Thy peace being made with Heaven, death's already vanquished. Bear a little longer the pains that attend this transitory life, and cease from pain for ever.

SCENE III

Barnwell

Barn. I find a power within that bears my soul above the fears of death, and, spite of conscious shame and guilt, gives me a taste of pleasure more than mortal.

SCENE IV

To him TRUEMAN *and Keeper*

Keeper. Sir, there's the prisoner.

SCENE V

BARNWELL *and* TRUEMAN

Barn. Trueman!—My friend, whom I so wished to see! yet now he's here, I dare not look upon him.   (*Weeps.*

True. Oh, Barnwell! Barnwell!

Barn. Mercy! Mercy! gracious Heaven! For death, but not for this, was I prepared.

True. What have I suffered since I saw thee last! What pain has absence given me!—But, oh, to see thee thus!——

Barn. I know it is dreadful! I feel the anguish of thy generous soul:—But I was born to murder all who love me.   (*Both weep.*

True. I came not to reproach you; I thought to bring you comfort; but I am deceived, for I have none to give. I came to share thy sorrow, but cannot bear my own.

Barn. My sense of guilt, indeed, you cannot know; 'tis what the good and innocent, like you, can ne'er conceive: but other griefs at present I have none, but what I feel for you. In your sorrow I read you love me still; but yet, methinks, 'tis strange, when I consider what I am.

True. No more of that; I can remember nothing but thy virtues; thy honest, tender friendship, our former happy state, and present misery. Oh, had you trusted me when first the fair seducer tempted you, all might have been prevented.

Barn. Alas! thou knowest not what a wretch I've been. Breach of friendship was my first and least offence. So far was I lost to goodness, so devoted to the author of my ruin, that had she insisted on my murdering thee—I think I should have done it.

True. Prithee aggravate thy faults no more.

Barn. I think I should! Thus good and generous as you are, I should have murdered you!

True. We have not yet embraced, and may be interrupted. Come to my arms.

Barn. Never, never will I taste such joys on earth; never will I so soothe my just remorse. Are those honest arms and faithful bosom fit to embrace and to support a murderer? These iron fetters only shall clasp, and flinty pavement bear me. (*Throwing himself on the ground.*) Even these too good for such a bloody monster.

True. Shall fortune sever those whom friendship joined? Thy miseries cannot lay thee so low but love will find thee. (*Lies down beside him.*) Upon this rugged couch then let us lie;

for well it suits our most deplorable condition. Here will we offer to stern calamity; this earth the altar, and ourselves the sacrifice. Our mutual groans shall echo to each other through the dreary vault; our sighs shall number the moments as they pass, and mingling tears communicate such anguish, as words were never made to express.

Barn. Then be it so. Since you propose an intercourse of woe, pour all your griefs into my breast, and in exchange take mine. (*Embracing.*) Where's now the anguish that you promised? You've taken mine, and make me no return. Sure peace and comfort dwell within these arms, and sorrow can't approach me while I'm here. This too is the work of Heaven, who, having before spoke peace and pardon to me, now sends thee to confirm it. O take, take some of the joy that overflows my breast!

True. I do, I do. Almighty Power, how have you made us capable to bear, at once, the extremes of pleasure and of pain?

SCENE VI

To them, Keeper

Keeper. Sir!
True. I come.

SCENE VII

BARNWELL *and* TRUEMAN

Barn. Must you leave me? Death would soon have parted us for ever.

True. Oh, my Barnwell! there's yet another talk behind. Again your heart must bleed for others' woes.

Barn. To meet and part with you I thought was all I had to do on earth. What is there more for me to do, or suffer?

True. I dread to tell thee, yet it must be known! Maria——

Barn. Our master's fair and virtuous daughter?

True. The same.

Barn. No misfortune, I hope, has reached that lovely maid! Preserve her, Heaven, from every will, to show mankind that goodness is your care!

True. Thy, thy misfortunes, my unhappy friend, have reached her. Whatever you and I have felt, and more, if more be possible, she feels for you.

Barn. (*aside*). I know he doth abhor a lie, and would not trifle with his dying friend. This is, indeed, the bitterness of death.

True. You must remember, for we all observed it, for some time past, a heavy melancholy weighed her down. Disconsolate she seemed, and pined and languished from a cause unknown; till, hearing of your dreadful fate, the long-stifled flame blazed out. She wept, she wrung her hands, and tore her hair, and, in the transport of her grief, discovered her own lost state, whilst she lamented yours.

Barn. Will all the pain I feel restore thy ease, lovely unhappy maid? (*Weeping.*) Why didn't you let me die and never know it?

True. It was impossible; she makes no secret of her passion for you, and is determined to see you ere you die. She waits for me to introduce her.

SCENE VIII

BARNWELL

Barn. Vain, busy thoughts, be still! What avails it to think on what I might have been? I now am what I've made myself.

SCENE IX

To him TRUEMAN *and* MARIA

True. Madam, reluctant I lead you to this dismal scene. This is the seat of misery and guilt. Here awful justice reserves her public victims. This is the entrance to shameful death.

Maria. To this sad place, then, no improper guest, the abandoned, lost Maria brings despair—and see the subject and the cause of all this world of woe! Silent and motionless he stands, as if his soul had quitted her abode, and the lifeless form alone was left behind—yet that so perfect that beauty and death, ever at enmity, now seem united there.

Barn. I groan, but murmur not. Just Heaven, I am your own; do with me what you please.

Maria. Why are your streaming eyes still fixed below, as though thou didst give the greedy earth thy sorrows, and rob me of my due? Were happiness within your power, you should bestow it where you pleased; but in your misery I must and will partake!

Barn. Oh! say not so, but fly, abhor, and leave me to my fate! Consider what you are—how vast your fortune, and how bright your fame; have pity on your youth, your beauty, and unequalled virtue, for which so many noble peers have sighed in vain! Bless with your charms some honourable lord! Adorn with your beauty, and by your example improve, the English Court, that justly claims such merit: so shall I quickly be to you as though I had never been.

Maria. When I forget you, I must be so indeed. Reason, choice, virtue, all forbid it. Let women, like Millwood, if there be more such women, smile in prosperity, and in adversity forsake! Be it the pride of virtue to repair, or to partake, the ruin such have made.

True. Lovely, ill-fated maid! Was there ever such generous distress before? How must this pierce his grateful heart, and aggravate his woes!

Barn. Ere I knew guilt or shame — when fortune smiled, and when my youthful hopes were at the highest—if then to have raised my thoughts to you, had been presumption in me, never to have been pardoned: think how much beneath yourself you condescend, to regard me now!

Maria. Let her blush, who, professing love, invades the freedom of your sex's choice. and meanly sues in hopes of a return! Your inevitable fate hath rendered hope impossible as vain. Then, why should I fear to avow a passion so just and so disinterested?

True. If any should take occasion, from Millwood's crimes, to libel the best and fairest part of the creation, here let them see their error! The most distant hopes of such a tender passion from so bright a maid add to the happiness of the most happy, and make the greatest proud. Yet here 'tis lavished in vain: though by the rich present the generous donor is undone, he on whom it is bestowed receives no benefit.

Barn. So the aromatic spices of the East, which all the living covet and esteem, are, with unavailing kindness, wasted on the dead.

Maria. Yes, fruitless is my love, and unavailing all my sighs and tears. Can they save thee from approaching death— from such a death? Oh, terrible idea! What is her misery and distress, who sees the first last object of her love, for whom alone she'd live—for whom she'd die a thousand, thousand deaths, if it were possible—expiring in her arms? Yet she is happy, when compared to me. Were millions of worlds mine, I'd gladly give them in exchange for her condition. The most consummate woe is light to mine. The last of curses to other miserable maids is all I ask; and that's denied me.

True. Time and reflections cure all ills.

Maria. All but this; his dreadful catastrophe virtue herself abhors. To give a holiday to suburb slaves, and passing entertain the savage herd, who, elbowing each other for a sight, pursue and press upon him like his fate! A mind with piety and resolution armed may smile on death. But public ignominy, everlasting shame—shame, the death of souls—to die a thousand times, and yet survive even death itself, in never dying infamy—is this to be endured? Can I who live in him, and must, each hour of my devoted life, feel all these woes renewed, can I endure this?

True. Grief has impaired her spirits; she pants as in the agonies of death.

Barn. Preserve her, Heaven, and restore her peace; nor let her death be added to my crime! (*Bell tolls.*) I am summoned to my fate.

SCENE X

To them, Keeper

Keeper. The officers attend you, sir. Mrs. Millwood is already summoned.

Barn. Tell 'em I am ready. And now, my friend, farewell! (*Embracing.*) Support and comfort the best you can this mourning fair.—No more! Forget not to pray for me! (*Turning to Maria.*) Would you, bright excellence, permit me the honour of a chaste embrace, the last happiness this world could give were mine. (*She inclines towards him; they embrace.*) Exalted goodness! O turn your eyes from earth, and me, to Heaven, where virtue, like yours, is ever heard. Pray for the peace of my departing soul! Early my race of wickedness began, and soon has reached the summit. Ere Nature has finished her work, and stamped me man—just at the time that others begin to stray— my course is finished. Though short my span of life, and few my days, yet, count my crimes for years, and I have lived whole ages. Justice and mercy are in Heaven the same: its utmost severity is mercy to the whole, thereby to cure man's folly and presumption, which else would render even infinite mercy vain and ineffectual. Thus justice, in compassion to mankind, cuts off a wretch like me, by one such example to secure thousands from future ruin.

> *If any youth, like you, in future times*
> *Shall mourn my fate, though he abhor my crimes;*
> *Or tender maid, like you, my tale shall hear,*
> *And to my sorrows give a pitying tear;*
> *To each such melting eye, and throbbing heart,*
> *Would gracious Heaven this benefit impart*
> *Never to know my guilt, nor feel my pain:*
> *Then must you own, you ought not to complain:*
> *Since you nor weep, nor shall I die, in vain.*

[SCENE XI.—*The place of execution.*[1] *The gallows and ladders at farther end of the stage. A crowd of spectators*

BLUNT *and* LUCY

Lucy. Heavens! what a throng!

Blunt. How terrible is death, when thus prepared!

Lucy. Support them, Heaven; thou only can support them; all other help is vain.

Officer (*within*). Make way there; make way, and give the prisoners room!

Lucy. They are here; observe them well! How humble and composed young Barnwell seems! But Millwood looks wild, ruffled with passion, confounded and amazed.

---

[1] This scene does not appear in the first edition, but was added later. Probably it was first printed in the fifth edition. It was often acted.

Enter BARNWELL, MILLWOOD, *Officers and Executioners*

Barn. See, Millwood, see: our journey's at an end. Life, like a tale that is told, is passed away; that short but dark and unknown passage, death, is all the space between us and endless joys, or woes eternal.

Mill. Is this the end of all my flattering hopes? Were youth and beauty given me for a curse, and wisdom only to insure my ruin? They were, they were! Heaven, thou hast done thy worst. Or, if thou hast in store some untried plague—somewhat that's worse than shame, despair and death, unpitied death, confirmed despair and soul-confounding shame—something that men and angels can't describe, and only fiends, who bear it, can conceive: now pour it now on this devoted head, that I may feel the worst thou canst inflict, and bid defiance to thy utmost power!

Barn. Yet, ere we pass the dreadful gulf of death—yet, ere you're plunged in everlasting woe: O bend your stubborn knees and harder heart, humbly to deprecate the wrath divine! Who knows but Heaven, in your dying moments, may bestow that grace and mercy which your life despised!

Mill. Why name you mercy to a wretch like me! Mercy's beyond my hope—almost beyond my wish. I can't repent, nor ask to be forgiven.

Barn. Oh, think what 'tis to be for ever, ever miserable! nor with vain pride oppose a Power that's able to destroy you!

Mill. That will destroy me; I feel it will. A deluge of wrath is pouring on my soul. Chains, darkness, wheels, racks, sharp-stinging scorpions, molten lead, and seas of sulphur, are light to what I feel.

Barn. Oh, add not to your vast account despair! a sin more injurious to Heaven than all you've yet committed.

Mill. Oh, I have sinned beyond the reach of mercy!

Barn. Oh, say not so! 'tis blasphemy to think it. As yon bright roof is higher than the earth, so, and much more, does Heaven's goodness pass our apprehension. Oh! what created being shall presume to circumscribe mercy, that knows no bounds?

Mill. This yields no hope. Though mercy may be boundless, yet 'tis free; and I was doomed, before the world began, to endless pains, and thou to joys eternal.

Barn. O gracious Heaven! extend thy pity to her! Let thy rich mercy flow in plenteous streams, to chase her fears and heal her wounded soul!

Mill. It will not be. Your prayers are lost in air, or else returned, perhaps with double blessing, to your bosom; but me they help not.

Barn. Yet hear me, Millwood!

Mill. Away! I will not hear thee. I tell thee, youth, I am by

Heaven devoted a dreadful instance of its power to punish. *Barnwell seems to pray.*) If thou wilt pray, pray for thyself, not me! How doth his fervent soul mount with his words, and both ascend to Heaven—that Heaven whose gates are shut with adamantine bars against my prayers, had I the will to pray. I cannot bear it! Sure, 'tis the worst of torments to behold others enjoy that bliss that we must never taste!

Officer. The utmost limit of your time's expired.

Mill. Incompassed with horror, whither must I go? I would not live—nor die. That I could cease to be, or ne'er had been!

Barn. Since peace and comfort are denied her here, may she find mercy where she least expects it, and this be all her hell! From our example may all be taught to fly the first approach of vice; but, if o'ertaken—

> *By strong temptation, weakness, or surprise,*
> *Lament their guilt and by repentance rise!*
> *The impenitent alone die unforgiven:*
> *To sin's like man, and to forgive like Heaven.*

(*Exeunt.*]

SCENE XI [XII]

TRUEMAN, BLUNT and LUCY

Lucy. Heart-breaking sight! O wretched, wretched Millwood!

True. You came from her, then; how is she disposed to meet her fate?

Blunt. Who can describe unalterable woe?

Lucy. She goes to death encompassed with horror, loathing life, and yet afraid to die; no tongue can tell her anguish and despair.

True. Heaven be better to her than her fears; may she prove a warning to others, a monument of mercy in herself!

Lucy. O sorrow insupportable! Break, break, my heart!

True. In vain

> *With bleeding hearts and weeping eyes we show*
> *A human gen'rous sense of others' woe,*
> *Unless we mark what drew their ruin on,*
> *And, by avoiding that, prevent our own.*

EPILOGUE

WRITTEN BY COLLEY CIBBER, ESQ.

AND SPOKE BY MRS. CIBBER

SINCE fate has robbed me of the hapless youth
For whom my heart had boarded up its truth;
By all the laws of love and honour, now
I'm free again to choose—and one of you.
But soft—With caution first I'll round me peep;
Maids, in my case, should look before they leap.
Here's choice enough, of various sorts and hue,
The cit, the wit, the rake cocked up in cue, }
The fair spruce mercer, and the tawny Jew. }

Suppose I search the sober gallery?—No; }
There's none but 'prentices and cuckolds all a-row; }
And these, I doubt, are those that make 'em so. }
(Pointing to the boxes.

'Tis very well, enjoy the jest.—But you, }
Fine powdered sparks—nay, I am told 'tis true, }
Your happy spouses—can make cuckolds too. }
'Twixt you and them the difference this, perhaps;
The cit's ashamed whene'er his duck he traps;
But you, when Madam's tripping, let her fall,
Cock up your hats, and take no shame at all.

What if some favoured poet I could meet,
Whose love would lay his laurels at my feet.
No—painted passion real love abhors—
His flame would prove the suit of creditors.

Not to detain you, then, with longer pause,
In short, my heart to this conclusion draws—
I yield it to the hand that's loudest in applause.

THE
CLANDESTINE MARRIAGE

GEORGE COLMAN, born at Florence in 1732, is known as "the Elder," to distinguish him from his son of the same name, who was also a dramatist. He was educated at Westminster and Oxford, and called to the Bar in 1755. In 1767 he bought with three others Covent Garden Theatre, and was manager for seven years, during which time he grudgingly produced Goldsmith's two comedies. Quarrels with his partners, with Macklin and with Garrick involved him in lawsuits and a pamphlet war. He bought the Haymarket Theatre from Foote in 1776. Besides writing many successful plays, some of them brilliant, he adapted plays of Shakespeare, Ben Jonson and others, translated Terence and Horace's *De Arte Poetica*, edited Beaumont and Fletcher, and Jonson, and wrote poems and essays. He died in 1785.

DAVID GARRICK, the great actor and theatre-manager, was born at Hereford on 20 February, 1717. After some years at Lichfield Grammar School and a few months under Dr. Johnson, Garrick went to London, with Johnson, to read for the Bar. But instead he became partner in a wine-business, and then abandoned this for the stage, achieving extraordinary success as Richard III. in 1741. His great genius and his astonishing versatility in both tragedy and comedy set him at once above all other actors of the day, and though he did not always stand so high in popular favour, he remained the dominating figure in the English theatre until his retirement in 1776, and made himself a great reputation on the Continent in 1763–5. While manager of Drury Lane Theatre, from 1747 to 1776, he did great things in developing his art, giving dignity to his profession, purifying the stage and reviving a number of Shakespeare's plays; and as a man, for all his faults, he was generous and honest.

He died on 20 January, 1779, and was buried in Westminster Abbey.

THE
Clandestine Marriage,
A
COMEDY.

As it is ACTED at the

Theatre-Royal in *Drury-Lane*.

BY

GEORGE COLMAN

AND

DAVID GARRICK.

Huc adhibe vultus, et in unâ parce duobus:
Vivat, et ejusdem simus uterque parens!   OVID.

===

LONDON:

Printed for T. BECKET and P. A. DE HONDT, in the Strand;
R. BALDWIN, in Pater-noster-Row; R. DAVIS, in Pic-
cadilly; and T. DAVIES, in Russel-Street, Covent-
Garden.
M.DCC.LXVI.

ADVERTISEMENT

HOGARTH'S *Marriage-à-la-Mode* has before furnished materials to the author of a novel, published some years ago, under the title of *The Marriage Act*. But as that writer pursued a very different story, and as his work was chiefly designed for a political satire, very little use could be made of it for the service of this comedy.

In justice to the person who has been considered as the sole author, the party who has hitherto lain concealed, thinks it incumbent on him to declare that the disclosure of his name was, by his own desire, reserved till the publication of the piece.

Both the authors, however, who have before been separately honoured with the indulgence of the public, now beg leave to make their joint acknowledgments for the very favourable reception of *The Clandestine Marriage*.

PROLOGUE

WRITTEN BY MR. GARRICK

SPOKEN BY MR. HOLLAND

Poets and painters, who from Nature draw
Their best and richest stores, have made this law:
That each should neighbourly assist his brother,
And steal with decency from one another.
To-night, your matchless Hogarth gives the thought,
Which from his canvas to the stage is brought.
And who so fit to warm the poet's mind,
As he who pictured morals and mankind?
But not the same their characters and scenes;
Both labour for one end, by different means:
Each, as it suits him, takes a separate road,
Their one great object, Marriage-à-la-mode!
Where titles deign with cits to have and hold,
And change rich blood for more substantial gold!
And honoured trade from interest turns aside,
To hazard happiness for titled pride.
The painter dead, yet still he charms the eye;
While England lives, his fame can never die:
But he who struts his hour upon the stage,
Can scarce extend his fame for half an age;
Nor pen nor pencil can the actor save,
The art, and artist, share one common grave.
  O let me drop one tributary tear
On poor Jack Falstaff's grave, and Juliet's bier!
You to their worth must testimony give;
'Tis in your hearts alone their fame can live.
Still as the scenes of life will shift away,
The strong impressions of their art decay.
Your children cannot feel what you have known;
They'll boast of Quins and Cibbers of their own:
The greatest glory of our happy few,
Is to be felt, and be approved by you.

DRAMATIS PERSONÆ

Lord Ogleby	. . . . .	Mr. King
Sir John Melvil	. . . .	Mr. Holland
Sterling	. . . . .	Mr. Yates
Lovewell	. . . . .	Mr. Powell
Canton	. . . . .	Mr. Baddeley
Brush	. . . . .	Mr. Palmer
Serjeant Flower	. . . .	Mr. Love
Traverse	. . . . .	Mr. Lee
Trueman	. . . . .	Mr. Aickin
Mrs. Heidelberg	. . . .	Mrs. Clive
Miss Sterling	. . .	Miss Pope
Fanny	. . . . .	Mrs. Palmer
Betty	. . . . .	Mrs. [? Abington]
Chambermaid	. . .	Miss Plym
Trusty	. . . . .	Miss Mills

THE CLANDESTINE MARRIAGE
A COMEDY

ACT I

SCENE.—*A Room in Sterling's House*

MISS FANNY *and* BETTY *meeting*

Betty (running in). Ma'am! Miss Fanny! Ma'am!

Fanny. What's the matter! Betty!

Betty. Oh la! ma'am! as sure as I'm alive, here is your husband——

Fanny. Hush! my dear Betty! if anybody in the house should hear you, I am ruined.

Betty. Mercy on me! it has frighted me to such a degree, that my heart is come up to my mouth.—But as I was a-saying, ma'am, here's that dear, sweet——

Fanny. Have a care Betty.

Betty. Lord! I'm bewitched, I think.—But as I was a-saying, ma'am, here's Mr. Lovewell just come from London.

Fanny. Indeed!

Betty. Yes, indeed, and indeed, ma'am, he is. I saw him crossing the courtyard in his boots.

Fanny. I am glad to hear it. But pray now, my dear Betty, be cautious. Don't mention that word again, on any account. You know we have agreed never to drop any expressions of that sort for fear of an accident.

Betty. Dear ma'am, you may depend upon me. There is not a more trustier creature on the face of the earth than I am. Though I say it, I am as secret as the grave—and if it's never told till I tell it, it may remain untold till Doomsday for Betty.

Fanny. I know you are faithful—but in our circumstances we cannot be too careful.

Betty. Very true, ma'am!—and yet I vow and protest there's more plague than pleasure with a secret; especially if a body mayn't mention it to four or five of one's particular acquaintance.

Fanny. Do but keep this secret a little while longer, and then I hope you may mention it to anybody. Mr. Lovewell will acquaint the family with the nature of our situation as soon as possible.

Betty. The sooner the better, I believe: for if he does not tell it, there's a little tell-tale, I know of, will come and tell it for him.

Fanny. Fie, Betty!   (*Blushing.*

Betty. Ah! you may well blush.—But you're not so sick, and so pale, and so wan, and so many qualms——

Fanny. Have done! I shall be quite angry with you.

Betty. Angry!—Bless the dear puppet! I am sure I shall love it as much as if it was my own.—I meant no harm, Heaven knows.

Fanny. Well—say no more of this—it makes me uneasy. All I have to ask of you is to be faithful and secret, and not to reveal this matter till we disclose it to the family ourselves.

Betty. Me reveal it!—if I say a word, I wish I may be burned. I would not do you any harm for the world.—And as for Mr. Lovewell, I am sure I have loved the dear gentleman ever since he got a tide-waiter's place for my brother. But let me tell you both, you must leave off your soft looks to each other, and your whispers, and your glances, and your always sitting next to one another at dinner, and your long walks together in the evening. For my part, if I had not been in the secret, I should have known you were a pair of loviers at least, if not man and wife, as——

Fanny. See there now again. Pray be careful.

Betty. Well—well—nobody hears me.—Man and wife—I'll say so no more. What I tell you is very true for all that——

Love. (*calling within*). William!

Betty. Hark! I hear your husband——

Fanny. What!

Betty. I say, here comes Mr. Lovewell. Mind the caution I give you—I'll be whipped now, if you are not the first person he sees or speaks to in the family. However, if you choose it, it's nothing at all to me—as you sow, you must reap—as you brew, so you must bake. I'll e'en slip down the back-stairs, and leave you together.   (*Exit.*

FANNY *alone*

Fanny. I see, I see I shall never have a moment's ease till our marriage is made public. New distresses crowd in upon me every day. The solicitude of my mind sinks my spirits, preys upon my health, and destroys every comfort of my life. It shall be revealed, let what will be the consequence.

Enter LOVEWELL

Love. My love!—How's this?—In tears?—Indeed this is too much. You promised me to support your spirits, and to wait the determination of our fortune with patience. For my sake, for your own, be comforted! Why will you study to add to our uneasiness and perplexity?

Fanny. Oh, Mr. Lovewell! the indelicacy of a secret marriage grows every day more and more shocking to me. I walk about the house like a guilty wretch: I imagine myself the object of the suspicion of the whole family; and am under the perpetual terrors of a shameful detection.

Love. Indeed, indeed, you are to blame. The amiable delicacy of your temper, and your quick sensibility, only serve to make you unhappy.—To clear up this affair properly to Mr. Sterling is the continual employment of my thoughts. Everything now is in a fair train. It begins to grow ripe for a discovery; and I have no doubt of its concluding to the satisfaction of ourselves, of your father, and the whole family,

Fanny. End how it will, I am resolved it shall end soon—very soon—I would not live another week in this agony of mind to be mistress of the universe.

Love. Do not be too violent neither. Do not let us disturb the joy of your sister's marriage with the tumult this matter may occasion!—I have brought letters from Lord Ogleby and Sir John Melvil to Mr. Sterling.—They will be here this evening —and, I dare say, within this hour.

Fanny. I am sorry for it.

Love. Why so?

Fanny. No matter. Only let us disclose our marriage immediately!

Love. As soon as possible.

Fanny. But directly.

Love. In a few days, you may depend on it.

Fanny. To-night—or to-morrow morning.

Love. That, I fear, will be impracticable.

Fanny. Nay, but you must.

Love. Must! why?

Fanny. Indeed, you must. I have the most alarming reasons for it.

Love. Alarming indeed! for they alarm me, even before I am acquainted with them. What are they?

Fanny. I cannot tell you.

Love. Not tell me?

Fanny. Not at present. When all is settled, you shall be acquainted with everything.

Love. Sorry they are coming!—Must be discovered! What can this mean! Is it possible you can have any reasons that need be concealed from me?

Fanny. Do not disturb yourself with conjectures—but rest assured, that though you are unable to divine the cause, the consequence of a discovery, be it what it will, cannot be attended with half the miseries of the present interval.

Love. You put me upon the rack.—I would do anything to make you easy.—But you know your father's temper.—Money (you will excuse my frankness) is the spring of all his actions, which nothing but the idea of acquiring nobility or magnificence can ever make him forgo — and these he thinks his money will purchase. — You know too your aunt's, Mrs. Heidelberg's, notions of the splendour of high life, her contempt for everything that does not relish of what she calls Quality, and that from the vast fortune in her hands, by her late husband, she absolutely governs Mr. Sterling and the whole family: now, if they should come to the knowledge of this affair too abruptly, they might, perhaps, be incensed beyond all hopes of reconciliation.

Fanny. But if they are made acquainted with it otherwise than by ourselves, it will be ten times worse: and a discovery grows every day more probable. The whole family have long suspected our affection. We are also in the power of a foolish maidservant; and if we may even depend on her fidelity, we cannot answer for her discretion. Discover it therefore immediately, lest some accident should bring it to light, and involve us in additional disgrace.

Love. Well—well—I meant to discover it soon, but would not do it too precipitately. I have more than once sounded Mr. Sterling about it, and will attempt him more seriously the next opportunity. But my principal hopes are these. My relationship to Lord Ogleby, and his having placed me with your father, have been, you know, the first links in the chain of this connection between the two families; in consequence of which, I am at present in high favour with all parties: while they all remain thus well-affected to me, I propose to lay our case before the old lord; and if I can prevail on him to mediate in this affair, I make no doubt but he will be able to appease your father; and, being a lord and a man of quality, I am sure he may bring Mrs. Heidelberg into good humour at any time. Let me beg you, therefore, to have but a little patience, as, you see, we are upon the very eve of a discovery that must probably be to our advantage.

Fanny. Manage it your own way. I am persuaded.

Love. But in the meantime make yourself easy.

Fanny. As easy as I can, I will.—We had better not remain together any longer at present.—Think of this business, and let me know how you proceed.

Love. Depend on my care! But, pray, be cheerful.

Fanny. I will.

As she is going out, enter STERLING.

Sterl. Hey-day! who have we got here?

Fanny (confused). Mr. Lovewell, sir!

Sterl. And where are you going, hussy!

Fanny. To my sister's chamber, sir! *(Exit.*

Sterl. Ah, Lovewell! What! always getting my foolish girl yonder into a corner! Well—well—let us but once see her elder sister fast-married to Sir John Melvil, we'll soon provide a good husband for Fanny, I warrant you.

Love. Would to heaven, sir, you would provide her one of my recommendation!

Sterl. Yourself? eh, Lovewell!

Love. With your pleasure, sir!

Sterl. Mighty well!

Love. And I flatter myself that such a proposal would not be very disagreeable to Miss Fanny.

Sterl. Better and better!

Love. And if I could but obtain your consent, sir——

Sterl. What! you marry Fanny!—no, no—that will never do, Lovewell!—You're a good boy, to be sure—I have a great value for you—but can't think of you for a son-in-law.—There's no *stuff* in the case, no money, Lovewell!

Love. My pretensions to fortune, indeed, are but moderate: but though not equal to splendour, sufficient to keep us above distress—add to which, that I hope by diligence to increase it—and have love, honour——

Sterl. But not the *stuff*, Lovewell!—Add one little round 0 to the sum total of your fortune, and that will be the finest thing you can say to me.—You know I've a regard for you—would do anything to serve you—anything on the footing of friendship—but——

Love. If you think me worthy of your friendship, sir, be assured that there is no instance in which I should rate your friendship so highly.

Sterl. Psha! psha! that's another thing, you know.—Where money or interest is concerned, friendship is quite out of the question.

Love. But where the happiness of a daughter is at stake, you would not scruple, sure, to sacrifice a little to her inclinations.

Sterl. Inclinations! why, you would not persuade me that the girl is in love with you—eh, Lovewell!

Love. I cannot absolutely answer for Miss Fanny, sir; but am sure that the chief happiness or misery of my life depends entirely upon her.

Sterl. Why, indeed now, if your kinsman, Lord Ogleby, would come down handsomely for you—but that's impossible.—No, no—'twill never do—I must hear no more of this.—Come, Lovewell, promise me that I shall hear no more of this.

Love. (*hesitating*). I am afraid, sir, I should not be able to keep my word with you, if I did promise you.

Sterl. Why you would not offer to marry her without my consent? would you, Lovewell!
(*Confused.*

Love. Marry her, sir!

Sterl. Ay, marry her, sir!—I know very well that a warm speech or two from such a dangerous young spark, as you are, will go much farther towards persuading a silly girl to do what she has more than a month's mind to do, than twenty grave lectures from fathers or mothers, or uncles or aunts, to prevent her.—But you would not, sure, be such a base fellow, such a treacherous young rogue, as to seduce my daughter's affections, and destroy the peace of my family in that manner.—I must insist on it that you give me your word not to marry her without my consent.

Love. Sir—I—I—as to that—I—I—I beg, sir—Pray, sir, excuse me on this subject at present.

Sterl. Promise then, that you will carry this matter no farther without my approbation.

Love. You may depend on it, sir, that it shall go no farther.

Sterl. Well—well—that's enough—I'll take care of the rest, I warrant you.—Come, come, let's have done with this nonsense!—What's doing in town?—Any news upon 'Change?

Love. Nothing material.

Sterl. Have you seen the currants, the soap, and Madeira, safe in the warehouses? Have you compared the goods with the invoice and bills of lading, and are they all right?

Love. They are, sir!

Sterl. And how are stocks?

Love. Fell one and a half this morning.

Sterl. Well—well—some good news from America, and they'll be up again.—But how are Lord Ogleby and Sir John Melvil? When are we to expect them?

Love. Very soon, sir! I came on purpose to bring you their commands. Here are letters from both of them. (*Giving letters.*

Sterl. Let me see—let me see—'Slife, how his lordship's letter is perfumed!—It takes my breath away. (*Opening it.*) And French paper too! with a fine border of flowers and flourishes —and a slippery gloss on it that dazzles one's eyes.—"My dear Mr. Sterling." (*Reading.*) Mercy on me! His lordship writes a worse hand than a boy at his exercise.—But how's this?— Eh!—"with you to-night"—(*Reading.*)—"Lawyers to-morrow morning."—To-night!—that's sudden indeed.—Where's my sister Heidelberg? She should know of this immediately.—Here, John! Harry! Thomas! (*Calling the Servants.*) Hark ye, Lovewell!

Love. Sir!

Sterl. Mind, now, how I'll entertain his lordship and Sir John. —We'll show your fellows at the other end of the town how we live in the city.—They shall eat gold—and drink gold—and lie in gold.—Here cook! butler! (*Calling.*) What signifies your birth and education, and titles? Money, money, that's the stuff that makes the great man in this country.

Love. Very true, sir!

Sterl. True, sir?—Why then have done with your nonsense of love and matrimony. You're not rich enough to think of a wife yet. A man of business should mind nothing but his business. —Where are these fellows? John! Thomas! (*Calling.*)—Get an estate, and a wife will follow of course.—Ah! Lovewell! an English merchant is the most respectable character in the universe, 'Slife, man, a rich English merchant may make himself a match for the daughter of a Nabob.—Where are all my rascals? Here, William! *(Exit, calling.*

LOVEWELL, *alone*

Love. So!—As I suspected.—Quite averse to the match, and likely to receive the news of it with great displeasure.—What's best to be done?—Let me see!—Suppose I get Sir John Melvil to interest himself in this affair. He may mention it to Lord Ogleby with a better grace than I can, and more probably prevail on him to interfere in it. I can open my mind also more freely to Sir John. He told me, when I left him in town, that he had something of consequence to communicate, and that I could be of use to him. I am glad of it: for the confidence he reposes in me, and the service I may do him, will ensure me his good offices.—Poor Fanny! It hurts me to see her so uneasy, and her making a mystery of the cause adds to my anxiety.—Something must be done upon her account; for at all events, her solicitude shall be removed. *(Exit.*

Scene changes to another chamber

Enter MISS STERLING and MISS FANNY

Miss Sterl. Oh, my dear sister, say no more! This is downright hypocrisy.—You shall never convince me that you don't envy me beyond measure.—Well, after all it is extremely natural. It is impossible to be angry with you.

Fanny. Indeed, sister, you have no cause.

Miss Sterl. And you really pretend not to envy me?

Fanny. Not in the least.

Miss Sterl. And you don't in the least wish that you was just in my situation?

Fanny. No, indeed, I don't. Why should I?

Miss Sterl. Why should you?—What! on the brink of marriage, fortune, title——But I had forgot.—There's that dear sweet creature Mr. Lovewell in the case.—You could not break your faith with your true love now for the world, I warrant you.

Fanny. Mr. Lovewell!—always Mr. Lovewell!—Lord, what signifies Mr. Lovewell, sister?

Miss Sterl. Pretty peevish soul!—Oh, my dear, grave, romantic sister!—a perfect philosopher in petticoats!—Love and a cottage!—Eh, Fanny!—Ah, give me indifference and a coach and six!

Fanny. And why not the coach and six without the indifference?—But, pray, when is this happy marriage of yours to be celebrated?—I long to give you joy.

Miss Sterl. In a day or two—I can't tell exactly.—Oh, my dear sister!—I must mortify her a little.—*(Aside.)* I know you have a pretty taste. Pray, give me your opinion of my jewels. How d'ye like the style of this esclavage? *(Showing jewels.*

Fanny. Extremely handsome indeed, and well fancied.

Miss Sterl. What d'ye think of these bracelets? I shall have a miniature of my father, set round with diamonds, to one, and Sir John's to the other.—And this pair of ear-rings! set transparent!—here, the tops, you see, will take off to wear in a morning, or in an undress—how d'ye like them?   (*Shows jewels.*

Fanny. Very much, I assure you.—Bless me; sister, you have a prodigious quantity of jewels—you'll be the very Queen of Diamonds.

Miss Sterl. Ha! ha! ha! very well, my dear! — I shall be as fine as a little queen indeed.—I have a bouquet to come home to-morrow—made up of diamonds, and rubies, and emeralds, and topazes, and amethysts—jewels of all colours, green, red, blue, yellow, intermixed—the prettiest thing you ever saw in your life!—The jeweller says I shall set out with as many diamonds as anybody in town, except Lady Brilliant, and Polly What-d'ye-call-it, Lord Squander's kept mistress.

Fanny. But what are your wedding-clothes, sister?

Miss Sterl. Oh, white and silver to be sure, you know.—I bought them at Sir Joseph Lutestring's, and sat above an hour in the parlour behind the shop, consulting Lady Lutestring about gold and silver stuffs, on purpose to mortify her.

Fanny. Fie, sister! how could you be so abominably provoking?

Miss Sterl. Oh, I have no patience with the pride of your city-knights' ladies.—Did you never observe the airs of Lady Lutestring dressed in the richest brocade out of her husband's shop, playing crown-whist at Haberdasher's Hall?—While the civil smirking Sir Joseph, with a smug wig trimmed round his broad face as close as a new-cut yew-hedge, and his shoes so black that they shine again, stands all day in his shop, fastened to his counter like a bad shilling?

Fanny. Indeed, indeed, sister, this is too much.—If you talk at this rate, you will be absolutely a by-word in the city.—You must never venture on the inside of Temple Bar again.

Miss Sterl. Never do I desire it—never, my dear Fanny, I promise you.—Oh, how I long to be transported to the dear regions of Grosvenor Square—far—far from the dull districts of Aldersgate, Cheap, Candlewick, and Farringdon Without and Within! — My heart goes pit-a-pat at the very idea of being introduced at Court!—gilt chariot!—piebald horses!—laced liveries!—and then the whispers buzzing round the circle: "Who is that young lady? Who is she?" "Lady Melvil, ma'am!" Lady Melvil! my ears tingle at the sound.—And then at dinner, instead of my father perpetually asking: "Any news upon 'Change?" to cry: Well, Sir John! anything new from Arthur's? —or to say to some other woman of quality: Was your ladyship at the Duchess of Rubber's last night?—Did you call in at Lady Thunder's? In the immensity of crowd I swear I did not see you

—Scarce a soul at the opera last Saturday.—Shall I see you at Carlisle House next Thursday?—Oh, the dear beau-monde! I was born to move in the sphere of the great world.

Fanny. And so, in the midst of all this happiness, you have no compassion for me—no pity for us poor mortals in common life.

Miss Sterl. (*affectedly*). You? — You're above pity. — You would not change conditions with me—you're over head and ears in love, you know.—Nay, for that matter, if Mr. Lovewell and you come together, as I doubt not you will, you will live very comfortably, I dare say.—He will mind his business— you'll employ yourself in the delightful care of your family— and once in a season perhaps you'll sit together in a front box at a benefit-play, as we used to do at our dancing-master's, you know—and perhaps I may meet you in the summer with some other citizens at Tunbridge.—For my part, I shall always entertain a proper regard for my relations.—You shan't want my countenance, I assure you.

Fanny. Oh, you're too kind, sister!

Enter MRS. HEIDELBERG

Mrs. Heidel. (*at entering.*) Here this evening!—I vow and pertest we shall scarce have time to provide for them—Oh, my dear! (*To* MISS STERL.) I am glad to see you're not quite in dishabille. Lord Ogleby and Sir John Mevil will be here to-night.

Miss Sterl. To-night, ma'am?

Mrs. Heidel. Yes, my dear, to-night.—Do put on a smarter cap, and change those ordinary ruffles!—Lord, I have such a deal to do, I shall scarce have time to slip on my Italian lute-string.—Where is this dawdle of a housekeeper?—(*Enter* MRS. TRUSTY.) Oh, here, Trusty! do you know that people of quality are expected here this evening?

Trusty. Yes, ma'am.

Mrs. Heidel. Well—Do you be sure now that everything is done in the most genteelest manner—and to the honour of the fammaly.

Trusty. Yes, ma'am.

Mrs. Heidel. Well—but mind what I say to you.

Trusty. Yes, ma'am.

Mrs. Heidel. His lordship is to lie in the chintz bedchamber —d'ye hear?—And Sir John in the blue damask room.—His lordship's valet-de-shamb in the opposite——

Trusty. But Mr. Lovewell is come down—and you know that's his room, ma'am.

Mrs. Heidel. Well—well—Mr. Lovewell may make shift—or get a bed at the George.—But hark ye, Trusty!

Trusty. Ma'am!

Mrs. Heidel. Get the great dining-room in order as soon as possible. Unpaper the curtains, take the covers off the couch and the chairs, and put the china figures on the mantelpiece immediately.

Trusty. Yes, ma'am.

Mrs. Heidel. Begone then! fly, this instant!—Where's my brother Sterling——

Trusty. Talking to the butler, ma'am.

Mrs. Heidel. Very well. (*Exit* TRUSTY.) Miss Fanny!—I pertest I did not see you before.—Lord, child, what's the matter with you?

Fanny. With me? Nothing, ma'am.

Mrs. Heidel. Bless me! Why your face is as pale, and black, and yellow—of fifty colours, I pertest.—And then you have dressed yourself as loose and as big—I declare there is not such a thing to be seen now as a young woman with a fine waist.— You all make yourselves as round as Mrs. Deputy Barter. Go, child!—You know the qualaty will be here by and by.—Go, and make yourself a little more fit to be seen. (*Exit* FANNY.) She is gone away in tears—absolutely crying, I vow and pertest.— This ridiculous love! we must put a stop to it. It makes a perfect nataral of the girl.

Miss Sterl. (*affectedly.*) Poor soul! she can't help it.

Mrs. Heidel. Well, my dear! Now I shall have an opportunity of convincing you of the absurdity of what you was telling me concerning Sir John Melvil's behaviour.

Miss Sterl. Oh, it gives me no manner of uneasiness. But, indeed, ma'am, I cannot be persuaded but that Sir John is an extremely cold lover. Such distant civility, grave looks, and lukewarm professions of esteem for me and the whole family! I have heard of flames and darts, but Sir John's is a passion of mere ice and snow.

Mrs. Heidel. Oh, fie, my dear! I am perfectly ashamed of you. That's so like the notions of your poor sister! What you complain of as coldness and indifference, is nothing but the extreme gentilaty of his address, an exact pictur of the manners of qualaty.

Miss Sterl. Oh, he is the very mirror of complaisance! full of formal bows and set speeches!—I declare, if there was any violent passion on my side, I should be quite jealous of him.

Mrs. Heidel. I say jealus indeed.—Jealus of who, pray?

Miss Sterl. My sister Fanny. She seems a much greater favourite than I am, and he pays her infinitely more attention, I assure you.

Mrs. Heidel. Lord! d'ye think a man of fashion, as he is, can't distinguish between the genteel and the wulgar part of the family?—Between you and your sister, for instance—or me and my brother?—Be advised by me, child! It is all politeness and good-breeding.—Nobody knows the qualaty better than I do.

Miss Sterl. In my mind the old lord, his uncle, has ten times more gallantry about him than Sir John. He is full of attentions to the ladies, and smiles, and grins, and leers, and ogles, and fills every wrinkle in his old wizen face with comical expressions of tenderness. I think he would make an admirable sweetheart.

Enter STERLING

Sterl. (*at entering*). No fish?—Why the pond was dragged but yesterday morning.—There's carp and tench in the boat.— Pox on't, if that dog Lovewell had any thought, he would have brought down a turbot, or some of the land-carriage mackerel.

Mrs. Heidel. Lord, brother, I am afraid his lordship and Sir John will not arrive while it's light.

Sterl. I warrant you.—But, pray, sister Heidelberg, let the turtle be dressed to-morrow, and some venison—and let the gardener cut some pine-apples—and get out some ice.—I'll answer for wine, I warrant you; I'll give them such a glass of champagne as they never drank in their lives—no, not at a duke's table.

Mrs. Heidel. Pray now, brother, mind how you behave. I am always in a fright about you with people of qualaty. Take care that you don't fall asleep directly after supper, as you commonly do. Take a good deal of snuff; and that will keep you awake.—And don't burst out with your horrible loud horse-laughs. It is monstrous wulgar.

Sterl. Never fear, sister!—Who have we here?

Mrs. Heidel. It is Monsieur Cantoon, the Swish gentleman, that lives with his lordship, I vow and pertest.

Enter CANTON

Sterl. Ah, Mounseer! your servant. — I am very glad to see you, Mounseer.

Canton. Mosh oblige to Monsieur Sterling.—Ma'am, I am yours—Matemoiselle, I am yours.   (*Bowing round.*

Mrs. Heidel. Your humble servant, Mr. Cantoon!

Canton. I kiss your hands, matam!

Sterl. Well, Mounseer!—and what news of your good family? —when are we to see his lordship and Sir John?

Canton. Monsieur Sterling! Milor Ogelby and Sir Jean Melvile will be here in one quarter-hour.

Sterl. I am glad to hear it.

Mrs. Heidel. Oh, I am perdigious glad to hear it. Being so late I was afeared of some accident.—Will you please to have anything, Mr. Cantoon, after your journey?

Canton. No, I tank you, ma'am.

Mrs. Heidel. Shall I go and show you the apartments, sir?

Canton. You do me great honeur, ma'am.

Mrs. Heidel. Come then!—come, my dear! (*To* Miss Sterl.)
(*Exeunt.*

Manent Sterling.

Sterl. Pox on't, it's almost dark—It will be too late to go round the garden this evening.—However, I will carry them to take a peep at my fine canal at least, I am determined. (*Exit.*

ACT II

SCENE I.—*An ante-chamber to Lord Ogleby's bedchamber. Table with chocolate, and small case for medicines*

Enter Brush, *my lord's valet-de-chambre, and Sterling's Chambermaid*

Brush. You shall stay, my dear, I insist upon it.
Chamber. Nay, pray, sir, don't be so positive; I can't stay indeed.
Brush. You shall take one cup to our better acquaintance.
Chamber. I seldom drinks chocolate; and if I did, one has no satisfaction, with such apprehensions about one—if my lord should wake, or the Swish gentleman should see one, or Madam Heidelberg should know of it, I should be frighted to death—besides I have had my tea already this morning.—I'm sure I hear my lord. (*In a fright.*
Brush. No, no, madam, don't flutter yourself—the moment my lord wakes, he rings his bell, which I answer sooner or later, as it suits my convenience.
Chamber. But should he come upon us without ringing——
Brush. I'll forgive him if he does.—This key (*Takes a phial out of the case.*) locks him up till I please to let him out.
Chamber. Law, sir! that's potecary's stuff.
Brush. It is so—but without this he can no more get out of bed—than he can read without spectacles (*Sips.*) What with qualms, age, rheumatism, and a few surfeits in his youth, he must have a great deal of brushing, oiling, screwing, and winding up to set him a-going for the day.
Chamber. (*sips.*) That's prodigious indeed. (*Sips.*) My lord seems quite in a decay.
Brush. Yes, he's quite a spectacle (*Sips.*), a mere corpse, till he is revived and refreshed from our little magazine here. When the restorative pills and cordial waters warm his stomach, and get into his head, vanity frisks in his heart, and then he sets up for the lover, the rake, and the fine gentleman.
Chamber. (*sips.*) Poor gentleman!—but should the Swish gentleman come upon us! (*Frightened.*
Brush. Why then the English gentleman would be very angry. No foreigner must break in upon my privacy. (*Sips.*

But I can assure you Monsieur Canton is otherwise employed. He is obliged to skim the cream of half a score newspapers for my lord's breakfast—ha, ha, ha. Pray, madam, drink your cup peaceably. My lord's chocolate is remarkably good, he won't touch a drop but what comes from Italy.

Chamber. (*sipping.*) 'Tis very fine indeed! (*Sips.*), and charmingly perfumed—it smells for all the world like our young ladies' dressing-boxes.

Brush. You have an excellent taste, madam, and I must beg of you to accept of a few cakes for your own drinking (*Takes them out of a drawer in the table.*), and in return I desire nothing but to taste the perfume of your lips. (*Kisses her.*) A small return of favours, madam, will make, I hope, this country and retirement agreeable to both. (*He bows, she curtsies.*) Your young ladies are fine girls, faith (*Sips.*): though upon my soul, I am quite of my old lord's mind about them; and were I inclined to matrimony, I should take the youngest.   (*Sips.*

Chamber. Miss Fanny's the most affablest and the most best-natered creter!

Brush. And the eldest a little haughty or so——

Chamber. More haughtier and prouder than Saturn himself—but this I say quite confidential to you, for one would not hurt a young lady's marriage, you know.   (*Sips.*

Brush. By no means; but you can't hurt it with us—we don't consider tempers—we want money, Mrs. Nancy. Give us enough of that, we'll abate you a great deal in other particulars—ha, ha, ha.

Chamber. Bless me, here's somebody. (*Bell rings.*)—Oh! 'tis my lord.—Well, your servant, Mr. Brush—I'll clean the cups in the next room.

Brush. Do so—but never mind the bell—I shan't go this half-hour. Will you drink tea with me in the afternoon?

Chamber. Not for the world, Mr. Brush—I'll be here to set all things to rights—but I must not drink tea indeed—and so your servant.   (*Exit Maid with tea-board.*
                                           (*Bell rings again.*

Brush. It is impossible to stupefy oneself in the country for a week without some little flirting with the Abigails: this is much the handsomest wench in the house, except the old citizen's youngest daughter, and I have not time enough to lay a plan for her. (*Bell rings.*) And now I'll go to my lord, for I have nothing else to do.   (*Going.*

Enter CANTON *with newspapers in his hand*

Canton. Monsieur Brush—Maistre Brush—My lor' stirra yet?

Brush. He has just rung his bell—I am going to him.

Canton. Dépêchez-vous donc.   (*Exit* BRUSH.
(*Puts on spectacles.*) I wish de deviel had all dese papiers—I forget as fast as I read.—De Advertise put out of my head

de Gazette, de Gazette de Chronique, and so dey all go l'un apres l'autre—I must get some nouvelle for my lor', or he'll be enragée contre moi—Voyons! (*Reads in the papers.*) Here is noting but Anti-Sejanus and advertise——

Enter Maid with chocolate things

Vat you vant, child?

Chamber. Only the chocolate things, sir.

Canton. O ver well—dat is good girl—and ver prit too!

(*Exit Maid.*

LORD OGLEBY, *within*

Lord Ogle. Canton, he, he—(*Coughs.*)—Canton!

Canton. I come, my lor'.—Vat shall I do?—I have no news.— He vil make great tintamarre!——

Lord Ogle. (*within*). Canton, I say, Canton! Where are you?—

Enter LORD OGLEBY *leaning on* BRUSH

Canton. Here, my lor'. I ask pardon, my lor', I have not finish de papiers——

Lord Ogle. Dem your pardon, and your papers—I want you here, Canton.

Canton. Den I run, dat is all. (*Shuffles along.* LORD OGLEBY *leans upon* CANTON *too, and comes forward.*

Lord Ogle. You Swiss are the most unaccountable mixture— you have the language and the impertinence of the French, with the laziness of Dutchmen.

Canton. 'Tis very true, my lor'—I can't help——

Lord Ogle. (*cries out*). O Diavolo!

Canton. You are not in pain, I hope, my lor'.

Lord Ogle. Indeed but I am, my lor'—That vulgar fellow Sterling, with his city politeness, would force me down his slope last night to see a clay-coloured ditch, which he calls a canal; and what with the dew, and the east wind, my hips and shoulders are absolutely screwed to my body.

Canton. A littel veritable eau d'arquibusade vil set all to right again.   (*My lord sits down,* BRUSH *gives chocolate.*

Lord Ogle. Where are the palsy-drops, Brush?

Brush. Here, my lord!   (*Pouring out.*

Lord Ogle. Quelle nouvelle avez vous, Canton?

Canton. A great deal of papier, but no news at all.

Lord Ogle. What! nothing at all, you stupid fellow?

Canton. Yes, my lor', I have littel advertise here vil give you more plaisir den all de lies about noting at all. La voila!

(*Puts on his spectacles.*

Lord Ogle. Come read it, Canton, with good emphasis, and good discretion.

Canton. I vil, my lor'. (CANTON *reads.*) Dere is no question,

but dat de Cosmetique Royale vil utterlie take away all heats,
pimps, frecks and oder eruptions of de skin, and likewise de
wrinque of old age, etc.—A great deal more, my lor'—be sure to
ask for de Cosmetique Royale, signed by de docteur own hand.
—Dere is more raison for dis caution dan good men vil tink.—
Eh bien, my lor'!

Lord Ogle. Eh bien, Canton!—Will you purchase any?

Canton. For you, my lor'?

Lord Ogle. For me, you old puppy! for what?

Canton. My lor'?

Lord Ogle. Do I want cosmetics?

Canton. My lor'!

Lord Ogle. Look in my face—come, be sincere.—Does it want
the assistance of art?

Canton (with his spectacles). En verité, non.—'Tis very smoose
and brillian'—but I tote dat you might take a little by way of
prevention.

Lord Ogle. You thought like an old fool, monsieur, as you
generally do——The surfeit-water, Brush! (BRUSH *pours out.*)
What do you think, Brush, of this family we are going to be
connected with?—Eh!

Brush. Very well to marry in, my lord; but it would not do
to live with.

Lord Ogle. You are right, Brush—There is no washing the
Blackamoor white—Mr. Sterling will never get rid of Black-
friars, always taste of the Borachio—and the poor woman his
sister is so busy and so notable, to make one welcome, that I
have not yet got over her first reception; it almost amounted to
suffocation! I think the daughters are tolerable.—Where's my
cephalic snuff? (BRUSH *gives him a box.*)

Canton. Dey tink so of you, my lor', for dey look at noting
else, ma foi.

Lord Ogle. Did they?—Why, I think they did a little.—Where's
my glass? (BRUSH *puts one on the table.*) The youngest is delect-
able.   (*Takes snuff.*

Canton. O, ouy, my lor'—very delect, inteed; she made doux
yeux at you, my lor'.

Lord Ogle. She was particular—the eldest, my nephew's lady,
will be a most valuable wife; she has all the vulgar spirits of her
father and aunt, happily blended with the termagant qualities
of her deceased mother.—Some peppermint water, Brush!—
How happy is it, Cant, for young ladies in general, that people
of quality overlook everything in a marriage contract but their
fortune.

Canton. C'est bien heureux, et commode aussi.

Lord Ogle. Brush, give me that pamphlet by my bedside.—
(BRUSH *goes for it.*) Canton, do you wait in the ante-chamber,
and let nobody interrupt me till I call you.

Canton. Mush goot may do your lordship!

Lord Ogle. (to BRUSH, *who brings the pamphlet.*) And now
Brush, leave me a little to my studies.   (*Exit* BRUSH.

LORD OGLEBY, *alone*

What can I possibly do among these women here, with this
confounded rheumatism? It is a most grievous enemy to gallantry
and address (*Gets off his chair.*) He!—Courage, my lor'! by
heavens, I'm another creature! (*Hums and dances a little.*) It
will do, faith.—Bravo, my lor'! these girls have absolutely inspired me.—If they are for a game of romps—me voila pret!
Sings and dances.) O!—that's an ugly twinge—but it's gone.—
I have rather too much of the lily this morning in my complexion; a faint tincture of the rose will give a delicate spirit to
my eyes for the day. (*Unlocks a drawer at the bottom of the glass,
and takes out rouge: while he's painting himself, a knocking at
the door.*) Who's there? I won't be disturbed.

Canton (without). My lor', my lor', here is Monsieur Sterling
to pay his devoir to you this morn in your chambre.

Lord Ogle. (softly). What a fellow! (*Aloud.*) I am extremely
honoured by Mr. Sterling. Why don't you see him in, monsieur?—I wish he was at the bottom of his stinking canal. (*Door
opens.*) Oh, my dear Mr. Sterling, you do me a great deal of
honour.

Enter STERLING *and* LOVEWELL

Sterl. I hope, my lord, that your lordship slept well in the
night.—I believe there are no better beds in Europe than I have
—I spare no pains to get 'em, nor money to buy 'em.—His
Majesty—God bless him—don't sleep upon a better out of his
palace; and if I had said in too, I hope no treason, my lord.

Lord Ogle. Your beds are like everything else about you,
incomparable! They not only make one rest well, but give one
spirits, Mr. Sterling.

Sterl. What say you then, my lord, to another walk in the
garden? You must see my water by daylight, and my walks,
and my slopes, and my clumps, and my bridge, and my flowering
trees, and my bed of Dutch tulips.—Matters looked but dim
last night, my lord; I feel the dew in my great toe—but I would
put on a cut shoe that I might be able to walk you about—I may
be laid up to-morrow.

Lord Ogle. (aside). I pray Heaven you may!

Sterl. What say you, my lord?

Lord Ogle. I was saying, sir, that I was in hopes of seeing the
young ladies at breakfast: Mr. Sterling, they are, in my mind,
the finest tulips in this part of the world—he, he.

Canton. Bravissimo, my lor'!—ha, ha, he.

Sterl. They shall meet your lordship in the garden—we won't
lose our walk for them; I'll take you a little round before break-

fast, and a larger before dinner, and in the evening you shall go
to the Grand Tower, as I call it, ha, ha, ha.

Lord Ogle. Not a foot, I hope, Mr. Sterling—consider your
gout, my good friend. You'll certainly be laid by the heels for
your politeness—he, he, he.

Canton. Ha, ha, ha—'tis admirable! en verité—

(Laughing very heartily.

Sterl. If my young man (*To* LOVEWELL) here, would but laugh
at my jokes, which he ought to do, as Mounseer does at yours,
my lord, we should be all life and mirth.

Lord Ogle. What say You, Cant, will you take my kinsman
under your tuition? you have certainly the most companionable
laugh I ever met with, and never out of tune.

Canton. But when your lordship is out of spirits.

Lord Ogle. Well said, Cant!—But here comes my nephew, to
play his part.

Enter SIR JOHN MELVIL

Well, Sir John, what news from the island of love? have you been
sighing and serenading this morning?

Sir John. I am glad to see your lordship in such spirits this
morning.

Lord Ogle. I'm sorry to see you so dull, sir. What poor things,
Mr. Sterling, these *very* young fellows are! They make love with
faces as if they were burying the dead—though, indeed, a
marriage sometimes may be properly called a burying of the
living—eh, Mr. Sterling?

Sterl. Not if they have enough to live upon, my lord—Ha,
ha, ha.

Canton. Dat is all Monsieur Sterling tink of.

Sir John. Prithee, Lovewell, come with me into the
garden; I have something of consequence for you, and
I must communicate it directly.　　　　　　　*Apart.*

Love. We'll go together—

If your lordship and Mr. Sterling please, we'll prepare the ladies
to attend you in the garden. (*Exeunt* SIR JOHN *and* LOVEWELL.

Sterl. My girls are always ready, I make 'em rise soon, and
to bed early; their husbands shall have 'em with good con-
stitutions, and good fortunes, if they have nothing else, my lord.

Lord Ogle. Fine things, Mr. Sterling!

Sterl. Fine things indeed, my lord!— Ah, my lord, had not
you run off your speed in your youth, you had not been so
crippled in your age, my lord.

Lord Ogle. Very pleasant, I protest—He, he, he.—

(Half-laughing.

Sterl. Here's Mounseer now, I suppose, is pretty near your
lordship's standing; but having little to eat, and little to spend,
in his own country, he'll wear three of your lordship out—eating
and drinking kills us all.

Lord Ogle. Very pleasant, I protest.—What a vulgar dog!

(*Aside*

Canton. My lor' so old as me!—He is shicken to me—and look like a boy to pauvre me.

Sterl. Ha, ha, ha. Well said, Mounseer—keep to that, and you'll live in any country of the world—Ha, ha, ha.—But, my lord, I will wait upon you into the garden: we have but a little time to breakfast.— I'll go for my hat and cane, fetch a little walk with you, my lord, and then for the hot rolls and butter!

(*Exit* STERLING.

Lord Ogle. I shall attend you with pleasure.—Hot rolls and butter in July!— I sweat with the thoughts of it.—What a strange beast it is!

Canton. C'est un barbare.

Lord Ogle. He is a vulgar dog, and if there was not so much money in the family, which I can't do without, I would leave him and his hot rolls and butter directly.—Come along, monsieur!

(*Exeunt.*

Scene changes to the Garden

Enter SIR JOHN MELVIL and LOVEWELL

Love. In my room this morning? Impossible!

Sir John. Before five this morning, I promise you.

Love. On what occasion?

Sir John. I was so anxious to disclose my mind to you, that I could not sleep in my bed.—But I found that you could not sleep neither—the bird was flown, and the nest long since cold.—Where was you, Lovewell?

Love. Pooh! prithee! ridiculous!

Sir John. Come now! which was it? Miss Sterling's maid?—a pretty little rogue!—or Miss Fanny's Abigail?—a sweet soul too!—or——

Love. Nay, nay, leave trifling, and tell me your business.

Sir John. Well, but where was you, Lovewell?

Love. Walking—writing—what signifies where I was?

Sir John. Walking! yes, I dare say. It rained as hard as it could pour. Sweet refreshing showers to walk in! No, no, Lovewell.—Now would I give twenty pounds to know which of the maids——

Love. But your business! your business, Sir John!

Sir John. Let me a little into the secrets of the family.

Love. Psha!

Sir John. Poor Lovewell! he can't bear it, I see. She charged you not to kiss and tell.—Eh, Lovewell! However, though you will not honour me with your confidence, I'll venture to trust you with mine.—What do you think of Miss Sterling?

Love. What do I think of Miss Sterling?

Sir John. Ay; what d'ye think of her?

Love. An odd question!—but I think her a smart, lively girl, full of mirth and sprightliness.

Sir John. All mischief and malice, I doubt.

Love. How?

Sir John. But her person—what d'ye think of that?

Love. Pretty and agreeable.

Sir John. A little grisette thing.

Love. What is the meaning of all this?

Sir John. I'll tell you. You must know, Lovewell, that notwithstanding all appearances.——(*Seeing* Lord Ogleby, *etc.*) We are interrupted.—When they are gone, I'll explain.

Enter Lord Ogleby, Sterling, Mrs. Heidelberg, Miss Sterling, *and* Fanny

Lord Ogle. Great improvements indeed, Mr. Sterling! wonderful improvements! The four Seasons in lead, the flying Mercury, and the basin with Neptune in the middle, are all in the very extreme of fine taste. You have as many rich figures as the man at Hyde Park Corner.

Sterl. The chief pleasure of a country house is to make improvements, you know, my lord. I spare no expense, not I.—This is quite another-guess sort of a place than it was when I first took it, my lord. We were surrounded with trees. I cut down above fifty to make the lawn before the house, and let in the wind and the sun — smack-smooth, as you see.—Then I made a greenhouse out of the old laundry, and turned the brew-house into a pinery.—The high octagon summer-house, you see yonder, is raised on the mast of a ship, given me by an East India captain who has turned many a thousand of my money. It commands the whole road. All the coaches and chariots, and chaises, pass and repass under your eye. I'll mount you up there in the afternoon, my lord. 'Tis the pleasantest place in the world to take a pipe and a bottle—and so you shall say, my lord.

Lord Ogle. Ay — or a bowl of punch, or a can of flip, Mr. Sterling; for it looks like a cabin in the air.—If flying chairs were in use, the captain might make a voyage to the Indies in it still, if he had but a fair wind.

Canton. Ha! ha! ha! ha!

Mrs. Heidel. My brother's a little comical in his ideas, my lord!—But you'll excuse him.—I have a little gothic dairy, fitted up entirely in my own taste.—In the evening I shall hope for the honour of your lordship's company to take a dish of tea there, or a sullabub warm from the cow.

Lord Ogle. I have every moment a fresh opportunity of admiring the elegance of Mrs. Heidelberg—the very flower of delicacy and cream of politeness.

Mrs. Heidel. O my lord!   } *Leering at each other.*
Lord Ogle. O madam!

Sterl. How d'ye like these close walks, my lord?

Lord Ogle. A most excellent serpentine! It forms a perfect maze, and winds like a true-lover's knot.

Sterl. Ay — here's none of your straight lines here — but all taste—zigzag—crinkum-crankum—in and out—right and left— to and again—twisting and turning like a worm, my lord!

Lord Ogle. Admirably laid out indeed, Mr. Sterling! one can hardly see an inch beyond one's nose anywhere in these walks.— You are a most excellent economist of your land, and make a little go a great way.—It lies together in as small parcels as if it was placed in pots out at your window in Gracechurch Street.

Canton. Ha! ha! ha! ha!

Lord Ogle. What d'ye laugh at, Canton?

Canton. Ah! que cette similitude est drole! So clever what you say, mi lor'.

Lord Ogle. (to Fanny). You seem mightily engaged, madam. What are those pretty hands so busily employed about?

Fanny. Only making up a nosegay, my lord!—Will your lordship do me the honour of accepting it?   (*Presenting it.*

Lord Ogle. I'll wear it next my heart, madam!—I see the young creature dotes on me.   (*Apart.*

Miss Sterl. Lord, sister, you've loaded his lordship with a bunch of flowers as big as the cook or the nurse carry to town on Monday morning for a beaupot.—Will your lordship give me leave to present you with this rose and a sprig of sweet brier?

Lord Ogle. The truest emblems of yourself, madam! all sweetness and poignancy.—A little jealous, poor soul!   (*Apart.*

Sterl. Now, my lord, if you please, I'll carry you to see my ruins.

Mrs. Heidel. You'll absolutely fatigue his lordship with overwalking, brother!

Lord Ogle. Not at all, madam! We're in the Garden of Eden, you know; in the region of perpetual spring, youth, and beauty.
        (*Leering at the women.*

Mrs. Heidel. Quite the man of qualaty, I pertest.   (*Apart.*

Canton. Take a my arm, mi lor'!

        (LORD OGLEBY *leans on him.*

Sterl. I'll only show his lordship my ruins, and the cascade, and the Chinese bridge, and then we'll go in to breakfast.

Lord Ogle. Ruins, did you say, Mr. Sterling?

Sterl. Ay, ruins, my lord! and they are reckoned very fine ones too. You would think them ready to tumble on your head. It has just cost me a hundred and fifty pounds to put my ruins in thorough repair.—This way, if your lordship pleases.

Lord Ogle. (going, stops). What steeple's that we see yonder? the parish church, I suppose.

Sterl. Ha! ha! ha! that's admirable. It is no church at all, my lord! it is a spire that I have built against a tree, a field or two off, to terminate the prospect. One must always have a church, or an obelisk, or a something, to terminate the prospect, you know. That's a rule in taste, my lord!

Lord Ogle. Very ingenious, indeed! For my part, I desire no finer prospect than this I see before me. (*Leering at the women.*) —Simple, yet varied; bounded, yet extensive.—Get away, Canton! (*Pushing away* CANTON.) I want no assistance.—I'll walk with the ladies.

Sterl. This way, my lord!

Lord Ogle. Lead on, sir!—We young folks here will follow you. —Madam!—Miss Sterling!—Miss Fanny! I attend you.

(*Exit after* STERLING, *gallanting the ladies.*

Canton (following). He is cock o'de game, ma foy! (*Exit.*

Manent SIR JOHN MELVIL and LOVEWELL

Sir John. At length, thank heaven, I have an opportunity to unbosom.—I know you are faithful, Lovewell, and flatter myself you would rejoice to serve me.

Love. Be assured, you may depend on me.

Sir John. You must know then, notwithstanding all appearances, that this treaty of marriage between Miss Sterling and me will come to nothing.

Love. How!

Sir John. It will be no match, Lovewell.

Love. No match?

Sir John. No.

Love. You amaze me. What should prevent it?

Sir John. I.

Love. You! wherefore?

Sir John. I don't like her.

Love. Very plain indeed! I never supposed that you was extremely devoted to her from inclination, but thought you always considered it as a matter of convenience, rather than affection.

Sir John. Very true. I came into the family without any impressions on my mind—with an unimpassioned indifference ready to receive one woman as soon as another. I looked upon love, serious, sober love, as a chimæra, and marriage as a thing of course, as you know most people do. But I, who was lately so great an infidel in love, am now one of its sincerest votaries. —In short, my defection from Miss Sterling proceeds from the violence of my attachment to another.

Love. Another! So! so! here will be fine work. And pray who is she?

Sir John. Who is she! who can she be? but Fanny, the tender, amiable, engaging Fanny.

Love. Fanny! What Fanny?

Sir John. Fanny Sterling. Her sister.—Is not she an angel, Lovewell?

Love. Her sister? Confusion!—You must not think of it, Sir John.

Sir John. Not think of it? I can think of nothing else. Nay, tell me, Lovewell, was it possible for me to be indulged in a perpetual intercourse with two such objects as Fanny and her sister, and not find my heart led by insensible attraction towards her?—You seem confounded.—Why don't you answer me?

Love. Indeed, Sir John, this event gives me infinite concern.

Sir John. Why so?—Is not she an angel, Lovewell?

Love. I foresee that it must produce the worst consequences. Consider the confusion it must unavoidably create. Let me persuade you to drop these thoughts in time.

Sir John. Never—never, Lovewell!

Love. You have gone too far to recede. A negotiation so nearly concluded cannot be broken off with any grace. The lawyers, you know, are hourly expected; the preliminaries almost finally settled between Lord Ogleby and Mr. Sterling; and Miss Sterling herself ready to receive you as a husband.

Sir John. Why the banns have been published, and nobody has forbidden them, 'tis true. But you know either of the parties may change their minds even after they enter the church.

Love. You think too lightly of this matter. To carry your addresses so far—and then to desert her—and for her sister too! —It will be such an affront to the family, that they can never put up with it.

Sir John. I don't think so: for as to my transferring my passion from her to her sister, so much the better!—for then, you know, I don't carry my affections out of the family.

Love. Nay, but prithee be serious, and think better of it.

Sir John. I have thought better of it already, you see. Tell me honestly, Lovewell! Can you blame me? Is there any comparison between them?

Love. As to that now—why that—that is just—just as it may strike different people. There are many admirers of Miss Sterling's vivacity.

Sir John. Vivacity! a medley of Cheapside pertness, and Whitechapel pride.—No—no—if I do go so far into the city for a wedding-dinner, it shall be upon turtle at least.

Love. But I see no probability of success; for granting that Mr. Sterling would have consented to it at first, he cannot listen to it now. Why did not you break this affair to the family before?

Sir John. Under such embarrassed circumstances as I have been, can you wonder at my irresolution or perplexity? Nothing but despair, the fear of losing my dear Fanny, could bring me to a declaration even now: and yet, I think I know Mr. Sterling so well, that, strange as my proposal may appear, if I can make it advantageous to him as a money transaction as I am sure I can, he will certainly come into it.

Love. But even suppose he should, which I very much doubt, I don't think Fanny herself would listen to your addresses.

Sir John. You are deceived a little in that particular.

Love. You'll find I am in the right.

Sir John. I have some little reason to think otherwise.

Love. You have not declared your passion to her already?

Sir John. Yes, I have.

Love. Indeed!—And—and—and how did she receive it?

Sir John. I think it is not very easy for me to make my addresses to any woman without receiving some little encouragement.

Love. Encouragement! did she give you any encouragement?

Sir John. I don't know what you call encouragement!—but she blushed—and cried—and desired me not to think of it any more; upon which I pressed her hand—kissed it—swore she was an angel—and I could see it tickled her to the soul.

Love. And did she express no surprise at your declaration?

Sir John. Why, faith, to say the truth, she was a little surprised—and she got away from me too, before I could thoroughly explain myself. If I should not meet with an opportunity of speaking to her, I must get you to deliver a letter from me.

Love. I!—a letter!—I had rather have nothing——

Sir John. Nay, you promised me your assistance—and I am sure you cannot scruple to make yourself useful on such an occasion.—You may, without suspicion, acquaint her verbally of my determined affection for her, and that I am resolved to ask her father's consent.

Love. As to that, I—your commands, you know—that is, if she——Indeed, Sir John, I think you are in the wrong.

Sir John. Well—well—that's my concern.—Ha! there she goes, by heaven! along that walk yonder, d'ye see? I'll go to her immediately.

Love. You are too precipitate. Consider what you are doing.

Sir John. I would not lose this opportunity for the universe.

Love. Nay, pray don't go! Your violence and eagerness may overcome her spirits.—The shock will be too much for her.
(Detaining him.

Sir John. Nothing shall prevent me.—Ha! now she turns into another walk.—Let me go! (*Breaks from him.*) I shall lose her.—(*Going, turns back.*) Be sure now to keep out of the way! If you interrupt us, I shall never forgive you. (*Exit hastily.*

LOVEWELL, *alone*

Love. 'Sdeath! I can't bear this. In love with my wife! acquaint me with his passion for her! make his addresses before my face! —I shall break out before my time.—This was the meaning of Fanny's uneasiness. She could not encourage him—I am sure she could not.—Ha! they are turning into the walk, and coming this way. Shall I leave the place?—Leave him to solicit my wife!

I can't submit to it.—They come nearer and nearer. If I stay it will look suspicious—it may betray us, and incense him.—They are here—I must go—I am the most unfortunate fellow in the world.   (*Exit.*

Enter FANNY *and* SIR JOHN

Fanny. Leave me, Sir John, I beseech you leave me!—Nay, why will you persist to follow me with idle solicitations, which are an affront to my character, and an injury to your own honour?

Sir John. I know your delicacy, and tremble to offend it: but let the urgency of the occasion be my excuse! Consider, madam, that the future happiness of my life depends on my present application to you; consider that this day must determine my fate; and these are perhaps the only moments left me to incline you to warrant my passion, and to entreat you not to oppose the proposals I mean to open to your father.

Fanny. For shame, for shame, Sir John! Think of your previous engagements! Think of your own situation, and think of mine!—What have you discovered in my conduct that might encourage you to so bold a declaration? I am shocked that you should venture to say so much, and blush that I should even dare to give it a hearing.—Let me be gone!

Sir John. Nay, stay, madam! but one moment!—Your sensibility is too great. — Engagements! what engagements have even been pretended on either side than those of family convenience? I went on in the trammels of matrimonial negotiation with a blind submission to your father and Lord Ogleby; but my heart soon claimed a right to be consulted. It has devoted itself to you, and obliges me to plead earnestly for the same tender interest in yours.

Fanny. Have a care, Sir John! do not mistake a depraved will for a virtuous inclination. By these common pretences of the heart, half of our sex are made fools, and a greater part of yours despise them for it.

Sir John. Affection, you will allow, is involuntary. We cannot always direct it to the object on which it should fix; but when it is once inviolably attached, inviolably as mine is to you, it often creates reciprocal affection.—When I last urged you on this subject, you heard me with more temper, and I hoped with some compassion.

Fanny. You deceived yourself. If I forbore to exert a proper spirit, nay if I did not even express the quickest resentment of your behaviour, it was only in consideration of that respect I wish to pay you, in honour to my sister: and be assured, sir, woman as I am, that my vanity could reap no pleasure from a triumph that must result from the blackest treachery to her.

                                                            (*Going.*

Sir John. One word, and I have done. (*Stopping her.*)—Your impatience and anxiety, and the urgency of the occasion, oblige me to be brief and explicit with you.—I appeal therefore from your delicacy to your justice.—Your sister, I verily believe, neither entertains any real affection for me, or tenderness for you.—Your father, I am inclined to think, is not much concerned by means of which of his daughters the families are united.— Now as they cannot, shall not be connected, otherwise than by my union with you, why will you, from a false delicacy, oppose a measure so conducive to my happiness, and, I hope, your own? I love you, most passionately and sincerely love you—and hope to propose terms agreeable to Mr. Sterling. If then you don't absolutely loathe, abhor, and scorn me—if there is no other happier man——

Fanny. Hear me, sir! hear my final determination.—Were my father and sister as insensible as you are pleased to represent them; were my heart for ever to remain disengaged to any other—I could not listen to your proposals.—What! You on the very eve of a marriage with my sister; I living under the same roof with her, bound not only by the laws of friendship and hospitality, but even the ties of blood, to contribute to her happiness,—and not to conspire against her peace—the peace of a whole family—and that my own too!—Away! away, Sir John!—At such a time, and in such circumstances, your addresses only inspire me with horror.—Nay, you must detain me no longer.—I will go.

Sir John. Do not leave me in absolute despair!—Give me a glimpse of hope!   (*Falling on his knees.*

Fanny. I cannot. Pray, Sir John!   (*Struggling to go.*

Sir John. Shall this hand be given to another? (*Kissing her hand.*) No—I cannot endure it.—My whole soul is yours, and the whole happiness of my life is in your power.

Enter MISS STERLING

Fanny. Ha! my sister is here. Rise for shame, Sir John!

Sir John. Miss Sterling!   (*Rising.*

Miss Sterl. I beg pardon, sir!—You'll excuse me, madam!— I have broke in upon you a little unopportunely, I believe; but I did not mean to interrupt you—I only came, sir, to let you know that breakfast waits, if you have finished your morning's devotions.

Sir John. I am very sensible, Miss Sterling, that this may appear particular, but——

Miss Sterl. Oh dear, Sir John, don't put yourself to the trouble of an apology. The thing explains itself.

Sir John. It will soon, madam!—In the meantime I can only assure you of my profound respect and esteem for you, and make no doubt of convincing Mr. Sterling of the honour and integrity of my intentions. And—and—your humble servant, madam!   (*Exit in confusion.*

Manent Fanny and Miss Sterling

Miss Sterl. Respect?—Insolence!—Esteem?—Very fine truly! —And you, madam! my sweet, delicate, innocent, sentimental sister! will you convince my papa too of the integrity of your intentions?

Fanny. Do not upbraid me, my dear sister! Indeed, I don't deserve it. Believe me, you can't be more offended at his behaviour than I am, and I am sure it cannot make you half so miserable.

Miss Sterl. Make me miserable! You are mightily deceived, madam! It gives me no sort of uneasiness, I assure you.—A base fellow!—As for you, miss! the pretended softness of your disposition, your artful good-nature, never imposed upon me. I always knew you to be sly, and envious, and deceitful.

Fanny. Indeed you wrong me.

Miss Sterl. Oh, you are all goodness, to be sure!—Did not I find him on his knees before you? Did not I see him kiss your sweet hand? Did not I hear his protestations? Was not I witness of your dissembled modesty?—No—no, my dear! don't imagine that you can make a fool of your elder sister so easily.

Fanny. Sir John, I own, is to blame; but I am above the thoughts of doing you the least injury.

Miss Sterl. We shall try that, madam!—I hope, miss, you'll be able to give a better account to my papa and my aunt—for they shall both know of this matter, I promise you.   (*Exit.*

FANNY, *alone*

How unhappy I am! my distresses multiply upon me.—Mr. Lovewell must now become acquainted with Sir John's behaviour to me—and in a manner that may add to his uneasiness. —My father, instead of being disposed by fortunate circumstances to forgive any transgression, will be previously incensed against me.—My sister and my aunt will become irreconcilably my enemies, and rejoice in my disgrace.—Yet, at all events, I am determined on a discovery. I dread it, and am resolved to hasten it. It is surrounded with more horrors every instant, as it appears every instant more necessary.   (*Exit.*

ACT III

SCENE I.—*A Hall*

Enter a Servant leading in SERJEANT FLOWER, *and Counsellors* TRAVERSE *and* TRUEMAN—*all booted*

Servant. This way, if you please, gentlemen! My master is at breakfast with the family at present—but I'll let him know, and he will wait on you immediately.

Flower. Mighty well. young man, mighty well.

Servant. Please to favour me with your names, gentlemen.

Flower. Let Mr. Sterling know that Mr. Serjeant Flower, and two other gentlemen of the bar, are come to wait on him according to his appointment.

Servant. I will, sir.   (*Going.*

Flower. And harkee, young man! (*Servant returns.*) Desire my servant—Mr. Serjeant Flower's servant—to bring in my green and gold saddle-cloth and pistols, and lay them down here in the hall with my portmanteau.

Servant. I will, sir.   (*Exit.*

Manent lawyers

Flower. Well, gentlemen! the sett[l]ing these marriage articles falls conveniently enough, almost just on the eve of the circuits. —Let me see—the Home, the Midland, and Western,—ay, we can all cross the country well enough to our several destinations. —Traverse, when do you begin at Hertford?

Traverse. The day after to-morrow.

Flower. That is commission-day with us at Warwick too. But my clerk has retainers for every cause in the paper, so it will be time enough if I am there the next morning.—Besides, I have about half a dozen cases that have lain by me ever since the Spring Assizes, and I must tack opinions to them before I see my country clients again—so I will take the evening before me—and then *currente calamo*, as I say—eh, Traverse!

Traverse. True, Mr. Serjeant—and the easiest thing in the world too—for those country attorneys are such ignorant dogs, that in case of the devise of an estate to A. and his heirs for ever, they'll make a query whether he takes in fee or in tail.

Flower. Do you expect to have much to do on the Home circuit these assizes?

Traverse. Not much *nisi prius* business, but a good deal on the Crown side, I believe.—The jails are brimful—and some of the felons in good circumstances, and likely to be tolerable clients.—Let me see! I'm engaged for three highway robberies, two murders, one forgery, and half a dozen larcenies, at Kingston.

Flower. A pretty decent jail-delivery! — Do you expect to bring off Darkin for the robbery on Putney Common? Can you make out your alibi?

Traverse. Oh, no! the Crown witnesses are sure to prove our identity. We shall certainly be hanged: but that don't signify.— But, Mr. Serjeant, have you much to do?—any remarkable cause on the Midland this circuit?

Flower. Nothing very remarkable—except two rapes, and Rider and Western at Nottingham, for *crim. con.*—but, on the whole, I believe a good deal of business.—Our associate tells me there are above thirty *venires* for Warwick.

Traverse. Pray, Mr. Serjeant, are you concerned in Jones and Thomas at Lincoln?

Flower. I am—for the plaintiff.

Traverse. And what do you think on't?

Flower. A non-suit.

Traverse. I thought so.

Flower. Oh, no manner of doubt on't—*luce clarius*—we have no right in us—we have but one chance.

Traverse. What's that?

Flower. Why, my Lord Chief does not go the circuit this time, and my brother Puzzle being in the commission, the cause will come on before him.

True. Ay, that may do, indeed, if you can but throw dust in the eyes of the defendant's counsel.

Flower. True.—Mr. Trueman, I think you are concerned for Lord Ogleby in this affair?   *(To* TRUEMAN.

True. I am, sir—I have the honour to be related to his lordship, and hold some courts for him in Somersetshire,—go the Western circuit, and attend the session at Exeter, merely because his lordship's interest and property lie in that part of the kingdom.

Flower. Ha!—and pray, Mr. Trueman, how long have you been called to the Bar?

True. About nine years and three-quarters.

Flower. Ha!—I don't know that I ever had the pleasure of seeing you before.—I wish you success, young gentleman!

Enter STERLING

Sterl. Oh, Mr. Serjeant Flower, I am glad to see you. Your servant, Mr. Serjeant! gentlemen, your servant!—Well, are all matters concluded? Has that snail-paced conveyancer, old Ferret of Gray's Inn, settled the articles at last? Do you approve of what he has done? Will his tackle hold? tight and strong?—Eh, Master Serjeant?

Flower. My friend Ferret's slow and sure, sir.—But then, *serius aut citius,* as we say,—sooner or later, Mr. Sterling, he is sure to put his business out of hand as he should do.—My clerk has brought the writings and all other instruments along with him, and the settlement is, I believe, as good a settlement as any settlement on the face of the earth!

Sterl. But that damn'd mortgage of £60,000.—There don't appear to be any other incumbrances, I hope?

Trav. I can answer for that, sir—and that will be cleared off immediately on the payment of the first part of Miss Sterling's portion.—You agree, on your part, to come down with £80,000.—

Sterl. Down on the nail.—Ay, ay, my money is ready to-morrow if he pleases—he shall have it in India-bonds, or notes, or how he chooses.—Your lords, and your dukes, and your people at the Court end of the town stick at payments sometimes—debts unpaid, no credit lost with them—but no fear of us substantial fellows—eh, Mr. Serjeant!

Flower. Sir John having last term, according to agreement, levied a fine, and suffered a recovery, has thereby cut off the entail of the Ogleby estate for the better effecting the purposes of the present intended marriage; on which above-mentioned Ogleby estate, a jointure of £2000 per ann. is secured to your eldest daughter, now Elizabeth Sterling, spinster, and the whole estate, after the death of the aforesaid earl, descends to the heirs male of Sir John Melvil on the body of the aforesaid Elizabeth Sterling lawfully to be begotten.

Trav. Very true—and Sir John is to be put in immediate possession of as much of his lordship's Somersetshire estate as lies in the manors of Hogmore and Cranford, amounting to between two and three thousands per ann., and at the death of Mr. Sterling, a further sum of seventy thousand——

Enter SIR JOHN MELVIL

Sterl. Ah, Sir John! Here we are—hard at it—paving the road to matrimony.—First the lawyers, then comes the doctor.—Let us but dispatch the long-robe, we shall soon set Pudding-sleeves to work, I warrant you.

Sir John. I am sorry to interrupt you, sir—but I hope that both you and these gentlemen will excuse me—having something very particular for your private ear, I took the liberty of following you, and beg you will oblige me with an audience immediately.

Sterl. Ay, with all my heart.—Gentlemen, Mr. Serjeant, you'll excuse it—business must be done, you know.—The writings will keep cold till to-morrow morning.

Flower. I must be at Warwick, Mr. Sterling, the day after.

Sterl. Nay, nay, I shan't part with you to-night, gentlemen, I promise you.—My house is very full, but I have beds for you all, beds for your servants, and stabling for all your horses.—Will you take a turn in the garden, and view some of my improvements before dinner? Or will you amuse yourselves on the green with a game of bowls and a cool tankard?—My servants shall attend you. Do you choose any other refreshment?—Call for what you please;—do as you please;—make yourselves quite at home, I beg of you.—Here,—Thomas, Harry, William, wait on these gentlemen!) (*Follows the lawyers out, bawling and talking, and then returns to Sir John.*) And now, sir, I am entirely at your service.—What are your commands with me, Sir John?

Sir John. After having carried the negotiation between our families to so great a length, after having assented so readily to all your proposals, as well as received so many instances of your cheerful compliance with the demands made on our part, I am extremely concerned, Mr. Sterling, to be the involuntary cause of any uneasiness.

Sterl. Uneasiness! what uneasiness?—Where business is transacted as it ought to be, and the parties understand one another, there can be no uneasiness. You agree, on such and such conditions, to receive my daughter for a wife; on the same conditions I agree to receive you as a son-in-law; and as to all the rest, it follows of course, you know, as regularly as the payment of a bill after acceptance.

Sir John. Pardon me, sir; more uneasiness has arisen than you are aware of. I am myself, at this instant, in a state of inexpressible embarrassment; Miss Sterling, I know, is extremely disconcerted too; and unless you will oblige me with the assistance of your friendship, I foresee the speedy progress of discontent and animosity through the whole family.

Sterl. What the deuce is all this? I don't understand a single syllable.

Sir John. In one word then—it will be absolutely impossible for me to fulfil my engagements in regard to Miss Sterling.

Sterl. How, Sir John? Do you mean to put an affront upon my family? What! refuse to——

Sir John. Be assured, sir, that I neither mean to affront nor forsake your family.—My only fear is, that you should desert me; for the whole happiness of my life depends on my being connected with your family by the nearest and tenderest ties in the world.

Sterl. Why, did you not tell me, but a moment ago, that it was absolutely impossible for you to marry my daughter?

Sir John. True.—But you have another daughter, sir——

Sterl. Well?

Sir John. Who has obtained the most absolute dominion over my heart. I have already declared my passion to her; nay, Miss Sterling herself is also apprised of it, and if you will but give a sanction to my present address, the uncommon merit of Miss Sterling will no doubt recommend her to a person of equal, if not superior rank to myself, and our families may still be allied by my union with Miss Fanny.

Sterl. Mighty fine, truly! Why, what the plague do you make of us, Sir John? Do you come to market for my daughters, like servants at a statute fair? Do you think that I will suffer you, or any man in the world, to come into my house, like the Grand Signior, and throw the handkerchief first to one, and then to t'other, just as he pleases? Do you think I drive a kind of African slave-trade with them? and——

Sir John. A moment's patience, sir! Nothing but the excess of my passion for Miss Fanny should have induced me to take any step that had the least appearance of disrespect to any part of your family; and even now I am desirous to atone for my transgression, by making the most adequate compensation that lies in my power.

Sterl. Compensation! what compensation can you possibly make in such a case as this, Sir John?

Sir John. Come, come, Mr. Sterling; I know you to be a man of sense, a man of business, a man of the world. I'll deal frankly with you; and you shall see that I do not desire a change of measures for my own gratification, without endeavouring to make it advantageous to you.

Sterl. What advantage can your inconstancy be to me, Sir John?

Sir John. I'll tell you, sir.—You know that by the articles at present subsisting between us, on the day of my marriage with Miss Sterling you agree to pay down the gross sum of eighty thousand pounds.

Sterl. Well!

Sir John. Now if you will but consent to my waiving that marriage——

Sterl. I agree to your waiving that marriage? Impossible, Sir John!

Sir John. I hope not, sir; as on my part, I will agree to waive my right to thirty thousand pounds of the fortune I was to receive with her.

Sterl. Thirty thousand. d'ye say?

Sir John. Yes, sir; and accept of Miss Fanny with fifty thousand, instead of fourscore.

Sterl. Fifty thousand—— *(Pausing.*

Sir John. Instead of fourscore.

Sterl. Why,—why,—there may be something in that.—Let me see; Fanny with fifty thousand instead of Betsey with four-score.—But how can this be, Sir John?—For you know I am to pay this money into the hands of my Lord Ogleby; who, I believe—between you and me, Sir John,—is not overstocked with ready money at present; and threescore thousand of it, you know, is to go to pay off the present incumbrances on the estate, Sir John.

Sir John. That objection is easily obviated.—Ten of the twenty thousand which would remain as a surplus of the four-score, after paying off the mortgage, was intended by his lord-ship for my use, that we might set off with some little *éclat* on our marriage; and the other ten for his own.—Ten thousand pounds, therefore, I shall be able to pay you immediately; and for the remaining twenty thousand you shall have a mortgage on that part of the estate which is to be made over to me, with whatever security you shall require for the regular payment of the interest, till the principal is duly discharged.

Sterl. Why—to do you justice, Sir John, there is something fair and open in your proposal; and since I find you do not mean to put an affront upon the family——

Sir John. Nothing was ever farther from my thoughts, Mr. Sterling.—And after all, the whole affair is nothing extraordinary —such things happen every day—and as the world has only heard generally of a treaty between the families, when this marriage takes place, nobody will be the wiser, if we have but discretion enough to keep our own counsel.

Sterl. True, true; and since you only transfer from one girl to another, it is no more than transferring so much stock, you know.

Sir John. The very thing.

Sterl. Odso! I had quite forgot. We are reckoning without our host here. There is another difficulty——

Sir John. You alarm me. What can that be?

Sterl. I can't stir a step in this business without consulting my sister Heidelberg.—The family has very great expectations from her, and we must not give her any offence.

Sir John. But if you come into this measure, surely she will be so kind as to consent——

Sterl. I don't know that—Betsey is her darling, and I can't tell how far she may resent any slight that seems to be offered to her favourite niece.—However, I'll do the best I can for you.— You shall go and break the matter to her first, and by that time that I may suppose that your rhetoric has prevailed on her to listen to reason, I will step in to reinforce your arguments.

Sir John. I'll fly to her immediately: you promise me your assistance?

Sterl. I do.

Sir John. Ten thousand thanks for it! and now success attend me!   (*Going.*

Sterl. Harkee, Sir John!   (SIR JOHN *returns.*

Sterl. Not a word of the thirty thousand to my sister, Sir John.

Sir John. Oh, I am dumb, I am dumb, sir.   (*Going.*

Sterl. You remember it is thirty thousand.

Sir John. To be sure I do.

Sterl. But, Sir John!—one thing more. (SIR JOHN *returns.*) My lord must know nothing of this stroke of friendship between us.

Sir John. Not for the world.—Let me alone! let me alone!
                                       (*Offering to go.*

Sterl. (*holding him.*) And when everything is agreed, we must give each other a bond to be held fast to the bargain.

Sir John. To be sure. A bond by all means! a bond, or whatever you please.   (*Exit hastily.*

STERLING, *alone*

I should have thought of more conditions—he's in a humour to give me everything.—Why, what mere children are your fellows of quality; that cry for a plaything one minute, and throw it by the next! as changeable as the weather, and as uncertain as the stocks.—Special fellows to drive a bargain! and yet they are to take care of the interest of the nation truly!—Here does this whirligig man of fashion offer to give up thirty thousand pounds in hard money, with as much indifference as if it was a china orange.—By this mortgage I shall have a hold on his *terra firma,* and if he wants more money, as he certainly will.

—let him have children by my daughter or no, I shall have his whole estate in a net for the benefit of my family.—Well, thus it is that the children of citizens, who have acquired fortunes, prove persons of fashion; and thus it is, that persons of fashion, who have ruined their fortunes, reduce the next generation to cits.   (*Exit.*

Scene changes to another apartment

Enter MRS. HEIDELBERG *and* MISS STERLING

Miss Sterl. This is your gentle-looking, soft-speaking, sweet-smiling, affable Miss Fanny for you!

Mrs. Heidel. My Miss Fanny! I disclaim her. With all her arts she could never insinuat herself into my good graces—and yet she has a way with her that deceives man, woman, and child, except you and me, niece.

Miss Sterl. O ay; she wants nothing but a crook in her hand, and a lamb under her arm, to be a perfect picture of innocence and simplicity.

Mrs. Heidel. Just as I was drawn at Amsterdam, when I went over to visit my husband's relations.

Miss Sterl. And then she's so mighty good to servants—*pray, John, do this—pray, Tom, do that—thank you, Jenny*—and then so humble to her relations—*to be sure, papa!—as my aunt pleases—my sister knows best.*—But with all her demureness and humility she has no objection to be Lady Melvil, it seems, nor to any wickedness that can make her so.

Mrs. Heidel. She Lady Melvil? Compose yourself, niece! I'll ladyship her indeed!—a little creepin, cantin——She shan't be the better for a farden of my money. But tell me, child, how does this intriguing with Sir John correspond with her partiality to Lovewell? I don't see a concatunation here.

Miss Sterl. There I was deceived, madam. I took all their whisperings and stealing into corners to be the mere attraction of vulgar minds; but, behold! their private meetings were not to contrive their own insipid happiness, but to conspire against mine.—But I know whence proceeds Mr. Lovewell's resentment to me. I could not stoop to be familiar with my father's clerk, and so I have lost his interest.

Mrs. Heidel. My spurrit to a T.—My dear child—(*Kissing her.*) Mr. Heidelberg lost his election for member of parliament because I would not demean myself to be slobbered about by drunken shoemakers, beastly cheesemongers, and greasy butchers and tallow-chandlers. However, niece, I can't help diffuring a little in opinion from you in this matter. My experunce and sagucity makes me still suspect that there is something more between her and that Lovewell, notwithstanding this affair of Sir John—I had my eye upon them the whole time of break-fast.—Sir John, I observed, looked a little confounded, indeed, though I knew nothing of what had passed in the garden. You seemed to sit upon thorns too: but Fanny and Mr. Lovewell made quite another-guess sort of a figur; and were as perfet a pictur of two distressed lovers, as if it had been drawn by Raphael Angelo.—As to Sir John and Fanny, I want a matter of fact.

Miss Sterl. Matter of fact, madam! Did not I come unexpectedly upon them? Was not Sir John kneeling at her feet and kissing her hand? Did not he look all love, and she all confusion? Is not that matter of fact? And did not Sir John, the moment that papa was called out of the room to the lawyermen, get up from breakfast and follow him immediately? And I warrant you that by this time he has made proposals to him to marry my sister.—Oh, that some other person, an earl, or a duke, would make his addresses to me, that I might be revenged on this monster!

Mrs. Heidel. Be cool, child! you *shall* be Lady Melvil, in spite of all their caballins, if it costs me ten thousand pounds to turn the scale. Sir John may apply to my brother, indeed; but I'll make them all know who governs in this fammaly.

Miss Sterl. As I live, madam, yonder comes Sir John. A base man! I can't endure the sight of him. I'll leave the room this instant.   (*Disordered.*

Mrs. Heidel. Poor thing! Well, retire to your own chamber, child; I'll give it him, I warrant you; and by and by I'll come and let you know all that has passed between us.

Miss Sterl. Pray do, madam!—(*Looking back.*) A vile wretch!
                                                  (*Exit in a rage.*

Enter Sir John Melvil

Sir John. Your most obedient humble servant, madam!
                                      (*Bowing very respectfully.*
Mrs. Heidel. Your servant, Sir John!
                              (*Dropping a half-curtsy, and pouting.*
Sir John. Miss Sterling's manner of quitting the room on my approach, and the visible coolness of your behaviour to me, madam, convince me that she has acquainted you with what passed this morning.

Mrs. Heidel. I am very sorry, Sir John, to be made acquainted with anything that should induce me to change the opinion which I could always wish to entertain of a person of quallaty.
                                                          (*Pouting.*
Sir John. It has always been my ambition to merit the best opinion from Mrs. Heidelberg; and when she comes to weigh all circumstances, I flatter myself——

Mrs. Heidel. You do flatter yourself, if you imagine that I can approve of your behaviour to my niece, Sir John.—And give me leave to tell you, Sir John, that you have been drawn into an action much beneath you, Sir John; and that I look upon

every injury offered to Miss Betty Sterling as an affront to
myself, Sir John.   (*Warmly.*

Sir John. I would not offend you for the world, madam! but
when I am influenced by a partiality for another, however ill-
founded, I hope your discernment and good sense will think it
rather a point of honour to renounce engagements which I could
not fulfil so strictly as I ought; and that you will excuse the
change in my inclinations, since the new object, as well as the
first, has the honour of being your niece, madam.

Mrs. Heidel. I disclaim her as a niece, Sir John; Miss Sterling
disclaims her as a sister, and the whole fammaly must disclaim
her for her monstrus baseness and treachery.

Sir John. Indeed she has been guilty of none, madam. Her
hand and heart are, I am sure, entirely at the disposal of yourself
and Mr. Sterling.

Enter STERLING *behind*

And if you should not oppose my inclinations, I am sure of Mr.
Sterling's consent, madam.

Mrs. Heidel. Indeed!

Sterl. (*behind*). So! they seem to be coming to terms already.
I may venture to make my appearance.

Mrs. Heidel. To marry Fanny?

(STERLING *advances by degrees.*

Sir John. Yes, madam.

Mrs. Heidel. My brother has given his consent, you say?

Sir John. In the most ample manner, with no other restric-
tion than the failure of your concurrence, madam. (*Sees* STER-
LING.) Oh, here's Mr. Sterling, who will confirm what I have
told you.

Mrs. Heidel. What! have you consented to give up your own
daughter in this manner, brother?

Sterl. Give her up! no, not give her up, sister; only in case
that you——Zounds, I am afraid you have said too much, Sir
John.   (*Apart to* SIR JOHN.

Mrs. Heidel. Yes, yes, I see now that it is true enough what
my niece told me. You are all plottin' and caballin against her.
—Pray, does Lord Ogleby know of this affair?

Sir John. I have not yet made him acquainted with it,
madam.

Mrs. Heidel. No, I warrant you. I thought so.—And so his
lordship and myself truly, are not to be consulted till the last.

Sterl. What! did not you consult my lord? Oh, fie for shame,
Sir John!

Sir John. Nay, but, Mr. Sterling——

Mrs. Heidel. We, who are the persons of most consequence
and experunce in the two fammalies, are to know nothing of the
matter till the whole is as good as concluded upon. But his
lordship, I am sure, will have more generosaty than to countenance such a perceeding.—And I could not have expected such

behaviour from a person of your quallaty, Sir John.—And as for you, brother——

Sterl. Nay, nay, but hear me, sister!

Mrs. Heidel. I am perfectly ashamed of you.—Have you no spurrit? no more concern for the honour of our fammaly than to consent——

Sterl. Consent?—I consent!—As I hope for mercy, I never gave my consent. Did I consent, Sir John?

Sir John. Not absolutely, without Mrs. Heidelberg's concurrence. But in case of her approbation——

Sterl. Ay, I grant you, if my sister approved.—But that's quite another thing, you know.   (*To* MRS. HEIDELBERG.

Mrs. Heidel. Your sister approve, indeed!—I thought you knew her better, brother Sterling!—What! approve of having your eldest daughter returned upon your hands, and exchanged for the younger?—I am surprised how you could listen to such a scandalus proposal.

Sterl. I tell you, I never did listen to it.—Did not I say that I would be governed entirely by my sister, Sir John? — And unless she agreed to your marrying Fanny——

Mrs. Heidel. I agree to his marrying Fanny? Abominable! The man is absolutely out of his senses.—Can't that wise head of yours foresee the consequence of all this, brother Sterling? Will Sir John take Fanny without a fortune? No.—After you have settled the largest part of your property on your youngest daughter, can there be an equal portion left for the eldest? No.— Does not this overturn the whole systum of the fammaly? Yes, yes, yes. You know I was always for my niece Betsey's marrying a person of the very first quallaty. That was my maxum. And, therefore, much the largest settlement was of course to be made upon her.—As for Fanny, if she could, with a fortune of twenty or thirty thousand pounds, get a knight, or a member of parliament, or a rich common-council-man for a husband, I thought it might do very well.

Sir John. But if a better match should offer itself, why should not it be accepted, madam?

Mrs. Heidel. What! at the expense of her elder sister! Oh, fie, Sir John!—How could you bear to hear of such an indignaty, brother Sterling?

Sterl. I! nay, I shan't hear of it, I promise you.—I can't hear of it indeed, Sir John.

Mrs. Heidel. But you *have* heard of it, brother Sterling. You know you have; and sent Sir John to propose it to me. But if you can give up your daughter, I shan't forsake my niece, I assure you. Ah! if my poor dear Mr. Heidelberg and our sweet babes had been alive, he would not have behaved so.

Sterl. Did I, Sir John? Nay, speak!—Bring me off, or we are ruined.   (*Apart to* SIR JOHN.

Sir John. Why, to be sure, to speak the truth——

Mrs. Heidel. To speak the truth, I'm ashamed of you both. But have a care what you are about, brother! have a care, I say. The lawyers are in the house, I hear; and if everything is not settled to my liking I'll have nothing more to say to you, if I live these hundred years.—I'll go over to Holland, and settle with Mr. Vanderspracken, my poor husband's first cousin; and my own fammaly shall never be the better for a farden of my money, I promise you. (*Exit.*

Manent SIR JOHN *and* STERLING

Sterl. I thought so. I knew she never would agree to it.

Sir John. 'Sdeath, how unfortunate! What can we do, Mr. Sterling?

Sterl. Nothing.

Sir John. What! must our agreement break off the moment it is made then?

Sterl. It can't be helped, Sir John. The family, as I told you before, have great expectations from my sister; and if this matter proceeds, you hear yourself that she threatens to leave us.—My brother Heidelberg was a warm man; a very warm man; and died worth a plum at least; a plum! ay, I warrant you, he died worth a plum and a half.

Sir John. Well; but if I——

Sterl. And then, my sister has three or four very good mortgages, a deal of money in the three per cents and old South Sea annuities, besides large concerns in the Dutch and French funds. —The greatest part of all this she means to leave to our family.

Sir John. I can only say, sir——

Sterl. Why, your offer of the difference of thirty thousand was very fair and handsome to be sure, Sir John.

Sir John. Nay, but I am even willing to——

Sterl. Ay, but if I was to accept it against her will, I might lose above a hundred thousand; so, you see, the balance is against you, Sir John.

Sir John. But is there no way, do you think, of prevailing on Mrs. Heidelberg to grant her consent?

Sterl. I am afraid not.—However, when her passion is a little abated—for she's very passionate—you may try what can be done: but you must not use my name any more, Sir John.

Sir John. Suppose I was to prevail on Lord Ogleby to apply to her, do you think that would have any influence over her?

Sterl. I think he would be more likely to persuade her to it than any other person in the family. She has a great respect for Lord Ogleby. She loves a lord.

Sir John. I'll apply to him this very day.—And if he should prevail on Mrs. Heidelberg, I may depend on your friendship, Mr. Sterling?

Sterl. Ay, ay, I shall be glad to oblige you, when it is in my power; but as the account stands now, you see it is not upon the figures. And so your servant, Sir John. (*Exit.*

SIR JOHN MELVIL, *alone*

What a situation am I in!—Breaking off with her whom I was bound by treaty to marry; rejected by the object of my affections; and embroiled with this turbulent woman, who governs the whole family.—And yet opposition, instead of smothering, increases my inclination. I must have her. I'll apply immediately to Lord Ogleby; and if he can but bring over the aunt to our party, her influence will overcome the scruples and delicacy of my dear Fanny, and I shall be the happiest of mankind. (*Exit.*

ACT IV

SCENE I.—*A Room*

Enter STERLING, MRS. HEIDELBERG, *and* MISS STERLING

Sterl. What! will you send Fanny to town, sister?

Mrs. Heidel. To-morrow morning. I've given orders about it already.

Sterl. Indeed?

Mrs. Heidel. Positively.

Sterl. But consider, sister, at such a time as this, what an odd appearance it will have.

Mrs. Heidel. Not half so odd as her behaviour, brother.—This time was intended for happiness, and I'll keep no incendaries here to destroy it. I insist on her going off to-morrow morning.

Sterl. I'm afraid this is all your doing, Betsey.

Miss Sterl. No, indeed, papa. My aunt knows that it is not.—For all Fanny's baseness to me, I am sure I would not do or say anything to hurt her with you or my aunt for the world.

Mrs. Heidel. Hold your tongue, Betsey!—I will have my way. —When she is packed off, everything will go on as it should do. —Since they are at their intrigues, I'll let them see that we can act with vigur on our part; and the sending her out of the way shall be the purlimunary step to all the rest of my perceedings.

Sterl. Well, but, sister——

Mrs. Heidel. It does not signify talking, brother Sterling, for I'm resolved to be rid of her. and I will.—Come along, child! (*To* MISS STERLING.)—The post-shay shall be at the door by six o'clock in the morning; and if Miss Fanny does not get into it, why *I* will, and so there's an end of the matter.

(*Bounces out with* MISS STERLING.

MRS. HEIDELBERG *returns*

Mrs. Heidel. One word more, brother Sterling!—I expect that you will take your eldest daughter in your hand, and make

a formal complaint to Lord Ogleby of Sir John Melvil's behaviour.
—Do this, brother; show a proper regard for the honour of your
fammaly yourself, and I shall throw in my mite to the raising
of it. If not—but now you know my mind. So act as you please,
and take the consequences. (*Exit.*

STERLING, *alone*

The devil's in the woman for tyranny—mothers, wives,
mistresses, or sisters, they always will govern us.—As to my
sister Heidelberg, she knows the strength of her purse, and
domineers upon the credit of it.—"I will do this"—and "you
shall do that"—and "you must do t'other, or else the fammaly
shan't have a farden of—" (*Mimicking.*) So absolute with her
money!—but to say the truth, nothing but money *can* make
us absolute, and so we must e'en make the best of her.

Scene changes to the Garden
Enter LORD OGLEBY *and* CANTON

Lord Ogle. What! Mademoiselle Fanny to be sent away!—
Why?—Wherefore?—What's the meaning of all this?

Canton. Je ne sais pas.—I know noting of it.

Lord Ogle. It can't be; it shan't be. I protest against the
measure. She's a fine girl, and I had much rather that the rest
of the family were annihilated than that she should leave us.—
Her vulgar father, that's the very abstract of 'Change Alley—
the aunt, that's always endeavouring to be a fine lady—and the
pert sister, forever showing that she is one, are horrid company
indeed, and without her would be intolerable. Ah, la petite
Fanchon! she's the thing. Isn't she, Cant?

Canton. Dere is very good sympatie entre vous and dat
young lady, mi lor'.

Lord Ogle. I'll not be left among these Goths and Vandals,
your Sterlings, your Heidelbergs, and Devilbergs.—If she goes,
I'll positively go too.

Canton. In de same post-shay, mi lor'? You have no object to
dat I believe, nor Mademoiselle neider too—ha, ha, ha.

Lord Ogle. Prithee hold thy foolish tongue, Cant. Does thy
Swiss stupidity imagine that I can see and talk with a fine girl
without desires?—My eyes are involuntarily attracted by
beautiful objects—I fly as naturally to a fine girl——

Canton. As de fine girl to you, my lor', ha, ha, ha; you alway
fly togedre like un pair de pigeons.——

Lord Ogle. Like un pair de pigeons. (*Mocks him.*)—Vous
etes un sot, Monsieur Canton—Thou art always dreaming of
my intrigues, and never seest me *badiner*, but you suspect mischief, you old fool, you.

Canton. I am fool, I confess, but not always fool in dat, my
lor', he, he, he.

Lord Ogle. He, he, he.—Thou art incorrigible, but thy ab-
surdities amuse one—Thou art like my rappee here (*Takes
out his box.*), a most ridiculous superfluity, but a pinch of thee
now and then is a most delicious treat.

Canton. You do me great honour, my lor'.

Lord Ogle. 'Tis fact, upon my soul.—Thou art properly my
cephalic snuff, and art no bad medicine against megrims, verti-
goes, and profound thinking—ha, ha, ha.

Canton. Your flatterie, my lor', vil make me too prode.

Lord Ogle. The girl has some little partiality for me, to be
sure. But prithee, Cant, is not that Miss Fanny yonder?

Canton (*looking with a glass*). En veritè, 'tis she, my lor'—
'tis one of de pigeons,—de pigeons d'amour.

Lord Ogle. (*smiling*). Don't be ridiculous, you old monkey.

Canton. I am monkeè, I am ole, but I have eye, I have ear,
and a little understand, now and den.——

Lord Ogle. Taisez-vous bête!

Canton. Elle vous attend, my lor'.—She vil make a love to you.

Lord Ogle. Will she? Have at her then! A fine girl can't
oblige me more.—Egad, I find myself a little enjouée. Come
along, Cant! she is but in the next walk—but there is such a
deal of this damned crinkum-crankum, as Sterling calls it, that
one sees people for half an hour before one can get to them.—
Allons, Monsieur Canton, allons donc! (*Exeunt, singing in French.*

Another part of the Garden

LOVEWELL *and* FANNY

Love. My dear Fanny, I cannot bear your distress; it over-
comes all my resolutions, and I am prepared for the discovery.

Fanny. But how can it be effected before my departure?

Love. I'll tell you.—Lord Ogleby seems to entertain a visible
partiality for you; and notwithstanding the peculiarities of his
behaviour, I am sure that he is humane at the bottom. He is
vain to an excess; but withal extremely good-natured, and would
do anything to recommend himself to a lady.—Do you open the
whole affair of our marriage to him immediately. It will come
with more irresistible persuasion from you than from myself;
and I doubt not but you'll gain his friendship and protection
at once.—His influence and authority will put an end to Sir
John's solicitations, remove your aunt's and sister's unkindness and suspicions, and, I hope, reconcile your father and the
whole family to our marriage.

Fanny. Heaven grant it! Where is my lord?

Love. I have heard him and Canton since dinner singing
French songs under the great walnut-tree by the parlour door.
If you meet with him in the garden, you may disclose the whole
immediately.

Fanny. Dreadful as the task is, I'll do it.—Anything is better than this continual anxiety.

Love. By that time the discovery is made, I will appear to second you.—Ha! here comes my lord.—Now, my dear Fanny, summon up all your spirits, plead our cause powerfully, and be sure of success.— (*Going.*

Fanny. Ah, don't leave me!

Love. Nay, you must let me.

Fanny. Well, since it must be so, I'll obey you, if I have the power. Oh. Lovewell!

Love. Consider, our situation is very critical. To-morrow morning is fixed for your departure, and if we lose this opportunity, we may wish in vain for another.—He approaches—I must retire.—Speak, my dear Fanny, speak, and make us happy!

(*Exit.*

FANNY, *alone*

Good heaven, what a situation am I in! what shall I do? what shall I say to him? I am all confusion.

Enter LORD OGLEBY *and* CANTON

Lord Ogle. To see so much beauty so solitary, madam, is a satire upon mankind, and 'tis fortunate that one man has broke in upon your reverie for the credit of our sex.—I say *one*, madam, for poor Canton here, from age and infirmities, stands for nothing.

Canton. Noting at all, inteed.

Fanny. Your lordship does me great honour.—I had a favour to request, my lord!

Lord Ogle. A favour, madam!—To be honoured with your command is an inexpressible favour done to me, madam.

Fanny. If your lordship could indulge me with the honour of a moment's——What is the matter with me? (*Aside.*

Lord Ogle. The girl's confused—he!—here's something in the wind, faith—I'll have a tête-à-tête with her—allez vous en!

(*To* CANTON.

Canton. I go—ah, pauvre Mademoiselle! my lor', have pitié upon de poor pigeone!

Lord Ogle. I'll knock you down, Cant, if you're impertinent. (*Smiling.*

Canton. Den 1 mus avay. (*Shuffles along.*)—You are mosh please, for all dat. (*Aside, and exit.*

Fanny. I shall sink with apprehension. (*Aside.*

Lord Ogle. What a sweet girl!—she's a civilised being, and atones for the barbarism of the rest of the family.

Fanny. My lord! I—— (*She curtsies, and blushes.*

Lord Ogle. (*addressing her*). I look upon it, madam, to be one of the luckiest circumstances of my life that I have this moment the honour of receiving your commands, and the satisfaction of confirming with my tongue what my eyes perhaps have but too weakly expressed—that I am literally—the humblest of your servants.

Fanny. I think myself greatly honoured by your lordship's partiality to me; but it distresses me that I am obliged in my present situation to apply to it for protection.

Lord Ogle. I am happy in your distress, madam, because it gives me an opportunity to show my zeal. Beauty to me is a religion, in which I was born and bred a bigot, and would die a martyr.—I'm in tolerable spirits, faith!   (*Aside.*

Fanny. There is not perhaps at this moment a more distressed creature than myself. Affection, duty, hope, despair, and a thousand different sentiments, are struggling in my bosom; and even the presence of your lordship, to whom I have flown for protection, adds to my perplexity.

Lord Ogle. Does it, madam?—Venus forbid!—My old fault; the devil's in me, I think, for perplexing young women. (*Aside and smiling.*) Take courage, madam! dear Miss Fanny, explain. —You have a powerful advocate in my breast, I assure you—my heart, madam—I am attached to you by all the laws of sympathy and delicacy.—By my honour, I am.

Fanny. Then I will venture to unburthen my mind.—Sir John Melvil, my lord, by the most misplaced and mistimed declaration of affection for me, has made me the unhappiest of women.

Lord Ogle. How, madam! Has Sir John made his addresses to you?

Fanny. He has, my lord, in the strongest terms. But I hope it is needless to say, that my duty to my father, love to my sister, and regard to the whole family, as well as the great respect I entertain for your lordship, (*curtsying*) made me shudder at his addresses.

Lord Ogle. Charming girl!—Proceed, my dear Miss Fanny, proceed!

Fanny. In a moment—give me leave, my lord!—But if what I have to disclose should be received with anger or displeasure——

Lord Ogle. Impossible, by all the tender powers!—Speak, I beseech you, or I shall divine the cause before you utter it.

Fanny. Then, my lord, Sir John's addresses are not only shocking to me in themselves, but are more particularly disagreeable to me at this time, as—as——   (*Hesitating.*

Lord Ogle. As what, madam?

Fanny. As—pardon my confusion—I am entirely devoted to another.

Lord Ogle. If this is not plain, the devil's in it—(*Aside.*) But tell me, my dear Miss Fanny, for I must know; tell me the how, the when, and the where. Tell me——

Enter CANTON *hastily*

Canton. My lor', my lor', my lor'!——

Lord Ogle. Damn your Swiss impertinence! how durst you

interrupt me in the most critical melting moment that ever
love and beauty honoured me with?

Canton. I demande pardonne, my lor'! Sir John Melvil, my
lor', sent me to beg you to do him the honour to speak a little
to your lorship.

Lord Ogle. I'm not at leisure—I'm busy.—Get away, you
stupid old dog, you Swiss rascal, or I'll——

Canton. Fort bien, my lor'.   (*Goes out [on] tiptoe.*

Lord Ogle. By the laws of gallantry, madam, this interruption
should be death; but as no punishment ought to disturb the
triumph of the softer passions, the criminal is pardoned and dismissed.—Let us return, madam, to the highest luxury of exalted
minds—a declaration of love from the lips of beauty.

Fanny. The entrance of a third person has a little relieved
me, but I cannot go through with it—and yet I must open my
heart with a discovery, or it will break with its burthen.

Lord Ogle. What passion in her eyes! I am alarmed to agitation. (*Aside.*) I presume, madam (and as you have flattered
me by making me a party concerned, I hope you'll excuse the
presumption), that——

Fanny. Do you excuse my making you a party concerned,
my lord, and let me interest your heart in my behalf, as my
future happiness or misery in a great measure depend——

Lord Ogle. Upon me, madam?

Fanny. Upon you, my lord!   (*Sighs.*

Lord Ogle. There's no standing this: I have caught the infection—her tenderness dissolves me.   (*Sighs.*

Fanny. And should you too severely judge of a rash action
which passion prompted, and modesty has long concealed——

Lord Ogle. (*taking her hand*). Thou amiable creature—command my heart, for it is vanquished.—Speak but thy virtuous
wishes, and enjoy them.

Fanny. I cannot, my lord—indeed, I cannot.—Mr. Lovewell
must tell you my distresses—and when you know them—pity
and protect me!——   (*Exit, in tears.*

LORD OGLEBY, *alone*

How the devil could I bring her to this? It is too much—too
much—I can't bear it—I must give way to this amiable weakness.
(*Wipes his eyes.*) My heart overflows with sympathy, and I feel
every tenderness I have inspired. (*Stifles the tear.*) How blind
have I been to the desolation I have made!—How could I
possibly imagine that a little partial attention and tender civilities
to this young creature should have gathered to this burst of
passion! Can I be a man and withstand it? No—I'll sacrifice
the whole sex to her.—But here comes the father, quite apropos.
I'll open the matter immediately, settle the business with him
and take the sweet girl down to Ogleby House to-morrow

morning.—But what the devil! Miss Sterling too! What mischief's in the wind now?

Enter STERLING *and* MISS STERLING

Sterl. My lord, your servant! I am attending my daughter here upon rather a disagreeable affair. Speak to his lordship, Betsey!

Lord Ogle. Your eyes, Miss Sterling—for I always read the eyes of a young lady—betray some little emotion. What are your commands, madam?

Miss Sterl. I have but too much cause for my emotion, my lord!

Lord Ogle. I cannot commend my kinsman's behaviour, madam. He has behaved like a false knight, I must confess. I have heard of his apostasy. Miss Fanny has informed me of it.

Miss Sterl. Miss Fanny's baseness has been the cause of Sir John's inconstancy.

Lord Ogle. Nay, now, my dear Miss Sterling, your passion transports you too far. Sir John may have entertained a passion for Miss Fanny, but believe me, my dear Miss Sterling, believe me, Miss Fanny has no passion for Sir John. She has a passion, indeed, a most tender passion. She has opened her whole soul to me, and I know where her affections are placed. (*Conceitedly.*)

Miss Sterl. Not upon Mr. Lovewell, my lord; for I have great reason to think that her seeming attachment to him is, by his consent, made use of as a blind to cover her designs upon Sir John.

Lord Ogle. Lovewell! No, poor lad! She does not think of him.   (*Smiling.*

Miss Sterl. Have a care, my lord, that both the families are not made the dupes of Sir John's artifice and my sister's dissimulation! You don't know her—indeed, my lord, you don't know her—a base, insinuating, perfidious!—It is too much.— She has been beforehand with me, I perceive. Such unnatural behaviour to me!—But since I see I can have no redress, I am resolved that some way or other I will have revenge.   (*Exit.*

Sterl. This is foolish work, my lord!

Lord Ogle. I have too much sensibility to bear the tears of beauty.

Sterl. It is touching indeed, my lord—and very moving for a father.

Lord Ogle. To be sure, sir!—You must be distressed beyond measure!—Wherefore, to divert your too exquisite feelings, suppose we change the subject, and proceed to business.

Sterl. With all my heart, my lord!

Lord Ogle. You see, Mr. Sterling, we can make no union in our families by the proposed marriage.

Sterl. And very sorry I am to see it, my lord.

Lord Ogle. Have you set your heart upon being allied to our house, Mr. Sterling?

Sterl. 'Tis my only wish, at present, my omnium, as I may call it.

Lord Ogle. Your wishes shall be fulfilled.

Sterl. Shall they, my lord!—but how—how?

Lord Ogle. I'll marry in your family.

Sterl. What! my sister Heidelberg?

Lord Ogle. You throw me into a cold sweat, Mr. Sterling. No, not your sister—but your daughter.

Sterl. My daughter!

Lord Ogle. Fanny!—Now the murder's out!

Sterl. What *you*, my lord?——

Lord Ogle. Yes—I, I, Mr. Sterling!

Sterl. No, no, my lord—that's too much.   (*Smiling.*

Lord Ogle. Too much?—I don't comprehend you.

Sterl. What, you, my lord, marry my Fanny!—Bless me, what will the folks say?

Lord Ogle. Why, what will they say?

Sterl. That you're a bold man, my lord—that's all.

Lord Ogle. Mr. Sterling, this may be city wit for aught I know. Do you court my alliance?

Sterl. To be sure, my lord.

Lord Ogle. Then I'll explain.—My nephew won't marry your eldest daughter—nor I neither.—Your youngest daughter won't marry him—I will marry your youngest daughter——

Sterl. What! with a younger daughter's fortune, my lord?

Lord Ogle. With any fortune, or no fortune at all, sir. Love is the idol of my heart, and the demon Interest sinks before him. So, sir, as I said before, I will marry your youngest daughter; your youngest daughter will marry me.——

Sterl. Who told you so, my lord?

Lord Ogle. Her own sweet self, sir.

Sterl. Indeed?

Lord Ogle. Yes, sir: our affection is mutual; your advantage double and treble—your daughter will be a countess directly—I shall be the happiest of beings—and you'll be father to an earl instead of a baronet.

Sterl. But what will my sister say ?—and my daughter?

Lord Ogle. I'll manage that matter—nay, if they won't consent, I'll run away with your daughter in spite of you.

Sterl. Well said, my lord!—your spirit's good—I wish you had my constitution!—but if you'll venture, I have no objection, if my sister has none.

Lord Ogle. I'll answer for your sister, sir. Apropos! the lawyers are in the house—I'll have articles drawn, and the whole affair concluded to-morrow morning.

Sterl. Very well: and I'll dispatch Lovewell to London immediately for some fresh papers I shall want, and I shall leave you to manage matters with my sister. You must excuse me, my lord, but I can't help laughing at the match—He! he! he! what will the folks say?   (*Exit.*

Lord Ogle. What a fellow am I going to make a father of?— He has no more feeling than the post in his warehouse.—But Fanny's virtues tune me to rapture again, and I won't think of the rest of the family.

Enter LOVEWELL *hastily*

Love. I beg your lordship's pardon, my lord; are you alone, my lord?

Lord Ogle. No, my lord, I am not alone! I am in company, the best company.

Love. My lord!

Lord Ogle. I never was in such exquisite enchanting company since my heart first conceived, or my senses tasted pleasure.

Love. Where are they, my lord?   (*Looking about.*

Lord Ogle. In my mind, sir.

Love. What company have you there, my lord?   (*Smiling.*

Lord Ogle. My own ideas, sir, which so crowd upon my imagination, and kindle it to such a delirium of ecstasy, that wit, wine, music, poetry, all combined, and each perfection, are but mere mortal shadows of my felicity.

Love. I see that your lordship is happy, and I rejoice at it.

Lord Ogle. You *shall* rejoice at it, sir; my felicity shall not selfishly be confined, but shall spread its influence to the whole circle of my friends. I need not say, Lovewell, that you shall have your share of it.

Love. Shall I, my lord?—Then I understand you—you have heard—Miss Fanny has informed you——

Lord Ogle. She has—I have heard, and she shall be happy— 'tis determined.

Love. Then I have reached the summit of my wishes.—And will your lordship pardon the folly?

Lord Ogle. O yes. Poor creature, how could she help it?— 'Twas unavoidable—Fate and necessity.

Love. It was indeed, my lord.—Your kindness distracts me.

Lord Ogle. And so it did the poor girl, faith.

Love. She trembled to disclose the secret, and declare her affections?

Lord Ogle. The world, I believe, will not think her affections ill-placed.

Love. (*bowing*). —You are too good, my lord.—And do you really excuse the rashness of the action?

Lord Ogle. From my very soul, Lovewell.

Love. Your generosity overpowers me. (*Bowing.*) I was afraid of her meeting with a cold reception.

Lord Ogle. More fool you then.

Who pleads her cause with never-failing beauty,
Here finds a full redress. (*Strikes his breast.*
She's a fine girl, Lovewell.

Love. Her beauty, my lord, is her least merit. She has an understanding——

Lord Ogle. Her choice convinces me of that.

Love. (*bowing*). That's your lordship's goodness. Her choice was a disinterested one.

Lord Ogle. No—no—not altogether—it began with interest, and ended in passion.

Love. Indeed, my lord, if you were acquainted with her goodness of heart, and generosity of mind, as well as you are with the inferior beauties of her face and person——

Lord Ogle. I am so perfectly convinced of their existence, and so totally of your mind touching every amiable, particular of that sweet girl, that were it not for the cold unfeeling impediments of the law, I would marry her to-morrow morning.

Love. My lord!

Lord Ogle. I would, by all that's honourable in man, and amiable in woman.

Love. Marry her!—Who do you mean, my lord?

Lord Ogle. Miss Fanny Sterling, that is—the Countess of Ogleby that shall be.

Love. I am astonished.

Lord Ogle. Why, could you expect less from me?

Love. I did not expect this, my lord.

Lord Ogle. Trade and accounts have destroyed your feeling.

Love. No, indeed, my lord. (*Sighs.*

Lord Ogle. The moment that love and pity entered my breast, I was resolved to plunge into matrimony, and shorten the girl's tortures—I never do anything by halves; do I, Lovewell?

Love. No, indeed, my lord. (*Sighs.*) What an accident!

Lord Ogle. What's the matter, Lovewell? thou seemest to have lost thy faculties. Why don't you wish me joy, man?

Love. Oh, I do, my lord. (*Sighs.*

Lord Ogle. She said that you would explain what she had not . power to utter—but I wanted no interpreter for the language of love.

Love. But has your lordship considered the consequences of your resolution?

Lord Ogle. No, sir; I am above consideration when my desires are kindled.

Love. But consider the consequences, my lord, to your nephew, Sir John.

Lord Ogle. Sir John has considered no consequences himself, Mr. Lovewell.

Love. Mr. Sterling, my lord, will certainly refuse his daughter to Sir John.

Lord Ogle. Sir John has already refused Mr. Sterling's daughter.

Love. But what will become of Miss Sterling, my lord?

Lord Ogle. What's that to you?—You may have her, if you will.—I depend upon Mr. Sterling's city-philosophy, to be reconciled to Lord Ogleby's being his son-in-law, instead of Sir John Melvil, Baronet. Don't you think that your master may be brought to that, without having recourse to his calculations? Eh, Lovewell!

Love. But, my lord, that is not the question.

Lord Ogle. Whatever is the question, I'll tell you my answer. —I am in love with a fine girl, whom I resolve to marry.

Enter SIR JOHN MELVIL

What news with you, Sir John?—You look all hurry and impatience—like a messenger after a battle.

Sir John. After a battle, indeed, my lord.—I have this day had a severe engagement, and wanting your lordship as an auxiliary, I have at last mustered up resolution to declare what my duty to you and to myself have demanded from me some time.

Lord Ogle. To the business then, and be as concise as possible; for I am upon the wing—eh, Lovewell?

(He smiles, and LOVEWELL *bows.*

Sir John. I find 'tis in vain, my lord, to struggle against the force of inclination.

Lord Ogle. Very true, nephew—I am your witness, and will second the motion—shan't I, Lovewell?

(Smiles, and LOVEWELL *bows.*

Sir John. Your lordship's generosity encourages me to tell you —that I cannot marry Miss Sterling.

Lord Ogle. I am not at all surprised at it—she's a bitter potion, that's the truth of it; but as you were to swallow it, and not I, it was your business, and not mine.—Anything more?

Sir John. But this, my lord—that I may be permitted to make my addresses to the other sister.

Lord Ogle. O yes—by all means—have you any hopes there, nephew?—Do you think he'll succeed, Lovewell?

(Smiles, and winks at LOVEWELL.

Love. I think not, my lord.   *(Gravely.*

Lord Ogle. I think so too, but let the fool try.

Sir John. Will your lordship favour me with your good offices to remove the chief obstacle to the match, the repugnance of Mrs. Heidelberg?

Lord Ogle. Mrs. Heidelberg!—Had you not better begin with the young lady first? it will save you a great deal of trouble; won't it, Lovewell? *(Smiles.)* But do what you please, it will be the same thing to me—won't it, Lovewell? *(Conceitedly.)* —Why don't you laugh at him?

Love. I do, my lord.   *(Forces a smile.*

Sir John. And your lordship will endeavour to prevail on Mrs. Heidelberg to consent to my marriage with Miss Fanny?

Lord Ogle. I'll go and speak to Mrs. Heidelberg about the adorable Fanny as soon as possible.

Sir John. Your generosity transports me.

Lord Ogle. Poor fellow, what a dupe! he little thinks who's in possession of the town. (*Aside.*

Sir John. And your lordship is not offended at this seeming inconstancy?

Lord Ogle. Not in the least. Miss Fanny's charms will even excuse infidelity—I look upon women as the *feræ naturæ*,—lawful game—and every man who is qualified, has a natural right to pursue them; Lovewell as well as you, and I as well as either of you.—Every man shall do his best, without offence to any—what say you, kinsmen?

Sir John. You have made me happy, my lord.

Love. And me, I assure you, my lord.

Lord Ogle. And I am superlatively so.—*Allons donc*—to horse and away, boys!—you to your affairs, and I to mine—*suivons l'amour!* (*Sings.*
  (*Exeunt severally.*

ACT V

SCENE I.—*Fanny's Apartment*

Enter LOVEWELL *and* FANNY, *followed by* BETTY

Fanny. Why did you come so soon, Mr. Lovewell? the family is not yet in bed, and Betty certainly heard somebody listening near the chamber-door.

Betty. My mistress is right, sir! evil spirits are abroad; and I am sure you are both too good not to expect mischief from them.

Love. But who can be so curious, or so wicked?

Betty. I think we have wickedness, and curiosity enough in this family, sir, to expect the worst.

Fanny. I do expect the worst.—Prithee, Betty, return to the outward door, and listen if you hear anybody in the gallery; and let us know directly.

Betty. I warrant you, madam—the Lord bless you both! (*Exit.*

Fanny. What did my father want with you this evening?

Love. He gave me the key of his closet, with orders to bring from London some papers relating to Lord Ogleby.

Fanny. And why did you not obey him?

Love. Because I am certain that his lordship has opened his heart to him about you, and those papers are wanted merely on that account—but as we shall discover all to-morrow, there will be no occasion for them, and it would be idle in me to go-

Fanny. Hark!—hark! bless me, how I tremble!—I feel the terrors of guilt—indeed, Mr. Lovewell, this is too much for me.

Love. And for me too, my sweet Fanny. Your apprehensions make a coward of me.—But what can alarm you? your aunt and sister are in their chambers, and you have nothing to fear from the rest of the family.

Fanny. I fear everybody, and everything, and every moment. —My mind is in continual agitation and dread;—indeed, Mr. Lovewell, this situation may have very unhappy consequences. (*Weeps.*

Love. But it shan't—I would rather tell our story this moment to all the house, and run the risk of maintaining you by the hardest labour, than suffer you to remain in this dangerous perplexity.—What! shall I sacrifice all my best hopes and affections, in your dear health and safety, for the mean, and in such a case, the meanest consideration—of our fortune! Were we to be abandoned by all our relations, we have that in our hearts and minds, will weigh against the most affluent circumstances.— I should not have proposed the secrecy of our marriage but for your sake; and with hopes that the most generous sacrifice you have made to love and me, might be less injurious to you by waiting a lucky moment of reconciliation.

Fanny. Hush! hush! for heaven sake, my dear Lovewell, don't be so warm!—your generosity gets the better of your prudence; you will be heard, and we shall be discovered.—I am satisfied, indeed I am.—Excuse this weakness, this delicacy— this what you will.—My mind's at peace—indeed it is—think no more of it, if you love me!

Love. That one word has charmed me, as it always does, to the most implicit obedience; it would be the worst of ingratitude in me to distress you a moment. (*Kisses her.*

Re-enter BETTY

Betty (*in a low voice*). I'm sorry to disturb you.

Fanny. Ha! what's the matter?

Love. Have you heard anybody?

Betty. Yes, yes, I have, and they have heard *you* too, or I am mistaken—if they had *seen* you too, we should have been in a fine quandary.

Fanny. Prithee don't prate now, Betty!

Love. What did you hear?

Betty. I was preparing myself, as usual, to take me a little nap.

Love. A nap!

Betty. Yes, sir, a nap; for I watch much better so than wide awake; and when I had wrapped this handkerchief round my head, for fear of the earache, from the keyhole I thought I heard a kind of a sort of a buzzing, which I first took for a gnat, and shook my head two or three times, and went so with my hand——

Fanny. Well—well—and so——

Betty. And so, madam, when I heard Mr. Lovewell a little loud, I heard the buzzing louder too—and pulling off my handkerchief softly—I could hear this sort of noise.

(Makes an indistinct noise like speaking.

Fanny. Well, and what did they say?

Betty. Oh! I could not understand a word of what was said.

Love. The outward door is locked?

Betty. Yes; and I bolted it too, for fear of the worst.

Fanny. Why did you? they must have heard you, if they were near.

Betty. And I did it on purpose, madam, and coughed a little too, that they might not hear Mr. Lovewell's voice—when I was silent, they were silent, and so I came to tell you.

Fanny. What shall we do?

Love. Fear nothing; we know the worst; it will only bring on our catastrophe a little too soon. But Betty might fancy this noise—she's in the conspiracy, and can make a man of a mouse at any time.

Betty. I can distinguish a man from a mouse, as well as my betters—I am sorry you think so ill of me, sir.

Fanny. He compliments you; don't be a fool!—Now you have set her tongue a-running, she'll mutter for an hour. (*To* Love-well.) I'll go and hearken myself. (*Exit.*

Betty. I'll turn my back upon no girl, for sincerity and service.

(Half aside, and muttering.

Love. Thou art the first in the world for both; and I will reward you soon, Betty, for one and the other.

Betty. I'm not marcenary neither—I can live on a little, with a good carreter.

Re-enter FANNY

Fanny. All seems quiet—suppose, my dear, you go to your own room.—I shall be much easier then—and to-morrow we will be prepared for the discovery.

Betty. You may discover, if you please; but, for my part, I shall still be secret. (*Half aside and muttering.*

Love. Should I leave you now,—if they still are upon the watch, we shall lose the advantage of our delay.—Besides, we should consult upon to-morrow's business.—Let Betty go to her own room, and lock the outward door after her; we can fasten this; and when she thinks all safe, she may return and let me out as usual.

Betty. Shall I, madam?

Fanny. Do! let me have my way to-night, and you shall command me ever after.—I would not have you surprised here for the world.—Pray leave me! I shall be quite myself again, if you will oblige me.

Love. I live only to oblige you, my sweet Fanny! I'll be gone this moment. (*Going.*

Fanny. Let us listen first at the door, that you may not be intercepted.—Betty shall go first, and if they lay hold of her——

Betty. They'll have the wrong sow by the ear, I can tell them that.   (*Going hastily.*

Fanny. Softly—softly—Betty! don't venture out, if you hear a noise.—Softly, I beg of you!—See, Mr. Lovewell, the effects of indiscretion!

Love. But love, Fanny, makes amends for all.

(*Exeunt all softly.*

Scene changes to a Gallery, which leads to several bedchambers

Enter Miss Sterling, *leading* Mrs. Heidelberg *in
a night-cap*

Miss Sterl. This way, dear madam, and then I'll tell you all.

Mrs. Heidel. Nay, but. niece—consider a little—don't drag me out in this figur—let me put on my fly-cap!—if any of my lord's fammaly, or the counsellors at law, should be stirring, I should be perdigus disconcarted.

Miss Sterl. But, my dear madam, a moment is an age, in my situation. I am sure my sister has been plotting my disgrace and ruin in that chamber—O she's all craft and wickedness!

Mrs. Heidel. Well, but softly, Betsey!—you are all in emotion —your mind is too much flustrated—you can neither eat nor drink, nor take your natural rest—compose yourself, child; for if we are not as warysome as they are wicked, we shall disgrace ourselves and the whole fammaly.

Miss Sterl. We are disgraced already, madam—Sir John Melvil has forsaken me; my lord cares for nobody but himself; or, if for anybody, it is my sister; my father, for the sake of a better bargain, would marry me to a 'Change-broker; so that if you, madam, don't continue my friend—if you forsake me— if I am to lose my best hopes and consolation—in your tender-ness—and affections—I had better—at once—give up the matter—and let my sister enjoy—the fruits of her treachery— trample with scorn upon the rights of her elder sister, the will of the best of aunts, and the weakness of a too interested father.

(*She pretends to be bursting into tears all this speech.*

Mrs. Heidel. Don't, Betsey—keep up your spurrit—I hate whimpering—I am your friend—depend upon me in every partickler—but be composed, and tell me what new mischief you have discovered.

Miss Sterl. I had no desire to sleep, and would not undress myself, knowing that my Machiavel sister would not rest till she had broke my heart—I was so uneasy that I could not stay in my room, but when I thought that all the house was quiet, I sent my maid to discover what was going forward; she imme-diately came back and told me that they were in high con-sultation; that she had heard only, for it was in the dark, my sister᾽s maid conduct Sir John Melvil to her mistress, and then lock the door.

Mrs. Heidel. And how did you conduct yourself in this dalimma?

Miss Sterl. I returned with her, and could hear a man's voice, though nothing that they said distinctly; and you may depend upon it, that Sir John is now in that room, that they have settled the matter, and will run away together before morning, if we don't prevent them.

Mrs. Heidel. Why the brazen slut! has she got her sister's husband (that is to be) locked up in her chamber! at night too? —I tremble at the thoughts!

Miss Sterl. Hush, madam! I hear something.

Mrs. Heidel. You frighten me—let me put on my fly cap— I would not be seen in this figur for the world.

Miss Sterl. 'Tis dark, madam, you can't be seen.

Mrs. Heidel. I protest there's a candle coming, and a man too.

Miss Sterl. Nothing but servants; let us retire a moment!

(*They retire.*

Enter BRUSH, *half drunk, laying hold of the Chambermaid, who has a candle in her hand*

Chamber. Be quiet, Mr. Brush; I shall drop down with terror!

Brush. But, my sweet and most amiable Chambermaid, if you have no love, you may hearken to a little reason; that cannot possibly do your virtue any harm.

Chamber. But you will do me harm, Mr. Brush, and a great deal of harm too—pray let me go—I am ruined if they hear you—I tremble like an asp.

Brush. But they shan't hear us—and if you have a mind to be ruined, it shall be the making of your fortune, you little slut, you!—therefore I say it again, if you have no love—hear a little reason!

Chamber. I wonder at your impurence, Mr. Brush, to use me in this manner; this is not the way to keep me company, I assure you.—You are a town rake I see, and now you are a little in liquor, you fear nothing.

Brush. Nothing, by heavens, but your frowns, most amiable Chambermaid; I am a little electrified, that's the truth on't; I am not used to drink port, and your master's is so heady, that a pint of it oversets a claret-drinker.

Chamber. Don't be rude! Bless me!—I shall be ruined—what will become of me?

Brush. I'll take care of you, by all that's honourable.

Chamber. You are a base man to use me so—I'll cry out, if you don't let me go—that is Miss Sterling's chamber, that Miss Fanny's and that Madam Heidelberg's.   (*Pointing.*

Brush. And that my Lord Ogleby's, and that my Lady What-d'ye-call-'em's: I don't mind such folks when I'm sober, much less when I am whimsical—rather above that too.

Chamber. More shame for you, Mr. Brush!—you terrify me—you have no modesty.

Brush. O but I have, my sweet spider-brusher!—for instance, I reverence Miss Fanny—she's a most delicious morsel and fit for a prince—with all my horrors of matrimony, I could marry her myself; but for her sister——

Miss Sterl. There, there, madam, all in a story!

Chamber. Bless me, Mr. Brush!—I heard something!

Brush. Rats, I suppose, that are gnawing the old timbers of this execrable old dungeon.—If it was mine, I would pull it down, and fill your fine canal up with the rubbish; and then I should get rid of two damned things at once.

Chamber. Law! law! how you blaspheme!—we shall have the house upon our heads for it.

Brush. No, no, it will last our time—but as I was saying, the eldest sister—Miss Jezabel——

Chamber. Is a fine young lady for all your evil tongue.

Brush. No—we have smoked her already; and unless she marries our old Swiss, she can have none of us—no, no, she won't do—we are a little too nice.

Chamber. You're a monstrous rake, Mr. Brush, and don't care what you say.

Brush. Why, for that matter, my dear, I am a little inclined to mischief; and if you won't have pity upon me, I will break open that door and ravish Mrs. Heidelberg.

Mrs. Heidel. (*coming forward*). There's no bearing this—you profligate monster!

Chamber. Ha! I am undone!

Brush. Zounds! here she is, by all that's monstrous.

(*Runs off*

Miss Sterl. A fine discourse you have had with that fellow!

Mrs. Heidel. And a fine time of night it is to be here with that drunken monster.

Miss Sterl. What have you to say for yourself?

Chamber. I can say nothing—I am so frightened, and so ashamed—but indeed I am vartuous—I am vartuous indeed.

Mrs. Heidel. Well, well—don't tremble so; but tell us what you know of this horrable plot here.

Miss Sterl. We'll forgive you, if you'll discover all.

Chamber. Why, madam—don't let me betray my fellow-servants—I shan't sleep in my bed, if I do.

Mrs. Heidel. Then you shall sleep somewhere else to-morrow night.

Chamber. Oh dear!—what shall I do?

Mrs. Heidel. Tell us this moment—or I'll turn you out of doors directly.

Chamber. Why our butler has been treating us below in his

pantry—Mr. Brush forced us to make a kind of a holiday night of it.

Miss Sterl. Holiday! for what?

Chamber. Nay, I only made one.

Miss Sterl. Well, well; but upon what account?

Chamber. Because as how, madam, there was a change in the family they said—that his honour, Sir John—was to marry Miss Fanny instead of your ladyship.

Miss Sterl. And so you made a holiday for that.—Very fine!

Chamber. I did not make it, ma'am.

Mrs. Heidel. But do you know nothing of Sir John's being to run away with Miss Fanny to-night?

Chamber. No, indeed, ma'am!

Miss Sterl. Nor of his being now locked up in my sister's chamber?

Chamber. No, as I hope for marcy, ma'am.

Mrs. Heidel. Well, I'll put an end to all this directly—do you run to my brother Sterling——

Chamber. Now, ma'am!—'Tis so very late, ma'am——

Mrs. Heidel. I don't care how late it is. Tell him there are thieves in the house—that the house is o' fire—tell him to come here immediately—go, I say!

Chamber. I will, I will, though I'm frightened out of my wits.   (*Exit.*

Mrs. Heidel. Do you watch here, my dear; and I'll put myself in order, to face them. We'll plot 'em, and counter-plot 'em too.
                                          (*Exit into her chamber.*

Miss Sterl. I have as much pleasure in this revenge, as in being made a countess!—Ha! they are unlocking the door.—Now for it!   (*Retires.*

(FANNY'S *door is unlocked and* BETTY *comes out with a candle.* MISS STERLING *approaches her.*

Betty (*calling within*). Sir, sir!—now's your time—all's clear. (*Seeing* MISS STERL.) Stay, stay—not yet—we are watched.

Miss Sterl. And so you are, Madam Betty!

(MISS STERLING *lays hold of her, while* BETTY *locks the door, and puts the key in her pocket.*

Betty (*turning round*). What's the matter, madam?

Miss Sterl. Nay, that you shall tell my father and aunt, madam.

Betty. I am no tell-tale, madam, and no thief; they'll get nothing from me.

Miss Sterl. You have a great deal of courage, Betty; and considering the secrets you have to keep, you have occasion for it.

Betty. My mistress shall never repent her good opinion of me, ma'am.

Enter STERLING

Sterl. What is all this? what's the matter? why am I disturbed in this manner?

Miss Sterl. This creature, and my distresses, sir, will explain the matter.

Re-enter MRS. HEIDELBERG, *with another head-dress*

Mrs. Heidel. Now I'm prepared for the rancounter—well, brother, have you heard of this scene of wickedness?

Sterl. Not I—but what is it? Speak! I was got into my little closet—all the lawyers were in bed, and I had almost lost my senses in the confusion of Lord Ogleby's mortgages, when I was alarmed with a foolish girl, who could hardly speak; and whether it's fire, or thieves, or murder, or a rape, I am quite in the dark.

Mrs. Heidel. No, no, there's no rape, brother!—all parties are willing, I believe.

Miss Sterl. Who's in that chamber?

        Detaining BETTY, *who seemed to be stealing away.*

Betty. My mistress.

Miss Sterl. And who is with your mistress?

Betty. Why, who should there be?

Miss Sterl. Open the door then, and let us see!

Betty. The door is open, madam. (MISS STERLING *goes to the door.*) I'll sooner die than peach!   *Exit hastily.*

Miss Sterl. The door 's locked; and she has got the key in her pocket.

Mrs. Heidel. There's impudence, brother! piping hot from your daughter Fanny's school!

Sterl. But, zounds! what is all this about? You tell me of a sum total, and you don't produce the particulars.

Mrs. Heidel. Sir John Melvil is locked up in your daughter's bedchamber.—There is the particular!

Sterl. The devil he is?—That's bad!

Miss Sterl. And he has been there some time too.

Sterl. Ditto!

Mrs. Heidel. Ditto! worse and worse, I say. I'll raise the house, and expose him to my lord and the whole family.

Sterl. By no means! we shall expose ourselves, sister!—The best way is to insure privately—let me alone!—I'll make him marry her to-morrow morning.

Miss Sterl. Make him marry her! this is beyond all patience!— You have thrown away all your affection; and I shall do as much by my obedience: unnatural fathers make unnatural children. —My revenge is in my own power, and I'll indulge it.—Had they made their escape, I should have been exposed to the derision of the world:—but the deriders shall be derided; and so: Help! help, there! Thieves! thieves!

Mrs. Heidel. Tit for tat, Betsey!—you are right, my girl.

Sterl. Zounds! you'll spoil all—you'll raise the whole family, —the devil's in the girl.

Mrs. Heidel. No, no; the devil's in *you,* brother. I am ashamed of your principles.—What! would you connive at your daughter's being locked up with her sister's husband? Help! thieves! thieves! I say.   (*Cries out.*

Sterl. Sister, I beg you!—daughter, I command you.—If you have no regard for me, consider yourselves!—we shall lose this opportunity of ennobling our blood, and getting above twenty per cent for our money.

Miss Sterl. What, by my disgrace and my sister's triumph! I have a spirit above such mean considerations; and to show you that it is not a low-bred, vulgar 'Change-alley spirit—Help! help! thieves! thieves! thieves! I say.

Sterl. Ay, ay, you may save your lungs—the house is in an uproar!—Women at best have no discretion; but in a passion they'll fire a house, or burn themselves in it, rather than not be revenged.

Enter CANTON, *in a night-gown and slippers*

Canton. Eh, diable! vat is de raison of dis great noise. dis tintamarre?

Sterl. Ask those ladies, sir; 'tis of their making.

Lord Ogle. (*calls within*). Brush!—Canton! where are you?—What's the matter? (*Rings a bell.*) Where are you?

Sterl. 'Tis my lord calls, Mr. Canton.

Canton. I com, mi lor'!—   (*Exit.* LORD OGLEBY *still rings.*

Serjeant Flower (*calls within*). A light! a light here!—Where are the servants? Bring a light for me and my brothers.

Sterl. Lights here! lights for the gentlemen!   (*Exit.*

Mrs. Heidel. My brother feels, I see—your sister's turn will come next.

Miss Sterl. Ay, ay, let it go round, madam! it is the only comfort I have left.

Re-enter STERLING, *with lights, before* SERJEANT FLOWER (*with one boot and a slipper*) *and* TRAVERSE

Sterl. This way, sir! this way, gentlemen!

Flower. Well, but, Mr. Sterling, no danger I hope.—Have they made a burglarious entry?—Are you prepared to repulse them?—I am very much alarmed about thieves at circuit-time. —They would be particularly severe with us gentlemen of the Bar.

Trav. No danger, Mr. Sterling?—No trespass, I hope?

Sterl. None, gentlemen, but of those ladies' making.

Mrs. Heidel. You'll be ashamed to know, gentlemen, that all your labours and studies about this young lady are thrown away—Sir John Melvil is at this moment locked up with this lady's younger sister.

Flower. The thing is a little extraordinary, to be sure—but, why were we to be frightened out of our beds for this? Could not we have tried this cause to-morrow morning?

Miss Sterl. But, sir, by to-morrow morning, perhaps, even your assistance would not have been of any service—the birds now in that cage would have flown away.

Enter LORD OGLEBY (*in his robe-de-chambre, night-cap, etc.— leaning on* CANTON)

Lord Ogle. I had rather lose a limb than my night's rest— what's the matter with you all?

Sterl. Ay, ay, 'tis all over!—Here's my lord too.

Lord Ogle. What is all this shrieking and screaming?—Where's my angelic Fanny? She's safe, I hope!

Mrs. Heidel. Your angelic Fanny, my lord, is locked up with your angelic nephew in that chamber.

Lord Ogle. My nephew! then will I be excommunicated.

Mrs. Heidel. Your nephew, my lord, has been plotting to run away with the younger sister; and the younger sister has been plotting to run away with your nephew: and if we had not watched them and called up the fammaly, they had been upon the scamper to Scotland by this time.

Lord Ogle. Look'ee, ladies!—I know that Sir John has conceived a violent passion for Miss Fanny; and I know too that Miss Fanny has conceived a violent passion for another person; and I am so well convinced of the rectitude of her affections, that I will support them with my fortune, my honour, and my life.—Eh, shan't I, Mr. Sterling? (*Smiling.*) What say you?——

Sterl. (*sulkily*). To be sure, my lord.—These bawling women have been the ruin of everything.   (*Aside.*

Lord Ogle. But come, I'll end this business in a trice—if you, ladies, will compose yourselves, and Mr. Sterling will ensure Miss Fanny from violence, I will engage to draw her from her pillow with a whisper through the keyhole.

Mrs. Heidel. The horrid creatures!—I say, my lord, break the door open.

Lord Ogle. Let me beg of your delicacy not to be too precipitate!—Now to our experiment! (*Advancing towards the door.*

Miss Sterl. Now, what will they do?—My heart will beat through my bosom.

Enter BETTY, *with the key*

Betty. There's no occasion for breaking open doors, my lord; we have done nothing that we ought to be ashamed of, and my mistress shall face her enemies.   (*Going to unlock the door.*

Mrs. Heidel. There's impudence.

Lord Ogle. The mystery thickens. Lady of the Bedchamber! (*to* BETTY) open the door, and entreat Sir John Melvil (for these ladies will have it that he is there) to appear and answer to high crimes and misdemeanours.—Call Sir John Melvil into the court!

Enter SIR JOHN MELVIL, *on the other side*

Sir John. I am here, my lord.

Mrs. Heidel. Heyday!

Miss Sterl. Astonishment!

Sir John. What is all this alarm and confusion? There is nothing but hurry in the house; what is the reason of it?

Lord Ogle. Because you have been in that chamber;—*have been!* nay you *are* there at this moment, as these ladies have protested, so don't deny it——

Trav. This is the clearest *alibi* I ever knew, Mr. Serjeant.

Flower. Luce clarius.

Lord Ogle. Upon my word, ladies, if you have often these frolics, it would be really entertaining to pass a whole summer with you. But come (*To* BETTY.), open the door, and entreat your amiable mistress to come forth, and dispel all our doubts with her smiles.

Betty (*opening the door*). Madam, you are wanted in this room.   (*Pertly.*

Enter FANNY, *in great confusion*

Miss Sterl. You see she's ready dressed—and what confusion she's in!

Mrs. Heidel. Ready to pack off, bag and baggage!—her guilt confounds her!

Flower. Silence in the court, ladies!

Fanny. I *am* confounded, indeed, madam!

Lord Ogle. Don't droop, my beauteous lily! but with your own peculiar modesty declare your state of mind.—Pour conviction into their ears, and raptures into mine.   (*Smiling.*

Fanny. I am at this moment the most unhappy—most distressed—the tumult is too much for my heart—and I want the power to reveal a secret, which to conceal has been the misfortune and misery of my—my—   (*Faints away.*

Lord Ogle. She faints! Help, help! for the fairest and best of women!

Betty (*running to her*). O my dear mistress!—help, help, there!——

Sir John. Ha! let me fly to her assistance.

} *Speaking all at once*

LOVEWELL *rushes out from the chamber*

Love. My Fanny in danger! I can contain no longer.— Prudence were now a crime; all other cares are lost in this!— Speak, speak to me, my dearest Fanny!—let me but hear thy voice, open your eyes, and bless me with the smallest sign of life!   (*During this speech they are all in amazement.*

Miss Sterl. Lovewell!—I am easy——

Mrs. Heidel. I am thunderstruck!

Lord Ogle. I am petrified!

Sir John. And I undone!

Fanny (recovering). O Lovewell!—even supported by thee, I dare not look my father nor his lordship in the face.

Sterl. What now! did not I send you to London, sir?

Lord Ogle. Eh!—What!—How's this?—by what right and title have you been half the night in that lady's bedchamber?

Love. By that right that makes me the happiest of men; and by a title which I would not forgo, for any the best of kings could give me.

Betty. I could cry my eyes out to hear his magnimity.

Lord Ogle. I am annihilated!

Sterl. I have been choked with rage and wonder; but now I can speak.—Zounds, what have you to say to me?—Lovewell, you are a villain.—You have broke your word with me.

Fanny. Indeed, sir, he has not.—You forbade him to think of me, when it was out of his power to obey you; we have been married these four months.

Sterl. And he shan't stay in my house four hours. What baseness and treachery! As for you, you shall repent this step as long as you live, madam.

Fanny. Indeed, sir, it is impossible to conceive the tortures I have already endured in consequence of my disobedience. My heart has continually upbraided me for it; and though I was too weak to struggle with affection, I feel that I must be miserable for ever without your forgiveness.

Sterl. Lovewell, you shall leave my house directly;—and you shall follow him, madam.   (*To* FANNY.

Lord Ogle. And if they do, I will receive them into mine. Look ye, Mr. Sterling, there have been some mistakes, which we had all better forget for our own sakes; and the best way to forget them is to forgive the cause of them; which I do from my soul.—Poor girl! I swore to support her affection with my life and fortune—'tis a debt of honour, and must be paid;—you swore as much too, Mr. Sterling; but your laws in the city will excuse you, I suppose; for you never strike a balance without errors excepted.

Sterl. I am a father, my lord; but for the sake of all other fathers, I think I ought not to forgive her, for fear of encouraging other silly girls like herself to throw themselves away without the consent of their parents.

Love. I hope there will be no danger of that, sir. Young ladies with minds like my Fanny's would startle at the very shadow of vice; and when they know to what uneasiness only an indiscretion has exposed her, her example, instead of encouraging, will rather serve to deter them.

Mrs. Heidel. Indiscretion, quoth a! a mighty pretty delicat word to express disobedience!

Lord Ogle. For my part, I indulge my own passions too much to tyrannise over those of other people. Poor souls, I pity them.

And you must forgive them too. Come, come, melt a little of your flint, Mr. Sterling!

Sterl. Why, why—as to that, my lord—to be sure he is a relation of yours, my lord—what say you, sister Heidelberg?

Mrs. Heidel. The girl's ruined, and I forgive her.

Sterl. Well—so do I then.—Nay, no thanks (*To* LOVEWELL *and* FANNY, *who seem preparing to speak.*) there's an end of the matter.

Lord Ogle. But, Lovewell, what makes you dumb all this while?

Love. Your kindness, my lord—I can scarce believe my own senses—they are all in a tumult of fear, joy, love, expectation, and gratitude; I ever was, and am now more bound in duty to your lordship. For you, Mr. Sterling, if every moment of my life, spent gratefully in your service, will in some measure compensate the want of fortune, you perhaps will not repent your goodness to me. And you, ladies, I flatter myself, will not for the future suspect me of artifice and intrigue—I shall be happy to oblige and serve you.—As for you, Sir John——

Sir John. No apologies to me, Lovewell, I do not deserve any. All I have to offer in excuse for what has happened, is my total ignorance of your situation. Had you dealt a little more openly with me, you would have saved me, and yourself, and that lady (who I hope will pardon my behaviour) a great deal of uneasiness. Give me leave, however, to assure you, that light and capricious as I may have appeared, now my infatuation is over, I have sensibility enough to be ashamed of the part I have acted, and honour enough to rejoice at your happiness.

Love. And now, my dearest Fanny, though we are seemingly the happiest of beings, yet all our joys will be damped, if his lordship's generosity and Mr. Sterling's forgiveness should not be succeeded by the indulgence, approbation, and consent of these our best benefactors.   (*To the audience.*

EPILOGUE

Written by Mr. Garrick

CHARACTERS OF THE EPILOGUE

Lord Minum	. .	. Mr. Dodd
Colonel Trill	.	. Mr. Vernon
Sir Patrick Mahony	.	. Mr. Moody
Miss Crotchet	. .	. Mrs. ——
Mrs. Quaver	. .	. Mrs. Lee
First Lady	. .	. Mrs. Bradshaw
Second Lady	. .	. Miss Mills
Third Lady	. .	. Mrs. Dorman

SCENE.—*An Assembly*

Several persons at cards, at different tables: among the rest
Col. Trill, Lord Minum, Mrs. Quaver, Sir Patrick
Mahony

At the quadrille table

Col. T. Ladies, with leave—
Second Lady. Pass!
Third Lady. Pass!
Mrs. Qu. You must do more.
Col. T. Indeed I can't.
Mrs. Q. I play in hearts.
Col. T. Encore!
Sec. Lady. What Luck!
Col. T. To-night at Drury Lane is played
A comedy, and *toute nouvelle*—a spade!
Is not Miss Crotchet at the play?
Mrs. Q. My niece.
Has made a party, sir, to damn the piece.

At the whist table

Lord Min. I hate a play-house—Trump!—It makes me sick.
First Lady. We're two by honours, ma'am.
Lord Min. And we the odd trick.
Pray do you know the author, Colonel Trill?
Col. T. I know no poets, Heaven be praised!—Spadille!
First Lady. I'll tell you who, my lord! (*Whispers my lord.*
Lord Min. What, he again?
"And dwell such daring souls in little men?"
Be whose it will, they down our throats will cram it!

334

Col. T. Oh, no.—I have a club—the best.—We'll damn it.
Mrs. Q. Oh bravo, Colonel, music is my flame.
Lord Min. And mine, by Jupiter!—We've won the game.
Col. T. What, do you love all music?
Mrs. Q.   No, not Handel's.
And nasty plays—
      Lord Min.   Are fit for Goths and Vandals.
                           (*Rise from the table and pay.*

From the piquette table

Sir Pat. Well, faith and troth! that Shakespeare was no fool!
Col. T. I'm glad you like him, sir!—So ends the pool!
                           (*Pay and rise from table.*

Song *by the* Colonel

> *I hate all their nonsense,*
> *Their Shakespeares and Johnsons,*
> *Their plays, and their playhouse, and bards ;*
> *'Tis singing, not saying :*
> *A fig for all playing,*
> *But playing, as we do, at cards !*
>
> *I love to see Jonas,*
> *Am pleased too with Comus :*
> *Each well the spectator rewards.*
> *So clever, so neat in*
> *Their tricks, and their cheating !*
> *Like them we would fain deal our cards.*

Sir Pat. King Lare is touching!—And how fine to see
Ould Hamlet's ghost!—"To be, or not to be."—
What are your op'ras to Othello's roar?
Oh, he's an angel of a Blackamoor!
      Lord Min. What, when he chokes his wife?—
      Col. T.   And calls her whore?
Sir Pat. King Richard calls his horse—and then Macbeth,
Whene'er he murders—takes away the breath.
My blood runs cold at ev'ry syllable,
To see the dagger—that's invisible.   (*All laugh.*
Sir Pat. Laugh if you please, a pretty play—
Lord Min.   Is pretty.
Sir Pat. And when there's wit in't—
Col. T.   To be sure 'tis witty.
Sir Pat. I love the playhouse now—so light and gay
With all those candles they have ta'en away!   (*All laugh.*
For all your game, what makes it so much brighter?
      Col. T. Put out the light, and then—
      Lord Min.   'Tis so much lighter.

Sir Pat. Pray do you mane, sirs, more than you express?
Col. T. Just as it happens—
Lord Min.   Either more, or less.
Mrs. Q. An't you ashamed, sir?   (*To* SIR PAT.
Sir Pat.   Me!—I seldom blush.—
For little Shakespeare, faith! I'd take a push!
Lord Min. News, news!—here comes Miss Crotchet from the
     play.

Enter MISS CROTCHET

Mrs. Q. Well, Crotchet, what's the news?
Miss Cro.   We've lost the day.
Col. T. Tell us, dear miss, all you have heard and seen.
Miss Cro. I'm tired—a chair—here, take my capuchin!
Lord Min. And isn't it damned, miss?
Miss Cro.   No, my lord, not quite:
But we shall damn it.
Col. T.   When?
Miss. Cro.   To-morrow night.
There is a party of us, all of fashion,
Resolved to exterminate this vulgar passion:
A playhouse, what a place!—I must forswear it.
A little mischief only makes one bear it.
Such crowds of city folks!—so rude and pressing!
And their horse-laughs, so hideously distressing!
Whene'er we hissed, they frowned and fell a-swearing,
Like their own Guildhall giants—fierce and staring!
Col. T. What said the folks of fashion? Were they cross?
Lord Min. The rest have no more judgment than my horse.
Miss Cro. Lord Grimly swore 'twas execrable stuff.
Says one, Why so, my lord?—My lord took snuff.
In the first act Lord George began to doze,
And criticised the author—through his nose;
So loud indeed, that as his lordship snored,
The pit turned round, and all the brutes encored.
Some lords, indeed, approved the author's jokes.
Lord Min. We have among us, miss, *some* foolish folks.
Miss Cro. Says poor Lord Simper, Well, now to my mind
The piece is good;—but he's both deaf and blind.
Sir Pat. Upon my soul, a very pretty story!
And Quality appears in all its glory!—
There was some merit in the piece, no doubt.
Miss Cro. Oh, to be sure!—if one could find it out.
Col. T. But tell us, miss, the subject of the play.
Miss Cro. Why, 'twas a marriage—yes, a marriage—Stay!
A lord, an aunt, two sisters, and a merchant—
A baronet—ten lawyers—a fat serjeant—
Are all produced—to talk with one another;
And about something make a mighty pother;

They all go in, and out; and to, and fro;
And talk, and quarrel—as they come and go;
Then go to bed, and then get up—and then—
Scream, faint, scold, kiss,—and go to bed again.   (*All laugh.*
Such is the play—your judgment! never sham it.

   Col. G. Oh damn it!
   Mrs. Q.   Damn it!
   First Lady.   Damn it!
   Miss Cro.   Damn it!
   Lord Min.   Damn it!
   Sir Pat. Well, faith, you speak your minds, and I'll be free—
Good night! this company's too good for me.   (*Going.*
   Col. T. Your judgment, dear Sir Patrick, makes us proud.
                                         (*All laugh.*

   Sir Pat. Laugh as you please, but pray don't laugh too loud.
                                           (*Exit.*

RECITATIVE

   Col. T. Now the Barbarian's gone, miss, tune your tongue,
And let us raise our spirits high with song!

RECITATIVE

   Miss Cro. Colonel, *de tout mon cœur*—I've one *in petto*,
Which you shall join, and make it a *duetto*.

RECITATIVE

   Lord Min. Bella Signora, et amico mio!
I too will join, and then we'll make a trio.—
   Col. T. Come all and join the full-mouthed chorus,
And drive all tragedy and comedy before us!

All the company rise, and advance to the front of the stage

AIR

   Col. T. Would you ever go to see a tragedy?
   Miss Cro.   Never, never.
   Col. T. A comedy?
   Lord Min.   Never, never,
                  Live for ever,
         Tweedle-dum and Tweedle-dee!
   Col. T., Lord M. and Miss Cro. Live for ever!
Tweedle-dum and Tweedle-dee!

CHORUS

Would you ever go to see, etc.

THE WEST INDIAN

RICHARD CUMBERLAND was born in the Master's Lodge of Trinity College, Cambridge, in 1732, grandson of a Bishop of Peterborough and of the great scholar, Richard Bentley. He began to "try his strength in several slight attempts towards the drama" while still at Bury St. Edmunds Grammar School, whence he passed to Westminster, where Warren Hastings, Cowper and Colman the Elder were his schoolfellows. At fourteen he returned to Trinity as an undergraduate, and at twenty was a fellow. The patronage of Lord Halifax secured him various offices, including that of Secretary to the Board of Trade, and his success as a dramatist presently brought him the acquaintance of the leading literary men of the day. After incurring a heavy financial loss on a diplomatic mission to Spain he retired to Tunbridge Wells, where he wrote epics, essays, comedies and tragedies, nearly all of poor quality. *The Brothers, The West Indian* and other plays of his were very successful, and show more merit than the novels he wrote later—*Arundel, Henry,* and *John de Lancaster.* These are much less interesting to-day than his *Memoirs,* which are entertaining, unreliable and full of unconscious revelations of the character of Sir Fretful Plagiary.

He died at Tunbridge Wells in 1811.

THE
WEST INDIAN:
A
COMEDY.

As it is Performed at the

THEATRE ROYAL

IN

DRURY LANE

BY THE
AUTHOR OF THE BROTHERS.

Quis novus hic Hospes?

LONDON:

Printed for W. GRIFFIN, at GARRICK's HEAD,
in CATHARINE-street, STRAND,
MDCCLXXI.

PROLOGUE

SPOKEN BY MR. REDDISH

CRITICS, hark forward! noble game and new;
A fine West Indian started full in view:
Hot as the soil, the clime which gave him birth,
You'll run him on a burning scent to earth;
Yet don't devour him in his hiding-place;
Bag him, he'll serve you for another chase;
For sure that country has no feeble claim,
Which swells your commerce, and supports your fame.
And in this humble sketch we hope you'll find
Some emanations of a noble mind;
Some little touches, which, though void of art,
May find perhaps their way into the heart.
Another hero your excuse implores,
Sent by your sister kingdom to your shores;
Doom'd by religion's too severe command
To fight for bread against his native land:
A brave, unthinking, animated rogue,
With here and there a touch upon the brogue;
Laugh, but despise him not, for on his lip
His errors lie; his heart can never trip.
Others there are—but may we not prevail
To let the gentry tell their own plain tale?
Shall they come in? They'll please you, if they can;
If not, condemn the bard—but spare the Man.
For speak, think, act, or write in angry times,
A wish to please is made the worst of crimes;
Dire slander now with black envenomed dart,
Stands ever armed to stab you to the heart.

Rouse, Britons, rouse, for honour of your isle,
Your old good humour; and be seen to smile.
You say we write not like our fathers—true,
Nor were our fathers half so strict as you,
Damned not each error of the poet's pen,
But judging man, remembered they were men.
Awed into silence by the time's abuse,
Sleeps many a wise and many a witty muse;
We that for mere experiment come out,
Are but the light armed rangers on the scout:
High on Parnassus' lofty summit stands
The immortal camp; there lie the chosen bands!
But give fair quarter to us puny elves,
The giants then will sally forth themselves;
With wit's sharp weapons vindicate the age,
And drive ev'n Arthur's magic from the stage.

DRAMATIS PERSONÆ

MEN

STOCKWELL	.	.	.	.	.	Mr. Aickin
BELCOUR	.	.	.	.	.	Mr. King
CAPTAIN DUDLEY	.	.	.	.	.	Mr. Packer
CHARLES DUDLEY	.	.	.	.	.	Mr. Cautherly
MAJOR O'FLAHERTY	.	.	.	.	.	Mr. Moody
STUKELY	.	.	.	.	.	Mr. J. Aickin
FULMER	.	.	.	.	.	Mr. Baddely
VARLAND	.	.	.	.	.	Mr. Parsons
SERVANT TO STOCKWELL	.	.	.	.	.	Mr. Wheeler

WOMEN

LADY RUSPORT	.	.	.	.	Mrs. Hopkins
CHARLOTTE RUSPORT	.	.	.	.	Mrs. Abington
LOUISA, *daughter to* DUDLEY	.	.	.	Mrs. Baddely
MRS. FULMER	.	.	.	.	Mrs. Egerton
LUCY	.	.	.	.	Mrs. Love
HOUSEKEEPER *belonging to* STOCKWELL	.	.	Mrs. Bradshaw

Clerks belonging to Stockwell, Servants, Sailors, Negroes, etc.

SCENE—London.

THE WEST INDIAN

ACT I

SCENE I

A Merchant's Compting-House

In an inner room, set off by glass doors, are discovered several Clerks, employed at their desks. A writing-table in the front room. STOCKWELL is discovered reading a letter: STUKELY comes gently out of the back room, and observes him some time before he speaks.

Stukely. He seems disordered: something in that letter, and, I'm afraid of an unpleasant sort. He has many ventures of great account at sea; a ship richly freighted for Barcelona; another for Lisbon; and others expected from Cadiz of still greater value. Besides these, I know he has many deep concerns in foreign bottoms, and underwritings to a vast amount. I'll accost him. Sir! Mr. Stockwell!

Stock. Stukely!—Well, have you shipped the cloths?

Stukely. I have, sir; here's the bill of lading, and copy of the invoice: the assortments are all compared: Mr. Traffick will give you the policy upon 'Change.

Stock. 'Tis very well; lay these papers by; and no more of business for a while. Shut the door, Stukely; I have had long proof of your friendship and fidelity to me; a matter of most intimate concern lies on my mind, and 'twill be a sensible relief to unbosom myself to you. I have just now been informed of the arrival of the young West Indian, I have so long been expecting; you know who I mean.

Stukely. Yes, sir; Mr. Belcour, the young gentleman who inherited old Belcour's great estates in Jamaica.

Stock. Hush, not so loud; come a little nearer this way. This Belcour is now in London; part of his baggage is already arrived; and I expect him every minute. Is it to be wondered at, if his coming throws me into some agitation, when I tell you, Stukely, he is my son?

Stukely. Your son!

Stock. Yes, sir, my only son; early in life I accompanied his grandfather to Jamaica as his clerk; he had an only daughter, somewhat older than myself, the mother of this gentleman: it was my chance (call it good or ill) to engage her affections: and, as the inferiority of my condition made it hopeless to expect her father's consent, her fondness provided an expedient, and we were privately married; the issue of that concealed engagement is, as I have told you, this Belcour.

Stukely. That event, surely, discovered your connection.

Stock. You shall hear. Not many days after our marriage old Belcour set out for England; and, during his abode here, my wife was, with great secrecy, delivered of this son. Fruitful in expedients to disguise her situation, without parting from her infant, she contrived to have it laid and received at her door as a foundling. After some time her father returned, having left me here; in one of those favourable moments that decide the fortunes of prosperous men, this child was introduced; from that instant, he treated him as his own, gave him his name, and brought him up in his family.

Stukely. And did you never reveal this secret, either to old Belcour or your son?

Stock. Never.

Stukely. Therein you surprise me; a merchant of your eminence, and a member of the British Parliament, might surely aspire, without offence, to the daughter of a planter. In this case, too, natural affection would prompt to a discovery.

Stock. Your remark is obvious; nor could I have persisted in this painful silence, but in obedience to the dying injunctions of a beloved wife. The letter you found me reading, conveyed those injunctions to me; it was dictated in her last illness, and almost in the article of death (you'll spare me the recital of it); she there conjures me, in terms as solemn as they are affecting, never to reveal the secret of our marriage, or withdraw my son, while her father survived.

Stukely. But on what motives did your unhappy lady found these injunctions?

Stock. Principally, I believe, from apprehension on my account, lest old Belcour, on whom at her decease I wholly depended, should withdraw his protection: in part from consideration of his repose, as well knowing the discovery would deeply affect his spirit, which was haughty, vehement, and unforgiving: and lastly, in regard to the interest of her infant, whom he had warmly adopted; and for whom, in case of a discovery, everything was to be dreaded from his resentment. And, indeed, though the alteration in my condition might have justified me in discovering myself, yet I always thought my son safer in trusting to the caprice than to the justice of his grandfather. My judgment has not suffered by the event; old Belcour is dead, and has bequeathed his whole estate to him we are speaking of.

Stukely. Now then you are no longer bound to secrecy.

Stock. True: but before I publicly reveal myself, I could wish to make some experiment of my son's disposition: this can only be done by letting his spirit take its course without restraint; by these means, I think I shall discover much more of his real character under the title of his merchant, than I should under that of his father.

SCENE II

A Sailor enters, ushering in several black Servants, carrying portmanteaux, trunks, etc.

Sailor. Save your honour! is your name Stockwell, pray?

Stock. It is.

Sailor. Part of my master Belcour's baggage an't please you; there's another cargo not far astern of us; and the coxswain has got charge of the dumb creatures.

Stock. Prithee, friend, what dumb creatures do you speak of; has Mr. Belcour brought over a collection of wild beasts?

Sailor. No, Lord love him; no, not he. Let me see; there's two green monkeys, a pair of grey parrots, a Jamaica sow and pigs, and a Mangrove dog; that's all.

Stock. Is that all?

Sailor. Yes, your honour; yes, that's all; bless his heart a' might have brought over the whole island if he would; a' didn't leave a dry eye in it.

Stock. Indeed! Stukely, show 'em where to bestow their baggage. Follow that gentleman.

Sailor. Come, bear a hand, my lads, bear a hand.

(*Exit with* STUKELY *and Servants.*)

Stock. If the principal tallies with his purveyors, he must be a singular spectacle in this place: he has a friend, however, in this seafaring fellow; 'tis no bad prognostic of a man's heart, when his shipmate gives him a good word.   (*Exit.*)

SCENE III

Scene changes to a drawing-room. A Servant discovered setting the chairs by, etc.; a Woman Servant enters to him

Housekeeper. Why, what a fuss does our good master put himself in about this West Indian: see what a bill of fare I've been forced to draw out: seven and nine I'll assure you, and only a family dinner as he calls it: why if my Lord Mayor was expected, there couldn't be a greater to-do about him.

Ser. I wish to my heart you had but seen the loads of trunks, boxes, and portmanteaux he has sent hither. An ambassador's baggage, with all the smuggled goods of his family, does not exceed it.

Housekeeper. A fine pickle he'll put the house into: had he been master's own son, and a Christian Englishman, there could not be more rout than there is about this Creolian, as they call 'em.

Ser. No matter for that; he's very rich, and that's sufficient. They say he has rum and sugar enough belonging to him, to make all the water in the Thames into punch. But I see my master's coming.   (*Exeunt.*

SCENE IV

STOCKWELL *enters, followed by a Servant*

Stock. Where is Mr. Belcour? Who brought this note from him?

Serv. A waiter from the London Tavern, sir; he says the young gentleman is just dressed, and will be with you directly.

Stock. Show him in when he arrives.

Serv. I shall, sir. I'll have a peep at him first, however; I've a great mind to see this outlandish spark. The sailor fellow says he'll make rare doings amongst us.   (*Aside.*

Stock. You need not wait; leave me.   (*Exit Servant.*
Let me see.   (*Reads.*
"SIR,

        "I write to you under the hands of the hairdresser; as soon as I have made myself decent, and slipped on some fresh clothes, I will have the honour of paying you my devoirs.

                                      "Yours,
                                          "BELCOUR."

He writes at his ease; for he's unconscious to whom his letter is addressed; but what a palpitation does it throw my heart into; a father's heart! 'Tis an affecting interview; when my eyes meet a son whom yet they never saw, where shall I find constancy to support it? Should he resemble his mother, I am overthrown. All the letters I have had from him, (for I industriously drew him into a correspondence with me) bespeak him of quick and ready understanding. All the reports I ever received, give me favourable impressions of his character, wild, perhaps, as the manner of his country is, but, I trust, not frantic or unprincipled.

SCENE V

Servant enters

Serv. Sir, the foreign gentleman is come.

Another Servant

Serv. Mr. Belcour.

BELCOUR *enters*

Stock. Mr. Belcour, I'm rejoiced to see you; you're welcome to England.

Bel. I thank you heartily, good Mr. Stockwell; you and I have long conversed at a distance; now we are met; and the

pleasure this meeting gives me, amply compensates for the perils
I have run through in accomplishing it.

Stock. What perils, Mr. Belcour? I could not have thought
you would have made a bad passage at this time o' year.

Bel. Nor did we: courier-like, we came posting to your shores,
upon the pinions of the swiftest gales that ever blew. 'Tis upon
English ground all my difficulties have arisen; 'tis the passage
from the riverside I complain of.

Stock. Ay, indeed! What obstructions can you have met
between this and the riverside?

Bel. Innumerable! Your town's as full of defiles as the Island
of Corsica; and, I believe, they are as obstinately defended: so
much hurry, bustle, and confusion on your quays; so many
sugar-casks, porter-butts, and common-council-men in your
streets, that, unless a man marched with artillery in his front,
'tis more than the labour of a Hercules can effect, to make any
tolerable way through your town.

Stock. I am sorry you have been so incommoded.

Bel. Why, faith, 'twas all my own fault: accustomed to a
land of slaves, and out of patience with the whole tribe of
custom-house extortioners, boatmen, tide-waiters, and water-
bailiffs, that beset me on all sides, worse than a swarm of mos-
quitoes, I proceeded a little too roughly to brush them away
with my rattan; the sturdy rogues took this in dudgeon, and
beginning to rebel, the mob chose different sides, and a furious
scuffle ensued; in the course of which, my person and apparel
suffered so much that I was obliged to step into the first tavern
to refit, before I could make my approaches in any decent trim.

Stock. All without is as I wish; dear Nature add the rest, and
I am happy. (*Aside*). Well, Mr. Belcour, 'tis a rough sample you
have had of my countrymen's spirit; but I trust you'll not think
the worse of them for it.

Bel. Not at all, not at all; I like 'em the better; was I only
a visitor, I might, perhaps, wish them a little more tractable;
but, as a fellow-subject, and a sharer in their freedom, I applaud
their spirit, though I feel the effects of it in every bone of my skin.

Stock. That's well; I like that well. How gladly I could fall
upon his neck, and own myself his father! (*Aside.*

Bel. Well, Mr. Stockwell, for the first time in my life, here am
I in England; at the fountain-head of pleasure, in the land of
beauty, of arts, and elegancies. My happy stars have given me
a good estate, and the conspiring winds have blown me hither
to spend it.

Stock. To use it, not to waste it, I should hope; to treat it,
Mr. Belcour, not as a vassal, over whom you have a wanton and
a despotic power; but as a subject, which you are bound to
govern with a temperate and restrained authority.

Bel. True, sir; most truly said; mine's a commission, not a
right: I am the offspring of distress, and every child of sorrow is

my brother; while I have hands to hold, therefore, I will hold them open to mankind: but, sir, my passions are my masters; they take me where they will; and oftentimes they leave to reason and to virtue nothing but my wishes and my sighs.

Stock. Come, come, the man who can accuse corrects himself.

Bel. Ah! that's an office I am weary of: I wish a friend would take it up: I would to Heaven you had leisure for the employ; but, did you drive a trade to the four corners of the world, you would not find the task so toilsome as to keep me free from faults.

Stock. Well, I am not discouraged: this candour tells me I should not have the fault of self-conceit to combat; that, at least, is not amongst the number.

Bel. No; if I knew that man on earth who thought more humbly of me than I do of myself, I would take up his opinion, and forgo my own.

Stock. And, was I to choose a pupil, it should be one of your complexion: so if you'll come along with me, we'll agree upon your admission, and enter on a course of lectures directly.

Bel. With all my heart.   (*Exeunt.*

SCENE VI

Scene changes to a room in Lady Rusport's house

LADY RUSPORT *and* CHARLOTTE

Lady R. Miss Rusport, I desire to hear no more of Captain Dudley and his destitute family: not a shilling of mine shall ever cross the hands of any of them: because my sister chose to marry a beggar, am I bound to support him and his posterity?

Char. I think you are.

Lady R. You think I am; and pray where do you find the law that tells you so?

Char. I am not proficient enough to quote chapter and verse; but I take a charity to be a main clause in the great statute of Christianity.

Lady R. I say, charity indeed! And pray, miss, are you sure that it is charity, pure charity, which moves you to plead for Captain Dudley? Amongst all your pity, do you find no spice of a certain anti-spiritual passion, called love? Don't mistake yourself; you are no saint, child, believe me; and, I am apt to think, the distresses of old Dudley, and of his daughter into the bargain, would never break your heart, if there was not a certain young fellow of two and twenty in the case; who, by the happy recommendation of a good person, and the brilliant appointments of an ensigncy, will, if I am not mistaken, cozen you out of a fortune of twice twenty thousand pounds, as soon as ever you are of age to bestow it upon him.

Char. A nephew of your ladyship's can never want any other recommendation with me; and, if my partiality for Charles

Dudley is acquitted by the rest of the world, I hope Lady Rusport will not condemn me for it.

Lady R. I condemn you! I thank Heaven, Miss Rusport, I am no ways responsible for your conduct; nor is it any concern of mine how you dispose of yourself; you are not my daughter; and, when I married your father, poor Sir Stephen Rusport, I found you a forward spoiled miss of fourteen, far above being instructed by me.

Char. Perhaps your ladyship calls this instruction.

Lady R. You're strangely pert; but 'tis no wonder; your mother, I'm told, was a fine lady; and according to the modern style of education you was brought up. It was not so in my young days; there was then some decorum in the world, some subordination, as the great Locke expresses it. Oh! 'twas an edifying sight, to see the regular deportment observed in our family: no giggling, no gossiping was going on there; my good father, Sir Oliver Roundhead, never was seen to laugh himself, nor ever allowed it in his children.

Char. Ay, those were happy times, indeed.

Lady R. But, in this forward age, we have coquettes in the egg-shell, and philosophers in the cradle; girls of fifteen that lead the fashion in new caps and new opinions, that have their sentiments and their sensations; and the idle fops encourage 'em in it. O' my conscience, I wonder what it is the men can see in such babies.

Char. True, madam; but all men do not overlook the maturer beauties of your ladyship's age, witness your admirer Major Dennis O'Flaherty; there's an example of some discernment; I declare to you, when your ladyship is by, the Major takes no more notice of me than if I was part of the furniture of your chamber.

Lady R. The Major, child, has travelled through various kingdoms and climates, and has more enlarged notions of female merit than falls to the lot of an English home-bred lover; in most other countries, no woman on your side forty would ever be named in a polite circle.

Char. Right, madam; I've been told that in Vienna they have coquettes upon crutches, and Venuses in their grand climacteric; a lover there celebrates the wrinkles. not the dimples, in his mistress's face. The Major, I think, has served in the imperial army.

Lady R. Are you piqued, my young madam? Had my sister, Louisa, yielded to the addresses of one of Major O'Flaherty's person and appearance, she would have had some excuse: but to run away, as she did, at the age of sixteen, too, with a man of old Dudley's sort——

Char. Was, in my opinion, the most venial trespass that ever girl of sixteen committed; of a noble family, an engaging person, strict honour, and sound understanding, what accomplishment was there wanting in Captain Dudley, but that which the prodigality of his ancestors had deprived him of?

Lady R. They left him as much as he deserves; hasn't the old man captain's half-pay? And is not the son an ensign?

Char. An ensign! Alas, poor Charles! Would to Heaven he knew what my heart feels and suffers for his sake.

Servant enters

Serv. Ensign Dudley to wait upon your ladyship.

Lady R. Who! Dudley! What can have brought him to town?

Char. Dear madam, 'tis Charles Dudley, 'tis your nephew.

Lady R. Nephew! I renounce him as my nephew; Sir Oliver renounced him as his grandson: wasn't he son of the eldest daughter, and only male descendant of Sir Oliver; and didn't he cut him off with a shilling? Didn't the poor dear good man leave his whole fortune to me, except a small annuity to my maiden sister, who spoiled her constitution with nursing him? And, depend upon it, not a penny of that fortune shall ever be disposed of otherwise than according to the will of the donor. (CHARLES DUDLEY *enters*.) So, young man, whence come you? What brings you to town?

Charles. If there is any offence in my coming to town, your ladyship is in some degree responsible for it, for part of my errand was to pay my duty here.

Lady R. I hope you have some better excuse than all this.

Charles. 'Tis true, madam, I have other motives; but, if I consider my trouble repaid by the pleasure I now enjoy, I should hope my aunt would not think my company the less welcome for the value I set upon hers.

Lady R. Coxcomb! And where is your father, child; and your sister? Are they in town too?

Charles. They are.

Lady R. Ridiculous! I don't know what people do in London who have no money to spend in it.

Char. Dear madam, speak more kindly to your nephew; how can you oppress a youth of his sensibility?

Lady R. Miss Rusport, I insist upon your retiring to your apartment; when I want your advice I'll send to you. (*Exit* CHARLOTTE.) So you have put on a red coat too, as well as your father; 'tis plain what value you set upon the good advice Sir Oliver used to give you; how often has he cautioned you against the army?

Charles. Had it pleased my grandfather to enable me to have obeyed his caution, I would have done it; but you well know how destitute I am; and 'tis not to be wondered at if I prefer the service of my king to that of any other master.

Lady R. Well, well, take your own course; 'tis no concern of mine: you never consulted me.

Charles. I frequently wrote to your ladyship, but could obtain no answer; and, since my grandfather's death, this is the first opportunity I have had of waiting upon you.

Lady R. I must desire you not to mention the death of that dear good man in my hearing; my spirits cannot support it.

Charles. I shall obey you: permit me to say, that, as that event has richly supplied you with the materials of bounty, the distresses of my family can furnish you with objects of it.

Lady R. The distresses of your family, child, are quite out of the question at present; had Sir Oliver been pleased to consider them, I should have been well content; but he has absolutely taken no notice of you in his will, and that to me must and shall be a law. Tell your father and your sister I totally disapprove of their coming up to town.

Charles. Must I tell my father that before your ladyship knows the motive that brought him hither? Allured by the offer of exchanging for a commission on full pay, the veteran, after thirty years' service, prepares to encounter the fatal heats of Senegambia; but wants a small supply to equip him for the expedition.

Servant enters

Serv. Major O'Flaherty to wait on your ladyship.

Major enters

Major. Spare your speeches, young man; don't you think her ladyship can take my word for that? I hope, madam, 'tis evidence enough of my being present, when I've the honour of telling you so myself.

Lady R. Major O'Flaherty, I am rejoiced to see you. Nephew Dudley, you perceive I'm engaged.

Charles. I shall not intrude upon your ladyship's more agreeable engagements. I presume I have my answer.

Lady R. Your answer, child! What answer can you possibly expect; or how can your romantic father suppose that I am to abet him in all his idle and extravagant undertakings? Come, Major, let me show you the way into my dressing-room; and let us leave this young adventurer to his meditation.   (*Exit.*

Major. I follow you, my lady. Young gentleman, your obedient! Upon my conscience, as fine a young fellow as I would wish to clap my eyes on: he might have answered my salute, however—well, let it pass: Fortune, perhaps, frowns upon the poor lad; she's a damned slippery lady, and very apt to jilt us poor fellows that wear cockades in our hats. Fare-thee-well, honey, whoever thou art.   (*Exit.*

Charles. So much for the virtues of a puritan; out upon it, her heart is flint; yet that woman, that aunt of mine, without one worthy particle in her composition, would, I dare be sworn, as soon set her foot in a pest-house, as in a playhouse.   (*Going.*

Miss Rusport *enters to him*

Char. Stop, stay a little, Charles, whither are you going in such haste?

Charles. Madam—Miss Rusport—what are your commands?

Char. Why so reserved? We had used to answer to no other names than those of Charles and Charlotte.

Charles. What ails you? You've been weeping.

Char. No, no; or if I have—your eyes are full too; but I have a thousand things to say to you; before you go, tell me, I conjure you, where you are to be found; here, give me your direction; write it upon the back of this visiting-ticket.—Have you a pencil?

Charles. I have: but why should you desire to find us out? 'Tis a poor little inconvenient place; my father has no apartment fit to receive you in.

Servant enters

Serv. Madam, my lady desires your company directly.

Char. I am coming.—Well, have you wrote it? Give it me. O Charles! either you do not, or you will not understand me.

(*Exeunt severally.*

ACT II

SCENE I

A room in Fulmer's *House*

Fulmer *and* Mrs. Fulmer

Mrs. F. Why, how you sit, musing and moping, sighing and desponding! I'm ashamed of you, Mr. Fulmer: is this the country you described to me, a second Eldorado, rivers of gold and rocks of diamonds? You found me in a pretty snug retired way of life at Boulogne, out of the noise and bustle of the world, and wholly at my ease; you, indeed, was upon the wing, with a fiery persecution at your back: but, like a true son of Loyola ¡you had then a thousand ingenious devices to repair your fortune: and this, your native country, was to be the scene of your performances. Fool that I was, to be inveigled into it by you: but, thank Heaven, our partnership is revocable: I am not your wedded wife, praised be my stars! For what have we got, whom have we gulled but ourselves; which of all your trains has taken fire; even this poor expedient of your bookseller's shop seems abandoned; for if a chance customer drops in, who is there, pray, to help him to what he wants?

Ful. Patty, you know it is not upon slight grounds that I despair; there had used to be a livelihood to be picked up in this country, both for the honest and dishonest: I have tried each walk, and am likely to starve at last: there is not a point to which the wit and faculty of man can turn that I have not set mine to; but in vain, I am beat through every quarter of the compass.

Mrs. Ful. Ah! common efforts all: strike me a master-stroke, Mr. Fulmer, if you wish to make any figure in this country.

Ful. But where, how, and what? I have blustered for prerogative; I have bellowed for freedom; I have offered to serve my country; I have engaged to betray it; a master-stroke, truly; why, I have talked treason, writ treason, and if a man can't live by that he can live by nothing. Here I set up as a bookseller, why men left off reading; and if I was to turn butcher, I believe, o' my conscience, they'd leave off eating.

CAPTAIN DUDLEY *crosses the stage*

Mrs. Ful. Why there now's your lodger, old Captain Dudley, as he calls himself; there's no flint without fire; something might be struck out of him, if you'd the wit to find the way.

Ful. Hang him, an old dry-skinned curmudgeon; you may as well think to get truth out of a courtier, or candour out of a critic: I can make nothing of him; besides, he's poor, and therefore not for our purpose.

Mrs. F. The more fool he! Would any man be poor that had such a prodigy in his possession?

Ful. His daughter, you mean; she is, indeed, uncommonly beautiful.

Mrs. F. Beautiful! Why she need only be seen, to have the first men in the kingdom at her feet. Egad, I wish I had the leasing of her beauty; what would some of our young Nabobs give—?

Ful. Hush! here comes the captain; good girl, leave us to ourselves, and let me try what I can make of him.

Mrs. F. Captain, truly! i' faith I'd have a regiment, had I such a daughter, before I was three months older.   (*Exit.*

SCENE II

CAPTAIN DUDLEY *enters to him*

Ful. Captain Dudley, good morning to you.

Dud. Mr. Fulmer, I have borrowed a book from your shop; 'tis the sixth volume of my deceased friend Tristram; he is a flattering writer to us poor soldiers; and the divine story of Le Fevre, which makes part of this book, in my opinion of it, does honour not to its author only, but to human nature.

Ful. He's an author I keep in the way of trade, but one I never relished: he is much too loose and profligate for my taste.

Dud. That's being too severe: I hold him to be moralist in

the noblest sense; he plays indeed with the fancy, and sometimes perhaps too wantonly; but while he thus designedly
masks his main attack, he comes at once upon the heart; refines,
amends it, softens it; beats down each selfish barrier from about
it, and opens every sluice of pity and benevolence.

Ful. We of the catholic persuasion are not much bound to
him.—Well, sir, I shall not oppose your opinion; a favourite
author is like a favourite mistress; and there you know, captain,
no man likes to have his taste arraigned.

Dud. Upon my word, sir, I don't know what a man likes in
that case; 'tis an experiment I never made.

Ful. Sir!—Are you serious?

Dud. 'Tis of little consequence whether you think so.

Ful. What a formal old prig it is! (*Aside.*) I apprehend you,
sir; you speak with caution; you are married?

Dud. I have been.

Ful. And this young lady, which accompanies you——

Dud. Passes for my daughter.

Ful. Passes for his daughter! humph.—(*Aside.*) She is exceed-
ingly beautiful, finely accomplished, of a most enchanting shape
and air.

Dud. You are much too partial; she has the greatest defect
a woman can have.

Ful. How so, pray?

Dud. She has no fortune.

Ful. Rather say that you have none; and that's a sore defect
in one of your years, Captain Dudley; you've served, no doubt?

Dud. Familiar coxcomb! But I'll humour him.   (*Aside.*

Ful. A close old fox! But I'll unkennel him.   (*Aside.*

Dud. Above thirty years I've been in the service, Mr. Fulmer.

Ful. I guessed as much; I laid it at no less: why 'tis a weari-
some time; 'tis an apprenticeship to a profession, fit only for a
patriarch. But preferment must be closely followed: you never
could have been so far behindhand in the chase, unless you had
palpably mistaken your way. You'll pardon me, but I begin to
perceive you have lived in the world, not with it.

Dud. It may be so; and you, perhaps, can give me better
counsel. I'm now soliciting a favour; an exchange to a company
on full pay; nothing more; and yet I meet a thousand bars to
that; though, without boasting, I should think the certificate
of services, which I sent in, might have purchased that indulgence
to me.

Ful. Who thinks or cares about 'em? Certificate of services,
indeed! Send in a certificate of your fair daughter; carry her in
your hand with you.

Dud. What! Who! My daughter! Carry my daughter! Well,
and what then?

Ful. Why, then your fortune's made, that's all.

Dud. I understand you: and this you call knowledge of the

world? Despicable knowledge; but, sirrah, I will have you
know——   (*Threatening him.*

Ful. Help! Who's within? Would you strike me, sir; would
you lift up your hand against a man in his own house?

Dud. In a church, if he dare insult the poverty of a man of
honour.

Ful. Have a care what you do; remember there is such a
thing in law as an assault and battery; aye, and such trifling
forms as warrants and indictments.

Dud. Go, sir; you are too mean for my resentment: 'tis that,
and not the law, protects you. Hence!

Ful. An old, absurd, incorrigible blockhead! I'll be revenged
of him.   (*Aside.*

SCENE III

Young Dudley *enters to him*

Charles. What is the matter, sir? Sure I heard an outcry as
I entered the house.

Dud. Not unlikely; our landlord and his wife are for ever
wrangling.—Did you find your aunt [Rusport] at home?

Charles. I did.

Dud. And what was your reception?

Charles. Cold as our poverty and her pride could make it.

Dud. You told her the pressing occasion I had for a small
supply to equip me for this exchange; has she granted me the
relief I asked?

Charles. Alas! sir, she has peremptorily refused it.

Dud. That's hard; that's hard, indeed! My petition was for
a small sum; she has refused it, you say: well, be it so; I must
not complain. Did you see the broker about the insurance on
my life?

Charles. There again I am the messenger of ill news; I can
raise no money, so fatal is the climate: alas! that ever my father
should be sent to perish in such a place!

SCENE IV

Miss Dudley *enters hastily*

Dud. Louisa, what's the matter? you seem frighted.

Louisa. I am, indeed: coming from Miss Rusport's, I met a
young gentleman in the streets, who has beset me in the strangest
manner.

Charles. Insufferable! Was he rude to you?

Louisa. I cannot say he was absolutely rude to me, but he was
very importunate to speak to me, and once or twice attempted
to lift up my hat: he followed me to the corner of the street, and
there I gave him the slip.

Dud. You must walk no more in the streets, child, without me or your brother.

Louisa. O Charles! Miss Rusport desires to see you directly; Lady Rusport is gone out, and she has something particular to say to you.

Charles. Have you any commands for me, sir?

Dud. None, my dear; by all means wait upon Miss Rusport. Come, Louisa, I shall desire you to go up to your chamber and compose yourself. (*Exeunt.*)

SCENE V

BELCOUR *enters, after peeping in at the door*

Bel. Not a soul, as I'm alive. Why, what an odd sort of a house is this! Confound the little jilt, she has fairly given me the slip. A plague upon this London, I shall have no luck in it: such a crowd, and such a hurry, and such a number of shops, and one so like the other, that whether the wench turned into this house or the next, or whether she went up stairs or down stairs (for there's a world above and a world below, it seems), I declare I know no more than if I was in the Blue Mountians. In the name of all the devils at once, why did she run away? If every handsome girl I meet in this town is to lead me such a wild-goose chase, I had better have stayed in the torrid zone: I shall be wasted to the size of a sugar-cane. What shall I do? give the chase up? Hang it, that's cowardly: shall I, a true-born son of Phœbus, suffer this little nimble-footed Daphne to escape me?—"Forbid it honour, and forbid it love." Hush, hush! here she comes! Oh! the devil! What tawdry thing have we got here?

MRS. FULMER *enters to him*

Mrs. F. Your humble servant, sir.

Bel. Your humble servant, madam.

Mrs. F. A fine summer's day, sir.

Bel. Yes, ma'am, and so cool, that if the calendar didn't call it July, I should swear it was January.

Mrs. F. Sir!

Bel. Madam!

Mrs. F. Do you wish to speak to Mr. Fulmer, sir?

Bel. Mr. Fulmer, madam? I haven't the honour of knowing such a person.

Mrs. Ful. No, I'll be sworn you have not; thou art much too pretty a fellow, and too much of a gentleman, to be an author thyself, or to have anything to say to those that are so. 'Tis the captain, I suppose, you are waiting for.

Bel. I rather suspect it is the captain's wife.

Mrs. F. The captain has no wife, sir.

Bel. No wife! I'm heartily sorry for it; for then she's his mistress; and that I take to be the more desperate case of the two. Pray, madam, wasn't there a lady just now turned into your house? 'Twas with her I wished to speak.

Mrs. F. What sort of a lady, pray?

Bel. One of the loveliest sort my eyes ever beheld; young, tall, fresh, fair; in short, a goddess.

Mrs. F. Nay, but dear, dear sir, now I'm sure you flatter; for 'twas me you followed into the shop-door this minute.

Bel. You! No, no, take my word for it, it was not you, madam.

Mrs. F. But what is it you laugh at?

Bel. Upon my soul, I ask your pardon; but it was not you, believe me; be assured it wasn't.

Mrs. F. Well, sir, I shall not contend for the honour of being noticed by you; I hope you think you wouldn't have been the first man that noticed me in the streets; however, this I'm positive of, that no living woman but myself has entered these doors this morning.

Bel. Why then I'm mistaken in the house, that's all; for 'tis not humanly possible I can be so far out in the lady.   (*Going.*

Mrs. F. Coxcomb! But hold—a thought occurs; as sure as can be he has seen Miss Dudley. A word with you, young gentleman; come back.

Bel. Well, what's your pleasure?

Mrs. F. You seem greatly captivated with this young lady; are you apt to fall in love thus at first sight?

Bel. Oh, yes: 'tis the only way I can ever fall in love; any man may tumble into a pit by surprise, none but a fool would walk into one by choice.

Mrs. F. You are a hasty lover it seems; have you spirit to be a generous one? They that will please the eye mustn't spare the purse.

Bel. Try me; put me to the proof; bring me to an interview with the dear girl that has thus captivated me, and see whether I have spirit to be grateful.

Mrs. F. But how, pray, am I to know the girl you have set your heart on?

Bel. By an undescribable grace that accompanies every look and action that falls from her: there can be but one such woman in the world, and nobody can mistake that one.

Mrs. F. Well, if I should stumble upon this angel in my walks, where am I to find you? What's your name?

Bel. Upon my soul, I can't tell you my name.

Mrs F. Not tell me! Why so?

Bel. Because I don't know what it is myself; as yet I have no name.

Mrs. F. No name!

Bel. None; a friend, indeed, lent me his; but he forbade me to use it on any unworthy occasion.

Mrs. F. But where is your place of abode?

Bel. I have none; I never slept a night in England in my life.

Mrs. F. Hey-day!

SCENE VI

FULMER *enters*

Ful. A fine case, truly, in a free country; a pretty pass things are come to, if a man is to be assaulted in his own house.

Mrs. F. Who has assaulted you, my dear?

Ful. Who! why this Captain Drawcansir, this old Dudley, my lodger; but I'll unlodge him; I'll unharbour him I warrant.

Mrs. F. Hush, hush! Hold your tongue, man; pocket the affront, and be quiet; I've a scheme on foot will pay you a hundred beatings. Why you surprise me, Mr. Fulmer. Captain Dudley assault you! Impossible.   [*Apart.*]

Ful. Nay, I can't call it an absolute assault; but he threatened me.   [*Apart.*]

Mrs. F. Oh, was that all? I thought how it would turn out— A likely thing, truly, for a person of his obliging compassionate turn: no, no, poor Captain Dudley, he has sorrows and distresses enough of his own to employ his spirits, without setting them against other people. Make it up as fast as you can. Watch this gentleman out; follow him wherever he goes; and bring me word who and what he is; be sure you don't lose sight of him; I've other business in hand.   [*Apart.*] (*Exit.*

Bel. Pray, sir, what sorrows and distresses have befallen this old gentleman you speak of?

Ful. Poverty, disappointment, and all the distresses attendant thereupon: sorrow enough of all conscience: I soon found how it was with him by his way of living, low enough of all reason; but what I overheard this morning put it out of all doubt.

Bel. What did you overhear this morning?

Ful. Why, it seems he wants to join his regiment, and has been beating the town over to raise a little money for that purpose upon his pay; but the climate, I find, where he is going, is so unhealthy that nobody can be found to lend him any.

Bel. Why then your town is a damned good-for-nothing town: and I wish I had never come into it.

Ful. That's what I say, sir; the hard-heartedness of some folks is unaccountable. There's an old Lady Rusport, a near relation of this gentleman's; she lives hard by here, opposite to Stockwell's, the great merchant; he sent to her a-begging, but to no purpose; though she is as rich as a Jew, she would not furnish him with a farthing.

Bel. Is the captain at home?

Ful. He is upstairs, sir.

Bel. Will you take the trouble to desire him to step hither? I want to speak to him.

Ful. I'll send him to you directly. [*Aside.*] I don't know what to make of this young man; but, if I live, I will find him out, or know the reason why. (*Exit.*

Bel. I've lost the girl it seems; that's clear: she was the first object of my pursuit; but the case of this poor officer touches me; and, after all, there may be as much true delight in rescuing a fellow-creature from distress, as there would be in plunging one into it.—But let me see; it's a point that must be managed with some delicacy—Apropos! there's pen and ink — I've struck upon a method that will do. (*Writes.*) Ay, ay, this is the very thing: 'twas devilish lucky I happened to have these bills about me. There, there, fare you well; I'm glad to be rid of you; you stood a chance of being worse applied. I can tell you.

(*Encloses and seals the paper.*

SCENE VII

FULMER *brings in* DUDLEY

Ful. That's the gentleman, sir. I shall make bold, however. to lend an ear.

Dud. Have you any commands for me, sir?

Bel. Your name is Dudley, sir——?

Dud. It is.

Bel. You command a company, I think, Captain Dudley?

Dud. I did: I am now upon half-pay.

Bel. You've served some time?

Dud. A pretty many years; long enough to see some people of more merit, and better interest than myself, made general officers.

Bel. Their merit I may have some doubt of; their interest I can readily give credit to; there is little promotion to be looked for in your profession, I believe, without friends, Captain?

Dud. I believe so too. Have you any other business with me, may I ask?

Bel. Your patience for a moment. I was informed you was about to join your regiment in distant quarters abroad.

Dud. I have been soliciting an exchange to a company on full-pay, quartered at James's Fort, in Senegambia; but, I'm afraid, I must drop the undertaking.

Bel. Why so, pray?

Dud. Why so, sir? 'Tis a home-question for a perfect stranger to put; there is something very particular in all this.

Bel. If it is not impertinent, sir, allow me to ask you whot reason you have for despairing of success?

Dud. Why really, sir, mine is an obvious reason for a soldier to have—Want of money; simply that.

Bel. May I beg to know the sum you have occasion for?

Dud. Truly, sir, I cannot exactly tell you on a sudden; nor is it, I suppose, of any great consequence to you to be informed; but I should guess, in the gross, that two hundred pounds would serve.

Bel. And do you find a difficulty in raising that sum upon your pay? 'Tis done every day.

Dud. The nature of the climate makes it difficult: I can get no one to insure my life.

Bel. Oh! that's a circumstance may make for you, as well as against; in short, Captain Dudley, it so happens that I can command the sum of two hundred pounds: seek no farther; I'll accommodate you with it upon easy terms.

Dud. Sir! do I understand you rightly?—I beg your pardon; but am I to believe that you are in earnest?

Bel. What is your surprise? Is it an uncommon thing for a gentleman to speak truth? Or is it incredible that one fellow-creature should assist another?

Dud. I ask your pardon—May I beg to know to whom? Do you propose this in the way of business?

Bel. Entirely: I have no other business on earth.

Dud. Indeed! you are not a broker, I'm persuaded.

Bel. I am not.

Dud. Nor an army agent I think?

Bel. I hope you will not think the worse of me for being neither; in short, sir, if you will peruse this paper, it will explain to you who I am, and upon what terms I act; while you read it, I will step home, and fetch the money; and we will conclude the bargain without loss of time. In the meanwhile, good day to you. (*Exit hastily.*

Dud. Humph! there's something very odd in all this—let me see what we've got here.—This paper is to tell me who he is, and what are his terms: in the name of wonder, why has he sealed it! Hey-day! what's here? Two bank-notes, of a hundred each! I can't comprehend what this means. Hold; here's a writing; perhaps that will show me. "Accept this trifle; pursue your fortune, and prosper." Am I in a dream? Is this a reality?

SCENE VIII

Enter MAJOR O'FLAHERTY

Major. Save you, my dear! Is it you now that are Captain Dudley, I would ask?—Whuh! What's the hurry the man's in? If 'tis the lad that run out of the shop you would overtake, you might as well stay where you are; by my soul he's as nimble as a Croat, you are a full hour's march in his rear—Ay, faith, you may as well turn back, and give over the pursuit. Well, Captain Dudley, if that's your name, there's a letter for you. Read, man; read it; and I'll have a word with you after you have done.

Dud. More miracles on foot! So, so, from Lady Rusport.

Major. You're right; it's from her ladyship.

Dud. Well, sir, I have cast my eye over it; 'tis short and peremptory; are you acquainted with the contents?

Major. Not at all, my dear; not at all.

Dud. Have you any message from Lady Rusport?

Major. Not a syllable, honey; only, when you've digested the letter, I've a little bit of a message to deliver you from myself.

Dud. And may I beg to know who yourself is?

Major. Dennis O'Flaherty, at your service; a poor major of grenadiers; nothing better.

Dud. So much for your name and title, sir; now be so good to favour me with your message.

Major. Why then, Captain, I must tell you I have promised Lady Rusport you shall do whatever it is she bids you to do in that letter there.

Dud. Ay, indeed; have you undertaken so much, Major, without knowing either what she commands, or what I can perform?

Major. That's your concern, my dear, not mine; I must keep my word, you know.

Dud. Or else, I suppose, you and I must measure swords.

Major. Upon my soul you've hit it.

Dud. That would hardly answer to either of us; you and I have, probably, had enough of fighting in our time before now.

Major. Faith and troth, Master Dudley, you may say that; 'tis thirty years, come the time, that I have followed the trade, and in a pretty many countries. Let me see—In the war before last I served in the Irish brigade, d'ye see; there, after bringing off the French monarch, I left his service, with a British bullet in my body, and this ribband in my button-hole. Last war I followed the fortunes of the German eagle, in the corps of grenadiers; there I had my belly full of fighting, and a plentiful scarcity of everything else. After six and twenty engagements, great and small, I went off, with this gash on my skull, and a kiss of the Empress Queen's sweet hand (Heaven bless it!) for my pains. Since the peace, my dear, I took a little turn with the Confederates there in Poland—but such another set of madcaps! —by the Lord Harry, I never knew what it was they were scuffling about.

Dud. Well, Major, I won't add another action to the list, you shall keep your promise with Lady Rusport; she requires me to leave London; I shall go in a few days, and you may take what credit you please from my compliance.

Major. Give me your hand, my dear boy! This will make her my own; when that's the case, we shall be brothers, you know, and we'll share her fortune between us.

Dud. Not so, Major; the man who marries Lady Rusport will have a fair title to her whole fortune without division. But, I hope your expectations of prevailing are founded upon good reasons.

Major. Upon the best grounds in the world. First, I think she will comply, because she is a woman; secondly, I am persuaded she won't hold out long, because she's a widow; and thirdly, I make sure of her, because I've married five wives (*en militaire,* Captain) and never failed yet; and, for what I know, they're all alive and merry at this very hour.

Dud. Well, sir, go on and prosper; if you can inspire Lady Rusport with half your charity, I shall think you deserve all her fortune; at present, I must beg your excuse: good morning to you.   (*Exit.*

Major. A good sensible man, and very much of a soldier; I did not care if I was better acquainted with him: but 'tis an awkward kind of country for that; the English, I observe, are close friends, but distant acquaintance. I suspect the old lady has not been over-generous to poor Dudley; I shall give her a little touch about that: upon my soul, I know but one excuse a person can have for giving nothing, and that is, like myself, having nothing to give.   (*Exit.*

SCENE IX

Scene changes to Lady Rusport's House. A dressing-room

Miss Rusport *and* Lucy

Char. Well, Lucy, you've dislodged the old lady at last; but methought you was a tedious time about it.

Lucy. A tedious time, indeed; I think they who have least to spare, contrive to throw the most away; I thought I should never have got her out of the house.

Char. Why, she's as deliberate in canvassing every article of her dress, as an ambassador would be in settling the preliminaries of a treaty.

Lucy. There was a new hood and handkerchief, that had come express from Holborn Hill on the occasion, that took as much time in adjusting——

Char. As they did in making, and she was as vain of them as an old maid of a young lover.

Lucy. Or a young lover of himself. Then, madam, this being a visit of great ceremony to a person of distinction, at the west end of the town, the old state chariot was dragged forth on the occasion, with strict charges to dress out the box with the leopard-skin hammer-cloth.

Char. Yes, and to hang the false tails on the miserable stumps of the old crawling cattle. Well, well, pray Heaven the crazy affair don't break down again with her!—at least till she gets to her journey's end.—But where's Charles Dudley? Run down,

dear girl, and be ready to let him in; I think he's as long in coming
as she was in going.

Lucy. Why, indeed, madam, you seem the more alert of the
two, I must say. (*Exit.*

Char. Now the deuce take the girl for putting that notion
into my head: I'm sadly afraid Dudley does not like me; so much
encouragement as I have given him to declare himself, I never
could get a word from him on the subject! This may be very
honourable, but upon my life it's very provoking. By the way,
I wonder how I look to-day. Oh! shockingly! hideously pale!
like a witch! This is the old lady's glass; and she has left some
of her wrinkles on it. How frightfully have I put on my cap! all
awry! and my hair dressed so unbecomingly! altogether, I'm a
most complete fright.

SCENE X

(CHARLES DUDLEY *comes in unobserved*)

Charles. That I deny.

Char. Ah!

Charles. Quarrelling with your glass, cousin? Make it up;
make it up and be friends; it cannot compliment you more than
by reflecting you as you are.

Char. Well, I vow, my dear Charles, that is delightfully said,
and deserves my very best curtsy: your flattery, like a rich
jewel, has a value not only from its superior lustre, but from its
extraordinary scarceness. I verily think this is the only civil
speech you ever directed to my person in your life.

Charles. And I ought to ask pardon of your good sense for
having done it now.

Char. Nay, now you relapse again: don't you know, if you
keep well with a woman on the great score of beauty, she'll
never quarrel with you on the trifling article of good sense?
But anything serves to fill up a dull yawning hour with an
insipid cousin; you have brighter moments, and warmer spirits,
for the dear girl of your heart.

Charles. Oh! fie upon you, fie upon you.

Char. You blush, and the reason is apparent: you are a novice
at hypocrisy; but no practice can make a visit of ceremony
pass for a visit of choice: love is ever before its time; friendship
is apt to lag a little after it. Pray, Charles, did you make any
extraordinary haste hither?

Charles. By your question, I see you acquit me of the impertinence of being in love.

Char. But why impertinence? Why the impertinence of being
in love? You have one language for me, Charles, and another
for the woman of your affection.

Charles. You are mistaken; the woman of my affection shall never hear any other language from me than what I use to you.

Char. I am afraid then you'll never make yourself understood by her.

Charles. It is not fit I should; there is no need of love to make me miserable; 'tis wretchedness enough to be a beggar.

Char. A beggar, do you call yourself! O Charles, Charles, rich in every merit and accomplishment, whom may you not aspire to? And why think you so unworthily of our sex, as to conclude there is not one to be found with sense to discern your virtue, and generosity to reward it?

Charles. You distress me; I must beg to hear no more.

Char. Well, I can be silent.—Thus does he always serve me, whenever I am about to disclose myself to him.

Charles. Why do you not banish me and my misfortunes for ever from your thoughts?

Char. Ay, wherefore do I not, since you never allowed me a place in yours? But go, sir, I have no right to stay you; go where your heart directs you; go to the happy, the distinguished fair one.

Charles. Now, by all that's good, you do me wrong: there is no such fair one for me to go to, nor have I an acquaintance among the sex, yourself excepted, which answers to that description.

Char. Indeed!

Charles. In very truth: there then let us drop the subject. May you be happy, though I never can!

Char. O Charles! give me your hand; if I have offended you, I ask your pardon: you have been long acquainted with my temper, and know how to bear with its infirmities.

Charles. Thus, my dear Charlotte, let us seal our reconciliation. (*Kissing her hand.*) Bear with thy infirmities! By Heaven, I know not any one failing in thy whole composition, except that of too great a partiality for an undeserving man.

Char. And you are now taking the very course to augment that failing. A thought strikes me: I have a commission that you must absolutely execute for me; I have immediate occasion for the sum of two hundred pounds; you know my fortune is shut up till I am of age; take this paltry box (it contains my ear-rings, and some other baubles I have no use for), carry it to our opposite neighbour, Mr. Stockwell (I don't know where else to apply), leave it as a deposit in his hands, and beg him to accommodate me with the sum.

Charles. Dear Charlotte, what are you about to do? How can you possibly want two hundred pounds?

Char. How can I possibly do without, it, you mean? Doesn't every lady want two hundred pounds? Perhaps I have lost it at play; perhaps I mean to win as much to it; perhaps I want it for two hundred different uses.

Charles. Pooh! pooh! all this is nothing; don't I know you never play?

Char. You mistake; I have a spirit to set not only this trifle, but my whole fortune, upon a stake; therefore make no wry faces, but do as I bid you: you will find Mr. Stockwell a very honourable gentleman.

LUCY *enters in haste*

Lucy. Dear madam, as I live, here comes the old lady in a hackney-coach.

Char. The old chariot has given her a second tumble. Away with you; you know your way out without meeting her: take the box, and do as I desire you.

Charles. I must not dispute your orders. Farewell!

(*Exeunt* CHARLES *and* CHARLOTTE.

SCENE XI

LADY RUSPORT *enters, leaning on* MAJOR O'FLAHERTY'S *arm*

Major. Rest yourself upon my arm; never spare it; 'tis strong enough: it has stood harder service han you can put it to.

Lucy. Mercy upon me, what is the matter; I am frightened out of my wits: has your ladyship had an accident?

Lady R. O Lucy; the most untoward one in nature: I know not how I shall repair it.

Major. Never go about to repair it, my lady; ev'n build a new one; 'twas but a crazy piece of business at best.

Lucy. Bless me, is the old chariot broke down with you again?

Lady R. Broke, child? I don't know what might have been broke, if, by great good fortune, this obliging gentleman had not been at hand to assist me.

Lucy. Dear madam, let me run and fetch you a cup of the cordial drops.

Lady R. Do, Lucy. Alas! sir, ever since I lost my husband, my poor nerves have been shook to pieces: there hangs his beloved picture; that precious relic, and a plentiful jointure, is all that remains to console me for the best of men.

Major. Let me see; i' faith a comely personage; by his fur cloak I suppose he was in the Russian service; and by the gold chain round his neck, I should guess he had been honoured with the Order of St. Catherine.

Lady R. No, no; he meddled with no St. Catherines: that's the habit he wore in his mayoralty; Sir Stephen was Lord Mayor of London: but he is gone, and has left me a poor, weak, solitary widow behind him.

Major. By all means, then, take a strong, able, hearty man to repair his loss: if such a plain fellow as one Dennis O'Flaherty can please you, I think I may venture to say, without any disparagement to the gentleman in the fur-gown there——

Lady R. What are you going to say? Don't shock my ears with any comparisons, I desire.

Major. Not I, by my soul; I don't believe there's any comparison in the case.

Lady R. Oh, are you come? Give me the drops; I'm all in a flutter.

Major. Hark'e, sweetheart, what are those same drops? Have you any more left in the bottle? I didn't care if I took a little sip of them myself.

Lucy. Oh, sir, they are called the cordial restorative elixir, or the nervous golden drops; they are only for ladies' cases.

Major. Yes, yes, my dear, there are gentlemen as well as ladies that stand in need of those same golden drops; they'd suit my case to a tittle.

Lady R. Well, Major, did you give old Dudley my letter, and will the silly man do as I bid him, and be gone?

Major. You are obeyed; he's on his march.

Lady R. That's well; you have managed this matter to perfection; I didn't think he would have been so easily prevailed upon.

Major. At the first word; no difficulty in life; 'twas the very thing he was determined to do, before I came; I never met a more obliging gentleman.

Lady R. Well, 'tis no matter, so I am but rid of him, and his distresses. Would you believe it, Major O'Flaherty, it was but this morning he sent a-begging to me for money to fit him out upon some wild-goose expedition to the coast of Africa, I know not where.

Major. Well, you sent him what he wanted?

Lady R. I sent him what he deserved, a flat refusal.

Major. You refused him!

Lady R. Most undoubtedly.

Major. You sent him nothing!

Lady R. Not a shilling.

Major. Good morning to you.—Your servant.   (*Going.*

Lady R. Hey-day! What ails the man? Where are you going?

Major. Out of your house, before the roof falls on my head— to poor Dudley, to share the little modicum that thirty years' hard service has left me; I wish it was more for his sake.

Lady R. Very well, sir; take your course; I shan't attempt to stop you; I shall survive it; it will not break my heart if I never see you more.

Major. Break your heart! No, o' my conscience will it not.— You preach, and you pray, and you turn up your eyes, and all the while you're as hard-hearted as a hyena—a hyena, truly! By my soul there isn't in the whole creation so savage an animal as a human creature without pity.   (*Exit.*

Lady R. A hyena, truly! Where did the fellow blunder upon that word? Now the deuce take him for using it, and the Macaronies for inventing it.

ACT III

SCENE I

A room in Stockwell's House

STOCKWELL and BELCOUR

Stock. Gratify me so far, however, Mr. Belcour, as to see Miss Rusport; carry her the sum she wants, and return the poor girl her box of diamonds, which Dudley left in my hands; you know what to say on the occasion better than I do; that part of your commission I leave to your own discretion, and you may season it with what gallantry you think fit.

Bel. You could not have pitched upon a greater bungler at gallantry than myself, if you had rummaged every company in the city, and the whole court of aldermen into the bargain. Part of your errand, however, I will do; but whether it shall be with an ill grace or a good one, depends upon the caprice of a moment, the humour of the lady, the mode of our meeting, and a thousand undefinable small circumstances that nevertheless determine us upon all the great occasions of life.

Stock. I persuade myself you will find Miss Rusport an ingenious, worthy, animated girl.

Bel. Why I like her the better as a woman; but name her not to me as a wife! No, if ever I marry, it must be a staid, sober, considerate damsel, with blood in her veins as cold as a turtle's; quick of scent as a vulture when danger's in the wind; wary and sharp-sighted as a hawk when treachery is on foot: with such a companion at my elbow, forever whispering in my ear— have a care of this man, he's a cheat; don't go near that woman, she's a jilt; overhead there's a scaffold, underfoot there's a well: Oh! sir, such a woman might lead me up and down this great city without difficulty or danger; but with a girl of Miss Rusport's complexion, heaven and earth, sir! we should be duped, undone, and distracted, in a fortnight.

Stock. Ha! ha! ha! Why you are become wondrous circumspect of a sudden, pupil; and if you can find such a prudent damsel as you describe, you have my consent—only beware how you choose; discretion is not the reigning quality amongst the fine ladies of the present time; and I think in Miss Rusport's particular I have given you no bad counsel.

Bel. Well, well, if you'll fetch me the jewels, I believe I can undertake to carry them to her; but as for the money, I'll have nothing to do with that; Dudley would be your fittest ambassador on that occasion; and, if I mistake not, the most agreeable to the lady.

Stock. Why, indeed, from what I know of the matter, it may not improbably be destined to find its way into his pockets.

(*Exit.*

Bel. Then, depend upon it, these are not the only trinkets she means to dedicate to Captain Dudley. As for me, Stockwell indeed wants me to marry; but till I can get this bewitching girl, this incognita, out of my head, I can never think of any other woman.

(*Servant enters, and delivers a letter*)

Hey-day! Where can I have picked up a correspondent already! 'Tis a most execrable manuscript.—Let me see— Martha Fulmer.—Who is Martha Fulmer? Pshaw! I won't be at the trouble of deciphering her damned pot-hooks. Hold, hold, hold; what have we got here!

"Dear Sir,

"I've discovered the lady you was so much smitten with, and can procure you an interview with her; if you can be as generous to a pretty girl as you was to a paltry old captain" (how did she find that out!), "you need not despair; come to me immediately; the lady is now in my house, and expects you.

"Yours,

"Martha Fulmer."

O thou dear, lovely, and enchanting paper, which I was about to tear into a thousand scraps, devoutly I entreat thy pardon! I have slighted thy contents, which are delicious; slandered thy characters, which are divine; and all the atonement I can make is implicitly to obey thy mandates.

Stockwell *returns*

Stock. Mr. Belcour, here are the jewels; this letter encloses bills for the money; and, if you will deliver it to Miss Rusport, you'll have no further trouble on that score.

Bel. Ah, sir! the letter which I've been reading disqualifies me for delivering the letter which you have been writing: I have other game on foot; the loveliest girl my eyes ever feasted upon is started in view, and the world cannot now divert me from pursuing her.

Stock. Hey-day! What has turned you thus on a sudden?

Bel. A woman: one that can turn, and overturn me and my tottering resolutions every way she will. Oh, sir, if this is folly in me, you must rail at Nature: you must chide the sun, that was vertical at my birth, and would not wink upon my nakedness, but swaddled me in the broadest, hottest glare of his meridian beams.

Stock. Mere rhapsody; mere childish rhapsody; the libertine's familiar plea.—Nature made us, 'tis true, but we are the responsible creators of our own faults and follies.

Bel. Sir!

Stock. Slave of every face you meet, some hussy has inveigled you, some handsome profligate (the town is full of them); and, when once fairly bankrupt in constitution, as well as fortune, nature no longer serves as your excuse for being vicious; necessity, perhaps, will stand your friend, and you'll reform.

Bel. You are severe.

Stock. It fits me to be so—it well becomes a father——I would say a friend. [*Aside.*] How strangely I forget myself—How difficult it is to counterfeit indifference, and put a mask upon the heart.—I've struck him hard; he reddens.

Bel. How could you tempt me so? Had you not inadvertently dropped the name of father, I fear our friendship, short as it has been, would scarce have held me.—But even your mistake I reverence.—Give me your hand—'tis over.

Stock. Generous young man—let me embrace you.—How shall I hide my tears? I have been to blame; because I bore you the affection of a father, I rashly took up the authority of one. I ask your pardon—pursue your course; I have no right to stop it.—What would you have me do with these things?

Bel. This, if I might advise. Carry the money to Miss Rusport immediately; never let generosity wait for its materials; that part of the business presses. Give me the jewels; I'll find an opportunity of delivering them into her hands; and your visit may pave the way for my reception. (*Exit.*

Stock. Be it so: good morning to you. Farewell advice! Away goes he upon the wing for pleasure. What various passions he awakens in me! He pains, yet pleases me; affrights, offends, yet grows upon my heart. His very failings set him off—forever trespassing, forever atoning, I almost think he would not be so perfect, were he free from fault. I must dissemble longer; and yet how painful the experiment!—Even now he's gone upon some wild adventure; and who can tell what mischief may befall him! O Nature, what it is to be a father! Just such a thoughtless headlong thing was I when I beguiled his mother into love. (*Exit.*

SCENE II

Scene changes to Fulmer's House

FULMER *and his* WIFE

Ful. I tell you, Patty, you are a fool to think of bringing him and Miss Dudley together; 'twill ruin everything, and blow your whole scheme up to the moon at once.

Mrs. F. Why, sure, Mr. Fulmer, I may be allowed to rear a

chicken of my own hatching, as they say. Who first sprung the thought but I, pray? Who first contrived the plot? Who proposed the letter, but I, I?

Ful. And who dogged the gentleman home? Who found out his name, fortune, connection; that he was a West Indian, fresh landed, and full of cash; a gull to our hearts' content; a hot-brained headlong spark, that would run into our trap like a wheatear under a turf?

Mrs. F. Hark! he's come. Disappear, march; and leave the field open to my machinations.   (*Exit* FULMER.

SCENE III

BELCOUR *enters to her*

Bel. O thou dear minister to my happiness, let me embrace thee! Why thou art my polar star, my propitious constellatoin, by which I navigate my impatient bark into the port of pleasure and delight.

Mrs. F. Oh, you men are sly creatures! Do you remember now, you cruel, what you said to me this morning?

Bel. All a jest, a frolic; never think on't; bury it for ever in oblivion; thou! why thou art all over nectar and ambrosia, powder of pearl and odour of roses; thou hast the youth of Hebe, the beauty of Venus, and the pen of Sappho. But in the name of all that's lovely, where's the lady? I expected to find her with you.

Mrs. F. No doubt you did, and these raptures were designed for her; but where have you loitered? The lady's gone, you are too late; girls of her sort are not to be kept waiting like negro slaves in your sugar plantations.

Bel. Gone! whither is she gone? Tell me that I may follow her.

Mrs. F. Hold, hold, not so fast, young gentleman, this is a case of some delicacy; should Captain Dudley know that I introduced you to his daughter, he is a man of such scrupulous honour——

. *Bel.* What do you tell me! is she daughter to the old gentleman I met here this morning?

Mrs. F. The same; him you was so generous to.

Bel. There's an end of the matter then at once; it shall never be said of me that I took advantage of the father's necessities to trepan the daughter.   (*Going.*

Mrs. F. So, so, I've made a wrong cast, he's one of your conscientious sinners I find; but I won't lose him thus—Ha! ha! ha!

Bel. What is it you laugh at?

Mrs. F. Your absolute inexperience: have you lived so very little time in this country as not to know that between young people of equal ages, the term of sister often is a cover for that of mistress? This young lady is, in that sense of the word, sister to young Dudley, and consequently daughter to my old lodger.

Bel. Indeed! are you serious?

Mrs. F. Can you doubt it? I must have been pretty well assured of that before I invited you hither.

Bel. That's true; she cannot be a woman of honour, and Dudley is an unconscionable young rogue to think of keeping one fine girl in pay, by raising contributions on another; he shall therefore give her up; she is a dear, bewitching, mischievous, little devil, and he shall positively give her up.

Mrs. F. Ay, now the freak has taken you again; I say give her up; there's one way, indeed, and certain of success.

Bel. What's that?

Mrs. F. Outbid him, never dream of out-blustering him; buy out his lease of possession, and leave her to manage his ejectment.

Bel. Is she so venal? Never fear me then; when beauty is the purchase, I shan't think much of the price.

Mrs. F. All things, then, will be made easy enough. Let me see; some little genteel present to begin with: what have you got about you? Ay, search; I can bestow it to advantage, there's no time to be lost.

Bel. Hang it, confound it; a plague upon't, say I! I haven't a guinea left in my pocket; I parted from my whole stock here this morning, and have forgot to supply myself since.

Mrs. F. Mighty well, let it pass then; there's an end; think no more of the lady, that's all.

Bel. Distraction! think no more of her? Let me only step home and provide myself, I'll be back with you in an instant.

Mrs. F. Pooh, pooh! that's a wretched shift: have you nothing of value about you? Money's a coarse slovenly vehicle, fit only to bribe electors in a borough; there are more graceful ways of purchasing a lady's favours—rings, trinkets, jewels!

Bel. Jewels! Gadso, I protest I had forgot; I have a case of jewels; but they won't do, I must not part from them; no, no, they are appropriated; they are none of my own.

Mrs. F. Let me see, let me see! Ay, now, this were something like: pretty creatures, how they sparkle! these would ensure success.

Bel. Indeed!

Mrs. F. These would make her your own for ever.

Bel. Then the deuce take 'em for belonging to another persons I could find in my heart to give 'em the girl, and swear I've lost them.

Mrs. F. Ay, do, say they were stolen out of your pocket.

Bel. No, hang it, that's dishonourable. Here, give me the paltry things, I'll write you an order on my merchant for double their value.

Mrs. F. An order! No; order for me no orders upon merchants, with their value received, and three days' grace; their noting, protesting, and endorsing, and all their counting-house formalities; I'll have nothing to do with them; leave your diamonds with me, and give your order for the value of them to the owner: the money would be as good as the trinkets, I warrant you.

Bel. Hey! how! I never thought of that; but a breach of trust! 'tis impossible; I never can consent therefore give me the jewels back again.

Mrs. F. Take 'em; I am now to tell you the lady is in this house!

Bel. In this house?

Mrs. F. Yes, sir, in this very house; but what of that? you have got what you like better; your toys, your trinkets. Go, go: Oh! you're a man of a notable spirit, are you not?

Bel. Provoking creature! Bring me to the sight of the dear girl, and dispose of me as you think fit.

Mrs. F. And of the diamonds too?

Bel. Damn 'em, I would there was not such a bauble in nature! But come, come, dispatch; if I had the throne of Delhi I should give it to her.

Mrs. F. Swear to me then that you will keep within bounds; remember she passes for the sister of young Dudley. Oh! if you come to your flights, and your rhapsodies, she'll be off in an instant.

Bel. Never fear me.

Mrs. F. You must expect to hear her talk of her father, as she calls him, and her brother, and your bounty to her family.

Bel. Ay, ay, never mind what she talks of, only bring her.

Mrs. F. You'll be prepared upon that head?

Bel. I shall be prepared, never fear; away with you.

Mrs. F. But hold, I had forgot: not a word of the diamonds; leave that matter to my management.

Bel. Hell and vexation! Get out of the room, or I shall run distracted. (*Exit* MRS. FULMER.) Of a certain, Belcour, thou art born to be the fool of woman: sure no man sins with so much repentance, or repents with so little amendment, as I do. I cannot give away another person's property, honour forbids me; and I positively cannot give up the girl; love, passion, constitution, everything protests against that. How shall I decide? I cannot bring myself to break a trust, and I am not at present in the humour to balk my inclinations. Is there no middle way? Let me consider.—There is, there is: my good genius has presented me with one; apt, obvious, honourable: the girl shall not go without her baubles, I'll not go without the girl, Miss Rusport shan't lose her diamonds, I'll save Dudley from destruction, and every party shall be a gainer by the project.

SCENE IV

Mrs. Fulmer *introducing* Miss Dudley

Mrs. F. Miss Dudley, this is the worthy gentleman you wish to see; this is Mr. Belcour.

Louisa. As I live, the very man that beset me in the streets!
                                                    (*Aside.*

Bel. An angel, by this light! Oh, I am gone past all retrieving!
                                                    (*Aside.*

Louisa. Mrs. Fulmer, sir, informs me you are the gentleman from whom my father has received such civilities.

Bel. Oh, never name 'em!

Louisa. Pardon me, Mr. Belcour, they must be both named and remembered; and if my father was here——

Bel. I am much better pleased with his representative.

Louisa. That title is my brother's, sir; I have no claim to it.

Bel. I believe it.

Louisa. But as neither he nor my father were fortunate enough to be at home, I could not resist the opportunity——

Bel. Nor I neither, by my soul, madam: let us improve it, therefore. I am in love with you to distraction; I was charmed at the first glance; I attempted to accost you; you fled; I followed; but was defeated of an interview; at length I have obtained one, and seize the opportunity of casting my person and my fortune at your feet.

Louisa. You astonish me! Are you in your senses, or do you make a jest of my misfortunes? Do you ground pretences on your generosity, or do you make a practice of this folly with every woman you meet?

Bel. Upon my life, no: as you are the handsomest woman I ever met, so you are the first to whom I ever made the like professions: as for my generosity, madam, I must refer you on that score to this good lady, who I believe has something to offer in my behalf.

Louisa. Don't build upon that, sir; I must have better proofs of your generosity, than the mere divestment of a little superfluous dross, before I can credit the sincerity of professions so abruptly delivered.   (*Exit hastily.*

Bel. O ye gods and goddesses, how her anger animates her beauty!   (*Going out.*

Mrs. F. Stay, sir; if you stir a step after her, I renounce your interest for ever: why you'll ruin everything.

Bel. Well, I must have her, cost what it will: I see she understands her own value though. A little superfluous dross, truly! She must have better proofs of my generosity.

Mrs. F. 'Tis exactly as I told you; your money she calls dross; she's too proud to stain her fingers with your coin; bait your hook well with jewels; try that experiment, and she's your own.

Bel. Take 'em; let 'em go; lay 'em at her feet; I must get out of the scrape as I can; my propensity is irresistible. There, you have 'em; they are yours; they are hers; but remember they are a trust; I commit them to her keeping till I can buy 'em off with something she shall think more valuable. Now tell me when shall I meet her?

Mrs. F. How can I tell that? Don't you see what an alarm you have put her into? Oh, you're a rare one! But go your ways for this while; leave her to my management, and come to me at seven this evening; but remember not to bring empty pockets with you—Ha, ha! ha! (*Exeunt severally.*)

SCENE V

Lady Rusport's House

MISS RUSPORT *enters, followed by a Servant*

Char. Desire Mr. Stockwell to walk in. (*Exit Servant.*

STOCKWELL *enters*

Stock. Madam, your most obedient servant. I am honoured with your commands, by Captain Dudley, and have brought the money with me as you directed; I understand the sum you have occasion for is two hundred pounds.

Char. It is, sir. I am quite confounded at your taking this trouble upon yourself, Mr. Stockwell.

Stock. There is a bank-note, madam, to the amount: your jewels are in safe hands, and will be delivered to you directly. If I had been happy in being better known to you, I should have hoped you would not have thought it necessary to place a deposit in my hands for so trifling a sum as you have now required me to supply you with.

Char. The baubles I sent you may very well be spared; and, as they are the only security in my present situation, I can give you, I could wish you would retain them in your hands: when I am of age (which, if I live a few months, I shall be) I will replace your favour, with thanks.

Stock. It is obvious, Miss Rusport, that your charms will suffer no impeachment by the absence of those superficial ornaments; but they should be seen in the suite of a woman of fashion, not as creditors to whom you are indebted for your appearance, but as subservient attendants, which help to make up your equipage.

Char. Mr. Stockwell is determined not to wrong the confidence I reposed in his politeness.

Stock. I have only to request, madam, that you will allow Mr. Belcour, a young gentleman in whose happiness I particularly interest myself, to have the honour of delivering you the box of jewels.

Char. Most gladly; any friend of yours cannot fail of being welcome here.

Stock. I flatter myself you will not find him totally undeserving your good opinion; an education not of the strictest kind, and strong animal spirits, are apt sometimes to betray him into youthful irregularities; but a high principle of honour, and an uncommon benevolence, in the eye of candour, will, I hope, atone for any faults by which these good qualities are not impaired.

Char. I dare say Mr. Belcour's behaviour wants no apology: we've no right to be over-strict in canvassing the morals of a common acquaintance.

Stock. I wish it may be my happiness to see Mr. Belcour in the list, not of your common, but particular acquaintance, of your friends, Miss Rusport—I dare not be more explicit.

Char. Nor need you, Mr. Stockwell: I shall be studious to deserve his friendship; and, though I have long since unalterably placed my affections on another, I trust I have not left myself insensible to the merits of Mr. Belcour; and hope that neither you nor he will, for that reason, think me less worthy your good opinion and regards.

Stock. Miss Rusport, I sincerely wish you happy: I have no doubt you have placed your affection on a deserving man; and I have no right to combat your choice.   (*Exit.*

Char. How honourable is that behaviour! Now, if Charles was here, I should be happy. The old lady is so fond of her new Irish acquaintance, that I have the whole house at my disposal.   (*Exit.*

SCENE VI

BELCOUR *enters, preceded by a Servant*

Serv. I ask your honour's pardon; I thought my young lady was here: who shall I inform her would speak to her?

Bel. Belcour is my name, sir; and pray beg your lady to put herself in no hurry on my account; for I'd sooner see the devil than see her face. (*Exit Servant.*) In the name of all that's mischievous, why did Stockwell drive me hither in such haste? A pretty figure, truly, I shall make: an ambassador without credentials. Blockhead that I was to charge myself with her diamonds; officious, meddling puppy! Now they are irretrievably gone: that suspicious jade Fulmer wouldn't part even with a sight of them, though I would have ransomed 'em at twice their value. Now must I trust to my poor wits to bring me off: a lamentable dependence. Fortune be my helper! Here comes the girl. —If she is noble minded, as she is said to be, she will forgive me; if not, 'tis a lost cause; for I have not thought of one word in my excuse.

SCENE VII

CHARLOTTE *enters*

Char. Mr. Belcour, I'm proud to see you: your friend, Mr. Stockwell, prepared me to expect this honour; and I am happy in the opportunity of being known to you.

Bel. A fine girl, by my soul! Now what a cursed hang-dog do I look like!   (*Aside.*

Char. You are newly arrived in this country, sir?

Bel. Just landed, madam; just set ashore, with a large cargo of Muscovado sugars, rum-puncheons, mahogany-slabs, wet sweetmeats, and green paroquets.

Char. May I ask you how you like London, sir?

Bel. To admiration: I think the town and the townsfolk are exactly suited: 'tis a great, rich, overgrown, noisy, tumultuous place: the whole morning is a bustle to get money, and the whole afternoon is a hurry to spend it.

Char. Are these all the observations you have made?

Bel. No, madam; I have observed the women are very captivating, and the men very soon caught.

Char. Ay, indeed! Whence do you draw that conclusion?

Bel. From infallible guides; the first remark I collect from what I now see, the second from what I now feel.

Char. Oh, the deuce take you! But to waive this subject; I believe, sir, this was a visit of business, not compliment; was it not?

Bel. Ay; now comes on my execution.

Char. You have some foolish trinkets of mine, Mr. Belcour; haven't you?

Bel. No, in truth; they are gone in search of a trinket, still more foolish than themselves.   (*Aside.*

Char. Some diamonds I mean, sir; Mr. Stockwell informed me you was charged with 'em.

Bel. Oh .yes, madam; but I have the most treacherous memory in life.—Here they are! Pray put them up; they're all right; you need not examine 'em.   (*Gives a box.*

Char. Hey-day! right, sir! Why these are not my diamonds; these are quite different, and, as it should seem, of much greater value.

Bel. Upon my life I'm glad on't; for then I hope you value 'em more than your own.

Char. As a purchaser I should, but not as an owner; you mistake; these belong to somebody else.

Bel. 'Tis yours, I'm afraid, that belong to somebody else.

Char. What is it you mean? I must insist upon your taking 'em back again.

Bel. Pray, madam, don't do that; I shall infallibly lose them; I have the worst luck with diamonds of any man living.

Char. That you might well say, was you to give me these in the place of mine. But pray, sir, what is the reason of all this? Why have you changed the jewels? and where have you disposed of mine?

Bel. Miss Rusport, I cannot invent a lie for my life; and, if it was to save it, I couldn't tell one. I am an idle, dissipated, unthinking fellow, not worth your notice: in short, I am a West Indian; and you must try me according to the charter of my colony, not by a jury of English spinsters. The truth is, I've given away your jewels; caught with a pair of sparkling eyes, whose lustre blinded theirs, I served your property as I should my own, and lavished it away. Let me not totally despair of your forgiveness: I frequently do wrong, but never with impunity; if your displeasure is added to my own, my punishment will be too severe. When I parted from the jewels, I had not the honour of knowing their owner.

Char. Mr. Belcour, your sincerity charms me; I enter at once into your character, and I make all the allowances for it you can desire. I take your jewels for the present, because I know there is no other way of reconciling you to yourself; but, if I give way to your spirit in one point, you must yield to mine in another: remember I will not keep more than the value of my own jewels: there is no need to be pillaged by more than one woman at a time, sir.

Bel. Now, may every blessing that can crown your virtues, and reward your beauty, be showered upon you; may you meet admiration without envy, love without jealousy, and old age without malady; may the man of your heart be ever constant, and you never meet a less penitent, or less grateful offender, than myself!

Servant enters and delivers a letter

Char. Does your letter require such haste?

Serv. I was bade to give it into your own hands, madam.

Char. From Charles Dudley, I see—have I your permission? Good Heaven, what do I read! Mr. Belcour, you are concerned in this—" Dear Charlotte, in the midst of our distress, Providence has cast a benefactor in our way, after the most unexpected manner. A young West Indian, rich, and with a warmth of heart peculiar to his climate, has rescued my father from his troubles, satisfied his wants, and enabled him to accomplish his exchange: when I relate to you the manner in which this was done, you will be charmed; I can only now add, that it was by chance we found out that his name is Belcour, and that he is a friend of Mr. Stockwell's. I lose not a moment's time in making you acquainted with this fortunate event, for reasons which delicacy obliges me to suppress; but, perhaps, if you have not received the money on your jewels, you will not think it necessary now to do it. I have the honour to be,

"Dear Madam,

"most faithfully yours,

"CHARLES DUDLEY."

Is this your doing, sir? Never was generosity so worthily exerted.

Bel. Or so greatly overpaid.

Char. After what you have now done for this noble, but indigent family, let me not scruple to unfold the whole situation of my heart to you. Know then, sir (and don't think the worse of me for the frankness of my declaration), that such is my attachment to the son of that worthy officer, whom you relieved, that the moment I am of age, and in possession of my fortune, I should hold myself the happiest of women to share it with young Dudley.

Bel. Say you so, madam! then let me perish if I don't love and reverence you above all womankind; and, if such is your generous resolution, never wait till you're of age; life is too short, pleasure too fugitive; the soul grows narrower every hour; I'll equip you for your escape; I'll convey you to the man of your heart, and away with you then to the first hospitable parson that will take you in.

Char. O blessed be the torrid zone for ever, whose rapid vegetation quickens nature into such benignity! These latitudes are made for politics and philosophy; friendship has no root in this soil. But, had I spirit to accept your offer, which is not improbable, wouldn't it be a mortifying thing for a fond girl to find herself mistaken, and sent back to her home like a vagrant! and such, for what I know, might be my case.

Bel. Then he ought to be proscribed the society of mankind for ever.—Ay, ay, 'tis the sham sister that makes him thus indifferent: 'twill be a meritorious office to take that girl out of the way.

SCENE VIII

Servant enters

Serv. Miss Dudley to wait on you, madam.

Bel. Who?

Serv. Miss Dudley.

Char. What's the matter, Mr. Belcour? Are you frighted at the name of a pretty girl? 'Tis the sister of him we were speaking of.—Pray admit her.

Bel. The sister! So, so; he has imposed upon her too—this is an extraordinary visit, truly. Upon my soul, the assurance of some folks is not to be accounted for.

Char. I insist upon your not running away; you'll be charmed with Louisa Dudley.

Bel. Oh, yes, I am charmed with her.

Char. You've seen her then, have you?

Bel. Yes, yes, I've seen her.

Char. Well, isn't she a delightful girl?

Bel. Very delightful.

Char. Why, you answer as if you was in a court of justice. O' my conscience! I believe you are caught; I've a notion she has tricked you out of your heart.

Bel. I believe she has, and you out of your jewels; for, to tell you the truth, she's the very person I gave 'em to.

Char. You gave her my jewels! Louisa Dudley my jewels? Admirable! inimitable! Oh, the sly little jade! But hush, here she comes; I don't know how I shall keep my countenance. (LOUISA *enters.*) My dear, I'm rejoiced to see you; how d'ye do? I beg leave to introduce Mr. Belcour, a very worthy friend of mine: I believe, Louisa, you have seen him before.

Louisa. I have met the gentleman.

Char. You have met the gentleman: well, sir, and you have met the lady; in short, you have met each other; why then don't you speak to each other? How you both stand! tongue-tied, and fixed as statues—Ha! ha! ha! Why you'll fall asleep by and by.

Louisa. Fie upon you; fie upon you; is this fair?

Bel. Upon my soul, I never looked so like a fool in my life, the assurance of that girl puts me quite down. *(Aside.*

Char. Sir — Mr. Belcour—was it your pleasure to advance anything? Not a syllable. Come, Louisa, women's wit, they say, is never at a loss.—Nor you neither? Speechless both.—Why you was merry enough before this lady came in.

Louisa. I am sorry I have been any interruption to your happiness, sir.

Bel. Madam!

Char. Madam! Is that all you can say? But come, my dear girl, I won't tease you. Apropos! I must show you what a present this dumb gentleman has made me. Are not these handsome diamonds?

Louisa. Yes, indeed, they seem very fine; but I am no judge of these things.

Char. Oh, you wicked little hypocrite, you are no judge of these things, Louisa; you have no diamonds, not you.

Louisa. You know I haven't, Miss Rusport: you know those things are infinitely above my reach.

Char. Ha! ha! ha!

Bel. She does tell a lie with an admirable countenance, that's true enough.

Louisa. What ails you, Charlotte? What impertinence have I been guilty of that you should find it necessary to humble me at such a rate? If you are happy, long may you be so; but, surely, it can be no addition to it to make me miserable.

Char. So serious! there must be some mystery in this.—Mr. Belcour, will you leave us together? You see I treat you with all the familiarity of an old acquaintance already.

Bel. Oh, by all means, pray command me, Miss Rusport, I'm your most obedient! By your condescension in accepting these poor trifles, I am under eternal obligations to you.—To you, Miss Dudley, I shall not offer a word on that subject: you despise finery; you have a soul above it; I adore your spirit; I was rather unprepared for meeting you here; but I shall hope for an opportunity of making myself better known to you. (*Exit.*)

SCENE IX

CHARLOTTE *and* LOUISA

Char. Louisa Dudley, you surprise me; I never saw you act thus before. Can't you bear a little innocent raillery before the man of your heart?

Louisa. The man of my heart, madam? Be assured I never was so visionary to aspire to any man whom Miss Rusport honours with her choice.

Char. My choice, my dear! Why we are playing at cross-purposes. How entered it into your head that Mr. Belcour was the man of my choice?

Louisa. Why, didn't he present you with those diamonds?

Char. Well, perhaps he did—and pray, Louisa, have you no diamonds?

Louisa. I diamonds truly! Who should give me diamonds?

Char. Who but this very gentleman. Apropos! here comes your brother——

SCENE X

CHARLES *enters*

I insist upon referring our dispute to him. Your sister and I, Charles, have a quarrel. Belcour, the hero of your letter, has just left us—somehow or other, Louisa's bright eyes have caught him; and the poor fellow's fallen desperately in love with her.—(Don't interrupt me, hussy.)—Well, that's excusable enough, you'll say; but the jet of the story is, that this hare-brained spark, who does nothing like other people, has given her the very identical jewels, which you pledged for me to Mr. Stockwell. And will you believe that this little demure slut made up a face, and squeezed out three or four hypocritical tears, because I rallied her about it!

Charles. I'm all astonishment! Louisa, tell me without reserve, has Mr. Belcour given you any diamonds?

Louisa. None, upon my honour.

Charles. Has he made any professions to you?

Louisa. He has; but altogether in a style so whimsical and capricious, that the best which can be said of them is to tell you, that they seemed more the result of good spirits than good manners.

Char. Ay, ay, now the murder's out; he's in love with her, and she has no very great dislike to him: trust to my observation, Charles, for that. As to the diamonds, there's some mistake about them, and you must clear it up: three minutes' conversation with him will put everything in a right train. Go, go, Charles, 'tis a brother's business; about it instantly; ten to one you'll find him over the way at Mr. Stockwell's.

Charles. I confess I'm impatient to have the case cleared up; I'll take your advice, and find him out. Good-bye to you.

Char. Your servant; my life upon it you'll find Belcour a man of honour. Come, Louisa, let us adjourn to my dressing-room; I've a little private business to transact with you, before the old lady comes up to tea and interrupts us.

ACT IV

SCENE I

Fulmer's House

FULMER *and* MRS. FULMER

Ful. Patty, wasn't Mr. Belcour with you?

Mrs. F. He was; and is now shut up in my chamber, in high expectation of an interview with Miss Dudley; she's at present with her brother, and 'twas with some difficulty I persuaded my hot-headed spark to wait till he has left her.

Ful. Well, child, and what then?

Mrs. F. Why then, Mr. Fulmer, I think it will be time for you and me to steal a march and be gone.

Ful. So this is all the fruit of your ingenious project; a shameful overthrow, or a sudden flight.

Mrs. F. Why, my project was a mere impromptu, and can at worst but quicken our departure a few days; you know we had fairly outlived our credit here, and a trip to Boulogne is no ways unseasonable. Nay, never droop, man.—Hark! hark! here's enough to bear charges.   (*Showing a purse.*

Ful. Let me see, let me see: this weighs well; this is of the right sort: why your West Indian bled freely.

Mrs. F. But that's not all: look here! Here are the sparklers! (*Showing the jewels.*) Now what d'ye think of my performances? Heh? a foolish scheme, isn't it—a silly woman——?

Ful. Thou art a Judith, a Joan of Arc, and I'll march under thy banners, girl, to the world's end. Come let's begone; I've little to regret; my creditors may share the old books amongst them; they'll have occasion for philosophy to support their loss; they'll find enough upon my shelves: the world is my library; I read mankind.—Now, Patty, lead the way.

Mrs. F. Adieu, Belcour!

(*Exeunt.*

SCENE II

Charles Dudley *and* Louisa

Charles. Well, Louisa, I confess the force of what you say: I accept Miss Rusport's bounty; and, when you see my generous Charlotte, tell her—but have a care, there is a selfishness even in gratitude, when it is too profuse; to be overthankful for any one favour, is in effect to lay out for another; the best return I could make my benefactress would be never to see her more.

Louisa. I understand you.

Charles. We that are poor, Louisa, should be cautious; for this reason, I would guard you against Belcour; at least till I can unravel the mystery of Miss Rusport's diamonds. I was disappointed of finding him at Mr. Stockwell's, and am now going in search of him again: he may intend honourably, but, I confess to you, I am staggered; think no more of him, therefore, for the present. Of this be sure, while I have life, and you have honour, I will protect you, or perish in your defence. (*Exit.*

Louisa. Think of him no more! Well, I'll obey; but if a wandering uninvited thought should creep by chance into my bosom, must I not give the harmless wretch a shelter? Oh yes! the great Artificer of the human heart knows every thread he wove into its fabric, nor puts his work to harder uses than it was made to bear. My wishes then, my guiltless ones, I mean, are free: how fast they spring within me at that sentence! Down, down, ye busy creatures! Whither would you carry me? Ah! there is one amongst you, a forward, new intruder, that, in the likeness of an offending, generous man, grows into favour with my heart. Fie, fie upon it! Belcour pursues, insults me; yet, such is the fatality of my condition, that what should rouse resentment, only calls up love.

SCENE III

Belcour *enters to her*

Bel. Alone, by all that's happy!

Louisa. Ah!

Bel. Oh! shriek not, start not, stir not, loveliest creature! but let me kneel and gaze upon your beauties.

Louisa. Sir! Mr. Belcour, rise! What is it you do?

Bel. See, I obey you; mould me as you will, behold your ready servant! New to your country, ignorant of your manners, habits, and desires, I put myself into your hands for instruction; make me only such as you can like yourself, and I shall be happy.

Louisa. I must not hear this, Mr. Belcour. Go! Should he that parted from me but this minute, now return, I tremble for the consequence.

Bel. Fear nothing; let him come. I love you, madam; he'll find it hard to make me unsay that.

Louisa. You terrify me; your impetuous temper frightens me; you know my situation; it is not generous to pursue me thus.

Bel. True; I do know your situation, your real one, Miss Dudley, and am resolved to snatch you from it. 'Twill be a meritorious act: the old captain shall rejoice; Miss Rusport shall be made happy; and even he, even your beloved brother, with whose resentment you threaten me, shall in the end applaud and thank me. Come, thou'rt a dear enchanting girl, and I'm determined not to live a minute longer without thee.

Louisa. Hold, are you mad? I see you are a bold assuming man, and know not where to stop.

Bel. Who that beholds such beauty can? By Heaven, you put my blood into a flame. Provoking girl! is it within the stretch of my fortune to content you? What is it you can further ask that I am not ready to grant?

Louisa. Yes, with the same facility that you bestowed upon me Miss Rusport's diamonds. For shame! for shame! was that a manly story?

Bel. So! so! these devilish diamonds meet me everywhere. —Let me perish if I meant you any harm. Oh! I could tear my tongue out for saying a word about the matter.

Louisa. Go to her, then, and contradict it; till that is done, my reputation is at stake.

Bel. Her reputation! Now she has got upon that, she'll go on forever.—What is there I will not do for your sake? I will go to Miss Rusport.

Louisa. Do so; restore her own jewels to her, which I suppose you kept back for the purpose of presenting others to her of a greater value. But for the future, Mr. Belcour, when you would do a gallant action to that lady, don't let it be at my expense.

Bel. I see where she points: she is willing enough to give up Miss Rusport's diamonds, now she finds she shall be a gainer by the exchange. Be it so! 'tis what I wished.—Well, madam, I will return Miss Rusport her own jewels, and you shall have others of tenfold their value.

Louisa. No, sir, you err most widely; it is my good opinion, not my vanity, which you must bribe.

Bel. Why, what the devil would she have now?—Miss Dudley,

it is my wish to obey and please you, but I have some apprehension that we mistake each other.

Louisa. I think we do: tell me, then, in few words, what it is you aim at.

Bel. In few words, then, and in plain honesty, I must tell you, so entirely am I captivated with you, that had you but been such as it would have become me to have called my wife, I had been happy in knowing you by that name; as it is, you are welcome to partake my fortune, give me in return your person, give me pleasure, give me love; free, disencumbered, anti-matrimonial love.

Louisa. Stand off, and let me never see you more.

Bel. Hold, hold, thou dear, tormenting, tantalising girl! Upon my knees I swear you shall not stir till you've consented to my bliss.

Louisa. Unhand me, sir! O Charles! protect me, rescue me, redress me.   (*Exit.*

SCENE IV

CHARLES DUDLEY *enters*

Charles. How's this! Rise, villain, and defend yourself.

Bel. Villain!

Charles. The man who wrongs that lady is a villain.—Draw!

Bel. Never fear me, young gentleman; brand me for a coward, if I balk you.

Charles. Yet hold! Let me not be too hasty. Your name, I think, is Belcour.

Bel. Well, sir.

Charles. How is it, Mr. Belcour, you have done this mean unmanly wrong; beneath the mask of generosity to give this fatal stab to our domestic peace? You might have had my thanks, my blessing; take my defiance now. 'Tis Dudley speaks to you, the brother, the protector of that injured lady.

Bel. The brother? Give yourself a true title.

Charles. What is't you mean?

Bel. Come, come, I know both her and you. I found you, sir (but how or why I know not), in the good graces of Miss Rusport (yes, colour at the name!); I gave you no disturbance there, never broke in upon you in that rich and plenteous quarter; but, when I could have blasted all your projects with a word, spared you, in foolish pity spared you, nor roused her from the fond credulity in which your artifice had lulled her.

Charles. No, sir, nor boasted to her of the splendid present you had made my poor Louisa; the diamonds, Mr. Belcour. How was that? What can you plead to that arraignment?

Bel. You question me too late; the name of Belcour and of villain never met before; had you inquired of me before you uttered that rash word, you might have saved yourself or me a mortal error; now, sir, I neither give nor take an explanation; so, come on!   (*They fight.*

SCENE V

LOUISA, *and afterwards* [MAJOR] O'FLAHERTY

Louisa. Hold, hold, for Heaven's sake hold! Charles! Mr. Belcour! Help! Sir, sir, make haste, they'll murder one another.

Major. Hell and confusion! What's all this uproar for? Can't you leave off cutting one another's throats, and mind what the poor girl says to you? You've done a notable thing, haven't you both, to put her into such a flurry? I think, o' my conscience, she's the most frighted of the three.

Charles. Dear Louisa, recollect yourself; why did you interfere? 'Tis in your cause.

Bel. Now could I kill him for caressing her.

Major. O sir, your most obedient! You are the gentleman I had the honour of meeting here before; you was then running off at full speed like a Calmuck, now you are tilting and driving like a Bedlamite with this lad here, that seems as mad as yourself. 'Tis pity but your country had a little more employment for you both.

Bel. Mr. Dudley, when you've recovered the lady, you know where I am to be found.   (*Exit.*

Major. Well, then, can't you stay where you are, and that will save the trouble of looking after yon? Yon volatile fellow thinks to give a man the meeting by getting out of his way: by my soul 'tis a roundabout method that of his. But I think he called you Dudley. Hark'e, young man, are you son of my friend the old captain?

Charles. I am. Help me to convey this lady to her chamber, and I shall be more at leisure to answer your questions.

Major. Ay will I: come along, pretty one. If you've had wrong done you, young man, you need look no farther for a second; Dennis O'Flaherty's your man for that: but never draw your sword before a woman, Dudley; damn it, never while you live draw your sword before a woman.   (*Exeunt.*

SCENE VI

Lady Rusport's House

LADY RUSPORT *and Servant*

Serv. An elderly gentleman, who says his name is Varland, desires leave to wait on your ladyship.

Lady R. Show him in; the very man I wish to see: Varland, he was Sir Oliver's solicitor, and privy to all his affairs; he brings some good tidings; some fresh mortgage, or another bond come to light; they start up every day. (VARLAND *enters*.) Mr. Varland, I'm glad to see you; you're heartily welcome, honest Mr. Varland; you and I haven't met since our late irreparable loss: how have you passed your time this age?

Var. Truly, my lady, ill enough: I thought I must have followed good Sir Oliver.

Lady R. Alack-a-day, poor man! Well, Mr. Varland, you find me here overwhelmed with trouble and fatigue; torn to pieces with a multiplicity of affairs; a great fortune poured upon me unsought for and unexpected: 'twas my good father's will and pleasure it should be so, and I must submit.

Var. Your ladyship inherits under a will made in the year forty-five, immediately after Captain Dudley's marriage with your sister.

Lady R. I do so, Mr. Varland; I do so.

Var. I well remember it; I engrossed every syllable; but I am surprised to find your ladyship set so little store by this vast accession.

Lady R. Why you know, Mr. Varland, I am a moderate woman; I had enough before; a small matter satisfies me; and Sir Stephen Rusport (Heaven be his portion!) took care I shouldn't want that.

Var. Very true, very true, he did so; and I am overjoyed at finding your ladyship in this disposition; for, truth to say, I was not without apprehension the news I have to communicate would have been of some prejudice to your ladyship's tranquillity.

Lady R. News, sir! What news have you for me?

Var. Nay, nothing to alarm you; a trifle, in your present way of thinking: I have a will of Sir Oliver's you have never seen.

Lady R. A will! Impossible! How came you by it, pray?

Var. I drew it up, at his command, in his last illness: it will save you a world of trouble: it gives his whole estate from you to his grandson, Charles Dudley.

Lady R. To Dudley? His estate to Charles Dudley? I can't support it! I shall faint! You've killed me, you vile man! I never shall survive it!

Var. Look'e there now: I protest, I thought you would have rejoiced at being clear of the incumbrance.

Lady R. 'Tis false; 'tis all a forgery, concerted between you and Dudley; why else did I never hear of it before?

Var. Have patience, my lady, and I'll tell you. By Sir Oliver's direction, I was to deliver this will into no hands but his grandson Dudley's: the young gentleman happened to be then in Scotland; I was dispatched thither in search of him: the hurry and fatigue of my journey brought on a fever by the way, which confined me in extreme danger for several days; upon my recovery, I pursued my journey, found young Dudley had left Scotland in the interim, and am now directed hither; where, as soon as I can find him, doubtless, I shall discharge my conscience, and fulfil my commission.

Lady R. Dudley then, as yet, knows nothing of this will?

Var. Nothing; that secret rests with me.

Lady R. A thought occurs: by this fellow's talking of his conscience, I should guess it was upon sale.—(*Aside.*) Come, Mr. Varland, if 'tis as you say, I must submit. I was somewhat flurried at first, and forgot myself; I ask your pardon. This is no place to talk of business; step with me into my room; we will there compare the will and resolve accordingly.—Oh! would your fever had you, and I had your paper.   (*Exeunt.*

SCENE VII

Miss Rusport, Charles, *and* [Major] O'Flaherty

Char. So, so! my lady and her lawyer have retired to close confabulation. Now, Major, if you are the generous man I take you for, grant me one favour.

Major. Faith will I, and not think much of my generosity neither; for, though it may not be in my power to do the favour you ask, look you, it can never be in my heart to refuse it.

Charles. Could this man's tongue do justice to his thoughts, how eloquent would he be!   (*Aside.*

Char. Plant yourself then in that room: keep guard, for a few moments, upon the enemy's motions, in the chamber beyond; and, if they should attempt a sally, stop their march a moment, till your friend here can make good his retreat down the back stairs.

Major. A word to the wise! I'm an old campaigner; make the best use of your time; and trust me for tying the old cat up to the picket.

Char. Hush! hush! not so loud.

Charles. 'Tis the office of a sentinel, Major, you have undertaken, rather than that of a field-officer.

Major. 'Tis the office of a friend, my dear boy, and therefore, no disgrace to a general.   (*Exit.*

SCENE VIII

Charles *and* Charlotte

Char. Well, Charles, will you commit yourself to me for a few minutes?

Charles. Most readily; and let me, before one goes by, tender you the only payment I can ever make for your abundant generosity.

Char. Hold, hold! so vile a thing as money must not come between us. What shall I say! O Charles! O Dudley! What difficulties have you thrown upon me? Familiarly as we have lived, I shrink not at what I'm doing; and, anxiously as I have sought this opportunity, my fears almost persuade me to abandon it.

Charles. You alarm me!

Char. Your looks and actions have been so distant, and at this moment are so deterring, that, was it not for the hope that delicacy, and not disgust, inspires this conduct in you, I should sink with shame and apprehension; but time presses, and I must speak, and plainly too.—Was you now in possession of your grandfather's estate, as justly you ought to be; and, was you inclined to seek a companion for life, should you, or should you not, in that case, honour your unworthy Charlotte with your choice?

Charles. My unworthy Charlotte! So judge me Heaven, there is not a circumstance on earth so valuable as your happiness, so dear to me as your person; but to bring poverty, disgrace, reproach from friends, ridicule from all the world, upon a generous benefactress; thievishly to steal into an open, unreserved, ingenuous heart—O Charlotte! dear, unhappy girl, it is not to be done.

Char. Nay, now you rate too highly the poor advantages fortune alone has given me over you: how otherwise could we bring our merits to any balance? Come, my dear Charles, I have enough; make that enough still more, by sharing it with me: sole heiress of my father's fortune, a short time will put it in my disposal. In the meanwhile you will be sent to join your regiment; let us prevent a separation, by setting out this very night for that happy country where marriage still is free: carry me this moment to Belcour's lodgings.

Charles. Belcour's—the name is ominous; there's murder in it: bloody inexorable honour!   (*Aside.*

Char. D'ye pause? Put me into his hands, while you provide the means of our escape: he is the most generous, the most honourable of men.

Charles. Honourable! most honourable!

Char. Can you doubt it? Do you demur? Have you forgot your letter? Why, Belcour 'twas that prompted me to this proposal, that promised to supply the means, that nobly offered his unasked assistance——

[MAJOR] O'FLAHERTY *enters hastily*

Major. Run, run, for holy St. Antony's sake, to horse and away! The conference is broke up, and the old lady advances upon a full Piedmontese trot, within pistol-shot of your encampment.

Char. Here, here, down the back-stairs! O Charles, remember me!

Charles. Farewell! Now, now I feel myself a coward.   (*Exit.*

Char. What does he mean?

Major. Ask no questions, but be gone. [*Exit.* CHARLOTTE.] She has cooled the lad's courage, and wonders he feels like a coward. There's a damned deal of mischief brewing between this hyena and her lawyer: egad, I'll step behind this screen and listen: a good soldier must sometimes fight in ambush as well as open field. (*Retires.*

SCENE IX

LADY RUSPORT *and* VARLAND

Lady R. Sure I heard somebody. Hark! No; only the servants going down the back stairs. Well, Mr. Varland, I think then we are agreed: you'll take my money, and your conscience no longer stands in your way.

Var. Your father was my benefactor; his will ought to be sacred; but, if I commit it to the flames, how will he be the wiser? Dudley, 'tis true, has done me no harm; but five thousand pounds will do me much good; so, in short, madam, I take your offer. I will confer with my clerk, who witnessed the will; and to-morrow morning put it into your hands, upon condition you put five thousand good pounds into mine.

Lady R. 'Tis a bargain: I'll be ready for you. Farewell. (*Exit.*

Var. Let me consider.—Five thousand pounds prompt payment for destroying this scrap of paper, not worth five farthings; 'tis a fortune easily earned; yes, and 'tis another man's fortune easily thrown away: 'tis a good round sum to be paid down at once for a bribe; but 'tis a damned rogue's trick in me to take it.

Major. So, so! this fellow speaks truth to himself, though he lies to other people—but hush. (*Aside.*

Var. 'Tis breaking the trust of my benefactor; that's a foul crime; but he's dead, and can never reproach me with it: and 'tis robbing young Dudley of his lawful patrimony; that's a hard case; but he's alive, and knows nothing of the matter.

Major. These lawyers are so used to bring off the rogueries of others, that they are never without an excuse for their own. (*Aside.*

Var. Were I assured now that Dudley would give me half the money for producing this will, that Lady Rusport does for concealing it, I would deal with him, and be an honest man at half price; I wish every gentleman of my profession could lay his hand on his heart and say the same thing.

Major. A bargain, old gentleman! Nay, never start, nor stare; you wasn't afraid of your own conscience, never be afraid of me.

Var. Of you, sir! who are you, pray?

Major. I'll tell you who I am. You seem to wish to be honest, but want the heart to set about it; now I am the very man in the world to make you so; for, if you do not give me up that paper this very instant, by the soul of me, fellow, I will not leave one whole bone in your skin that shan't be broken.

Var. What right have you, pray, to take this paper from me?

Major. What right have you, pray, to keep it from young Dudley? I don't know what it contains, but I am apt to think it will be safer in my hands than in yours; therefore give it me without more words, and save yourself a beating: do now; you had best.

Var. Well, sir, I may as well make a grace of necessity. There! I have acquitted my conscience, at the expense of five thousand pounds.

Major. Five thousand pounds! Mercy upon me! When there are such temptations in the law, can we wonder if some of the corps are a disgrace to it?

Var. Well, you have got the paper; if you are an honest man, give it to Charles Dudley.

Major. An honest man! Look at me, friend; I am a soldier, this is not the livery of a knave; I am an Irishman, honey; mine is not the country of dishonour. Now, sirrah, begone; if you enter these doors, or give Lady Rusport the least item of what has passed, I will cut off both your ears, and rob the pillory of its due.

Var. I wish I was once fairly out of his sight.   (*Exeunt.*

SCENE X

A room in Stockwell's House

Stock. I must disclose myself to Belcour; this noble instance of his generosity, which old Dudley has been relating, allies me to him at once; concealment becomes too painful; I shall be proud to own him for my son.—But see, he's here.

BELCOUR *enters, and throws himself upon a sofa*

Bel. O my cursed tropical constitution! Would to Heaven I had been dropped upon the snows of Lapland, and never felt the blessed influence of the sun, so I had never burnt with these inflammatory passions!

Stock. So, so, you seem disordered, Mr. Belcour.

Bel. Disordered, sir! Why did I ever quit the soil in which I grew; what evil planet drew me from that warm sunny region, where naked nature walks without disguise, into this cold contriving artificial country?

Stock. Come, sir, you've met a rascal; what o' that? general conclusions are illiberal.

Bel. No, sir, I've met reflection by the way; I've come from folly, noise, and fury, and met a silent monitor.—Well, well, a villain! 'twas not to be pardoned.—Pray never mind me, sir.

Stock. Alas! my heart bleeds for him.

Bel. And yet, I might have heard him: now, plague upon that blundering Irishman for coming in as he did; the hurry of the deed might palliate the event: deliberate execution has less to plead.—Mr. Stockwell, I am bad company to you.

Stock. Oh, sir, make no excuse. I think you have not found me forward to pry into the secrets of your pleasures and pursuits; 'tis not my disposition; but there are times when want of curiosity would be want of friendship.

Bel. Ah, sir, mine is a case wherein you and I shall never think alike; the punctilious rules by which I am bound are not to be found in your ledgers, nor will pass current in the compting-house of a trader.

Stock. 'Tis very well, sir; if you think I can render you any service, it may be worth your trial to confide in me; if not, your secret is safer in your own bosom.

Bel. That sentiment demands my confidence: pray, sit down by me. You must know, I have an affair of honour on my hands with young Dudley; and though I put up with no man's insult, yet I wish to take away no man's life.

Stock. I know the young man, and am apprised of your generosity to his father; what can have bred a quarrel between you?

Bel. A foolish passion on my side, and a haughty provocation on his. There is a girl, Mr. Stockwell, whom I have unfortunately seen, of most uncommon beauty; she has withal an air of so much natural modesty, that had I not had good assurance of her being an attainable wanton, I declare I should as soon have thought of attempting the chastity of Diana.

Servant enters

Stock. Hey-dey, do you interrupt us?

Serv. Sir, there's an Irish gentleman will take no denial; he says he must see Mr. Belcour directly, upon business of the last consequence.

Bel. Admit him; 'tis the Irish officer that parted us, and brings me young Dudley's challenge; I should have made a long story of it, and he'll tell you in three words.

[MAJOR] O'FLAHERTY enters

Major. Save you, my dear; and you, sir! I have a little bit of a word in private for you.

Bel. Pray deliver your commands; this gentleman is my intimate friend.

Major. Why then, Ensign Dudley will be glad to measure swords with you, yonder, at the London Tavern, in Bishops-gate Street, at nine o'clock—you know the place?

Bel. I do; and shall observe the appointment.

Major. Will you be of the party, sir? We shall want a fourth hand.

Stock. Savage as the custom is, I close with your proposal; and though I am not fully informed of the occasion of your quarrel, I shall rely on Mr. Belcour's honour for the justice of it, and willingly stake my life in his defence.

Major. Sir, you're a gentleman of honour, and I shall be glad of being better known to you.—But hark'e, Belcour, I had like to have forgot part of my errand: there is the money you gave old Dudley; you may tell it over, faith; 'tis a receipt in full; now the lad can put you to death with a safe conscience, and when he has done that job for you, let it be a warning how you attempt the sister of a man of honour.

Bel. The sister?

Major. Ay, the sister; 'tis English, is it not? Or Irish; 'tis all one; you understand me—his sister, or Louisa Dudley, that's her name I think, call her which you will. By St. Patrick, 'tis a foolish piece of a business, Belcour, to go about to take away a poor girl's virtue from her, when there are so many to be met in this town who have disposed of theirs to your hands.

(Exit.

Stock. Why I am thunderstruck! What is it you have done, and what is the shocking business in which I have engaged? If I understood him right, 'tis the sister of young Dudley you've been attempting: you talked to me of a professed wanton; the girl he speaks of has beauty enough indeed to inflame your desires, but she has honour, innocence and simplicity to awe the most licentious passion. If you have done that, Mr. Belcour, I renounce you, I abandon you, I forswear all fellowship or friendship with you for ever.

Bel. Have patience for a moment; we do indeed speak of the same person, but she is not innocent, she is not young Dudley's sister.

Stock. Astonishing! who told you this?

Bel. The woman where she lodges; the person who put me on the pursuit and contrived our meetings.

Stock. What woman? What person?

Bel. Fulmer her name is. I warrant you I did not proceed without good grounds.

Stock. Fulmer, Fulmer! Who waits? (A *Servant enters.*) Send Mr. Stukely hither directly; I begin to see my way into this dark transaction. Mr. Belcour, Mr. Belcour, you are no match for the cunning and contrivances of this intriguing town. (STUKELY *enters.*) Prithee, Stukely, what is the name of the woman and her husband who were stopped upon suspicion of selling stolen diamonds at our next-door neighbour's, the jeweller?

Stukely. Fulmer.

Stock. So!

Bel. Can you procure me a sight of those diamonds?

Stukely. They are now in my hand; I was desired to show them to Mr. Stockwell.

Stock. Give 'em to me. What do I see? As I live, the very diamonds Miss Rusport sent hither, and which I entrusted to you to return.

Bel. Yes, but I betrayed that trust, and gave 'em Mrs. Fulmer to present to Miss Dudley.

Stock. With a view no doubt to bribe her to compliance?

Bel. I own it.

Stock. For shame, for shame! And 'twas this woman's intelligence you relied upon for Miss Dudley's character?

Bel. I thought she knew her. By Heaven! I would have died sooner than have insulted a woman of virtue, or a man of honour.

Stock. I think you would; but mark the danger of licentious courses; you are betrayed, robbed, abused, and, but for this providential discovery, in a fair way of being sent out of the world with all your follies on your head.—Dear Stukely, go to my neighbour, tell him I have an owner for the jewels, and beg him to carry the people under custody to the London Tavern, and wait for me there. (*Exit* STUKELY.

I fear the law does not provide a punishment to reach the villainy of these people. But how in the name of wonder could you take anything on the word of such an informer?

Bel. Because I had not lived long enough in your country to know how few informers' words are to be taken. Persuaded, however, as I was of Miss Dudley's guilt, I must own to you I was staggered with the appearance of such innocence, especially when I saw her admitted into Miss Rusport's company.

Stock. Good Heaven! did you meet her at Miss Rusport's, and could you doubt her being a woman of reputation?

Bel. By you perhaps such a mistake could not have been made; but in a perfect stranger, I hope it is venial; I did not know what artifices young Dudley might have used to conceal her character; I did not know what disgrace attended the detection of it.

Stock. I see it was a trap laid for you, which you have narrowly escaped. You addressed a woman of honour with all the loose incense of a profane admirer, and you have drawn upon you the resentment of a man of honour who thinks himself bound to protect her. Well, sir, you must atone for this mistake.

Bel. To the lady the most penitent submission I can make is justly due, but in the execution of an act of justice it never shall be said my soul was swayed by the least particle of fear. I have received a challenge from her brother; now, though I would give my fortune, almost my life itself, to purchase her happiness, yet I cannot abate her one scruple of my honour; I have been branded with the name of villain.

Stock. Ay, sir, you mistook her character, and he mistook yours; error begets error.

Bel. Villain, Mr. Stockwell, is a harsh word.

Stock. It is a harsh word, and should be unsaid.

Bel. Come, come, it shall be unsaid.

Stock. Or else what follows? Why the sword is drawn, and to heal the wrongs you have done to the reputation of the sister, you make an honourable amends by murdering the brother.

Bel. Murdering!

Stock. 'Tis thus religion writes and speaks the word; in the vocabulary of modern honour there is no such term.—But come, I don't despair of satisfying the one without alarming the other; that done, I have a discovery to unfold that you will then, I hope, be fitted to receive.

ACT V

SCENE I

The London Tavern

[MAJOR] O'FLAHERTY, STOCKWELL, CHARLES, *and* BELCOUR

Major. Gentlemen, well met! you understand each other's minds, and as I see you have brought nothing but your swords, you may set to without any further ceremony.

Stock. You will not find us backward in any worthy cause; but before we proceed any farther, I would ask this young gentleman whether he has any explanation to require of Mr. Belcour.

Charles. Of Mr. Belcour none; his actions speak for themselves: but to you, sir, I would fain propose one question.

Stock. Name it.

Charles. How is it, Mr. Stockwell, that I meet a man of your character on this ground?

Stock. I will answer you directly, and my answer shall not displease you. I come hither in defence of the reputation of Miss Dudley, to redress the injuries of an innocent young lady.

Major. By my soul the man knows he's to fight, only he mistakes which side he's to be of.

Stock. You are about to draw your sword to refute a charge against your sister's honour; you would do well, if there were no better means within reach; but the proofs of her innocence are lodged in our bosoms, and if we fall, you destroy the evidence that most effectually can clear her fame.

Charles. How's that, sir?

Stock. This gentleman could best explain it to you, but you have given him an undeserved name that seals his lips against you: I am not under the same inhibition, and if your anger can keep cool for a few minutes, I desire I may call in two witnesses, who will solve all difficulties at once. Here, waiter! bring those people in that are without.

Major. Out upon it, what need is there for so much talking about the matter! Can't you settle your differences first, and dispute about 'em afterwards?

FULMER *and* MRS. FULMER *brought in*

Charles. Fulmer and his wife in custody?

Stock. Yes, sir, these are your honest landlord and landlady, now in custody for defrauding this gentleman of certain diamonds intended to have been presented to your sister. Be so good, Mrs. Fulmer, to inform the company why you so grossly scandalised the reputation of an innocent lady, by persuading Mr. Belcour that Miss Dudley was not the sister, but the mistress, of this gentleman.

Mrs. F. Sir, I don't know what right you have to question me, and I shall not answer till I see occasion.

Stock. Had you been as silent heretofore, madam, it would have saved you some trouble; but we don't want your confession. This letter, which you wrote to Mr. Belcour, will explain your design; and these diamonds, which of right belong to Miss Rusport, will confirm your guilt: the law, Mrs. Fulmer, will make you speak, though I can't. Constable, take charge of your prisoners.

Ful. Hold a moment. Mr. Stockwell, you are a gentleman that knows the world, and a member of parliament; we shall not attempt to impose upon you; we know we are open to the law, and we know the utmost it can do against us. Mr. Belcour has been ill-used to be sure, and so has Miss Dudley; and, for my own part, I always condemned the plot as a very foolish plot, but it was a child of Mrs. Fulmer's brain, and she would not be put out of conceit with it.

Mrs. F. You are a very foolish man, Mr. Fulmer, so prithee hold your tongue.

Ful. Therefore, as I was saying, if you send her to Bridewell, it won't be amiss; and if you give her a little wholesome discipline, she may be the better for that too: but for me, Mr. Stockwell, who am a man of letters, I must beseech you, sir, not to bring any disgrace upon my profession.

Stock. 'Tis you, Mr. Fulmer, not I, that disgrace your profession, therefore begone, nor expect that I will betray the interests of mankind so far as to show favour to such incendiaries. Take 'em away; I blush to think such wretches should have the power to set two honest men at variance.

(*Exeunt* FULMER, *etc.*

Charles. Mr. Belcour, we have mistaken each other; let us exchange forgiveness. I am convinced you intended no affront to my sister, and ask your pardon for the expression I was betrayed into.

Bel. 'Tis enough, sir; the error began on my side, and was Miss Dudley here, I would be the first to atone.

Stock. Let us all adjourn to my house, and conclude the evening like friends: you will find a little entertainment ready for you; and, if I am not mistaken, Miss Dudley and her father will make part of our company. Come, Major, do you consent?

Major. Most readily, Mr. Stockwell; a quarrel well made up is better than a victory hardly earned. Give me your hand, Belcour; o' my conscience you are too honest for the country you live in. And now, my dear lad, since peace is concluded on all sides, I have a discovery to make to you, which you must find out for yourself, for deuce take me if I rightly comprehend it, only that your aunt Rusport is in a conspiracy against you, and a vile rogue of a lawyer, whose name I forget, at the bottom of it.

Charles. What conspiracy? Dear Major, recollect yourself.

Major. By my soul, I've no faculty at recollecting myself; but I've a paper somewhere about me, that will tell you more of the matter than I can. When I get to the merchant's, I will endeavour to find it.

Charles. Well, it must be in your own way; but I confess you have thoroughly roused my curiosity.   (*Exeunt.*

SCENE II

Stockwell's House

CAPT. DUDLEY, LOUISA *and* STUKELY

Dud. And are those wretches, Fulmer and his wife, in safe custody?

Stukely. They are in good hands; I accompanied them to the tavern, where your son was to be, and then went in search of you. You may be sure Mr. Stockwell will enforce the law against them as far as it will go.

Dud. What mischief might their cursed machinations have produced, but for this timely discovery!

Louisa. Still I am terrified; I tremble with apprehension lest Mr. Belcour's impetuosity and Charles's spirit should not wait for an explanation, but drive them both to extremes before the mistake can be unravelled.

Stukely. Mr. Stockwell is with them, madam, and you have nothing to fear; you cannot suppose he would ask you hither for any other purpose but to celebrate their reconciliation and to receive Mr. Belcour's atonement.

Dud. No, no, Louisa; Mr. Stockwell's honour and discretion guard us against all danger or offence; he well knows we will endure no imputation on the honour of our family, and he certainly has invited us to receive satisfaction on that score in an amicable way.

Louisa. Would to Heaven they were returned!

Stukely. You may expect them every minute; and see, madam, agreeable to your wish, they are here.   (*Exit.*

SCENE III

CHARLES *enters, and afterwards* STOCKWELL *and* [MAJOR] O'FLAHERTY

Louisa. O Charles, O brother, how could you serve me so; how could you tell me you was going to Lady Rusport's and then set out with a design of fighting Mr. Belcour? But where is he: where is your antagonist?

Stock. Captain, I am proud to see you, and you, Miss Dudley, do me particular honour. We have been adjusting, sir, a very extraordinary and dangerous mistake, which I take for granted my friend Stukely has explained to you.

Dud. He has; I have too good an opinion of Mr. Belcour to believe he could be guilty of a designed affront to an innocent girl, and I am much too well acquainted with your character to suppose you could abet him in such design; I have no doubt, therefore, all things will be set to rights in very few words when we have the pleasure of seeing Mr. Belcour.

Stock. He has only stepped into the compting-house and will wait upon you directly. You will not be over-strict, madam, in weighing Mr. Belcour's conduct to the minutest scruple; his manners, passions and opinions are not as yet assimilated to this climate; he comes amongst you a new character, an inhabitant of a new world, and both hospitality as well as pity recommend him to our indulgence.

SCENE IV

BELCOUR *enters, bows to* MISS DUDLEY

Bel. I am happy and ashamed to see you; no man in his senses would offend you; I forfeited mine and erred against the light of the sun, when I overlooked your virtues; but your beauty was predominant, and hid them from my sight; I now perceive I was the dupe of a most improbable report, and humbly entreat your pardon.

Louisa. Think no more of it; 'twas a mistake.

Bel. My life has been composed of little else; 'twas founded in mystery, and has continued in error. I was once given to hope, Mr. Stockwell, that you was to have delivered me from these difficulties, but either I do not deserve your confidence, or I was deceived in my expectations.

Stock. When this lady has confirmed your pardon, I shall hold you deserving of my confidence.

Louisa. That was granted the moment it was asked.

Bel. To prove my title to his confidence, honour me so far with yours as to allow me a few minutes' conversation in private with you.   (*She turns to her father.*

Dud. By all means, Louisa. Come, Mr. Stockwell, let us go into another room.

Charles. And now, Major O'Flaherty, I claim your promise of a sight of the paper that is to unravel this conspiracy of my aunt Rusport's: I think I have waited with great patience.

Major. I have been endeavouring to call to mind what it was I overheard; I've got the paper, and will give you the best account I can of the whole transaction.   (*Exeunt.*

SCENE V

BELCOUR *and* LOUISA

Bel. Miss Dudley, I have solicited this audience to repeat to you my penitence and confusion. How shall I atone? What reparation can I make to you and virtue?

Louisa. To me there's nothing due, nor anything demanded of you but your more favourable opinion for the future, if you should chance to think of me. Upon the part of virtue I'm not empowered to speak, but if hereafter, as you range through life, you should surprise her in the person of some wretched female, poor as myself and not so well protected, enforce not your advantage, complete not your licentious triumph, but raise her, rescue her from shame and sorrow, and reconcile her to herself again.

Bel. I will, I will; by bearing your idea ever present in my thoughts, virtue shall keep an advocate within me; but tell me, loveliest, when you pardon the offence, can you, all-perfect as you are, approve of the offender? As I now cease to view you in that false light I lately did, can you, and in the fulness of your bounty will you, cease also to reflect upon the libertine addresses I have paid you, and look upon me as your reformed, your rational admirer?

Louisa. Are sudden reformations apt to last? and how can I be sure the first fair face you meet will not ensnare affections so unsteady, and that I shall not lose you lightly as I gained you?

Bel. Because though you conquered me by surprise, I have no inclination to rebel; because since the first moment that I saw you, every instant has improved you in my eyes; because by principle as well as passion I am unalterably yours; in short there are ten thousand causes for my love to you—would to Heaven I could plant one in your soft bosom that might move you to return it!

Louisa. Nay, Mr. Belcour——

Bel. I know I am not worthy your regard; I know I'm tainted with a thousand faults, sick of a thousand follies; but there's a healing virtue in your eyes that makes recovery certain; I cannot be a villain in your arms.

Louisa. That you can never be; whomever you shall honour with your choice, my life upon't that woman will be happy; it is not from suspicion that I hesitate, it is from honour; 'tis the severity of my condition, it is the world that never will interpret fairly in our case.

Bel. Oh, what am I, and who in this wide world concerns himself for such a nameless, such a friendless thing as I am? I see, Miss Dudley, I've not yet obtained your pardon.

Louisa. Nay, that you are in full possession of.

Bel. Oh, seal it with your hand then, loveliest of women, confirm it with your heart; make me honourably happy, and crown your penitent not with your pardon only, but your love.

Louisa. My love!——

Bel. By Heaven, my soul is conquered with your virtues more than my eyes are ravished with your beauty! Oh, may this soft, this sensitive alarm be happy, be auspicious! Doubt not, deliberate not, delay not. If happiness be the end of life, why do we slip a moment?

SCENE VI

[MAJOR] O'FLAHERTY *enters, and afterwards* DUDLEY *and* CHARLES *with* STOCKWELL

Major. Joy, joy, joy! sing, dance, leap, laugh for joy! Ha done making love and fall down on your knees to every saint in the calendar, for they're all on your side, and honest St. Patrick at the head of them.

Charles. O Louisa, such an event! By the luckiest chance in life we have discovered a will of my grandfather's made in his last illness, by which he cuts off my aunt Rusport with a small annuity, and leaves me heir to his whole estate, with a fortune of fifteen thousand pounds to yourself.

Louisa. What is it you tell me? O sir, instruct me to support this unexpected turn of fortune.   (*To her father.*

Dud. Name not fortune; 'tis the work of Providence, 'tis the justice of Heaven that would not suffer innocence to be oppressed, nor your base aunt to prosper in her cruelty and cunning.

            (*A Servant whispers* BELCOUR, *and he goes out.*

Major. You shall pardon me, Captain Dudley, but you must not overlook St. Patrick neither, for by my soul if he had not put it into my head to slip behind the screen when your righteous aunt and the lawyer were plotting together, I don't see how you would ever have come at the paper there, that Master Stockwell is reading.

Dud. True, my good friend, you are the father of this discovery; but how did you contrive to get this will from the lawyer?

Major. By force, my dear, the only way of getting anything from a lawyer's clutches.

Stock. Well, Major, when he brings his action of assault and battery against you, the least Dudley can do is to defend you with the weapons you have put into his hands.

Charles. That I am bound to do, and after the happiness I shall have in sheltering a father's age from the vicissitudes of life, my next delight will be in offering you an asylum in the bosom of your country.

Major. And upon my soul, my dear, 'tis high time I was there, for 'tis now thirty long years since I set foot in my native country, and by the power of St. Patrick I swear I think it's worth all the rest of the world put together.

Dud. Ay, Major, much about that time have I been beating the round of service, and 'twere well for us both to give over; we have stood many a tough gale and abundance of hard blows, but Charles shall lay us up in a little private but safe harbour, where we'll rest from our labours, and peacefully wind up the remainder of our days.

Major. Agreed, and you may take it as a proof of my esteem, young man, that Major O'Flaherty accepts a favour at your hands, for by Heaven I'd sooner starve than say I thank you to the man I despise. But I believe you are an honest lad, and I'm glad you've trounced the old cat, for on my conscience I believe I must otherwise have married her myself to have let you in for a share of her fortune.

Stock. Hey-day, what's become of Belcour?

Louisa. One of your servants called him out just now, and seemingly on some earnest occasion.

Stock. I hope, Miss Dudley, he has atoned to you as a gentleman ought.

Louisa. Mr. Belcour, sir, will always do what a gentleman ought, and in my case I fear only you will think he has done too much.

Stock. What has he done; and what can be too much?—Pray Heaven, it may be as I wish!   (*Aside.*)

Dud. Let us hear it, child.

Louisa. With confusion for my own unworthiness, I confess to you he has offered me——

Stock. Himself.

Louisa. 'Tis true.

Stock. Then I am happy; all my doubts, my cares are over, and I may own him for my son.—Why these are joyful tidings. Come, my good friend, assist me in disposing your lovely daughter to accept this returning prodigal; he is no unprincipled, no hardened libertine; his love for you and virtue is the same.

Dud. 'Twere vile ingratitude in me to doubt his merit.— What says my child?

Major. Begging your pardon now, 'tis a frivolous sort of a question, that of yours; for you may see plainly enough by the young lady's looks, that she says a great deal, though she speaks never a word.

Charles. Well, sister, I believe the Major has fairly interpreted the state of your heart.

Louisa. I own it; and what must that heart be, which love, honour and beneficence like Mr. Belcour's can make no impression on?

Stock. I thank you. What happiness has this hour brought to pass!

Major. Why don't we all sit down to supper then and make a night on't?

Stock. Hold, here comes Belcour.

SCENE VII

BELCOUR *introducing* MISS RUSPORT

Bel. Mr. Dudley, here is a fair refugee who properly comes under your protection; she is equipped for Scotland, but your good fortune, which I have related to her, seems inclined to save you both the journey.—Nay, madam, never go back; you are amongst friends.

Charles. Charlotte!

Char. The same; that fond officious girl that haunts you everywhere; that persecuting spirit——

Charles. Say rather, that protecting angel; such you have been to me.

Char. O Charles, you have an honest, but proud heart.

Charles. Nay, chide me not, dear Charlotte.

Bel. Seal up her lips then; she is an adorable girl; her arms are open to you, and love and happiness are ready to receive you.

Charles. Thus then I claim my dear, my destined wife.

(*Embracing her.*

SCENE VIII

LADY RUSPORT *enters*

Lady R. Hey-day! mighty fine! wife truly! mighty well! kissing, embracing—did ever anything equal this? Why you shameless hussy!—But I won't condescend to waste a word upon you.—You, sir, you, Mr. Stockwell, you fine, sanctified, fair-dealing man of conscience, is this the principle you trade upon? Is this your neighbourly system, to keep a house of reception for runaway daughters, and young beggarly fortune-hunters?

Major. Be advised now, and don't put yourself in such a passion; we were all very happy till you came.

Lady R. Stand away, sir; haven't I a reason to be in a passion?

Major. Indeed, honey, and you have, if you knew all.

Lady R. Come, madam, I have found out your haunts; dispose yourself to return home with me. Young man, let me never see you within my doors again.—Mr. Stockwell, I shall report your behaviour, depend on it.

Stock. Hold, madam, I cannot consent to lose Miss Rusport's company this evening, and I am persuaded you won't insist upon it; 'tis an unmotherly action to interrupt your daughter's happiness in this manner, believe me it is.

Lady R. Her happiness truly; upon my word! and I suppose it's an unmotherly action to interrupt her ruin; for what but ruin must it be to marry a beggar?—I think my sister had a proof of that, sir, when she made choice of you. (*To* CAPTAIN DUDLEY.

Dud. Don't be too lavish of your spirits, Lady Rusport.

Major. By my soul you'll have occasion for a sip of the cordial elixir by and by.

Stock. It don't appear to me, madam, that Mr. Dudley can be called a beggar.

Lady R. But it appears to me, Mr. Stockwell; I am apt to think a pair of colours cannot furnish settlement quite sufficient for the heiress of Sir Stephen Rusport.

Char. But a good estate in aid of a commission may do something.

Lady R. A good estate, truly! where should he get a good estate, pray?

Stock. Why suppose now a worthy old gentleman on his death-bed should have taken it in mind to leave him one——

Lady R. Hah! what's that you say?

Major. O ho! you begin to smell a plot, do you?

Stock. Suppose there should be a paper in the world that runs thus—"I do hereby give and bequeath all my estates, real and personal, to Charles Dudley, son of my late daughter Louisa, etc., etc., etc."

Lady R. Why I am thunder-struck! By what contrivance, what villainy did you get possession of that paper?

Stock. There was no villainy, madam, in getting possession of it; the crime was in concealing it, none in bringing it to light.

Lady R. Oh, that cursed lawyer, Varland!

Major. You may say that, faith, he is a cursed lawyer, and a cursed piece of work I had to get the paper from him; your ladyship now was to have paid him five thousand pounds for it, I forced him to give it me of his own accord for nothing at all, at all.

Lady R. Is it you that have done this? Am I foiled by your blundering contrivances, after all?

Major. 'Twas a blunder, faith, but as natural a one as if I'd made it o' purpose.

Charles. Come, let us not oppress the fallen; do right even now, and you shall have no cause to complain.

Lady R. Am I become an object of your pity then? Insufferable! confusion light amongst you! marry and be wretched; let me never see you more.   [*Exit.*

Char. She is outrageous; I suffer for her, and blush to see her thus exposed.

Charles. Come, Charlotte, don't let this angry woman disturb our happiness: we will save her in spite of herself; your father's memory shall not be stained by the discredit of his second choice.

Char. I trust implicitly to your discretion, and am in all things yours.

Bel. Now, lovely but obdurate, does not this example soften?

Louisa. What can you ask for more? Accept my hand, accept my willing heart.

Bel. O bliss unutterable! brother, father, friend, and you the author of this general joy——

Major. Blessing of St. Patrick upon us all! 'tis a night of wonderful and surprising ups and downs. I wish we were all fairly set down to supper and there was an end on't.

Stock. Hold for a moment! I have yet one word to interpose. Entitled by my friendship to a voice in your disposal, I have approved your match; there yet remains a father's consent to be obtained.

Bel. Have I a father?

Stock. You have a father. Did not I tell you I had a discovery to make? Compose yourself: you have a father, who observes, who knows, who loves you.

Bel. Keep me no longer in suspense; my heart is softened for the affecting discovery, and nature fits me to receive his blessing.

Stock. I am your father.

Bel. My father! Do I live?

Stock. I am your father.

Bel. It is too much; my happiness o'erpowers me; to gain a friend and find a father is too much; I blush to think how little I deserve you.   (*They embrace.*

Dud. See, children, how many new relations spring from this night's unforeseen events, to endear us to each other.

Major. O' my conscience, I think we shall be all related by and by.

Stock. How happily has this evening concluded, and yet how threatening was its approach! Let us repair to the supper room, where I will unfold to you every circumstance of my mysterious story. Yes, Belcour, I have watched you with a patient, but inquiring eye, and I have discovered through the veil of some irregularities, a heart beaming with benevolence, an animated nature, fallible indeed, but not incorrigible; and your election of this excellent young lady makes me glory in acknowledging you to be my son.

Bel. I thank you, and in my turn glory in the father I have gained: sensibly impressed with gratitude for such extraordinary dispensations, I beseech you, amiable Louisa, for the time to come, whenever you perceive me deviating into error or offence, bring only to mind the Providence of this night, and I will turn to reason and obey.

EPILOGUE

WRITTEN BY D[AVID] G[ARRICK] ESQ.

SPOKEN BY MRS. ABINGTON

N.B.—*The lines in italics are to be spoken in a catechise tone.*

CONFESS, good folks, has not Miss Rusport shown,
Strange whims for SEVENTEEN HUNDRED SEVENTY-ONE?
What, pawn her jewels!—there's a precious plan!
To extricate from want a brave *old* man;
And fall in love with poverty and honour;
A girl of fortune, fashion!—Fie upon her.
But do not think we females of the stage
So dead to the refinements of the age,
That we agree with our old-fashioned poet:
I am point-blank against him, and I'll show it:
And that my tongue may more politely run,
Make me a lady—Lady Blabington.
Now, with a rank and title to be free,
I'll make a catechism—and you shall see,
What is the *véritable Beaume de Vie*:
As I change place, I stand for that, or this,
My Lady questions first—then answers Miss.

(She speaks as my Lady)

"Come, tell me, child, what were our modes and dress
In those strange times of that old fright Queen Bess?"—

And now for Miss:

(She changes place, and speaks for Miss)

When Bess was England's queen,
Ladies were dismal beings, seldom seen :
They rose betimes, and breakfasted as soon
On beef and beer, then studied Greek till noon :
Unpainted cheeks with blush of health did glow,
B ruffed and fardingal'd from top to toe,
Nor necks, nor ankles would they ever show.

Learnt Greek!—(*Laughs.*)—Our outside head takes half
a day;
Have we much time to dress the inside, pray?
No heads dressed *à la Grecque*; the ancients quote,

There may be learning in a *papillote*:
Cards are *our* classics; and I, Lady B.,
In learning will not yield to any she
Of the late founded female university. }

But now for Lady Blab—

(*Speaks as my Lady*)

"Tell me, Miss Nancy,
What sports and what employments did they fancy?"

(*Speaks as Miss*)

The vulgar creatures seldom left their houses,
But taught their children, worked, and loved their spouses:
The use of cards at Christmas only knew,
They played for little, and their games were few, }
One-and-thirty, Put, All-Fours, and Lantera-Loo:
They bore a race of mortals stout and bony,
And never heard the name of Macaroni.—

(*Speaks as my Lady*)

"Oh brava, brava! that's my pretty dear—
Now let a modern, modish fair appear;
No more of these old dowdy maids and wives
Tell how superior beings pass their lives."—

(*Speaks as Miss*)

Till noon they sleep, from noon till night they dress,
From night till morn they game it more or less,
Next night the same sweet course of joy run o'er, }
Then the night after as the night before,
And the night after that, encore, encore!

(*She comes forward*)

Thus with our cards we *shuffle* off all sorrow,
To-morrow, and to-morrow, and to-morrow!
We *deal apace*, from youth unto our prime,
To the last moment of our *tabby*-time;
And all our yesterdays, from rout and drum,
Have lighted fools with empty pockets home.
Thus do our lives with rapture roll away,
Not with the nonsense of our author's play;
This is true life—true spirit—give it praise;
Don't snarl and sigh for good Queen Bess's days!
For all you look so sour, and bend the brow,
You all rejoice with me you're living now.